THE CONTESSA'S EASEL

THE CONTESSA'S EASEL

Book Three of the

ORLA PAINTS QUARTET

by

Mary Sharnick

www.penmorepress.com

The Contessa's Easel by Mary Donnarumma Sharnick

Copyright © 2021 Mary Donnarumma Sharnick

ISBN-13: 978-1-950586-81-3(Paperback)
ISBN   978-1-950586-82-0(e-book)

BISAC Subject Headings:
FIC045000 / FICTION / Family Life
FIC011000 / FICTION / Gay
FIC107000 / FICTION / Italy

Editing: Lauren McElroy, Chris Wozney
Cover Illustration by Christine Horner

Address all correspondence to:

Penmore Press LLC
920 N Javelina Pl
Tucson AZ 85748

Dedication

For Wayne

and

For our families on both sides of the Atlantic

Musée des Beaux Arts

About suffering they were never wrong
The Old Masters: how well they understood
Its human position; how it takes place
While someone else is eating or opening a window or just
    walking dully along;
How, when the aged are reverently, passionately waiting
For the miraculous birth, there always must be
Children who did not specially want it to happen, skating
On a pond at the edge of the wood:
They never forgot
That even the dreadful martyrdom must run its course
Anyhow in a corner, some untidy spot
Where the dogs go on with their doggy life and the torturer's
    horse
Scratches its innocent behind on a tree,
In Brueghel's *Icarus* for instance: how everything turns
    away
Quite leisurely from the disaster; the ploughman may
Have heard the splash, the forsaken cry,
But for him it was not an important failure; the sun shone
As it had to on the white legs disappearing into the green
Water; and the expensive delicate ship that must have seen
Something amazing, a boy falling out of the sky,
Had somewhere to get to and sailed calmly on.

—W. H. Auden

"The past is never dead. It's not even past."

—William Faulkner

Note to Readers

This novel was written during the Coronavirus Pandemic of 2020. Sheltering in place in Beacon Falls, Connecticut, I often thought of Giovanni Boccaccio's *The Decameron*, published in Italian in 1353. Boccaccio's seven young men and three young women narrate their one hundred tales in a secluded villa in the town of Fiesole, high above Florence, where they had traveled to escape the Black Death.

For a very long time Fiesole has been a go-to place for many besides Boccaccio's characters. Etruscans, Romans, artists, writers, film makers, lovers of antiquities, historians, religious pilgrims, Nazi occupiers during the Second World War, and the *partigiani* who resisted them, all deemed the town essential for their disparate purposes and goals. Harvard and Georgetown, among other universities, have long brought students and scholars to properties there, so conducive is the atmosphere to inquiry and exploration. In October of 1986 Pope John Paul II visited the San Francesco Monastery at the very top of the town. And fortunate "slow travelers" with sturdy shoes and a disposition for walking find that Fiesole promises discoveries large and small, among the most noteworthy a spectacular and expansive view of Florence below.

So it was no surprise to me that when Orla Castleberry, the fictional "voice in my head," told me she wanted to spend some time there too, I found myself with her in her New Orleans home from May through July of 1989 preparing for an exhibit in Fiesole scheduled for August 15th. While all Italians celebrate the Feast of the Assumption of Mary on that mid-August date, in 1989 the Fiesolani also commemorated the 45th anniversary of the town's liberation from its Nazi occupiers.

In the third novel of the *Orla Paints Quartet* Orla finds herself immersed in, susceptible to, and transformed by the seductive force of Fiesole. Several characters from *Orla's Canvas* and *Painting Mercy*, the first two novels of the series, travel from New Orleans to join her there, and several others, both native Fiesolani and a transplant or two, meet up with them. The intersections of their lives give voice to this book.

The historical dates in the novel are factual, as are several edifices and persons. They include:

In New York City—
The former St. Vincent's Hospital in Greenwich Village, considered to be "ground zero" of the 1980s AIDS epidemic. The director of the AIDS program there was Doctor Ramon A. Gabriel Torres, and the hospital was administrated and staffed by the Sisters of Charity and their secular personnel.

The Rizzoli Bookstore, formerly located on 57th St. in Manhattan

In New Orleans—
Project Lazarus, an HIV/AIDS hospice/shelter/aid facility and its programs, established in 1985 by Father Paul Desrosiers and Father Bob Pawell

Café Maspero, New Orleans Museum of Art (NOMA)

In the District of Columbia—
The National Institutes of Health (NIH) and Dr. Anthony S. Fauci, Director of the National Institute of Allergy and Infectious Diseases (NIAID) since 1984, and the primary voice

of the U. S. government's response to the AIDS crisis during the 1980s

In Vietnam—
Chí Hòa Prison, Lycée Marie Curie, the Majestic Saigon Hotel, all in Ho Chi Minh City (formerly Saigon)
Tan Son Nhut Air Base

In Arkansas—
Fort Chaffee Army Base; Fort Smith

In Assisi—
The Basilica of San Francesco d'Assisi; the Basilica of Santa Chiara; Rocca Maggiore

In Florence—
Ospedale di Santa Maria Nuova; il Duomo; Galleria dell'Accademia; Istituto del Sacro Cuore; l'Universita degli Studi di Firenze

In Fiesole—
The former Hotel Villa Aurora, the Cathedral of San Romolo; Villa le Balze; Villa I Tatti; the Etruscan and Roman ruins. The Martyrs of Fiesole (Carabinieri Alberto LaRocco, Vittorio Marandola, Fulvio Sbaretti) indeed gave their young lives on August 12th 1944, so that their ten imprisoned fellow townsmen might escape death at the hands of the Nazis.

Villa d'Annunzio and its outbuildings, chapel, and grounds are imagined settings. The narrative is fictional and is not intended as a documentary. The characters and story are my own. I hope they will capture your interest and offer you an escape to Fiesole, whether you are sheltering in place or free to roam.

Part One—Orphans

"Never think you've seen the last of anything."

—Eudora Welty

Chapter One
Laps

Fourteen laps and I'm done for. I feel like a Beauceron bitch gone bad, having abandoned the herd I'm charged with leading home. I haven't served family meals in our Garden District dining room but for Christmas, New Year's Day, and Easter Sunday. Instead, I've been making monthly commutes from New Orleans to New York City and back again. New York University, my alma mater, named me Artist-in-Residence for the 1988-89 academic year. And since 9 in the evening on February 1st at Le Cirque in Manhattan, the moment thirty-eight candles blazed on my birthday cake (flourless chocolate drizzled with raspberry sauce) courtesy of my eighty-five-years-young Tante Yvette DuBois, I've ditched domestic(ated) life and its trainer-proscribed menu for a four-month-long marathon run through the City, sniffing out succulent feasts of the fat and the fried, lapping amber and russet liquids in dog-bowl quantities, barking and grrr-ing and keening my absolute pleasure until now—bloated, sated, and in need of tedious grooming—I pant.

3

At 7 a.m. on this Saturday May morning—the 27th, to be precise—New Orleans is all blues, cumulous clouds, and lush greenery. Low humidity still, though the temperature should reach a steamy 95 degrees Fahrenheit later on.

So when I lift myself out of the pool, remove my mint-colored bathing cap, and shake my head to let my hair loose, I don't bother to towel myself, instead letting the sun do its job. If I continue doing twenty-five sit-ups a day after my swim and before my shower, the disturbing bulge above my waist should disappear within the month. Sigh. I spread a turquoise beach towel on the flagstone surrounding the pool, kneel, then use my arms and hands to turn and lie down on my back. I clasp my hands behind my head, bend my knees, then, ugh, lift myself up. One. Two. Three. Four....

My tenure at the university is over. I flew home last evening. And I'm awaiting tomorrow's arrival of my daughter Mercy, just-graduated from Georgetown with degrees in biology and the fine arts. Mercy has been staying with friends in D.C. post-commencement for what she terms an "extended baccalaureate bacchanal." And if I do not relish her participation in the orgiastic goings-on associated with the aforementioned, I certainly do admire my daughter's word choices for them. At any rate, once she arrives the spacious second-floor apartment above collector/agent/friend Luke Segreti's art gallery that we have called home for fourteen years will no longer feel like a kennel for two yapping, transient canines.

By now, you probably think I adore dogs, what with the extended metaphor. I don't. Too much slobbering. What I do relish, though, are the traditional weekly Sunday gatherings of my clan—a few blood relatives, plus more who are not—with whom Mercy and I will convene non-stop, at least until we leave again on the 31st of July. Then Mercy will head back to D.C., find an apartment, and do some temp work at

Georgetown. Come September, she'll intern for a year in the graphics department at *National Geographic*.

My work for an art exhibit in Fiesole, Italy, scheduled for mid-August, will take me to the Contessa Beatrice d'Annunzio's villa overlooking that storied Tuscan town. I'll stay there through October, maybe even November. I want to experience autumn in Tuscany to see if doing so will expand my repertoire. The contessa tells me I may stay for as long as I wish. She has always been a most generous supporter.

Now seventy-five years of age, during the Second World War she had an affair with my late paternal grandfather, Peter Clemson Castleberry, M. D., when he was ostensibly stationed with the 300th American Mobile Surgical Unit. His unit was first in Tunisia, then in Naples, Italy. However, we have recently learned from the contessa herself that he never served in Naples at all, but instead carried on intelligence work in and around Florence while attending to patients, actual and contrived, some at the art critic Bernard Berenson's Villa I Tatti in Settignano, close to Florence. That is where he first met the Conte and Contessa d'Annunzio, who were frequent guests. But more about that later.

The d'Annunzios were anti-Fascists. Conte d'Annunzio was driving his eight-year-old son Paolo home from a dentist's appointment in Florence when his car was targeted and grenaded by Fascist supporters. While the conte died instantly, the boy lingered for several days. My grandfather had been the one to tell the contessa her son would not survive. Within a year's time, he and the contessa had a daughter together.

News of that daughter, Gabriella Castello, an ill-conceived pun if I ever heard one, came late to my grandmother, Bellefleur DuBois Castleberry. At eleven years of age I was with her when the envelope documenting Gabriella's birth and paternity slipped out of a packing crate containing an Angel Gabriel statue. The statue was part of the crèche collection the contessa added to every Christmas. Though Grandfather Castleberry had died of lung cancer at age forty-five, well before I was born, Grandmother was deeply wounded by the news of his infidelity. I suspect she'd been cognizant of it, for I was told she never accompanied him on his annual visits to Fiesole and the orphanage the contessa had opened during the war. But being aware of her husband's affair was different from holding in her own hands indisputable proof of his daughter's existence. The certainty killed my grandmother, made me an heiress, and resulted in my learning my own true paternity. Providence? The irony of life? Divine humor? Who knows? As I've told you in my earlier narratives, that's why I paint, to try and figure out what eludes me.

At any rate, the way I look and feel right now is not the way I need to look and feel when the handsome and exacting contessa greets me. I do not at present resemble "...America's svelte, sometimes acerbic mid-career artist whose social critiques on canvas cut to the bone while at the same time dazzling the viewer." Or at least so wrote Barkley Peckingham in last Sunday's *New York Times*, reviewing my latest show, the "Portraits of AIDS" exhibit NYU sponsored.

Other critics were not so kind. "What is suitable for portraiture? Certainly not grotesque dying men who have no one but their perverted selves to blame for their disgusting predicament. Artist Orla Castleberry ought to be ashamed of herself," opined gallery owner Gatley Spooner of Roanoke, Virginia. I'm told I've even been critiqued in a Sunday church sermon or two. Last time I saw her for a trim, my hairdresser Liz Murchison said, "Our minister told us that celebrities like you just glorify behaviors that demean human life and destroy Christian values. 'And worse still,' he said, 'they call it art.'" But I digress.

No, of late I have been an over-indulging bitch. Attribute it to my daughter's graduating from college, to the imminent approach of middle age—recently, after a shower, I yanked several gray hairs, uncoiling themselves among my otherwise auburn head hair the way earthworms stretch to their full lengths in the grass after rain—or to a myriad of unsatisfied bodily and spiritual appetites. However, I am known to be capable of discipline. Have been disciplined before. And shall be disciplined again. So I do laps, sit-ups, and ingest protein, fiber, calcium, water, and caffeine. I'll be ready to "show" by the time the contessa's mustachioed driver Marciano opens the navy sedan's door and I step out onto the worn cobblestone drive and confront Beatrice d'Annunzio's penetrating gaze.

*****

"Impressive."

It's Tad, thank God.

"Hardly," I say, groan, turn over, rest a moment on all fours, then prepare to lift myself up. Fortunately, Tad reaches out his right hand. I take it with my left and lurch myself upright (Really, there is no other word for it).

"Quite a workout you're attempting," Tad says. His twinkling eyes tell me he's amused. I've always loved him watching me through that look.

I suck in my stomach and stand as erect as I can, even though I don't have to. Tad knows all a person can know about me. He's been my one and only since we were children in St. Suplice, our misspelled hometown just twenty miles north of NOLA. One year older than I, he was the boy I planned to marry. We were to be a couple extraordinaire, renowned for my artistry and his historical acumen, two of America's best and brightest. Back in 1975, the weekend that left no doubt he was gay, the trajectory I had charted for us veered out of its original orbit. The shift felt meteoric. (You can read about it in my second narrative.) But neither of us wanted to or could let go of

7

the other. As if we couldn't trust ourselves to act in the world alone. As if we understood before we could admit our understanding that we were and are each other's lodestar, true confessor, harbor, flag. Emergency room friends. The one you want to pull the plug and deliver your eulogy when the time comes.

Don't misunderstand me. Though I was initially devastated by the news and furious at Tad for ruining my life plan—ego is one of my strong suits, as you'll learn if you haven't already—it's not as if we haven't gone on. Tad has become an immigration law expert whose first history book will be published come August. And I, well, my Vietnam painting dedicated to our late childhood friend Denny Cowles hangs in the Oval Office, and I don't mean the room the senior partner occupies at Ciampi and Vester, where Tad practices downtown. As for Tad's lover and might-as-well-be-husband of fifteen-plus years, the aforementioned Luke Segreti, he turned out to be the kick-ass catalyst for my career as a painter. I guess I should believe that things have a way of working out. Or that Divine Providence is real. Because the two of them, gay Tad and gay Luke, have been boons to me and Mercy in all ways but the one I'd initially imagined. That said, I still and always want Tad. Even though I know what his body does with Luke's, it inevitably attracts me with its tennis-toned legs, square chin just the right height above me to rest a moment on my head when we say hello and good-bye, smooth hands with manicured nails never bitten, and an Adam's apple that bobs as naturally as an ice cube in a glass of gin and tonic.

And if you were to think I've been living like a nun since Tad's coming out to me, you'd be misled. I've had plenty of sex. Just not sex with Tad. You know, the kind with enduring love in an admirable marriage (think Abigail and John Adams), the kind I'd figured on, the gold-standard kind. First there was five-year Diego, the talented and charming Argentinian sculptor I met during college. You'll recall him from my last story where, for sure, I admit I did him wrong in the end. Then saxophonist Todd. Hardly worth mentioning, as he was my failed attempt at livening up the winter doldrums when my parents entertained Mercy in St. Suplice during her February school break some ten years ago. Next, steady, uniformed Tyrone, one of the installation crew at the New Orleans Museum of Art. Hands down the sexiest man I've met so far. Not a talker in the act, just focused intention and physical grace. And if he did tell any museum folk about us, not a one ever let on. I'm telling you now that if NOMA's walls could speak, they would have several titillating tales to tell. We conducted all our business right there during visiting hours in all manner of secluded, angled spaces. When Tyrone left for Detroit and his ailing mother—so he said, anyway—we shook hands by Charles Giroux's *Louisiana Road Scene.* "It's been a real pleasure, ma'am," he drawled. "Same, sir," I told him. And I meant it. And now, for four of the eight years since we met, there's been Don.

But please don't think me a harlot, or a woman without a nesting instinct. Be assured that back in 1975, after I adopted Mercy, I swore off men for quite some time, focused on being a devoted and doting mother to a little girl who had suffered. But, yet again, Divine Providence intervened when, in September of 1981, it led me to Don Wainwright. He's the fellow I'll probably have sex with tonight. Don and I met at "Back to School Night" in homeroom—how quaint, I didn't even have to try—when both our daughters entered the Ursuline Academy in ninth grade. "What line of work are you in?" he had asked. (Clearly, he had no idea who I was. HE HAD NO IDEA WHO I WAS!) "Paint," I said, "I work in paint. And you?" He smiled a white-toothed smile that contrasted nicely with his mess of red hair. "Dough," he answered. "I work with dough." Was he mocking me? I couldn't tell. I crossed my legs in what I thought a fetching manner and imagined eating a jellied cruller with him,

9

his mouth at one end, mine at the other. Our lips would meet in a sugary strawberry kiss. "So you're a baker?" He showed those white Chiclets again. "No, a financial planner." I liked him right away.

How he managed to smile I'll never understand. As I learned from Mercy not a day later, then from Don himself at the September Parent Coffee, just a couple of years earlier his landscape-designer wife Carlotta had heard voices that prompted her to set their Garden District house on fire and, soon after that conflagration had been stomped out, to go after their daughter Lily with a hedge clipper. Carlotta has been institutionalized since, with no discernible signs of improvement, if improvement is even possible. The voices in her head dulled by drugs, she shuffles and hums, according to Don. When he mentions her, he stares off, I wonder if in memory of former good times or not. Don and Lily live in a condominium downtown now, the only garden a rooftop one with flower-boxes surrounding a pool and sun deck. And while Don is his wife's devoted weekly visitor, Lily has elected not to see her mother even once in the last decade. Don doesn't make her. And how can I presume to judge her choice?

Lily and Mercy latched onto one another as members of their school's social justice group. They made hundreds of sandwiches weekly for the folks at the Catholic Charity shelter where they did crafts with elementary-school children every Tuesday after classes. They spent countless overnights here and at the Wainwright condo, developing rituals as steady as Sunday Mass: microwaving popcorn, baking brownies, and watching DVDs. Among their favorites: *The Princess Bride*, *Spaceballs*, and *Dirty Dancing*. Truth be told, Mercy got no grief from American-as-baseball-and-apple-pie Lily the way she did from two full-blooded Vietnamese students who on the second day of school had used Magic Markers to scrawl "*Bui Doi*," "Dust of Life," on Mercy's locker. (The phrase, maybe you've heard, refers to children of Vietnamese mothers and American fathers, like my Mercy, who along with hundreds of others had been airlifted to the United States before the Fall of Saigon.) Though the two miscreants who confessed—I refuse to invoke their names here—were disciplined, they were allowed to continue at the school, where they remained a constant burden during Mercy's high school years.

I know I've often indulged my daughter, perhaps in ways I shouldn't have, to compensate for what she's endured. So she's become a spoiled kid who hails from less-than-ideal circumstances, a real handful when she doesn't get her way. She's got a closet full of Keds and jelly shoes, enough to rival any department store, not to mention a jewelry case devoted entirely to watches, seventeen at last count. And the irony is she's always late. She's a manicure/pedicure junkie, but never ("I will n-e-v-e-r, Mamma!") frequents one of the many Vietnamese-owned salons. She can and does whine effectively in four languages—her native Vietnamese, French, the Neapolitan dialect that Luke's mother taught her, and New Orleans English. But her foibles are mostly of my making. And her anger at having been abandoned is completely understandable, even if her birth mother's intention had been to keep Mercy safe. At any rate, you can probably understand why Don and I and our beautiful, damaged girls initially connected and immediately clicked. The four of us don't have to explain ourselves to one another.

Although the physical attraction between Don and me was instantly charged, we didn't go beyond school-sponsored group pool parties and Sunday suppers with my folks, Tad, and the Segreti family, pats on the back, or friendly hugs until the girls graduated. Only during the post-commencement lock-in, when the chaperoned students stayed on the Ursuline campus to celebrate from dusk to dawn, did we take to bed at my place. Then—and still—neither of us has ever sought or pretended anything more from each other than congenial company, mutual kindness, shared understanding, and satisfying bodily release. I know our relationship is legally and morally reprehensible. But there it is. I am not as heartily sorry as a proper Catholic woman should be. Actually, I'm not sorry at all.

Do our daughters know? Of course. We told them we were dating over supper at Café Maspero the day after the lock-in. Mercy and Lily were sitting adjacent to one another, as were Don and I, at a table for four. Mercy instantly admonished us.

"You're too old." She sighed and rolled her eyes at the same time. "And for God's sake, don't dare tell me anything you do." She gulped ice water from a sweating glass. "It's embarrassing and disgusting."

"Well, now," Don chuckled, "be sure to tell us how you feel, Mercy."

My daughter then snorted. Good God, she sounded like a piglet.

"Mercy!" I said, and she stuck out her tongue at me.

Don tried to hide his smile with his napkin.

"I'm only thirty-four, and Don's forty. We're youngsters."

Don put his napkin down and covered my right hand with his.

"I'm deeply wounded." He pretended distress as he looked to Mercy. Then he winked at the two of us.

Mercy rolled her eyes again and stared at her dish, the remains of a shrimp po' boy decorating the plate like deep-fried golden confetti.

Completely silent and emotionless until then, Lily spoke. "Well, I understand why they need each other," she said to Mercy. "Think about it. Parents are actually just people. If you think about them as just people, even they can get lonely."

"I suppose," Mercy said, tapping an unused dessert fork on the table in slow, even beats.

The Contessa's Easel

Lily sounded aged, wise, sensible, and looked right at her father as she spoke. Then she looked across the table to me and smiled. Her eyes never lose their sadness.

Mercy livened up again, letting go the fork. She turned to her friend.

"Say what you think, Lily. I understand the loneliness part, but it's still gross to think of parents..." Here Mercy paused and covered her eyes with her hands. I couldn't tell whether she was laughing or crying or both. Lily guffawed and play-punched Mercy on her shoulder.

"Having sex?" she whispered.

"Lily!" Mercy jumped up from her seat. "May we be excused, at least?" Mercy asked. "I don't want to hear any more."

Lily stood up as well.

Don blew a kiss as the two girls pushed in their chairs none too softly.

"Go," I said. I remember waving them off.

Now Tad's voice interrupted my memory.

"Where were you?' he asked. "Already imagining Italy?"

"Oh, just remembering something," I said. "Do you want to go for a quick swim?"

He smiled. "Sure."

He went to the pool house to change. By the time he dove in I was already floating on my back. The clouds were moving fast, giving way to the sun that would burn me if I stayed in it too long. I thought back again, this time to when I'd told Tad and Luke. Don wasn't with me at the time. Frankly, I'm glad he wasn't, because for that duo the news of our arrangement was a source of disagreement.

The three of us had been drinking Negronis by the pool just before Don was to join us for the first post-high school Sunday supper. We sat three in a row, separated by two little round, glass-topped tables on either side of my middle chair, as if awaiting an aquatic choral performance by the cricket frogs that frequented the pool. The girls had gone off to another schoolmate's house for a birthday sleepover.

"For Christ's sake, Orla, this won't end well," Luke said, patting the top of his ancient straw sun hat as he spoke. Pat, pat, pat, as if his hand were flattening a big old bale of hay. His tone was jovial enough. Expansive, even. "One of you will fall in love, or the wife will miraculously recover, or the girls will have a spat and you'll take sides. You're famous, dammit." Pat, pat, pat. "Can't you find some unencumbered fellow who appreciates your work, who's got his own big gig going?"

I grinned and wiggled my toes. Mercy had asked the pedicurist to paint them lilac to match the linen dress I wore to her graduation.

"Actually, it's quite nice not to have to talk about my work," I said. "A bit of a breather, you know? Food, conversation, and sex—that's it. Nice, no?"

I looked right and smiled at him. He shrugged. Then I breathed in through my nose and out from my mouth three times, the way psychologists suggest to relax and lower blood pressure instantly. I didn't want to defend myself or make a big deal out of what felt so easy and pleasant.

"I suppose," Luke said. He clicked the nails of his left hand against his glass.

"At least we're heterosexual," I teased.

"Bitch," Luke said, and pinched my arm.

"Ow!"

"You know you deserved it."

We both laughed, clicked our glasses together, and drank.

I finished my drink and watched Tad stare into the pool.

"You're awfully quiet, Tad," I said. I wanted his approval. As if he were my conscience. Or the better part of myself.

He ran a hand through his wavy hair, then turned his face toward me. He looked tan and relaxed, but his prolonged sigh, like a heavy, unsatisfying waft of summer wind off the Mississippi, told me he was annoyed.

"Don's married," he said.

A statement, simple and direct. His voice measured and calm. His eyes holding mine in their gaze.

"To a zombie," Luke snorted, and shifted in his seat. "A schizophrenic zombie." He continued the clicking. "She tried to murder their kid, for God's sake!"

I hoped the two of them weren't going to get prickly with each other. When they did, they fed into the stereotype of the melodramatic gay couple. Luke, flamboyant and huffy. Tad, subdued and injured.

"Nonetheless," Tad said. His tone didn't waver, but his eyes pleaded with Luke.

Luke took a drink from his glass, then glared at his lover.

"Give the guy a break, Tad," he said. He crossed and uncrossed his legs. "He visits what's her name—Carlotta, right Orla?"

"Yes," I said. "Every Wednesday afternoon."

"He takes care of her."

Tad folded his fingers together, then cracked them.

"Even so," said Tad.

"You expect too much from him," said Luke. His tone was harsh. "Too much."

Tad didn't reply. Instead he walked barefoot in front of us to the far end of the pool. That's where the sandbox-sized bin of beach balls and rubber rafts were kept. He picked up the raft shaped like a white swan and dropped it into the pool.

"They mate for life, you know, swans do."

"Good Lord," said Luke.

I didn't like where this was heading. The swan bobbed on the water. The water was clear, and the raft made a shadow at the bottom of the pool. Luke stuck his right forefinger into his glass and stirred and stirred. For some unfathomable reason, I envisioned the three witches in *Macbeth*. *"Toil and trouble, toil and trouble. Fair is foul, and foul is fair."*

I stood up, picked up my empty glass, walked to the main table we used for dining, and made myself a second drink. Tad returned to his chair and stared into the water.

"Anyone else want another?" I asked, trying for insouciance.

Luke stood up and joined me.

"I'll do it," he growled.

When Luke was done, going heavier on the gin than on the Campari and vermouth, I sliced into the half-orange left on the well-used cutting board, cut two half-moons and, after wedging a slice onto each of our glasses, returned to my chair.

"He's married, Orla," Tad repeated. He tilted his head and looked at me with a "come on, now" expression. I hate it when someone tells me a truth I'd rather not acknowledge.

"I heard you the first time," I said. Even I cringed at my tone.

Luke laughed out loud, though of course nothing was funny now.

I felt the haughty in me rise. The part of me I wasn't proud of, but understood was as real as my very vitals. The part of me that readily expressed outrage at anyone and everyone but myself.

"You can be a prig, you know," I told Tad. I crossed and uncrossed my legs. "You are a gay prig."

"Well, now," Luke said. He chortled and downed his drink in two swift swigs.

"That may be, Orla," Tad continued, rubbing his right forefinger under his nose, "but it doesn't change the fact. Don made a promise, took a vow."

Luke rolled his eyes. Tad ignored him.

While my dearest friend was accustomed to my pronouncements, he rarely outwardly angered at them. That acknowledged, he always said his piece. This time was no different.

"I know," I said. "For better or worse. Even if the worse lasts a lifetime."

Luke made fake coughing sounds.

"You just want the guy to masturbate his whole life, Tad?" Luke asked. "Or maybe I underestimate you. Maybe you expect him to be celibate. To tame his carnal appetite." He flung his orange peel onto the grass behind us.

"I'm just stating the facts."

"Can you not be a lawyer for five minutes!" Luke protested. "It gets tiring."

"*Mihi meditandam ergo sum,*" Tad replied.

"Christ," Luke muttered.

I took my orange wedge off the edge of my glass and gnawed on it, chewing my way through the peel, finally swallowing it. Bitter and sweet at the same time.

"You're right, of course," I said to Tad. "And good. A good prig."

Tad smiled. Luke did not.

"I've been called worse, Orla." He pointed at Luke, who raised his middle finger.

I decided not to be angry. I stood, rested my left hand on Tad's chair, leaned over, and kissed him on his forehead.

"Much more good than I am. My name should be Magdalene."

"Don't let him bully you, Orla," Luke said. "Ask him what he would do in the same circumstances. Go ahead, ask him."

Tad didn't respond. Instead, he reached up and caressed my arm the way a mother would to calm a fussy child. There was my punishment, the one that would no doubt last my lifetime. The touch I wanted only for me and could never have. Mine to keep. To have and to hold. For better or worse.

My eyes watered in regret. Not in contrition, as perhaps Tad hoped. As he had numerous times before, he took his ever-ready handkerchief from the right pocket in his shorts and wiped my eyes with it. The cotton square was soft and pressed.

Then he looked to Luke.

"You know I wouldn't," he said.

Luke weakened then, and nodded. Pressing his right hand to his lips, he blew a kiss to Tad.

That was when Don's car had pulled into the drive.

This morning, the only cars in the driveway are Tad's and mine. Tad's by the pool with me again, and still. He sees my flab and my efforts to get back into shape. He's always been kind to Don and me both, as we continue to dabble in something significantly less than committed love. And he's just about ready for the culmination of our own three-year history/art collaboration come August, in Fiesole.

Don's Lily has gone off to an equestrian camp near Dublin after four years at Hollins College in Roanoke, Virginia, where she rode every day. Mercy's not home yet, and I'm here for a couple of months. When I got in after 11 last night I listened to Don's message on the answering machine: "Let me know when you're back." I did. So after hair color and cut, pedicure (never a manicure, as I don't like the texture of polish on my nails distracting me when I paint), and maybe a bikini wax, I'll see him at his place. Perhaps I'll stay the night. That, and he'll join the rest of the crew for Sunday dinner here tomorrow.

"They've arrived," Tad said, climbing out of the pool.

I followed suit.

He shook the water off himself and ran his fingers through his hair, putting each strand back into place. I stood legs apart and arms fully stretched in front of me. Having neglected my bathing cap this time around, I just let my hair dry however nature deemed it would.

I looked up toward the property's guest cottage and patio, expecting to see Luke helping his mother, the infirm Signora Segreti, who made her home there. Signora has used a walker since her stroke in March, but her loss of mobility has not diminished her enjoyment of the outdoors or her son's daily visits. Since we buried Signor Segreti two years ago, Bredice Noyes has become nonagenarian Signora's full-time companion and caretaker. Bredice is a retired maid from the Jesuit residence over at Loyola University where Mamma Segreti cooked for four decades. The two get along famously, as they always did, and Bredice's three grandchildren—Lester and Quince, twin boys of eight, and their four-year-old sister, Favorly—are frequent visitors to the pool they call "our country club." Every now and then Luke gets a nasty letter from one neighbor or another who still believes the "coloreds" shouldn't taint the pool water or set foot in a Garden District back yard unless they're mowing it. I've seen him rip a couple of these missives up, put the shredded paper into properly addressed envelopes, and send them right on back to their authors. Love the guy. Even though he is a thief.

"Who's here? Some folks besides Luke and Signora?"

"No," Tad said. "All is quiet at the cottage, and Luke is still in bed at my place. (Tad owns a shotgun house right across from the Ursuline Convent in the French Quarter. The house Mercy and I will inherit should Tad, Mercy's godfather, and the man she calls "Uncle Luke," go to their heavenly reward before either of us.)

19

"Oh?" I said.

"He's feeling a bit under the weather." Tad said. "He tells me it's the flu. But I say it's last evening's excesses. He went out while I read and re-read my manuscript at home. We both overdid it, albeit quite differently. Thankfully I was still up when he made his way to my place, though I can't imagine how. He literally fell inside when I opened the door. A car full of costumed boys dropped him off. He says they were part of a private drag show at the Blue Room. It was the third time in as many weeks somebody or other has dumped him with me."

Tad's tone was not sympathetic.

"What's up, Tad?"

He grimaced.

"A bit of a lovers' quarrel, I'm afraid, my friend."

I waited for him to go on.

"Well?" I said.

Tad looked away long enough to watch a funeral cortège ease past the front of the house, then his eyes focused back on mine.

"There is nothing more to tell you, Orla."

I raised my eyebrows and twisted my mouth in dissatisfaction at his answer.

"Be that way," I said, and crossed my arms in front of me.

A crow cawed high above the row of magnolia trees that separated the pool area from the neighboring yard. I couldn't see it flying.

"I'm serious," Tad replied. "Don't press me. Please."

He was upset for real.

Caw, caw, again.

Tad shifted his weight from one foot to the other.

"I'll try not to feel hurt, then."

I softened my tone.

But Tad didn't smile.

Luke had always liked his cocktails. For that matter, all three of us do. But I'd never seen him unable to hold his liquor. In fact, he's the one who usually drives our trio home from our intermittent revels.

"You weren't with him, you said?"

Now the crow dipped and flapped furiously over the pool.

"Please, Orla. I don't want to talk about it. I'm going to get dressed."

He walked away from me to the pool house.

When he returned he took his proverbial handkerchief from the right pocket of his khaki Bermuda shorts. Unfolding it to wipe the dew off one of the wrought-iron chairs that matched a glass-topped table large enough to seat twenty, he sat down.

"Want some breakfast?" I asked, still standing.

"No. I told you. I had work to do. And now so do you."

He didn't look at me when he spoke. And his voice wavered. I wanted to hug him, to hold him. But I spoke instead.

"What are you really here about?" I asked. "What's the matter, Tad?"

He played his fingers one against the other long enough for me to spell M-i-s-s-i-s-s-i-p-p-i in my mind and ignored my second question.

"The final galleys of my book and the contessa's copies of your grandfather's photographs arrived this week. The galleys on Wednesday, and the photos yesterday afternoon."

"That's why you didn't go out?"

I pulled another chair out and sat down as well.

"I just didn't, Orla."

Clearly, we weren't going to converse further about last night. I shifted my focus.

"All right, then, I guess I can get going on my interpretations of the photographs I favor."

I scanned the tabletop, but didn't see any sign of either the galleys or the photos.

"Where are they?"

He crossed his right leg over his left.

"When I saw you down here, I let myself in and left them on the foyer table," he said. "I didn't want to risk wetting anything."

I stood up.

"Coffee, at least?"

He ran his right hand through his drying hair, the brown on the way to salt-and-pepper the last few months.

"No, thanks, I've got to go to the office and get rid of some paperwork before Monday."

He worked a few hours almost every Saturday morning. From the start of their relationship, Luke had had little patience for it. But Tad told me he liked the silence and the solitude of Vester and Ciampi on a Saturday. And he always met up with Luke for lunch somewhere afterward.

"Too bad to lose a morning like this one, though," I said.

He shrugged.

"I am just doing what I need to in order to be up to date with my work."

Something was amiss, for sure. But I'd need to wait to learn what it was. That much was clear.

Tad stood up and put his hands in his pockets as we strolled toward the house. He whistled "Always". There was still no sign of Signora Segreti or Bredice from the guest cottage. All the blinds were drawn.

"You and Luke will be here for supper tomorrow, right?"

I looked down at my toes and cringed. The graduation violet had chipped, as if birds had pecked at several of my toenails. A pedicure was certainly in order.

"No doubt," he said. "Luke assured me even as he held his head in his hands this morning that he would be 'not only sober, but also super' by dinnertime Sunday."

Tad managed a smile at the telling. "By the way, who else is coming?" he asked.

We stopped by the back steps of the main house.

"Mercy, of course, Don Wainwright, Signora Segreti, and Bredice."

He laughed.

"Only seven people? I won't even have to drag the folding chairs out of the garage?"

I punched his left arm.

"Invite your parents if you want, and I'll ask Mamma, Daddy, and baby brother, aka King Arthur, to come, too. Then we can have an even dozen, maybe get a good fight going."

He pretended to consider. His mood had lightened.

"Done," he said. "I'll phone my folks as soon as I get to the office."

I walked up the back steps.

"I'll call Mamma now."

He took his car keys from his right pocket and returned to the matter for which he had come.

"Study the photos, decide if you'd like to paint portraits based on any of them, and I'll see you tomorrow at five. Don't buy any wine. I'll take care of it."

He started for his car. "Oh, and why don't I pick up Mercy at the airport?"

I raised my eyebrows. "You mean it?

He jangled his keys.

"Yes, that way you can prepare Signora Segreti's sauce."

I licked my lips. Signora had stopped cooking. She just can't balance on her feet well enough to ensure her safety, though she still rolls meatballs, stuffs sausage casings, and slices vegetables for a salad as long as she can do so seated at the kitchen table.

"Deal," I said.

"Deal, then," he answered.

"I'll phone you as soon as I check with Mercy to confirm her flight number and arrival time."

He nodded. "Good."

"Tell Luke I look forward to catching up with him."

"Will do," he called back to me, "though I don't know if he'll be up to meeting me for lunch today. He barely lifted himself up from the couch this morning. You may run into him here when he comes to his mother's to regroup. God knows he needs to."

I realized he had said "couch" instead of "bed." Hmmm.

Then he was gone. And I was perplexed. He and Luke had seemed fine at Easter. I shrugged, trying to force patience to trump curiosity. I opened the door, stepped inside, and went right to the gallery's phone on the first floor to dial my mamma's number. The line was busy. I'd have to try her again. With little time to lose before my 10 o'clock appointment at the Hotel Portanova Spa, I walked upstairs, dropped my swimsuit and towel in the laundry room, then headed to the bathroom. Though I needn't have, I closed the door tight, turned the shower faucet to its hottest level, and waited for the room to fill with steam.

Chapter Two
An Appointment at the Spa

I brought the galleys and photos to the Portanova Hotel Spa with me. They didn't fit into the almond-colored calf briefcase I had carried all semester in New York, so I stuffed them into a fan-shaped straw beach bag instead. The bag made sense with my seashell-decorated shift and white leather flip-flops. The day had rapidly heated up, so I was glad both for the air-conditioned car and the almost too-cold hotel lobby. As I made my way to the elevators, I looked over to the registration desk to see if my favorite bellhop, Ignazio, was there. He was, and we exchanged our usual greeting—hands to lips followed by simultaneous dramatic flings outward, the way he had taught Mercy when she was just six, soon after her arrival in NOLA. I had taken her to a Catholic Charities fashion show in the hotel ballroom. All she could talk about after was the "kisses man." Since then, Ignazio has never missed an opportunity to ask after Mercy and visit my intermittent exhibits at NOMA. I know because he always sends a note on Portanova stationery to let me know what he likes or doesn't, offers praise, horror, or surprise. He's a true fan, and I appreciate him.

"Mercy will be home tomorrow," I called to him.

He applauded and called back, "Be sure to bring her by, then. I'll be here all week. First drink at the Floating Bar is on me."

"Promise," I answered, and waved again.

Not wanting to put up with the idle chatter that was part and parcel of the main hair and nail salons, I had phoned ahead to request a private room for my overdue ablutions. My regular stylist, Liz Murcheson, had arranged for one just the other side of the open corridor from the rooftop pool.

"Nobody will even know you're here, Miss Castleberry," she'd said when I phoned.

I must have urged her, "Please, call me Orla," each and every visit for the past decade, but she never has. I've never figured out why. The other stylists do. She's always as brisk and pristine in her white uniform as a well-trained nurse. All business.

"Would you like your pedicure done while the color takes hold?" she asked. "Or would you rather have the girl come in after we finish?"

I put my bag on an end table by the pink-and-peppermint-striped loveseat in the room, then eased into the white-leather chair while Liz robed me.

"After, please," I said. "Then I can do my research."

Liz nodded.

"Let's go with something that resembles the warm browns of Siena," I said, "something with a touch of red in it. I'll be off to Tuscany at the end of July. I'll come by again just before and, if the color doesn't suit me, we can change it then."

"Fine."

She unpinned a color chart from a bulletin board on the far wall. I pretended to study it, but the color I liked popped right out at me.

"There," I pointed to a rich burnished tone.

"Good," she said, went over to a narrow stand of aluminum drawers that reminded of a doctor's office instrument drawer. From the top drawer she pulled out two small plastic jars, one with a mahogany-colored liquid, the second with one that looked like butter. I wiggled my neglected toes while she went over to the counter/sink area and mixed both concoctions together in a third, larger plastic container. Then she took a brush not unlike a mid-sized artist's brush from a lower drawer and, arranging herself behind my head, began her task.

She dabbed the dye around my hairline at neck, ears, and forehead, then worked it into my hair completely. I watched her purposeful, sure ministrations in the mirror across from me.

"Done," she said when she was, and put her brush and the third container into the sink next to the drawer stand. "I'll disappear for thirty minutes or so. Would you like your bag?"

I nodded.

She brought it to me.

"Thanks, Liz."

"My pleasure, Miss Castleberry," she said, tiptoed to the door, opened and closed it quietly, and left me to my work.

First I took the galleys from their long envelope. Tad's book was entitled *The Orphans of Fiesole: A World War II Physician's Photographs and Letters*. Tad and I had discovered Dr. Castleberry's diaries way back in 1962, when my grandmother Castleberry had hired us to organize her late husband's study. At eleven, I couldn't have been less interested in Dr. Castleberry's writings, but twelve-year-old Tad was already exhibiting the historian's tendencies. He was besotted with them. Obsessed. History is to him what paint is to me.

But Tante Yvette had seen to it that I spent lots of time with the contessa when I studied in Florence every summer during my college years, so the photos as well as the events and people that had inspired them came to mean a great deal to me as well. It hadn't been but three years before, at dinner one night, that Luke had suggested, "Why don't you two collaborate on a book?" And so we have.

Acting as our agent, Luke pitched the idea of the coffee-table-style history book in photographs. Rizzoli was enthusiastic about the project, as was the contessa. In the end, after numerous conference calls between New York and New Orleans, New Orleans and Fiesole, it was decided that I would mount an exhibit in conjunction with the release of Tad's book to celebrate the 45th anniversary of the liberation of Fiesole from the Nazis. I'd paint portraits based on photographs, as I had done years ago with my Vietnam collection, and just this academic year with my AIDS series. The contessa would sponsor the gala event at her villa on August 15th, 1989 (an Italian holiday, both the Feast of the Assumption and *Ferragosto*, "Iron August"). Between Rizzoli's publicity machine and the contessa's international coterie, a two-continent promotional campaign was well underway. Needless to say, a crowd was expected.

Though I hadn't even heard the door open, I realized Liz had come back in to check on the status of the dye.

"Ten more minutes, Miss Castleberry," she said, and left the room as quietly as she had entered it.

The photos in the book were Dr. Castleberry's own, taken between 1944 and 1945. Tad had initially discovered them in my grandfather's collection of five scrapbooks back in St. Suplice. The contessa had made copies of them so the originals could be preserved. The four most compelling photographs to me were:

The Music Teacher: A full-length shot of a short, stern-looking, middle-aged woman holding a baton and standing by an upright piano in what appears to be a classroom. She wears a dark shirtwaist dress with white detachable lace collar and cuffs. Her hair is cut like an aristocratic man's, with substantial waves softening what would otherwise be termed a visage instead of a face. A nameplate on a bookshelf behind her reads "*Dottoressa* Antonella Ghiraschi."

The One-armed Girl: A child no more than six years old with a stump wrapped in muslin instead of a healthy left arm. Her face is wreathed in short blonde curls. She is smiling and holding a battered naked doll to her chest with her right arm. Her dress is a tattered plaid smock with buttons shaped like daisies. Her eyes are wide open and glisten, as if she is unaware of the tragedy that has befallen her.

The Nazi Violinist: A high-cheek-boned young officer, in full German uniform, with impeccably groomed hair and nails, his side part as straight as a ruler, his nails rounded and smooth. His eyes are closed and his violin is tucked under his chin. His calm demeanor leads one to believe he has left the war and successfully escaped into a completely musical realm. Beside him is **The Girl Violinist with the Rapunzel-like Braid.** She sits next to the Nazi violinist. Their knees—his left, her right—touch. Her thick braid, which reaches all the way to her waist, is tied with a wide ribbon that has been starched and pressed. She wears a peasant's coarse apron over her simple smock. Her eyes tend toward his lidded ones even as she balances her instrument under her chin. Her lips are slightly open and voluptuous, though her breasts might as well be flatbreads. Her nails are bitten to the quick.)

A Priest and a Bishop at an Altar:The priest on the left wears a finely sewn lace surplice over his regulation cassock. On his left shoulder is a pin designating him as a member of the Third Reich. On the right stands the Bishop in his hierarchical regalia, including miter and staff, Penned in ornate script beneath the photograph: "Padre Ernst Adenauer, Military Chaplain of the Third Reich, Roman Catholic; His Excellency Giovanni Giorgis, Bishop of Fiesole".

Liz entered the room to the sound of a timer going off in the adjoining main salon.

"Time to wash out the dye, Miss Castleberry," she said. "Were you able to concentrate?"

"Yes," I said, and readjusted myself as she took the photographs from me and walked them back over to the loveseat. If she had anything to say about what she saw, she kept it to herself. Then she came back and tipped the chair back to the edge of the deep sink.

As the warm water rushed over my head, a similar rush of thoughts flooded my imagination. *What if some of the people in the photographs were still alive? Some even in Fiesole. I certainly should be able to locate the Germans and the bishop. No doubt the contessa could help.*

"Up you go," said Liz, and she wrapped a towel around my head while she went after the scissors.

"Chin-length, and layered, please," I said.

She returned to the chair.

"As always, Miss Castleberry."

I laughed.

"I am boringly predictable, I know."

Liz clipped with speed and precision.

"Not at all. You know your style, that's all."

As she continued to clip with purpose and precision, I imagined how I might gather any surviving people from the earlier photographs. I'd ask them to sit for me at the contessa's.

"There," Liz said.

She spun the chair around and gave me a hand mirror so I could check the length in back against the wall mirror.

"Good," I said. "Just right." I ran my hand down the silky wet back of my head.

Then she took a black blow dryer out of a deep cabinet drawer on the right side of the sink.

What if I can find most of them? I thought. *They might not only be willing to sit for portraits, but may also be able to speak with Tad. We might find out what my grandfather's secret missions were. There could be another book.*

The blow dryer shut off. Liz spun the chair again.

"Well, what do you think, Miss Castleberry?"

I looked in the mirror. My hair felt soft against my scalp and ears. I could blend right in with the buildings of Siena. Burnt umber, bronzed brown, baked brick.

"Excellent. Thanks."

I reached into my beach bag to pay her.

"You don't want us to put it on your tab?' she asked.

I took out a twenty.

"This is for you."

Liz looked surprised. I was feeling generous.

"Well, thank you—thank you very much, Miss Castleberry."

I stood for a moment to gather the galleys and the photos and inserted them back into their respective envelopes.

"Jilly will be right in. She's new, but she's good."

I nodded, sat down again, slipped off my flip-flops, and waited. Jilly came in rolling a mobile footbath contraption and tray of polish selections—I chose Red Earth. As soon as she turned on the automatic massage function in the chair I dozed off. It seemed only a moment had passed when I felt a hand on my arm, wakened in surprise, realized where I was, and heard Jilly, tiny as a sparrow, chirp, "All set, Miss Castleberry."

She reached down for my flip-flops and slid my feet onto them before dabbing each deep-toned toenail with oil. My toes looked much better.

"Thank you," I said, and dug a ten-dollar bill out of my bag.

"The thanks are all mine," she chirped again. "Is there anything else we can do for you today?"

I stood to leave. "I'm all set. The bikini wax can wait." I wanted to get home, phone Luke about my portrait ideas, and make sure Mercy's room was ready for her. "See you next month."

I started for the main salon, but Jilly stopped me.

"You can go right out here," she opened a door leading to the corridor that shared the pool area. "The elevators are down the corridor and to your right."

She giggled, catching herself.

"But you know that," she said. "I'm the one who's new here."

She was adorable. A Disney animation personified. Flitting from task to task as if from one tree branch to another. I'd have to let Liz know.

"Thanks—have a good weekend," I said, and made my way out and into the heat of the open, columned corridor.

I walked briskly, thinking about both Mercy's bed to be made up and the possibilities for another collaboration with Tad. Rizzoli might go for it. Luke would certainly be game to pitch the idea. *Let's see,* I thought, *it's almost 1 o'clock in New Orleans, so it'll be early evening in Fiesole—after speaking with Luke, if he's up to it, I'll put a call in to the contessa before I get a fresh set of Mercy's sheets from the linen closet.*

All of a sudden, a familiar voice made me stop short. It was Luke's. From a distance, though. I looked backwards down the open corridor, then forward and around the corner toward the elevators. No dice. So I looked directly out to the pool area beyond the rounded arches and columns separating the pool from the corridor. There he was in swim trunks, sitting at the pool's edge next to a much younger man—a boy, really—who was sitting, too. They were close together, shoulder to shoulder, their feet churning the water. And Luke, I kid you not, was rubbing the boy's left leg, knee to crotch, knee to crotch, with his right hand while the boy looked up towards the sky. No one else was in sight except a long-legged woman in a red bikini lying face down on a flattened lounge chair, her bathing suit top undone, and her wide-brimmed straw hat resting on top of her head.

I jolted, then seized. My body became a pregnant pause. My mouth a gaping O. My mind seeing what it saw and obliterating it. I didn't know what to do. O, O, O.

What I did do was scrunch myself against the wall and stare. Tad's name drummed in my ears. This was what was wrong. This.

In a few moments, Luke reached behind himself, picked up a key on the pavement, and gave it to the boy. The boy looked down at Luke and smiled. "Thank you," he said. His voice trilled. He took the key, their two hands touching as he did, eased his long legs out of the pool, stood up, and, then, wrapping a hotel towel around his neck, left Luke. He walked like a runway model, turning his neck to smile back at Luke.

"I'll be there shortly," I heard Luke say.

The boy didn't reply, but waved back at Luke, and then with the key traced the curve of his right buttock. Luke laughed out loud.

My heart pounded, and I almost called out, "No—just no." But instead, I stared, my open mouth a repository of hot, humid air.

The unsuspecting boy noticed me as he entered the corridor. He nodded. I nodded back before he turned the corner perpendicular to where I was standing. He wore a gold chain with a heavy cross around his neck. He couldn't have been more than eighteen. He was beautiful, Botticelli's St. Sebastian before the arrows. Yes, he was slim and tall with dark curls, but it was

33

youth, raw youth, that radiated from him. The words "graceful limbs" formed on my lips. I listened for the elevator door. It opened and closed.

In a bit, as the reclining lady in red rolled over, exposing her breasts to the sun while protecting her face with her hat, Luke stood up and walked over to the lounge chair where his things were. He picked up his sandals, put on the green and turquoise terrycloth robe he sometimes wore poolside at home, and took his favorite black-ribboned straw hat in hand. He, too, made his way to the corridor. Before he reached it, though, I fled back into the room I had just left. Jilly was cleaning up.

"Oh, hi, Miss Castleberry. Did you forget something?' Her hands fluttered like small wings.

I looked around the room, pretending I had. Then I put my bag down on a counter and stuck my hands into it.

"There they are," I said, pulled out a pair of sunglasses, and put them on.

"Bye, again, then," Jilly said. She had nested her tools in a straw basket lined with a hand towel.

This time I walked out the door to the main salon as if on a mission.

"Bye, now, Miss Castleberry," Liz Murcheson called out from behind a counter filled with hair products for sale.

I waved, avoided the elevators, and speed-walked down the stairs to be used in case of fire. I found my car in the parking garage, unlocked it, turned on the engine, and blasted cold air onto my face.

"Jesus," I said out loud. "Jesus, have mercy."

When I banged my hands on the steering wheel, the noise from the horn made me jump.

I'd have to find out from Ignazio if Luke Segreti had taken rooms here before.

Chapter Three
What's Cooking?

By Sunday noon my domesticity was reasserting itself, with the darks swirling in the dryer, the delicates drying on the wooden rack in the bathroom, and a peach pie baking in the oven. Sunday evening's obligatory sauce was simmering on the stove. Garlic, olive oil imported from La Fontana, a *fattoria* owned by the contessa, meatballs I had mixed from ground veal, pork, and beef with day-old bits of bread dipped in whole milk, and some grated Asiago cheese. Rolled strips of beef *bracciole* seasoned with basil, crushed garlic, salted and peppered and held together with string. Sweet and hot sausages hand-stuffed into natural casings by Signora Segreti at her table in a marathon-long day of chopping, spicing, and casing with Bredice. (I'd found a package of them awaiting my return in my refrigerator. The accompanying note, in Bredice's handwriting, had read, "Done Thursday.") And, for good measure, I added a stick of spicy pepperoni cut into bite-size pieces. I was hungry—not so much for nourishment, but for the sensate pleasures the gustatory realm provides and the motley community that would gather with me to enjoy it.

I'd yet to set out the store-bought fennel wine biscuits, olives, peppers, and cheeses for the antipasti, and I needed to decide between arugula with lemon or romaine and balsamic for the salad. But there was plenty of time. As I moved about the kitchen, I was painting in my mind, seeing my grandfather's photographs translated onto canvas. As always, an opera—this time *La Bohème*—accompanied my thoughts as I strode repeatedly from stove to island, refrigerator to counter, counter to pantry.

My work was the only antidote to the spectacle that had tossed me into tumult at the Portanova the morning before. Art had always superseded everything else, at least ideally, its primacy a blessing for an artist and a curse for an artist with a family and friends. To avoid continually failing Mercy, I had taken to setting multiple alarm clocks around the apartment while she was in school. If I hadn't, I'd never have shown up at her basketball games or dance recitals. I missed her Brownie installation when she was seven and, another time, arrived late to an honors convocation for the fifth grade, when she won a "diligent worker" medal. I lied to her both times, the first time telling her that I had gotten a flat tire two blocks from the recreation center, the second describing in dramatic and colorful detail how I had vomited after eating shrimp lo mein gone bad. (I have to say that I *should be*—rather than I *am*—ashamed of myself, as such is my habitual behavior whenever I behave badly. This moral failing never changes. I am the personification of original sin. Someone must have replaced my baptismal holy water with brackish tap.) Truth be told, I always swore when the alarms went off. I'd have to stop painting in the middle of a nose or shading a sky.

This morning, I knew my artistic focus would shift the second I encountered Luke. At least Tad is in charge of fetching

Mercy from the airport. That will afford me a couple of hours to work. Plus, she'll be glad to see him. But as soon as Luke shows up, as he always does after visiting his mother, I will have to forget about portraiture and choose between two options: ignoring or confronting the reality that will surely prove a crushing blow to Tad, and that had already grossly tarnished my perception of the gorgeous, generous man who has offered nothing but good to all of us for the past decade and a half.

Though I hadn't planned on talking about Luke's indiscretion to Don, he had immediately picked up on my agitation. My concern for Tad had made for a more subdued reunion than either of us had anticipated. I did end up spending the night at Don's place, and we did enjoy one another, parting after early Mass this morning at Saint Louis Cathedral. (I know, I know, vexing contradictions abound.)

Don and the others were due to arrive at five. As it turned out, neither Tad's folks nor mine could join us. The Charbonneaus had been invited to The Links, St. Suplice's country club, by the Drs. Cormier—Hank and Elaine, a husband and wife dental team who'd opened a practice in St Suplice the previous November. Evidently Tad's father had handled the closings of both their home and office. And my parents had to attend "yet another soccer match down in Convent," Mamma complained. My much younger brother Arthur (younger by twenty-four years) was a rising star. "He is good, you know, Orla," Daddy had insisted once again when I phoned. Ashamed as I am about it, I don't think I'll ever stop resenting Arthur's having two parents to cheer him on simultaneously. Daddy hadn't shown up in my life until I was eleven, and then only because his mother had died. (I'll never resolve that issue. Abandonment is a biggie, that's for damn sure. Mercy and I share that affliction, though for different reasons. How Mercy might eventually explain her experience is up to her. As for me, Daddy's not acknowledging me had felt like a vital organ gone missing. I once painted myself as a jellyfish floundering in foamy seawater, searching for him. The longing for him to call me "my daughter" had been physical. When he finally did—after a tragedy which I told about in my first story—I was literally re-born.)

I still hadn't heard from Signora Segreti and Bredice, which is unusual. They could usually be found out in the garden before ten. I hoped Signora was not feeling too poorly. But, of course, even if no one else at all arrived, my daughter would be here. I'd missed her. If her flight was on time, she should arrive with Tad just in time for cocktails. And tonight my "family"—Tad, Luke, Signora Segreti, Bredice, Don, and Mercy—would be those who share not an ounce of my own blood. Go figure.

Thud. Something heavy dropped on the veranda, interrupting the opera and my imaginings.

I went into the living room and looked out the front window and down to see if a delivery truck was outside. I had ordered a *Welcome Home, Graduate!* flower-and-balloon arrangement for Mercy. Nothing. The front door squeaked open, then closed.

"Something's cooking!" Luke's voice boomed up the stairwell.

His flip-flops on the stairs made me see ducks in an uphill parade, and I smiled. Maybe I'd paint some notecards with that image. A nice Christmas gift for my St. Suplice friends.

But as soon as I walked back into the kitchen, the darling image disappeared. My teeth clenched—involuntarily, it seemed. I tried adjusting my face to greet him. It proved an effort to let my jaw go slack, never mind softening my attitude, already cement-like in judgment.

"Ah, the aromas of heaven, and music just as celestial. Indisputable cures for life's ailments," Luke went on, his voice getting closer and closer.

I felt like piss and vinegar. Wanted to spit. Slap him all over. Bastard. Son of a bitch.

The dryer beeped. I'd see to the clothes later, even though I'd need to iron some of them if I didn't take them out and arrange them on hangers now. Oh, well. Maybe I'd just re-start on "wrinkle release" instead.

"*Buon giorno.*" I drew out the vowels, speaking as melodically as I could, as if all were well. But my racing pulse told me I was gearing up for an attack.

The door to the apartment was open, the way I like it for the sun that comes through the windowed stairwell. Luke would have to walk through the living and dining rooms to get to me in the kitchen.

"Come right in!" I called out.

Agitated, I grabbed the long wooden spoon from the spoon rest shaped like an ear of corn on the counter. Plunging it too hard into the aluminum cauldron, I splashed pasta sauce onto the stovetop, making the flames leap up and the burner hiss. The odor of burnt sauce overwhelmed the aroma of simmering Luke had commented on.

"Your angel of cuisine at your service," I responded, though not without self-reproach for my false gaiety. My words did *not* match the staccato beats of my heart.

I put the wooden spoon onto the spoon rest again. Luke's footsteps were even, and his flip-flops beat a rhythm like a ticking clock.

"My mother sends you your mid-morning *café*," he said, entering the kitchen and handing me my summer's favorite pick-me-up in a tall, frosted glass. As always, his smile was magnificent. He didn't notice my right hand shaking when I took the glass from him. He eyed the stove to his right instead.

Luke was dressed for the pool, just like yesterday. And he exhibited no signs of a hangover, lingering or recent. He typically cleaned up well. This morning appeared to be no different.

"Oh, good. So she's feeling well?"

I sipped. Luke slid out of his flip-flops and placed them next to the metallic trash can by the door to the dining room.

Never one to waste food or drink, for her entire life Signora Segreti had frozen leftover espresso in ice trays. Mid-morning and mid-afternoon, she'd put five or six espresso cubes into a tall glass, add some light cream and sugar, and sprinkle with cinnamon. Whenever I cooked in her stead, she made sure to send the drink my way. When Luke enjoyed her barista ministrations, he added sambuca.

"Mmmm," I murmured as I drank the coffee. "How is she? I've yet to see her about since I got back home."

My acting skills appeared to have been successful thus far, for, as he always did when I cooked Sunday sauce, Luke walked to the corner china cabinet and got a soup spoon from the silverware drawer. He came back to the stove and dipped it into the sauce. Lifting spoon to mouth in a graceful motion, he faced me and slurped in ostentatious and unabashed appreciation. It seemed an ordinary Sunday.

"Delicious," he said. "As for my mamma—not so great. Bredice made her sit with her feet up all day yesterday because her ankles were swollen and she became short of breath when they meandered around the garden."

"Sorry to hear that," I said, placing my half-empty glass on the table. "She evidently stuffed sausages on Thursday."

I pointed at the simmering pot.

"Yes, so she told me." He licked his lips. "I wish people didn't get old."

I uttered a "Hmm" in agreement, glad I'd had my hair colored.

"Do you think we all want to be Merlin so we can 'youthen' rather than age?" I asked.

It was a trick question.

"True for me, anyway," he said, then pointed to the oven. "Peach pie?" he asked, stooping and squinting to see through the rectangular glass in the oven door.

"Yes," I answered, pushed him aside, and opened the door to check on the crust.

"Nice," he said.

"Four minutes more." I talked to myself the way Faulkner claimed women naturally do. I had been reading *As I Lay Dying* on the plane. I looked to the clock on the wall.

"Mamma says she has a doctor's appointment Monday. But they'll both be here for supper."

"Good," I said. "I mean about their being here for supper."

"Understood," he said.

He scooped up another spoonful of sauce.

"And you, how are you?" I stared at his eyeballs.

I was playing with him. Felt myself go clammy even though the air conditioning was on full blast.

"What do you mean?"He looked at me quizzically, holding the soupspoon in abeyance. "Do I look sick?"

"Tad said you were feeling under the weather yesterday morning, when he came by with the galleys and photographs."

He made for the sauce a third time, but I grabbed his arm mid-reach.

"Hey, there won't be any left for the pasta."

"My apologies"—he smiled his wonderful smile. "I guess I'll have to exercise restraint."

There it was. A segue as slick as the olive oil I'd later pour into the dipping bowl.

"I was overcome by deliciousness." He walked around me and put the soupspoon into the sink.

No doubt about his charm. But today charm would not win.

He pointed to a second, smaller lidded pan on the stove.

"Escarole and beans," I said. "Don't touch."

He put up both hands and backed away.

"So how are you?"

He scrunched and unscrunched his shoulders. Scratched his nose.

"Oh, I've recovered. Sad to say, my comeback from a night out takes longer. My half-century looms. No Merlin here," he said, thwacking his hands on his chest.

He pulled a chair out from under the table and sat down. The flip-flops had left inverted Vs on his otherwise tanned feet.

"Old man," I teased. "Too old for a young man's shenanigans."

So far my voice was controlled. Still, I felt my anger rising. I turned away from him and took two oven mitts from the shelf above the stove, opened the oven, and pulled out the peach pie. I turned back and placed it on the pie rack I had set on the table earlier.

Luke made to grab a piece of the crust, but I slapped his hand. Harder than I should have.

"No, no touching."

I played with him as if he were a mouse I held by the tail.

"You are brutal today. Everything's a no-no."

He raised his eyebrows and showed those white teeth in an exaggerated grin.

"Don didn't welcome you home properly last night?" He leered. Lech.

"Don is just fine," I countered. "More than fine. Even went to church with me."

Luke laughed out loud.

"Precious," he said. "What a pair you are. The very picture of propriety."

I put my hands on my waist, spread my feet apart, and had at him.

"It's your shenanigans that are making me brutal," I said.

Luke looked up at me, his face a question mark.

"What are you talking about?"

He eyed the pie again and I glared. Raised my right forefinger. Then I wagged it right in front of his face.

"Schoolmarm," he said, wagging a finger back at me.

"I saw you at your shenanigans." I was taunting him. "Saw you."

I turned away, went to the stove, took up the wooden spoon, and stirred the sauce frenetically. The pan was my cauldron.

"What are you talking about?" he asked.

He stood up as well, came over to me, and wrested the wooden spoon away. He scooped up and slurped another serving of sauce, dripping some as he did. I grabbed the spoon back.

"I'm talking about your shenanigans. Your shenanigans at the Portanova."

He let the spoon fall back into the sauce and backed away from me. I took two steps toward him. I was close enough to bite his nose.

"Is that why you were with the boy? To deny your age? To relive your youth? I'm sure he hasn't even reached his quarter century. You could be his father, for God's sake!"

I lifted the wooden spoon out of the steaming cauldron and, as if I were a bishop flinging holy water over his congregants, I pitched hot dollops of sauce at him.

"Ow," he protested. "It's hot."

"No kidding," I said. "And you're a stinking bastard."

He was sprinkled in red, fending me off with his arms crisscrossed in front of his face.

"What boy?" he asked.

43

I wielded the spoon that had become my weapon. He dodged me like a fighter attempting to ward off my blows.

"Don't try to deny it. The boy at the Portanova pool. The young, young boy."

Luke lunged at me, grabbed the spoon, and threw it to the floor. The black and white tiles looked like a stabbing was taking place. We both stared at the spreading red. Then, after standing as motionless as the costumed street performers posing in the Quarter do, Luke drew in a long, deep breath, turned around slowly, sat down again, and put his head in his hands.

"Oh, that boy. Shit."

I took up the wooden spoon, and buying time, went to the sink where I soaped and washed it. Then I laid it across the cauldron of sauce. I pulled too many paper towels off the roll on the wall, wet them, knelt, and wiped up the red puddle and several splashes. I threw the sopped towels in the trash and pulled a chair from the other side of the table and sat down, too. I was exhausted.

"Is he your new one and only, or are there others?" I asked. I drummed my fingers on the table.

"A few," he said, looking up. "Three, maybe four."

"Jesus," I muttered.

His mouth was tight. His lips formed a straight line of purplish pink where no white teeth sparkled through.

"Since when?" I asked.

Drum, drum, drum.

I was the prosecutor, he the accused.

"Since the gala at NOMA in February to raise funds for the AIDS hospice, if you must know."

I remembered the event. I'd missed it because I'd been in Manhattan.

"Where the servers were dressed as if they were from classical paintings or sculptures. Where Donatello's David kept my champagne glass full."

He smiled a Mona Lisa smile as he told me. He wasn't sorry, the son of a bitch.

I pressed my top teeth into my bottom lip. Stopped drumming.

"I took your yesterday's trick for Botticelli's Sebastian." I was as bad as he was, relishing the allusions as much as I hated what he was doing to Tad.

Luke's smile turned into a grimace.

"You do know your art, Orla," he said.

He never let a conversation flag, Luke didn't—not even this one.

He took a deep breath and exhaled. I held my head up with both hands under my chin.

"Does Tad know?"

Luke said nothing. The sauce simmered and *O soave fanciulla* sounded in the background, the lovers' voices blending one into the other, soaring, then slowing to a sustained and aching close.

I found myself crying. Couldn't help it. I was crying for Tad.

Luke's eyes teared, too. Why, I couldn't know. Because he was sorry I'd caught him? Or sorry because he knew he was a lout? I was too angry to let up.

"Does he?" My voice was as sharp as a scalpel. I wiped my eyes with both hands.

Luke put his head into his hands again and sighed.

"I told him," he said, looking up quickly. "I had to be drunk to do it. But I told him. Three months ago."

I gasped, then recovered myself. Poor Tad.

"Oh, good for you. So you're an honest cheater."

He slammed his fists on the table. Then silence, long enough to hear the wall clock tick tock forty seconds. I waited, seething.

"Do you want to know what he said?" His voice was an appeal.

I shook my head and imagined Tad slumped and hurting.

"'I love you,' he said. 'I hope you'll let them go and come back to me.'"

Luke was crying out loud now. "I don't deserve him. I know I don't deserve him."

True. He didn't. He wouldn't get an argument from me.

I stood up, grabbed the wooden spoon and stirred and stirred the sauce. *Toil and trouble, toil and trouble.*

"And you haven't sworn them off?" I asked.

"I haven't."

I stamped my feet and slapped the side of his head like a caricature of an Italian kitchen hag.

"Jesus, Luke, why not? Are you crazy? Not to mention you could die. Jesus, half the men we know have died, are dying right now. Are you trying—God dammit—to kill yourself?"

He rubbed his reddening ear and covered his eyes with both hands.

"I don't know," he said, looking up. "I can't help it. I meet them, we fuck, I pay them money, then I get blasted and crawl back to Tad's place. Tad lets me in and fixes me up on the couch." He wrung his hands. "He takes care of me, but won't let me get into our bed. We hardly touch anymore."

Snot dripped from his nose as he sobbed openly now. He wiped it with the sleeve of his beach robe.

"Jesus, Luke! How can you do this? To yourself, to Tad?" I yelled at him. "How can you?"

His body shook and he wrapped his arms around his middle. All I could hear was bubbling on the stove. I turned both burners off. Then, all of a sudden, he sat up tall and his voice boomed, as if he had snapped to with an epiphany.

"Here's the blasted, blessed difference between me and Tad, Orla. He thought only of me. Me. You know what he said? You know what he asked?" Luke stood up and paced from stove to doorway and back again. "'How can you hate yourself this way, Luke? Why do you loathe yourself when you know my loving you proves you're wonderful? Wonderful.'"

I was flummoxed. Couldn't think of a thing to say. And I knew Luke was right. Tad was better than the both of us.

"I love him, I tell myself. But the truth is, Orla, I don't. I love what I want. What *I* want. Not a thing more."

He clapped his hands together as he paced, then had at his own cheeks as if his face were a punching bag.

"I want to feel young—I want novelty, Orla. I want Tad and me more than a decade ago."

He grabbed me by the shoulders and looked right into my eyes.

"But that's past, Orla. Even I know that. And Tad..."

Luke was weeping now. No holds barred. Weeping for what was gone, for what he had let go.

"Tad loves me. He really loves me. Loves me the way happily married people love each other, like my parents loved each other, each season a good one, even when they disappointed each other, even when they started failing. Even, —no, *especially*—then."

I seethed with jealousy.

He sat down again and banged his forehead on the tabletop three times. He might have been autistic Timmy Hawes from Mercy's seventh-grade summer camp down at Grand Isle.

It wasn't until I heard Bredice scream our names over and over from downstairs that I realized a siren was blaring from the ambulance pulling into our driveway.

Chapter Four
Other Mothers' Milk

We buried Signora Segreti Friday, June 9th. Her neurologist told Luke she had been the victim of a massive stroke that had rendered her brain-dead even before the ambulance had pulled into the drive. It took Luke three days to pull her off life support. ("But she looks alive. Her chest is moving up and down. They're wrong. She'll come back.") Tad went in with him when Doctor Taddeo arrived to turn off the breathing apparatus. Mercy and I, sitting just outside the closed door on two wooden folding chairs, had come after Tad phoned to say that Luke wanted us there at the end. I still had paint on my hands—the sunny yellow I had selected for the center of the enamel daisy buttons on the one-armed girl's dress in the contessa's photograph. Mercy was in her usual summer uniform—white Keds, khaki short shorts, and a blue cotton top with spaghetti straps. We had left Bredice back at the cottage, where she prayed with her three grandchildren. "I'll be here talking to the Lord," she had assured us, while Lester, Quince, and Favorly, each dressed in shorts and cowboy hats for the barbeque she'd promised them, stood hunched and quiet behind her, knowing from our faces that life and death were surely shaking hands. Favorly had hiccuped and shed some tears, but the twins' voices rose with their grandmother's—"Lord, deliver us. Lord, drop your mercy down."Quince took off his hat and held it against his chest. As we got into my car and pulled out of the driveway, Favorly was blowing kisses. Mercy reciprocated. As we sped downtown, I watched Mercy sideways while I drove. She was wringing her hands and tapping her right foot on the floor mat the entire way. Was she remembering Vietnam? Signora Segreti's death throes and final breath would certainly not be the first she had witnessed.

Signora was still being kept alive when we arrived at University Medical Center, but we knew instantly when she breathed her last: Luke's outcry, a sound he might have made otherwise if someone were bludgeoning his knees, penetrated the translucent glass between us. Mercy gripped both my hands, we stood, and Tad opened the heavy wooden door to let us in. Luke was lying face down on the bed with his mother, his face buried in her neck while Dr. Taddeo, tight-lipped and crisp at the foot of the bed, wrote on a chart. He nodded as we entered. Mercy walked around him to the other side of the bed, kissed Signora on her forehead, then ran her hand down her arm to her wrinkled fingers. "She's still warm," Mercy whispered, before turning away. I put my arms around my daughter, stroked her black silk hair, breathed in the scents of pine and mint from her favorite lotion. I stared down at the corpse of the woman who had become my second mother from the first day we two had walked into her vegetable garden in the summer of 1975. As if by a telepathic connection, she understood at once that her son had stolen my dream of Tad. She taught me how to bear it. Not accept it, mind you, but bear it. The way I do the weight of Daddy's abandonment, which, even after all these years of his earnest atonement, sits on my shoulders, a certain and immutable burden.

Luke's mother died just as dusk was descending over the city on Tuesday, June 6th. From then on Luke might as well have been comatose himself. For several weeks after his mother's burial he made her favorite rocking chair in the cottage his home. Never had I seen him so enervated. Not even Tad's devoted attention could rouse him to attempt conversation or take in sustenance. He just sat and stared at the floor in his mother's kitchen, while Bredice, herself in mourning for the loss of her friend, companion, and patient, wiped and swept and dusted around him. He moved only to use the toilet. Didn't shower or shave. Sipped water from time to time, ignoring his favorite foods, which Bredice prepared for him. Even Tad's threat to call social services did not rouse him.

It was Luke who needed a lifeline then. Tad saw to it that Bredice never left. In fact, he read her the portion of Signora Segreti's will that ensured lifetime use of the cottage for "my loyal friend and companion." Even at Bredice's emotional response to Signora's unanticipated gift, when she had gasped and lifted her apron to her eyes to wipe her copious tears, Luke remained impassive. Tad, Signora Segreti's lawyer and—even though it could not be spoken of in public—her longtime virtual son-in-law, spent part of each work day seeing to her wishes, which had been articulated and codified soon after the death and burial of Luke's father, Signor Segreti.

In addition to Bredice's ministrations and Tad's legal work, for at least two weeks after Signora's funeral Mass at the Loyola University chapel, more than a few of "our Jesuits," as she always called them, paid daily consolation calls to the cottage. Their visits were not unusual. Long after Signora Segreti and Bredice officially retired from the Jesuit residence's kitchen, they often invited the men they had served to what had become joyous, coveted suppers. A birthday, an anniversary, a leave-taking as a man of the cloth, a retirement, a consultation, sometimes even a confession to the two trusted women. The priests visited frequently. Still, Luke would not, could not, be drawn out.

His only words, spoken *sotto voce* and repeatedly, were "My fault, my fault."

The times I tried to awaken his senses, pulling a chair close to his, he said, "I'm tired," and closed his eyes.

On a Friday—June 30th, to be precise—Mercy went down to the cottage at nine to take care of Lester, Quince, and Favorly, who of course were on summer break by then, so that Bredice could run some errands. You know, the usual chores—bank, grocery, hairdresser, drug store. Mercy planned to watch the children by the pool and do the same sorts of crafts she and Lily Wainwright were used to facilitating over at Catholic Charities. Honestly, I was glad of it. I love Mercy, no doubt about that, but the incessant music booming from her bedroom and her unending phone conversations with friends both local and not (I dread the next phone bill) do not make for the best painting atmosphere. Now, with her and her charges out in the yard, I could replace 2 Live Crew's *As Nasty as They Wanna Be* with *La Traviata*. The deadline for my August 15h exhibit in Fiesole was beginning to feel as oppressive as a New Orleans' hazy, hot, and humid day.

But no sooner did Act I end, right after I had finished painting the Nazi musician's hair, ensuring that his left-side part was as straight as a razor's edge, just the way it appeared in the contessa's photograph, than Mercy bounded up the stairs and into my studio. Favorly came right behind her. Lester and Quince followed at a more measured pace.

"He's gone," Mercy said.

I sighed aloud at the interruption. Didn't turn to look.

"Who's gone?" I asked, still appraising my work. I liked the soldier's hair. It was nuanced by four colors, with a glow that attested to the fellow's attention to grooming, even as grimy and grim battles swirled outside the music room where he and his (looked like, however unlikely) lover held their instruments.

"Mr. Luke!" shouted Favorly. "Mr. Luke!"

At Luke's name, I finally turned away from the canvas and looked at Mercy. The three children stood behind her like backup singers.

"Oh?" I said. "He's decided to come back into the world, has he?"

I spoke jauntily, imagining that Luke had showered, dressed, and maybe gone to see his barber for a shave, a haircut, and whatever other primping he required to look as gleaming and fine as he usually did. I twirled my brush in my right hand.

Mercy shook her head. Her just-trimmed chin-length hair afforded a lovely view of her graceful swan's neck. Her mother had to have been a beauty. I'd seen a photo of her alleged father in Tad's office. Her upturned nose and freckles would have been his. I needed to paint her again in her early adulthood, I thought. I'd dress her in a simple shift—silvery, perhaps.

The sound of her voice interrupted my painter's vision of her.

"I don't know where he is, Mamma. Really. We can't find him."

She seemed upset. I, on the other hand, was relieved. Luke was not a man who stayed still for long. He had re-bounded from his father's death just fine. It wasn't as if Signora Segreti had been young. He knew that she was losing the capacity to do the things she loved best—garden, cook, walk. He had probably gone off to the barber or perhaps the gym.

"Where did you look?" I asked.

I wanted to get back to painting.

Mercy shifted her weight from one leg to the other.

"When he wasn't in the rocking chair, I assumed he was in the bathroom or the bedroom," she said.

"Mercy sent us to look," Lester said. "I went into Signora Segreti's bedroom first, then into Nanna's. Mr. Luke weren't in either one."

Quince giggled.

"What are you—stupid?!" his brother said, shoving Quince. "Show some respect."

Quince pushed back at his brother.

"I'm not laughing about Mr. Luke gone missing," he said. He giggled some more. "Just that you said you didn't want to have to smell him stink if he was on the toilet."

Mercy and I both laughed now. Favorly raised her eyebrows and held her nose, dancing in circles as she did. I had to smile. They were all three wet from the pool, each with boldly striped towels wrapped around them. The floor was puddled with their foot prints.

With reluctance, I went to the stereo against the windowless wall and turned off the opera. Then I placed my brush into one of the plastic cups lined up on the center windowpane to the right of my canvas.

"Maybe this is good news," I said, looking to Mercy, who didn't seem to have gone into the pool at all. "Maybe Luke went out with Bredice in her car."

Favorly peeked around Mercy.

"We was already in the pool before they left," Favorly said. "I didn't hear Mr. Luke or Nanna say good-bye."

"Us, neither," the twins said together. "We was divin' for quarters," Lester said, and Quince took two out from a pocket in his swimming trunks.

"I see," I said, and looked to Mercy again.

My daughter kept quiet. She had one forefinger to her lips and seemed to be going through something in her mind. The children watched her as closely as they did Saturday morning cartoons.

"I was keeping my eyes on the children in the water," she said. She strode between the canvas and the doorway as she spoke. "And I did hear the kitchen door close and the car start. But I didn't look."

"Okay. So everything seemed normal."

"I suppose. It's just that he's been so depressed."

"Yes," I said. "No doubt about that."

"He hasn't been willing to speak with me for weeks now," Mercy said.

"That's so unlike him," I said. "And sad for you, I imagine."

Mercy nodded. "Very," she said. "I like him better than most everybody else."

"Duly noted," I replied, and turned the opera back on. It didn't appear there was anything to be concerned about. At least not yet. Though I did wonder if Luke had found his way to the Portanova and his boy or boys.

"He might have gone off with Bredice, right?" I said.

"Maybe," Mercy said.

"Tell you what. If Bredice can't tell us where he's gone to, I'll do some investigating myself. How does that sound? I certainly don't want to disturb Tad unless or before we have cause to."

Mercy perked up a bit. She cracked her knuckles. Quince did the same.

"I guess that's a plan, then," she said.

But she didn't make a move, just stood still in the middle of my studio.

"So let's not worry until then." I tried to sound reassuring. Convinced myself, anyway, that Luke had simply decided that enough languishing was enough. I wouldn't have been surprised if he were strolling about the neighborhood or had phoned for a cab. I only hoped he wasn't seeking solace in the embrace of a trick who could kill as easily as kiss him.

I turned away from Mercy and the children and prepared to paint the girl in the photograph, arranging the colors I'd need for her face. But as I selected my first brush, an uneasiness seized me. I could actually feel Mercy and the children watching silently from behind. I couldn't understand why they weren't leaving. So I turned back toward them, brush still in hand, and, opening my arms wide enough to engulf all of them in a wing-like spread, started moving them towards the doorway.

"So, let's just assume he's with Bredice. We'll find out soon enough. She said she'd be back in two hours or so."

Walking, walking.

"I guess we should," Mercy said. She paused. "But like I already said, he's been so depressed. I can't even imagine him having the energy to get cleaned up and dressed to go out."

I couldn't think of anything more to offer her. We were standing in the doorway. Good. Slow progress. But in the right direction.

"Maybe Nanna helped him like she does me," Favorly piped up.

"She helps you 'cause you're still a babychile." Quince stuck out his tongue at his sister.

Favorly put her hands on her hips and stood on tiptoe.

"You're just jealous Nanna makes you dress yourself," she said, not without some satisfaction in her voice. "She give me more 'tention."

I liked Favorly's spunk.

Keeping my arms outspread, I made shoo-ing motions with my hands to Mercy, who said, sarcasm as thick as hot molasses, "Ah, yes, the great artist has been disturbed." She bowed ostentatiously and backed into the hallway.

I should have apologized, but couldn't manage to. Instead, I shrugged my shoulders. Mercy glared.

Just then, as if tweaked with a magic wand, Favorly jumped up and down.

"I know! I know what they're doing."

I lowered my wings.

Even her brothers looked interested.

"What?' Mercy asked. "Tell us," she said, getting low and bouncing on her Keds in front of the little girl.

"They're pro'ly getting mothers' milk. That's what Nanna said Mr. Luke needed." Favorly was as sure as a person could be. "Even without his own mother's milk, 'cause his mamma be dead and gone, Nanna can get him some milk from lots of other mothers. Cow and goat mothers. Right, Mercy? You said Nanna told you that in the kitchen where she and Signora worked when you were missing your first mother, the lady who borned you, right? The lady in Veenam, right, Mercy? Right?" Favorly spun around and around. "She told you your new mother, this lady, Miss Orla,"—the little girl pointed at me—"Miss Orla made sure she got you mothers' milk from other mothers, from cow and goat mothers. Then you didn't have to miss your own mamma so much."

The words were an arrow to my heart. I went limp, a balloon losing its air. I hadn't heard this story. Not from Bredice. Not from Mercy. Not from anyone at all. Who else knew it? When was it told? Why wasn't it mine? Mercy's and mine.

Other mothers' milk.

I looked at my daughter, who was rising from Favorly now to face me. Slow. Everything felt slow. I felt myself sinking to the floor.

"Mamma," Mercy said, grabbing onto my arms to steady me and keep me standing.

56

"Why you crying, Miss Orla?" Favorly asked. "Is you sad about Mr. Luke being lost?"

"All right, I'm all right, Favorly," I mumbled.

I nodded to Mercy that she could let go, that I could stand by myself. I took a moment, breathed deeply, then turned away from them all and faced the canvas. The opera music filled the room and the Nazi soldier's parted hair undulated before my tears. Nobody said another word. The children tip-toed out of the studio and padded down the stairs.

When they were gone, Mercy spoke to my back. I stared at the Nazi's part.

"I was just a little girl," she said. "You were at an exhibit and Signora brought me to the priests' kitchen to cook with her. She stood me on a chair and I stirred pea soup for the priests. I remember stirring the soup."

I stiffened, took in a breath, held it. I was afraid to move.

"After, when Signora was done preparing supper, Bredice brought out some sugar snaps. Cookies and milk. We all sat down at a round table. And she told me the story, Bredice did."

I tilted my head, waiting to hear more.

"Go on," I said, still facing the canvas.

"She told me how sometimes a person needs other mothers' milk if her mother's got none of her own to give."

I crossed my arms over my breasts, at last turning from the canvas to face my daughter, the child I was supposed to have saved. No doubt about it, I was exposed, found out, discovered to be a fraud.

"Right before she handed me over to the flight attendants," Mercy was talking with tears streaming down her face, "I was screaming, thrashing and screaming, but it didn't stop her. 'I've got to, got to,' she said. She told me my father would find me in America. And that she would join us later. That he and I would meet her at another plane. Then the three of us would be together. That we would make our home in America and be a complete family."

Mercy squeezed her eyes tight. Tears dotted her cheeks.

"She must have wanted that desperately," I whispered. "Must have believed it would come to pass."

My breaths were coming fast, too fast.

Mercy continued. She wiped her face with her hands, opened her eyes, breathed a long sigh, and spoke with the authority of an ancient sage.

"But it wasn't true. None of it was true."

Done with crying, then, she didn't waver or whimper, just stood there speaking the truth of her life. She rubbed her swan's neck as if she were caressing down instead of human skin. She looked into my longing, sorry, terribly imperfect eyes. Eyes that valued my portraits more than the people who sat for them.

"And then I got you."

"Oh, Mercy!" I cried. I dropped my paintbrush and grabbed her hard, swaddling her in a too-tight grip.

"Mercy, when are you coming?" Lester called from downstairs. "Nanna says we can't go in the water unless you be with us."

"I've got to go," Mercy said, wriggling from my hold.

"Yes," I answered. "I know. You've got to."

She turned toward the doorway.

"Coming!" she called down to the children.

"Wait. Please," I said, and she looked back at me.

"You know I love you, right?"

She paused, bent down, and picked up my brush from the floor. She offered it to me and I took it.

"As much as you can," she answered, and walked away.

Her sneakers thumped, thumped, like heartbeats on the stairs.

Chapter Five
Hide and Seek

"Yes, indeed, Mister Luke came downtown with me," Bredice said. "I was just fixin' to go when he asked, 'Might you wait on me ten minutes?'"

"Thank the Lord," I said. I watched Mercy's body relax, become pliable again, ridding itself of the rigidity it had suffered in my studio earlier.

Bredice was unpacking groceries. As soon as she'd pulled into the drive, Mercy, the children, and I had run to the guest cottage—Mercy and the children from the pool, me from my studio. Between putting the milk, eggs, and fresh chicory into the refrigerator and lining up boxes of pasta and rice on the pantry shelves, Bredice kept us apprised of the heretofore missing Luke.

"Mind you, it was as if an alarm went off in his head," she said. "Him sitting there nearly in a coma for three weeks, uglifyin' himself without washing or shaving, then, boom, up like a flash."

She shooed the children out to the patio, handing them the deck of cards she kept handy on the windowsill over the sink.

"Whyn't you all play Go Fish while we organize in here."

She took three tall glasses already dried on the dish rack and set them on the table. Then she reached into the refrigerator for the always-ready pitcher of iced tea. Mercy selected a lemon from the fruit bowl and found a cutting board and plate on which she sliced quarter wedges for us. I pulled out a kitchen chair and sat down, lifting three napkins from the napkin holder in the center of the table, and waited for more information.

"All of a sudden, he jumped up from that rocking chair—she pointed at Signora's favorite seat—and practically ran barefoot into Signora's room. I heard the shower, the blow dryer, and lots of banging around." She poured the tea, filling the three glasses. "When he came back in here, he seemed his own self again. He was dressed in his 'going to make some money' outfit, you know how he calls it, the one he kept here in Signora's wedding armoire in case a client came by the gallery in the big house and he was down here."

I imagined Luke in his oatmeal linen suit, his lilac and pink bow tie of *fleurs de lis*, and the vanilla leather loafers he always wore without socks. Couldn't help smiling.

Mercy leaned against the counter by the sink and Bredice sat beside me.

"Where did he go?" I asked.

Bredice took a long, slow swallow of tea.

"The bank."

Now Mercy sat down, as well.

"Do you know what he planned to do after that?" I asked.

"He," she began, but something caught her eye and she stopped speaking.

"Go on," Mercy said, but our eyes followed Bredice as she stood up from her chair and walked toward the rolled manila envelope sticking like a cylinder out of the flat-backed straw basket Signora had always kept hanging right next to the wall phone.

"What's that? Mercy asked.

Bredice drew out the envelope, unrolled it, paused, and said, "My name's on it."

Mercy stood up, went over to Bredice, and looked.

"It's Luke's handwriting," she said. "I'd recognize it anywhere. He always sent me checks at school so I could 'enjoy some entertainment your mamma doesn't need to know about.'"

"It figures," I said. "Party pooper you both think I am. He's always spoiled you."

"'That's what uncles, even adopted ones, are for,'" Mercy quoted Luke's oft-stated mantra.

I never knew what Luke and Mercy were conspiring to do. Even Tad wasn't party to their *tête-à-têtes* and letter writing. They shared a bond I could only describe as visceral. Sometimes they didn't even need to speak. As if they shared a brain. Or, more likely, a heart.

"Cheater!" Favorly shouted from the patio, to whoops of laughter from her brothers.

"Don't be a baby," Lester said.

"But she is," Quince insisted.

"Am not!" Favorly protested.

Bredice opened the sealed envelope, using the brass letter opener also in the basket. From the envelope she pulled out four smaller envelopes, ecru, all the same, the size of thank you notes or party invitations. Each one showed Luke's handwriting again. The notes were addressed to *Bredice, Mercy, Orla,* and *Tad.* Bredice laid them on the table.

Sudden dread rose from my gut. Quick, God awful, sickly dread.

"Oh, no," I said, grabbing the envelope addressed to me and tearing it open.

Mercy picked up hers, as well. Then she watched me, at the same time pressing her own unopened missive between her palms.

I read it aloud.

> *I am sorry to have disappointed you, dearest friend. You are a first-rate artist. I'm glad we made money together. Paint my found body as a cautionary tale to other ne'er do wells.*
>
> *As ever,*
> *Luke*

I screamed, ran to the phone, dialed Tad, and waited. Bredice put her hands on both sides of her face.

"Good Lord," Bredice said, just as a receptionist answered. "He told me he had an appointment on the Chartres River."

"He's gone to St. Suplice, then!" Mercy cried. "To their cottage on the river."

She spotted Bredice's car keys on the counter by the breadbox and pointed. Bredice nodded for her to take them. While Mercy sprinted to grab them, Bredice ripped open her note, read it, then shoved it under my nose.

> *No one could have cared for my mother better. Thank you. Soon a check will arrive in the mail for your grandchildren.*

Tad picked up his phone.

"Tad, Luke's going to kill himself. He's gone to the cottage. He's got a two-hour lead."

"I'm leaving now," Tad said, no questions asked. "Phone your father. He'll know what to do."

Favorly came into the kitchen. "Why's everybody yelling? What's goin' on? I got to go to the bathroom."

"We're going to get Luke," Mercy answered. "Mamma, I'll get our handbags up at the big house."

She grabbed Tad's note even as she held onto hers.

Daddy picked right up when his office nurse said it was me calling.

"Please, please drive carefully," he said. "I'll get the ambulance and what all. See you there."

Bredice followed me to the car and Mercy came running from the big house with our pocketbooks. I reached out so Mercy could throw me the keys over the Buick's hood, but my hands were shaking so much that she didn't. I couldn't control them. Not one bit.

"I'm driving," Mercy said. "Get in."

I couldn't argue.

"Here," Mercy said, lifting her and Tad's notes from her brassiere. "Hold them. That should steady you."

I grasped them, watched the envelopes quiver with my hands. Once we were on the road, the motion and hum of the car's engine calmed me some, so that I could trace my right forefinger over the *Mercy* and *Tad* Luke had penned. I wanted to open the envelopes. I turned Mercy's envelope over and slid my right forefinger toward the glued triangular flap. Mercy saw me from the corner of her right eye just as we got onto the interstate.

"Don't even think about it," she warned.

Her voice was hard and curt, so much so that I snatched my finger away, reached down and picked my purse up from the floor beneath the passenger seat, and unlatched it. Then, making sure she could see me doing so, I slid both notes into a zippered compartment inside my purse. They remained sealed and unread, just as she had insisted. As if not opening them might matter, as if not seeing Luke's words would slow things down, as if not reading his good-byes could ensure there wouldn't be any.

Chapter Six
On the Chartres River

Luke stood barefoot and rigid at the end of the wooden dock. He could have been a totem pole. The dock, long and wide enough for three tables for eight to be set in a row every Fourth of July, until now had been a symbol of *laissez les bon temps rouler*. Luke was still dressed in his making money suit and had his pant legs rolled to his knees. His turquoise-rimmed sunglasses glinted in the early afternoon sun. His back was to the water, and the Chartres River was running fast. It was blanket hot. No breeze. A police boat made circles in the brownish current far enough away from him so as not to be a threat. Its presence there at the ready, along with its persistent *chuggachugga*, reassured me somewhat. Luke was shouting to Daddy, who also stood on the dock, but as far away from Luke and as close to the cottage as possible. I think I heard Luke holler that something was "all my fault." Daddy was wearing his doctor's coat over his shirt and khakis. "Well, let's talk about that, Luke," he shouted back. "Let's see if we can make things right." Tad stood right next to Daddy. "Impossible," Luke shouted. "I've ruined everything. Nobody can ever trust me again." Daddy kept talking. "Will you at least give it a chance?" Daddy asked. "As a favor to me? For friendship's sake?" While the two of them kept up their conversation, Tad undid his tie and slipped off his suit jacket, dropping them both without looking to see where they fell. Lifting one leg at a time, he removed his cordovans and started toward Luke with slow, deliberate steps.

I don't rightly know if any of them knew that Mercy and I had arrived. First thing we saw in front of the cottage was the village ambulance, its motor running and lights flashing. The two EMTs—pot-bellied veteran Carver LaValle holding the keys, and just-married Kacey used-to-be Coltrain, now Kacey Metzger, her pony tail reaching down to her waist—stood watching on the leafy slope at the water's edge. Mercy and I scrambled down to them. Right beside Carver, as familiar as a supersized beer cooler, their rectangular medical case showed red and white amidst the ferns and branches.

"Luke!" Tad called out. "I'm coming to stand with you. I want to be with you."

He kept up his slow, measured steps and held his hands in the air.

Luke sobbed and put his left hand to his mouth. He lowered his right hand into his pants pocket and pulled out something black.

"I've got a gun," he yelled.

"Oh, no," Mercy whispered and grabbed my arm.

"Hail Mary!" I blurted. "Holy Mother of God. Help us."

"What did you say?" Kacey said.

"Nothing," I answered.

Mercy let go and we both watched Carver turn away from the water and run up the slope.

66

This was as bad as when the Klan had busted up the church picnic in St. Suplice and tried to kill Reverend Makepeace and my grandmother. I felt exactly the same, helpless and scared, thinking folks were about to die, just like that. Feeling what a sorry bunch all of us human beings can be.

Luke held the pistol up in the air. I held my breath. Tad paused.

"I see!" Tad hollered back, walking again. Slowly, slowly. "I see it. I'll be careful. You be careful, too."

I was begging Blessed Mother Mary to help. "Pay attention, will you? Listen and do something, please."

Carver radioed somebody about the potential suicide having a weapon and asked for backup. Pretty soon I heard the wail of sirens, and Sheriff Bob Metcalf's car and a squad car both screeched to a stop across the street. Sheriff Metcalf's hand was on his holster when he got down to us. Bill Taggert, the rookie cop, came down out of the squad car, his hand on his gun, as well.

"Orla, Mercy." Bob tipped his cowboy hat.

Mercy let go of my arm. She looked up at Bob, then over at Bill.

"Don't shoot him," she said. "Please don't shoot him."

"We don't want to, honey," Bob said. "We won't if we don't have to."

But he kept his hand on his gun.

"He ever act like this before?" Bill asked me.

I paused from my praying, turned to him, and said, "Not in the time I've known him, and that's about fifteen years."

"Huh," said Bill. "Wonder what's got into him."

I might have blabbed what I knew, but it wasn't my story to tell, so I kept quiet, silently imploring the Blessed Virgin instead.

Both Bob and Bill climbed onto the dock and stood near Daddy, both of them poised to run and grab Luke.

Tad was now but one rowboat's length from him when, with a wave of his free hand, Luke motioned us all to go away.

"Leave me! Go on now!" he yelled out.

Then he turned around and faced the water.

My already-folded hands clenched. Turned clammy with dread.

"I'm right here," Tad said. "I'm not going anywhere. I'm right here with you. Wait for me. I want to be with you."

Luke's whole body was shaking now. He still held the gun aloft. But it wasn't steady anymore.

"I don't deserve you. Let me go, Tad."

"Not yet, Luke. Not yet. I've got to tell you something. Something important. Something I don't want anyone else to hear."

It was then that Mercy said, "Enough."

She dropped to the ground, sat for a moment, and yanked off her Keds. Then she strode into the water. Didn't so much as flinch from the rocks that were certainly cutting her feet.

"Mercy," I called after her, "he's got a gun," but she was already swimming. Dogpaddling to Luke.

"Mother of God, protect her." I prayed out loud now.

"Hope somebody can," Kacey said.

I wanted to slap Kacey's smart-ass face.

I thought better than to go after my daughter. She swims faster than I do anyway. And we'd just make a second scene, another potential disaster for everybody. All I could do was hope Luke wouldn't start shooting. That and keep praying, trusting that the Virgin would overlook my lousy mothering and keep my daughter from getting hurt or killed.

"Okay, Tad," Luke answered, "I'm listening. I'll wait for you. But hurry. Hurry, now."

The gun seesawed in his hand.

"I love you," Tad said. "I need you. We can work things out. I promise you."

Luke swayed from side to side. Left. Right. Left. Right. The police boat moved in. Luke waved his left hand at it as if he were shooing away an annoying poodle. The boat's engine quieted and it bobbed on the water.

Mercy paddled parallel to the dock. Arriving at its left corner, she splashed and splashed, her arms pounding the water up and down, up and down.

"Uncle Luke!" she screamed. "Uncle Luke! Help me!"

Distracted, Luke turned and looked down.

"Mercy!" he yelled her. "Get away! Go away!"

"I can't, Uncle Luke!" she cried. "I'm hurt! Help me! Help me!"

Luke stared down at my daughter in the water. He looked up at the gun in his right hand. He angled it to the right, pointing it away from her and out at the river.

Tad said, "I don't want to lose you, Luke."

"Please help me!" Mercy called.

She flailed and flailed, head under water, then up again. Pretending to drown for Luke, she was, betting he would save her. Sure he would. I was sure, too. He'd never let her go. Never.

Maybe the Virgin *was* helping. Maybe she would come through this time. "Hail Mary, Mother of God. Save them both, please."

Still holding the gun up and away from her, Luke knelt down on his left knee.

"Thank you," I whispered. "Thank you."

"My leg, Uncle Luke. Something's happened to my leg. I can't get up there myself."

Tad was nearly there.

Luke looked to his right at the police boat but a few yards from the dock. Then to his left and Tad just an arm's length from him now. He laid the gun on the dock at his right side so it rested between him and the river. Mercy raised both her arms. He reached down for her. As he lifted her, Tad lunged, tackling him. Mercy fell back into the water. Luke fought like a gator, but Tad held on. And with his right foot he pushed the pistol off of the dock and into the river.

"Bastard!" Luke screamed. "Bastard."

The police boat met the dock.

Daddy and Bob and Bill dashed to Luke and Tad, Daddy's unbuttoned doctor's coat flapping behind him.

Though Luke was bigger than Tad, I knew Tad would not let him go. Jesus, he hadn't thrown him out for becoming a drunk, for fucking other men. He sure as hell wasn't going to let him loose this way, either.

Luke tried to get up. He growled and bit, but Tad stayed on him. They struggled so much that pretty soon he and Tad had their feet toward the river and their heads toward us. They looked like human bodies keeping rough time on a clock that read 12:30.

Bob and Bill got either side of them, two human pillars blocking Luke from the water.

Mercy swam away from the edge of the dock, just far enough to get clear of where the sheriff was. Then she hoisted herself up and crawled onto the dock. Lying down on her stomach, she inched her way to Luke as if she were training for combat. She brought her head to his.

"I love you, I love you!" she cried, caressing his hair while he writhed.

"Let's get him up," Daddy said. "Stand up, Mercy."

Mercy stood while Daddy and Tad each gripped one of Luke's arms and pulled him upward. He kicked and cursed.

70

They dragged him to his feet. Mercy crouched under them and wrapped both her arms around his waist. Then the three of them hauled him back to us, the sheriff and his rookie striding sideways on each side of the dock, their arms outspread in case Luke broke free.

Carver and Kacey were ready. They'd run up the slope, gotten the stretcher out of the ambulance, and raised and locked it. They donned masks and rubber gloves and met the others when they reached the road. I'd run up the rise as soon as I saw that Mercy was okay.

"Sorry," I wanted to tell Luke, so he would hear me. I needed to apologize. I'd been too hard on him. Too hard. I'm no paragon of virtue, either. *Like you*, I wanted to say, *I want what I want. I'm so very sorry. Part of this is my fault, too.*

Wet and bloodied about her feet and legs, Mercy was begging now, her voice become a plea.

"Don't hurt him," she begged, as Carver and Kacey jacketed Luke tight, his spittle pinging their faces like summer hail. "Don't hurt him."

She stood so close that Kacey elbowed her away.

"Let me do my job," Kacey said in a raised voice.

"Bitch!" Mercy yelled at her, tears streaming down her face.

Kacey ignored her, but Bill Taggert grabbed Mercy by her elbows from behind and backed her away.

"Calm down now," he said, sounding the way he had to.

"Don't, Mercy," I called out to her. "Here, come here. Please."

I held out my arms.

But my daughter didn't obey. Instead she nodded and said, "Sorry," to Bill, who asked, "You sure?" She nodded again, so he unhanded her. Rubbing both her arms, she turned her attention to my daddy then.

"We're going to help him, not hurt him," he assured her. "Don't you worry, now."

He knelt to his doctor's bag while the EMTs strapped Luke onto the stretcher. Luke struggled in vain, wrapped in the straitjacket. He was howling, enraged.

I put my hands over my ears and watched Daddy fill a syringe with some liquid.

Mercy was sobbing. When Daddy was ready, he stood, his gloved hand holding the syringe aloft the way Luke had held the pistol. Still sobbing, Mercy followed Daddy to the stretcher. He let her stay beside him.

"You're safe now, Luke," Daddy said. He held the needle in his right hand and rubbed Luke's forehead with his left. "You're with Mercy and me and the others. You're safe now. We're not going to leave you. We won't let you go."

As he spoke softly now, reassuring him, Daddy covered Luke's eyes for just a moment while he jabbed the needle into Luke's imprisoned arm. Then Daddy eased the sedative in, its incipient balm guaranteeing at least a temporary oblivion.

"Safe now," Daddy kept crooning, as all of us watched Luke's shoulders relax.

Mercy's Keds were still by the water's edge. Since Luke wouldn't hear me now if I spoke to him, I ran down and got them, then came back up the slope with one sneaker dangling from my left hand, the other from my right. Luke was completely still as Carver and Kacey slid him into the ambulance. Daddy got in right after. We all waited while both EMTs went down the slope to retrieve their cooler.

"Thank you, fellows!" he called to the sheriff and Bill. "I got him now."

"You betcha," said the sheriff, and gave a wave. "Nice going, Tad and Mercy," he said. "You both did good."

Tad looked like a human rag.

"You take care of yourself, now," Bill said to Mercy, patting her on the back before he left.

"Let's go," Bob said to Bill. "It's almost 3:00, about time for church camp to let out for the afternoon. Let all those mothers pickin' up their kids make googly eyes at you and ignore a has-been like me."

Even Tad smiled.

"Yessir," answered Bill, grinning big and blushing, and they left, Bill showing off when he squealed the squad car tires on purpose.

Daddy leaned out of the ambulance. "I'll meet you all at home soon," he said. Stay together on the road and head on there. Minerva will be expecting you. I expect you could all use a stiff drink."

Kacey closed the ambulance's back doors as Carver walked to the driver's seat.

"I'm sorry," Mercy called out to Kacey.

"It ain't the first time," Kacey answered. "And won't be the last."

She didn't so much as glance at Mercy. I sure didn't like her. Apology not accepted.

They drove off, no siren needed now.

Tad lowered himself onto the grass by the cottage's eucalyptus-wreathed front door and, with his knees up to his chin, put his head in his hands. He was as disheveled and forlorn as I'd ever seen him—his shirt more sweat-drenched than not, his ankles starting bruises where Luke had kicked him, a bite with teeth marks on his left cheek. I dropped Mercy's sneakers, sat down to Tad's right, stretched out my legs, and draped my left arm over his shoulder. After the ambulance was out of sight, Mercy joined us. She sat cross-legged facing us both. She was wet and grimy.

"Our heroine," I said. "You were brave. Probably foolish. Definitely brave."

She was only sniffling now. She'd seen better days. And probably worse. Seen things I'd never know about.

Tad lifted his head.

"Thank you, Mercy," he said, and tousled her hair the way he used to when she only reached his waist.

She lost control then. Let herself go.

"Oh, Mamma!" she cried.

She crawled to me, got as close to my torso as she could, then burrowed into my arms the way she might have if she hadn't been another mother's baby.

Chapter Seven
An Unexpected Gathering

"I can't believe he tried to off himself," my baby brother Arthur said, banging the screen door and coming into the kitchen. He dropped his soccer bag by the umbrella stand. He was almost as tall as our daddy and had our mamma's smirky smile. He'd graduated eighth grade at the regional middle school in Convent last month and would turn 14 on December 25th. "I heard about the commotion when I stopped by the firehouse for lunch with Benny."

Benny was Arthur's best friend on the traveling soccer team. And Benny's dad was Todd Markham, the fire chief and station-appointed cook. Evidently, he made lunch for any of the fellows on the team when their schedule matched the noon meal at the firehouse.

"You're an asshole," Mercy replied. "My too-young uncle, nothing but an asshole."

Sad to say, such were their usual niceties.

Mercy was standing by the sink drinking lemon water from a crystal pitcher, one glass after another. Her knees were scraped and crusted with dried blood from when she had clambered onto the dock and lain down with Luke. She hadn't yet cleaned up and changed. I was sitting at the kitchen table with my mamma.

"Nice to see you, too, Merce," Arthur said. He looked her up and down. "Christ, what happened to you? You look like shit."

Mercy didn't even have to think.

"Saved Uncle Luke's life," she said, and poured herself a third or fourth glass—I couldn't keep count.

"Goddam heroine, then. I'm impressed. Way to go. No flies on you, Merce."

He high-fived her.

"She did," I sighed in relief as I spoke, as did my mamma Minerva, aka "Mamerva," as Mercy had christened her some years ago to differentiate between us and confer grandmother status upon her.

Arthur came over to the table and kissed me on both cheeks.

"Gone European on us now?" I teased.

He scratched his head, his hair the color of shaved ginger.

"If you say so," he said. "All I know is you get to hug and kiss any girl you want this way and she thinks you're a gentleman instead of a lech."

"You're incorrigible," Mamerva sighed.

"*Are* you a lech?" I asked.

Mamerva hardly ever reprimanded him.

"Me?" Arthur stooped down and wrapped me in a bear hug. "Why, I'm a perfect gentleman, Big Sis." Then he straightened up and scratched his crotch. Jesus, did they all do that?

He turned to look at Mercy.

"But what if he's angry at you for saving him? What if he really wanted to die?" Scratch, scratch. "Seriously."

Mercy shifted from one leg to the other and sipped from her glass.

"What if you're still an asshole for asking?" Mercy said. She put her glass into the sink. "Nobody wants to die. Not really, anyway. They only try to, to see if anybody cares enough to keep them alive."

I wondered if that were so. Thought about Denny Cowles. How the blood rushed right out of him and none of us could save him that night in the bayou after his sister's wedding. I think he really meant to die. Otherwise he wouldn't have fixed it so the gators would make his death certain. That's what serving in Vietnam did to him. Vietnam and his stinking father. Now *there* was a man who made an ordinary lech look like a prince.

"Jesus, you're a philosopher, too," Arthur said.

He laughed as if he had said something witty and sat down.

My mamma and I were drinking gin and tonics. I know I was on my third. Mamerva was, too, I was pretty sure. It had been an unnerving day so far, if I needed an excuse. What hers was I couldn't tell. The acidity of the lime quarters I kept sucking on was consoling.

I must say that Mercy's assessment of Arthur was mostly correct. Though six years younger than she, Arthur was Mercy's legitimate uncle and my frequent nemesis. He, the boy wonder of the soccer field—if you believe my parents—has never experienced a day of want or loss in his life. He was born into Castleberry-ness, our parents properly married and rich before his birth, thereby immediately conferring upon him the societal and material benefits befitting St. Suplice royalty. Not to mention that he shares the day of his birth with none other than the Lord himself. He struts around town like an heir apparent. I call him King Arthur when he pontificates, which is nearly always.

Love and jealousy characterize my warring feelings for him. And his flippant manner annoys me to no end. Mercy deals with him much more effectively than I do. Perhaps because she doesn't seek approval from Mamerva and Pappa Prout nearly as much as I do. So much for my maturity. You'd think my public celebrity status, at least in the art world, would have endowed me with enough confidence to face down an arrogant teenager. But family skullduggery, alliances and misalliances trump worldly success every time, don't you know. Mercy's got her own proven posse of fans in NOLA—me, Tad, Luke, Bredice, Don, Lily, and, until their deaths, the late Signora and Signor Segreti. But I'm still and always seeking assurances that Mamma and Daddy value me as much as they do their sole legitimate offspring.

"Do you want Tad to hear you talk about Luke like that?" Mercy asked.

"Where is Tad, by the way?" Arthur asked, looking around the kitchen.

What did he think? That Tad was playing hide and seek? That he'd pop out of the broom closet and say "Boo!"?

"I don't mean any harm. I'm merely stating a fact," Arthur continued. "Tad deals in facts, and the fact is Luke tried to off himself. I can just see tomorrow's headline: 'Fag Art Dealer Saved by Adopted Daughter of Notorious Artist.'"

Hmm. I took some pride in Arthur's knowing that I was sometimes considered a provocateur because of my subject matter and interpretations. And I did have to admit that Arthur was probably not too far off in his prediction. Fact and opinion were kissing cousins in the *St. Suplice Daily*.

Arthur got up, went to the kitchen door, and grabbed his soccer bag that was by the umbrella stand. Then he opened the door to the laundry room and flung the bag in. He stood by the door, every now and again cracking his knuckles.

"Tad's right upstairs," I said.

"Tad is?"

"What are you, deaf, too?" asked Mercy.

She looked down at her knees.

"Yes, and he nearly lost Luke," Mamerva continued. "Remember, he loves him."

She got up and walked to the dishwasher, opened its door, and collected the cleaned utensils first. She bustled about the kitchen from silverware drawer to the dish cabinets to the right of the stove, and the glass cabinets on either side of the sink. Her legs and arms were still slim and shapely, but her middle had expanded significantly over the last few years. I cringed inwardly. I was determined to thwart that development in my own body. Thus far, my summer regimen was working effectively. May's muffin top of flesh no longer protruded over my waist.

"His lover," Arthur said. "Jesus. How embarrassing." Arthur scrunched up his face in apparent disgust.

"Asshole again," Mercy said. "Embarrassing, how? Are you embarrassed that Luke tried to kill himself or are you embarrassed that he and Tad are lovers?"

Arthur shrugged his shoulders. "Both, I guess," he said.

"Well, I'm embarrassed to be related to you," Mercy went on.

Arthur didn't miss a beat. "Only by law," he said. "Not by blood."

"Good God!" I said. I wanted to slap him. "Sometimes I actually hate you, King Arthur," I said. I couldn't help myself.

"Oh, he's only kidding, Orla," Mamerva said.

She was wiping the sink with a paper towel. She always took his side.

"I'm only kidding," Arthur mimicked her.

I stood up from my chair, went over to Mercy, and stood next to her. "Doubt it," I said.

"Who cares?" Mercy said, and edged away from me.

I went back to my seat at the table. Sad. Sad and disappointed in my family much of the time. Now I was angry as well.

Arthur walked over to the refrigerator, opened it, and took out a peach from a round plastic bowl of peaches. My ire was up. Nonetheless, I tried for a temperate tone.

"Have some compassion, little bro'," I said. "You never know when you might need some yourself. And Mercy will likely be among the first to offer it."

He turned from the refrigerator.

"I don't need you to defend me, you know," Mercy said. She glared at me. I struggled to hold back tears.

"Yeah," Arthur said, "like I'm gonna throw myself into a river or do it with a guy."

He bit into the peach and its juice ran down his chin. He wiped it away with the back of his left hand.

"More likely someone will push you in," I said.

"I concur," Mercy said. There was no sarcasm in her tone.

Arthur gyrated and snapped his fingers as if he were keeping time to music the rest of us couldn't hear, then stopped to turn and open the refrigerator again. This time he pulled out a quart carton of orange juice, opened it, drank its entire contents, then made a show of taking three giant steps across the kitchen to toss the carton into the trash under the sink.

"Don't the flavors compete?" I asked. I was trying for playfulness.

Arthur shook his head no. His belch would have been applauded had he still been a nursing baby.

"My boy," Mamerva said, acknowledging his action and appearing not to mind it.

Mercy found the paper towels hung over the sink, unrolled a few, and wet them. She wiped dried blood off her knees. "I need to shower," she said.

"Go on up," Mamerva said. "You know we've got a supply of your clothes in the guest room."

"Pretty soon," Mercy answered. "I'm ready for a beer first."

"Help yourself," Mamerva said.

We'd arrived home at "the Castleberry place," as everyone called it, just after 5. This was the grand house my mamma and I had worked in until Grandmother Belle DuBois Castleberry had died and willed it to us, finally acknowledging me as her granddaughter, her son Prout's child. Although I'd lived in it since I was eleven, had come back to it during the college vacations I didn't spend in Italy with the contessa, and moved out permanently only after Luke had opened his gallery and apartment to Mercy and me when her adoption was finalized, the place always felt like a mirage to me. I thought it could and would disappear upon my every arrival. For Arthur, on the other hand, the place was as solid as the iron door knockers on the long double front doors that had kept my mamma and me out for over a decade before they had ultimately opened to let us in.

Tad was upstairs with Daddy and the heavily sedated Luke. After checking out Luke's vitals in the ambulance, Daddy had announced he would take responsibility for him rather than send him down to Convent's little hospital and the one locked room that passed for a psychiatric ward. Luke was in Daddy's childhood bedroom now. There were two single beds there, so Tad could stay if he wanted to. Of course I knew he would.

All of a sudden, the door from the dining room swung open into the kitchen.

"Hello, son," Daddy said, offering Arthur a high-five.

"How's the patient?" Arthur asked. For once, his tone was neutral.

"He won't wake up 'til evening," Daddy said.

He looked to me, and then Mercy.

"Say, why don't you all plan on staying here with the three of us tonight. Calm down some. Decide next steps. Tad's already agreed. We certainly have the space."

"Yes, good idea," Mercy said.

I wouldn't have been so quick. I needed to work on my World War II portraits, and I was almost done with the Nazi-and-his-Italian peasant-lover painting at home. But Mercy had endured enough upset today. So I kept my preference to myself.

"Mamerva," I said instead, "might I have the key to the bridal salon? I want to phone Bredice and Don, let them know what's going on."

We all knew to keep the house phone free for emergency calls that came at all hours for my daddy.

"Gonna pick out a wedding dress and get married to Don?" Mercy taunted me.

I stuck out my tongue.

"Wouldn't that be nice!" my mamma said.

I mock-scowled at her.

"Wouldn't he have to divorce his crazy wife first?" asked Arthur.

"First of all, she's ill, not crazy. And Don's not about to do that," I answered.

Mamerva pointed to the iron key latches on the wall by the back door.

"Third one from the left," she said. "And Sam will be delivering dinner from his fish shack around six-thirty. So you'll want to be ready by then."

If we had to stay overnight, I knew I could and would paint over at the salon. It was just a short walk from the kitchen past the garage to the freestanding building we had named *Easels and Lace* when my mamma had set up her bridal business. Luke and Tad had hosted my first big exhibit there just before I adopted Mercy. Mamma had chosen many of my paintings as decorations over the years. Every now and again, somebody bought one. I always kept supplies, including large and small canvases, in the storage room. But if Mercy found out I was even considering keeping on with my work while her Uncle Luke languished, I'd have to endure another ordeal like the one this morning, though this morning felt light years away. Well, too bad for her. She doesn't understand that you can't call yourself an artist if you don't paint.

Chapter Eight
An Unusual Night

By the time I had updated Bredice and Don and gotten cleaned up, Tad's parents had arrived. With Luke still out cold upstairs, the lot of us gathered in the dining room and we commiserated together over dinner. I know some folks might wonder how we could eat, or might frown upon our fervor for spiritual libations, but the truth is that we are a communal culture here that marries the commonplace with the unexpected, the sacred with the profane, the grotesque with the beautiful. So together we mourned Luke's despair at the same time we celebrated his salvation. We held each other up. Expressed our gratitude for each other. Rounded up the wagons, as it were, to keep at bay the terrors of life's frontiers that could not be tolerated alone.

Over the shrimp gumbo, Daddy had suggested to Tad—after all, who else could be considered Luke's next of kin?—that he and Luke be Castleberry houseguests, with Tad commuting to work for the next few weeks, until he and I took off for Fiesole on July 31st. Tad concurred. Helen Acheson, M.D., a psychiatrist and former colleague of Daddy's, lived not too far from Daddy's office in the center of town, and she had agreed to a consult with Luke on Monday. "Then," Tad said, with a nod to Daddy and his own parents, "we'll see how to proceed from there."

Mercy and I cleared the soup plates and brought in platters of shrimp, catfish, and cabbage slaw. If you ask me, there's nothing like a ritual meal for offering hope going forward. The habitual movements and routines allow folks to put one step in front of the other without having to think. However, Tad did make me pause as I was about to go through the door to the kitchen.

"I'd like to prevent Luke's having to spend time in an institution," he said. "I don't want him locked up."

His voice wavered a bit, and his mother, sitting at his left, placed her right hand on top of his left. Her rounded nails were polished so that they seemed like valuable pearls. Though several strands of her graying hair had strayed from the chignon at her neck, that did not detract from her steady calm. At his right, Tad's father tipped his silver dinner fork forward then back, forward then back, then stopped to take the catfish platter from Mamerva.

"Take it day by day, son," he said, looking at Tad. His voice was sonorous and the platter shook a little. "Your well-being is just as important as Luke's, you know."

Tad nodded, and his cheeks reddened.

"Darling," his mother said, though I couldn't tell if she spoke to her husband or her son, if she were reprimanding or agreeing.

I continued into the kitchen to replace an empty platter of slaw with a full one. When I returned to my seat we continued passing the platters among ourselves as smoothly as a practiced assembly line of factory workers. Arthur was unusually quiet. I saw him watch the several tears that slid from Tad's eyes onto his cheeks even as he put fork to mouth. For a bit, no one spoke, and the dining room's sounds were those of people eating: the clicking of forks and knives removing shells from shrimp, the *zzzz-ing* of bread knives slicing through the pleasing crust of loaves, beer and wine glasses clinking against each other as if to say, "Thank you for being here."

Then, all of a sudden, holding his knife and fork aloft, Arthur blurted, "I'm really sorry, man," addressing his words directly across the table to Tad.

"Thank you," Tad said. "Thank you very much, Arthur."

He managed a smile at my brother.

Daddy put down his fork and knife, wiped his mouth with one of my grandmother's monogrammed napkins, and nodded his approval from the head of the table. Arthur blushed briefly. Mamerva winked at him from her chair, nearest the kitchen. Next she looked at me, then at Mercy, her eyebrows raised, I supposed, in pleasure and surprise.

Maybe Arthur would turn out all right.

I was drinking too much coffee, though I was able to demur when offered Mrs. Charbonneau's perfectly baked apple pie, its fluted crust sculpture-like in its symmetry.

After dinner, Daddy, Tad, and Mr. Charbonneau conferred on the porch, the two older men smoking stogies that my mamma would not have tolerated inside. I set out a tray of after-dinner drinks for them and made several unnecessary trips, one with napkins, another with peanuts, just so I could listen to what they said. I knew that while Daddy and Tad were set on making the best medical decisions on Luke's behalf, Mr. Charbonneau was razor-focused on his son's well-being. I couldn't blame him. As if Luke's attempt to end his own life wasn't traumatic enough for Tad, I wondered if Mr.

Charbonneau had any idea about the months-long domestic troubles that had preceded it.

By 10 o'clock, most all of us were tuckered out. Tad walked his parents to their car and the three of them chatted in hushed voices in the dark. Soon after, everybody but Arthur and me had gone upstairs and shut the door to their respective bedrooms. I knew Arthur would be going out soon, to do whatever teenagers now did in St. Suplice after dark. Luke had still not awakened. "His vitals are fine," Daddy reassured us all. He had checked on Luke every thirty minutes all night. Before he left, Arthur told me he had decided to meet up with Benny, ostensibly to "find some chicks, Big Sis," at *Felicia's Candies and Cones*, two doors down from Daddy's office. The fire chief and his wife Corinne had told Daddy that Arthur could spend the night at their place, and they'd see to it he got to soccer practice come early morning, "given the circumstances and the crowd at your place," Corinne had said. On the phone she'd sounded like a cheerleader. I heard every word she uttered to my mamma because her voice carried through the wires so that Mamerva had to hold the phone away from her ear. "She's wonderful," Mamerva had said. "Perhaps a little deaf. But wonderful, nonetheless."

I knew I wouldn't be able to settle down to sleep yet, so I walked out onto the front porch and sat down, kicked off my sandals, and stretched my legs all the way out on one of the pillowed teak lounge chairs. I'd showered before dinner and exchanged my splattered morning painting clothes for one of the nicer shifts I kept here for when we stayed over on a weekend. The grit of the tumultuous day washed away, I felt the kind of clean I usually took for granted. At last alone in the dark, I listened to the night insects buzz. I let the ceiling fans whir me to calmness. I watched the potted citronella candles flicker along the length of the flat-topped wooden railings. I inhaled the intoxicating scent of camellias that my mamma cossetted along the pebble pathway to the porch steps.

God, I loved it here. Home. In the end, home.

St. Marguerite's church bells roused me from my quasi-soporific state. It was 11 o'clock and most of St. Suplice was sleeping. I was ready now, alone and composed. I felt I was myself again, knowing Mercy, Luke, and Tad were, at least for the present, safe. Finally, it was time to paint.

Cat-like, I stretched my arms and legs and rose from the lounge chair and put on my sandals. I took up one of the two flashlights Daddy always kept on the outside windowsill to the right of the double front doors. Making sure not to shine the light upward, where everyone else was sleeping, I made my way over to *Easels and Lace*. I'd have to move a couple of the standing spotlights from the sewing room to my studio at the back of the building. While they wouldn't provide natural light, they'd give me the brightness and clarity I needed to work with any success. I'd switch my mamma's record stack on the hi-fi system, too—from easy listening to opera arias.

I thought I would begin the next portrait, this one featuring the severe-looking music instructor standing next to her grand piano in her 1944 Fiesole studio. But try as I might to work from memory, to outline her torso and the detachable lace collar that drew the eye to her neck and face, I couldn't focus. Not one bit. Another subject kept intruding, flooding my mind, as if it were painting itself, as if its colors were running in my imagination, stream-like strands of liquid silk. It interrupted, rattled, and compelled me. I sighed, deciding to give myself over to it. So I abandoned the music instructor for the time being. Leaving her just-begun canvas on its own easel, I went to the wall closet, opened its double louvered doors, and took out a second easel, then set a three-foot by five-foot canvas vertically on it. I'd use acrylics rather than oils for this one. I lifted the music instructor's easel and carried it over to lean against the wall by the doorway to the sewing room.

When all was ready I stood up straight and faced the empty canvas. The painting, not yet even begun, was calling itself *Mother of the Chartres*, its name repeating itself like an advertising jingle that won't stop. This repetition wasn't annoying, though—more soothing than singsong-y. The "m" and the "r" sounds lengthened and slowed it. I imagined the painting completed, framed, and displayed, and had now only to transfer it to the canvas. I picked up a brush and began. Joan Sutherland's voice as Lucia in *Lucia di Lammermoor* accompanied me. She was transporting, and I remembered reading that she had once received a 12-minute standing ovation for her performance in that role. I forgot myself, moving my brushes as she sang. Then, in the middle of a second aria, as if she had decided to take a sudden intermission, she stopped, and another voice replaced hers. It spoke rather than sang. Its clarity startled me, at once a crystal bell and a caressing balm. The voice belonged to a lady. She felt close by. She was with me in the studio, though I could not see her. I sensed her, the way one does a butterfly's wings or oncoming rain. The beginning of love, or lilacs releasing their fragrance.

"Paint me," she said.

I felt sanctuary, hopefulness, purpose, and joy. Most of all, joy.

Some of you will doubt me, I know. Dismiss what I'm saying and call me mad. Think what you want. I tell you, she made my fingers fly.

Chapter Nine
Come Morning

I put down my brush as Mr. Dolan's milk truck pulled into the drive. Outside, the sky had already turned from black to pale blue, salmon, and yellow. Dawn had come and I was exhausted. So I doused the spotlights, lowered the navy-and-white-striped Roman shades on the windows either side of my easel, and flung myself on the daybed across the room. My mamma had installed it when she was expecting Arthur. She had covered it in a vivid print of tiny easels and paintbrushes. It was where she'd rested between brides. Almost fifteen years ago now she'd told me, "I'm too darn old to be expecting again." (She'd been forty-two then. Can't say I'd disagreed with her.) As soon as I settled into the soft pillows that had cradled her then, the painting and all that had preceded it receded from my consciousness. I felt my left arm fall over the mattress's side.

Footsteps. Shushing. I did not want to wake or be bothered.

"Let her sleep," a voice said.

It sounded like Luke, but Luke whispering. I couldn't be sure. Something bad had happened to him. But he hadn't died. I could rest because he hadn't died.

The *whoosh* of people walking by. The scent of Irish Spring soap and shaving lotion.

It must be full morning already. Still, I wanted to sleep some more.

I decided to ignore whoever it was, Luke and somebody else, so I turned toward the white-washed wall. Two black-and-white baby portraits, one of me, the other of Arthur, were framed identically and hung side by side above the bed. Knowing this consoled me. For once we were acknowledged as equals. I didn't look at them. I just knew they were there. Now I was here bodily, too. I drew my knees up and in toward my chest, and lowered my head to my breasts. I was curled and curving. A fetus. Alone, and not. Completely at ease.

"Okay"—I think it was Tad whispering now—"she doesn't know we're here."

I breathed deeply, in and out. Heard myself groan.

Someone said, "Shhh."

Then it was quiet again. Shade and silence and warmth. I felt cocooned.

All of a sudden, an exclamation. "My God, Oh! Jesus Christ!"

Luke, it was definitely Luke. He wasn't whispering now, dammit.

"What?" I asked, turning away from the wall and rubbing my eyes.

It took me a bit to focus. My back hurt, so I stood up slowly, blinking and blinking, scrunched my shoulders, made circles with my neck. I shook each leg—one, two, three, four. One, two, three, four. Then I started toward the window on the right of my easel to raise the linen shade.

"Orla," Tad said, "I'm sorry we woke you."

I looked around the room. Where was he?

"Down here."

I forced myself to wake fully, then stared down at the floor. Just to the left of me, Tad and Luke sat cross-legged. They were arm in arm, staring at the painting. The one I had finished just before dawn.

"Oh," I said. "You're both here. Sorry, I must have dozed off."

I tried not to be annoyed that I'd had to wake up. Then, looking at the two of them next to each other, I changed my attitude. Luke was alive, for God's sake. He and Tad were together again. Clearly, this was not a bad start to a day.

I yawned and yawned.

"You must have painted all night," Tad said.

I shrugged, then remembered. Tingled inside with my secret of the Lady. But it was just the three of us here now. No sensation of her presence. I decided to tell them.

"You can't imagine what it was like," I said. "I couldn't stop." I made brushing motions with my right hand. "What a workout. I was totally jazzed up." I looked down at them and smiled what I thought was a radiant smile. "And without chemical assistance other than coffee."

Luke grunt-laughed.

"Now I feel like I could sleep forever. She really knocked the wind out of me."

"Who did?" Tad asked.

Then he stopped talking and sat still as a Buddha. He looked up at me as if he were about to ask another question. He tilted his head sideways and asked, "Have you looked at what you've done?"

"You mean the painting, I assume," I said. I rubbed my eyes again. "Not really. When I put down my brush, it was as if the lights went out in my brain. I couldn't even step back and give the work my usual once-over."

I wanted to lie down again. "In fact, I'm still not completely with you," I said. I felt my face. "As if I'm hung over, but not really."

"Well, take a look at your work now," Tad said. He pointed to the easel and the painting that had put me into this stupor.

My eyes followed his finger.

The long dock loomed outward and up from the bottom of the canvas. It was all grays and slivers of black. Mercy's head poked above the water to the left of the dock's edge. Her ebony hair framed her face in a flat cap. Her olive arms were pushing upward, their hands raised in supplication, two cups of hopeful expectation. Luke, red-faced against his beige linen suit and carnation-white shirt, was kneeling to her, his arms reaching for her even as they shook. His sunglasses, the turquoise-rimmed pair he favored, were forever falling now, from his face into the brown, white-frothed Chartres. Closer to the bottom-center of the canvas Tad was mid-stride in his walk toward Luke, both arms bent at the elbow and palms open. The back of his shirt was drenched with sweat. Above them all, at the top right of the painting, was the Lady who had told me what to paint. She was full of light. No, that's wrong. She was light itself, and she was lighting us so we could see. In those terrifying moments, I understand now, she had helped us to see. She looked like an ordinary new mother, her wavy, dark brown hair framing her pleasant, walnut-colored face. She wore a one-piece pistachio swimsuit and held her baby, a boy in tiny purple swim trunks, to her breast, cradling him with her left arm. Her right arm reached downward, its fingers spread in the luminescent light. Her lips were parted, waiting to speak, or having just spoken—I couldn't tell. Her frank, wide-open eyes made me smile. I smiled big and wide.

"Orla," Tad said. He uncrossed his legs and stood up. He looked at the painting, then at me. Twice more.

I was smiling and crying, raining tears. Overcome. The Lady knew me. Even so—or maybe *because*—she had shared her light.

Tad reached out his right hand and Luke took it with his left. Wobbling a bit, so that Tad had to steady him, he stood up as well. He stared a long while at the painting. Then he turned to me and grabbed my cheeks between his forefingers and thumbs like Signor Segreti used to do to Mercy when she first was ours. Finally, he planted a kiss on my forehead as if he were greeting me from the gangplank after a far too long absence at sea.

"One of your best," he said. "And to think I was your Muse for this one."

"Helluva way to inspire her," said Tad.

"All for art, my sweet," Luke replied, and he pinched Tad on the cheeks, too.

All of a sudden, as spontaneously as applause at the final note of a glorious symphony, Tad put his hands on top of Luke's so he couldn't budge them. Then he leaned in and kissed him on the mouth in a way that made me turn away in jealousy and joy. I tiptoed toward the door to the main salon. Silence.

"Wait," Tad finally called.

He was breathless and Luke had tears in his eyes.

"Please, come be with us."

"Yes, do," echoed Luke.

I walked back to them.

The three of us grasped hands and held each other tight.

Chapter Ten
Intermezzo

I came home alone the Monday after Luke had tried to kill himself and lived solo until July 29th, just two days before my departure to Fiesole. Can't say I wasn't glad. I was able to complete the paintings that needed to be shipped to the contessa. Went back to my exercise routine. Every now and then met Bredice at the vegetable garden. And didn't have to deal with Mercy's music blaring or her making me feel guilty for being a full-time artist and a part-time mom. Saw Don a couple of nights ago. He's considering coming to Fiesole for the show if he can get enough time off work to take a two-week vacation. He could spend a week with Lily in Dublin and another with me in Florence.

Meanwhile, Mercy had become her Uncle Luke's full-time *aide-de-camp* as he adjusted to his antidepressant meds, sessions with the shrink Daddy's friend had paired him with, and a better-health regimen. Three weeks into all that, with lots of support and a schedule that made him tired in all the right ways, he had backed away from the edge of the dock.

95

Mercy and I spoke by phone every night.

"We've been jogging every morning at seven," Mercy had told me.

Grabbing the ear piece away from her then, Luke had said, "I shouldn't have bothered attempting suicide. Mercy will be the death of me yet. It's just a matter of time."

I know better than to equate joviality with well-being, especially with Showman Segreti, my unspoken name for him when he'd first begun publicizing my work. I never saw someone else so able to light up just one second before he went on stage. So I knew we'd have to hope his improved states of body and mind would continue.

At any rate, you get the picture. Luke was eating, sleeping, exercising, drinking "mocktails" instead of cocktails, and enjoying—so I was told by my mamma—verbal sparring with Arthur. The subject of the most contention between them was whether or not comic-book drawings ought to be considered art. Good of them all to look after him. Really generous, in fact. So much for my being disappointed in my blood relations. Sometimes I'm just plain wrong-headed. Ornery, too.

Tad has decided that I should head to Fiesole on the 31st, as planned, but that he would follow, with Luke in tow, just one day before our August 15th book-signing and exhibition. I can't say that I was thrilled at his decision, but, then again, nobody was dead. So there's that.

Luke and Mercy would come back to the apartment the following day. If all went as planned, Luke would stay in the cottage so he and Mercy could continue their regimen while Tad was at work. Where Tad would spend his nights I didn't yet know. That kiss in the studio in St. Suplice had made me think they'd reconciled. And, of course, Bredice would keep an eye on the whole shebang. Fingers crossed, in the coming days there would be no further drama other than arguing about what to eat for dinner or whether to go to the movies.

The Contessa's Easel

I was packed, with all my stuff taking up a corner of my studio and, just that morning, I'd once again submitted myself to the healing ministrations of the Portanova Spa. All I had left to do was switch pocketbooks. I'd purchased a large satchel, attractive and practical enough both to project a fashion-forward image as well as house my passport, back issues of *Vogue* and *The New Yorker*, Atwood's novel *Cat's Eye*, and one complete outfit in case Alitalia saw fit to send my checked luggage somewhere other than its intended destination.

All I had scheduled for the following day were a few chores before an afternoon meeting in the Quarter, supper with the family, and bedtime no later than eleven. "*Finito*," as Signora Segreti used to say.

Chapter Eleven
Homecoming, Leave-taking, and Now What?

"Thanks for going with me, Luke," I said.

We had just emerged from five laps in the pool after having visited Project Lazarus, the HIV-AIDS hospice in the Quarter. The hospice had been founded in 1985 by two priests, diocesan prelate Father Paul Derosiers and Franciscan Bob Pawell. Recently the two had heard about my AIDS display in Manhattan and wondered if I'd be willing to let the exhibition travel to NOLA for a fundraiser next Mardi Gras. The Project Lazarus team had raised over 15,000 dollars at a Halloween gala in 1987, and they were keen to host another successful fund-raising event, this one during Mardi Gras, with me and my work as the draw.

Needless to say, I was pleased to help. God knows, the epidemic continues to be a death sentence. I can personally name thirty dead friends and acquaintances, including colleagues, fellow artists, and men I'd met on the HIV-AIDS ward at St. Vincent Catholic Medical Center in Greenwich Village. Dr. Ramon Gabriel Torres, who directs the St. Vincent clinic, and the Sisters of Charity, who manage the hospital, were my mentors. So intent were they to educate and assist that they gave me free rein to interview, visit, and paint any patients who were willing to be my subjects. My former landlords in Manhattan, wall-paper store owners Charley Thompson and Evan Childs, whom I visit whenever I'm in Manhattan, had told me not to fret about them. Even their characteristic good humor seemed strained, and could not lighten the atmosphere.

"Honey," Evan said, when they came to the exhibit's opening, "Don't you worry about us. We haven't had sex with each other let alone anybody else for practically the last decade." Charley had tried to hush him, going so far as to put a hand over his lover's mouth, to no avail. We were all standing by the painting of a mother holding a baby photo of her son as she wept over his hospital bed. "We're older than sin, and been together over forty years," Evan had continued. "And be honest, Charley"—he'd planted a kiss on his lover's lips—"the only thing you can get up these days is your ire." Charley pretended to glare at Evan. Then he shrugged and said, "True." Then he'd pointed to another of the paintings, the one that showed an almost comatose man on a stretcher, skeletal and full of Kaposi sarcoma sores on his bony arms and hollow cheeks. "At least we're alive. Not like these poor fuckers."

Although I'd at first been hesitant about asking for Luke's help, I went ahead and did so. Maybe a distraction like this— big, important, challenging—would help him focus outward rather than inward. Plus, I reasoned, if he used his considerable talents and connections to help eradicate or at least lessen the obscene suffering caused by what was being called a plague, he would have found purpose and exhilaration again.

"Of course," he'd said instantly when I'd asked him over the phone the previous Thursday evening. "After all, these are my people. And your paintings may shock some members of the *glitterati* enough that they will empty their purses on our behalf."

I tossed imaginary confetti into the air at his answer.

"I'm very grateful, Luke. Plus, you'll coach me so I don't screw up with the obligatory speechifying."

He laughed. "Duly noted. One favor I need from you, though. For this meeting, you'll have to choose some clothes for me. I seem to have ruined my making-money get up."

Even before he continued, I knew I'd pick his beige and white seersucker suit and add citrus-y accents. His orange bow tie dotted with bright lemons. A lime pocket handkerchief. A persimmon pair of loafers. A soft calf-skin belt. And, of course, forget about socks.

"Glad to do so," I'd replied. "I'll invade your wardrobe and have your duds at the ready."

Really, the meeting couldn't have gone better. Not only had Luke charmed the board members and donors, mostly females of a certain age, but he'd also exuded palpable and unsurprising compassion for those in need of the hospice's care. In short, he commanded the room. Only once did I see his own fear of the killer surface.

"Despite our name, none of our patients have yet survived, let alone come back to life," said Molly LeVigne, whose own grandson Scott had passed away only a few months before.

At her comment, Luke gulped the air, then exhaled audibly. We'd locked eyes across the conference table. He took up the glass of water by his place and sipped. "Pardon me," he said. Others might have thought him simply parched.

As frightening and too close for comfort as this endeavor might be for him, I selfishly hoped Luke would be able to be deeply involved. Chairing the publicity committee would be a boost to his ego, not to mention re-ignite his talent and creativity for event-planning. Once he'd toured the facility in the former Benedictine convent next door to Holy Trinity Church, he bought in.

I wouldn't be able to be at the hospice again until autumn, upon my return from Italy, but Luke had promised that in the meanwhile he would draw up a detailed proposal, all anticipated publicity costs and legal requirements included.

"The need is so great, but they've got only ten beds," Luke told Tad when he arrived from work and changed into a swimsuit to join us. "You know I'm going to drag you in on this."

"Of course," Tad said. "How would you ever not?"

They smiled at each other the way I first remembered them doing.

"How about I drag you into the pool right now? A little dip before dinner," Luke suggested.

"Hey!" Mercy called to us from the cottage, "Supper will be ready in fifteen."

She and Bredice had teamed up all afternoon to prepare a mixed grill, a *fritto misto*. The aroma of grilling sausages, chicken legs, and sirloin were making my gastric juices jump for joy.

"Okay!" I called back.

"Good," Tad said, turning to Luke, "we have just enough time."

They jumped into the pool together.

I got up from my poolside seat, threw a fern-patterned cover-up over my bathing suit, and walked over to the patio to get ready for supper. While I set the two turbo fans whirring at either end of the glass-topped table we dined at most evenings, I was also glad for the shade that double rows of bamboo provided on the long perimeter of the side yard. I'd brought out five ceramic platters earlier, and placed forks, knives, and spoons in each of the tall coffee mugs that read "Loyola," "Georgetown," and "NYU." Hot pink napkins popped out from stem glasses we'd soon fill with a seltzer water, mashed raspberries, and a lemon concoction we all enjoyed. We were trying to help Luke stay away from alcohol. But I couldn't help thinking, like it or not, he'd have to learn to stay away from both booze and boys himself.

I sighed, listening to Luke and Tad talk, though not able to glean their words, hoping they could manage a long relationship like Evan and Charley. Only time would tell.

I was glad Luke had still been chatting up several women who were friends of Project Lazarus when Father Pawell had told me, "Sadly, our hospice is still and only a place of death." His hope was that soon, if enough funding were available to catalyze research, there'd be a way to manage if not cure what he correctly called "this insidious disease." Though I tried to suppress my fears, I worried most every day about Luke's recklessness of the past few months. I'd have to call on my Lady again and hope she'd have another miracle up her sleeve, and not just for Luke's safety, but for Tad's as well.

But tonight was no time for fatalism. It was instead an evening to celebrate a homecoming and a leave-taking.

"Ready!" Mercy shouted, and we gathered at the table that over the years we had come to appreciate as pilgrims do their shrine.

By the time we had all had our fill of supper, there were but two sausages and half a New York strip left over. Some mayonnaise smearing the side of a serving bowl with several stray strands of parsley clinging to it was a reminder of a potato salad that used to be. And a long wooden salad bowl that hardly needed cleansing left us diners with a scrumptious aftertaste of its marvelous mix of shaved fennel, chopped oranges, Vidalia onions, and plum tomatoes with horseradish-laced mustard dressing.

"How about espresso?" Luke asked.

"Good idea," I said.

"I'll make it," Mercy chimed in, and she made off for the cottage while Bredice and Tad cleared.

I stood up.

"Be right back," I said. "I've got some things up at the big house to bring down here."

Luke stood up, too. "May I help?" he asked.

"Yes," I said. "Just stay here so they don't follow me."

"A bit crusty you are tonight. Sorry to be leaving us?"

I pretended to consider. Put a forefinger to my chin. "Excited, actually."

"Good," Luke said. "I'll look after Mercy,"

"Thanks," I said. "And she you."

He tapped his fingers on the table lightly. "Yes," he said. "We are a pair. A pair of what, I can't say. But a pair."

I laughed. "She really loves you, you know," I said.

He nodded. "God knows, I owe her."

"And I owe you," I said, my voice trailing as I went.

I sprinted from the patio, past the cottage and the vegetable garden, to the big house.

Early that morning, right after it had opened at nine, I'd driven over to Elisa's Confections to pick out a peach *crostata*, one of Luke's favorite desserts. That, and I needed to slip both Tad and Mercy their unopened suicide notes from Luke lest Mercy send the Italian authorities after me. I'd forgotten all about them in our weeks-ago rush to St. Suplice. I'd inadvertently found them just the day before while emptying out my usual go-to handbag to stash my necessities in my new bag. Obviously, I couldn't let Luke see. But, call me superstitious, I didn't want to get on an airplane without having all my relationships in order.

By the time I'd put the notes in the right-side pocket of my cover-up, picked up the *crostata* in its ribboned box, and walked back down to the patio, I could smell the espresso.

"Be right there," I called to Luke.

Then I stepped into the cottage, where Bredice, Mercy, and Tad hardly noticed me while they fussed with the coffee maker and discussed which cups and saucers to use. I went into Signora Segreti's bedroom and placed the envelopes marked *Mercy* and *Tad* on Signora's dresser. I didn't care who found them, only that whoever did saw them unopened by me. Satisfied with myself, I walked back outside and sat down at my usual place with my back toward the bamboo.

"And what's in there?" Luke pointed to the cake box, opening his eyes wide.

"Let's wait for Mercy," I said.

Bredice came back outside and over to the table.

"She insists on serving us herself," she said, trying unsuccessfully to suppress a smile.

She sat down, too.

"Have a good trip, Mamma," Mercy said, as she came out of the cottage holding a candlelit flourless chocolate cake, my absolute favorite.

"Mercy," I said, "thank you."

I saw that she'd made a stencil of an easel so that the confectioner's sugar outlined it.

"How beautiful!' I said, and leapt from my chair to grab and kiss her.

She wriggled away, but smiled nonetheless. "Well, blow out the candles."

Candles were our family joke. During the first year that Mercy was with us, in 1975, it seemed we celebrated a birthday at every family gathering, whether with just several of us or all members of the Segreti, Charbonneau, and Castleberry families. There came a point when Mercy had suggested, "Why don't we have candles all the time?" Naturally, everyone assented. So with this cake, on this evening, I closed my eyes, made a wish—for health, safety, and imagination for all—and blew.

Wisps of smoke rose as if from a genie's lamp.

"Now, your turn, Luke." I slid the cake box across the table.

He took his time with the ribbon and lifted the box top carefully, carefully, as though it might tear in his hands.

"Aha!" he exclaimed. "This is perfectly peachy."

We all laughed at his corny comment. You'd have thought us punch drunk with happiness.

"Wait, the candles," Mercy said.

She lifted the four she had placed on the cake she'd baked, wiped the chocolate off their wickless ends with a napkin, then stuck them into the peach *crostata*, and lit a match from the matchbox Bredice brought to the table every suppertime precisely for this exercise.

"To all of us, at home and abroad," Luke said before he blew the flames away.

"Good," Mercy said, "just the way we're supposed to do dessert."

For a moment, I forgot she was not still a little girl.

"Does everyone want espresso?" she asked, walking backwards to the cottage until she got a show of hands.

"Not for me, thank you kindly," Bredice said. "At least one of us is going to sleep tonight. Plus, I got the children come early morning." And she took off her apron and folded it, making a neat square of muslin on the tabletop.

"Okay," Mercy said, "four, then."

"I'll get the dessert plates and forks, et cetera," Tad said, and he followed Mercy inside.

"'Et cetera,'" Luke mimicked him. "Goddam lawyer." But he smiled.

"And so forth," Tad teased back.

The screen door slammed behind Mercy and Tad just as a taxi pulled into the drive and stopped by the big house.

"Expecting anybody?" Luke asked.

He picked at the crust of the *crostata*, sneaking flaky pieces into his mouth and mumbling "Yummm!"

"Not that I know of," I said. "You, Bredice?"

"No, ma'am, not me," she said. "My daughter would have told me if she had to send the children. She don't have to work tonight, far as I know."

We all three watched.

"Wrong address, maybe," said Luke, and stood up. "I'll go see."

It was still light, only a little after eight, though the sun was already slanting toward setting. A lady got out of the back seat of the cab and motioned for the driver to wait. He turned off the ignition. The lady carried a large suitcase. It was robin's egg blue and had lots of stickers on it, no doubt indicating where she had traveled. She was wearing a muted pink shirtwaist dress, taupe pumps, and a matching handbag, the kind of bag Queen Elizabeth II carries. Her hair was dark, chin length. Classic rather than contemporary.

She saw us and started walking.

"Good evening!" she called out. "Good evening!"

"Good evening," Luke and I parroted.

We were nothing if not polite.

She stopped at the vegetable garden, closer to the big house than to the cottage. She put her suitcase and pocketbook down right next to the cucumbers. Then she stood up, took a lace kerchief from her breast pocket, and patted her neck.

I stood up, too, and walked toward her, wondering who she was and why she was here. Bredice was on her feet now, as well. I heard her push her chair back on the flagstone.

The lady gave a nod of her head before she spoke. Then she said, "The sisters, the sisters at the Ursuline convent, tell me I might find my daughter here. I am looking for my daughter."

I stopped short and held my breath. Then I gazed at her face.

In an instant, Luke was beside me. He took my arm in his.

"Steady now," he said. "Steady."

"I'm okay," I said. "I can do this. I have to do this. It was bound to happen."

"You sure?" he asked.

I nodded, and he let me go.

"Come, join us," I said, and extended my right hand as I walked toward her. I had only to walk past the tomatoes, and then my hand would touch hers.

I saw that she was beautiful. She was real—realized, now. Here. I wanted both to scrutinize her and to see her vanish. Poof.

"Thank you," she said, and smiled.

She spoke a learned, correct English. She was impeccable, even as her neck and face glowed from the evening damp.

She took several sure and small steps toward me. Her neck was a swan's. Lithe, she was. So lithe. A reed both supple and strong. Her posture estimable, as if a puppeteer held her erect with an invisible string. Had she been a ballerina, I wondered?

I heard Grandmother Castleberry in my head.

"Strong," she was saying. "For your child, you must be strong. You must be her example, no matter how or what you feel."

107

"I'm Orla Castleberry," I heard myself say. "These are my friends. Please, come join us. We were just about to have coffee."

The woman took two more steps toward me. We were only a yard apart. But before our hands could touch, the cottage door squeaked open and I turned to look. Tad had placed the dessert plates and some silverware in a basket he held in one hand. With his other hand he supported the screen door so that Mercy could carry out the tray of espresso cups, saucers, sugar cubes, and lemon peels.

I turned back to the woman and forced myself to smile. I surveyed her face closely. Then I stared back at Mercy. The woman looked at Mercy, too. There could be no doubt whatsoever.

I couldn't catch my breath. I was suffocating from pretending grace.

"If you practice graceful habits, you will soon own them. You will be grace itself," Grandmother had said when she'd taught me how to walk across the school stage for a French language competition.

"Dear God," I said, the words just slipping out of my mouth.

I heard myself, wished I hadn't blurted.

"Yes," the woman said. "Dear God."

She spoke the words as if they were a thank you.

I'm sure it was only a moment, but it felt like a moment unending. In that moment we all stood still. Then the woman spoke again.

"There is my daughter," she said. She pointed to Mercy. A long scar from elbow to wrist marred her right arm. Then she folded her hands together at her waist.

"My daughter!" she called to the girl in the doorway. Then, moving her hands to her sides, she bowed low from her waist, as if she were presenting herself to royalty. When she raised herself up, she stood as still as stone.

Silence, but for the hum and buzz of night insects tuning up, the slow passage of a maroon sedan in front of the main house, a siren winding down far away.Then a keening that rose as if from the earth's center. Next, a crash of china and glass followed by a series of bleats, a lamb's plaintive bleats.

"*May ouy, may ouy,*" is what the lamb said.

And Mercy was tripping over broken cups and saucers, her sneakers turning brown with coffee, and she was running, running to the woman next to the garden.

Luke and Bredice stood apart from me, yet close on either side. Tad laid his basket on the ground and waited, keeping his eyes trained on both Mercy and the woman. He was ready to do whatever was called for.

When Mercy reached the woman, she stopped short, rising on her sneakered toes. She put her hands each side of her head, her elbows outward like handles on a teacup. She said not a word. Circling the woman three times, she studied her the way a doctor or a sculptor might. Then, she put her nose to the woman's hair and sniffed. Oh, God, she did. Sniffed. Pure animal she was. She took the woman's two hands in hers, inhaled them, too, then turned them, first palms up, then palms down. She brought them to her cheeks. Holding them there, she looked long into the woman's eyes. Then, as if zapped by an electric current, she raised her arms and brought them down hard on the woman's shoulders. She pummeled her, bleating and bleating, "*May ouy, may ouy.*"

The woman absorbed the blows. She never wavered. Stood straight in her proper, modest dress, ladylike pumps, kerchief in hand, and suffered Mercy's rage. The cab driver got out of his car and sprinted down to them.

"You want I should get the police?" he asked. "Or an ambulance?"

Tad walked over to him and they talked so we could not hear them.

"God bless you all," the driver said, and walked back to his cab. He made the Sign of the Cross as he went.

By the time he had backed out of the driveway and driven away, Mercy was still once more. Her hands were at her sides, as were the woman's. She looked downward, appeared to be thinking, considering. Another car, this one a station wagon with a child's feet sticking out the back, passed by the big house. The sky was streaking pink and violet and gray. Bats made circles in the sky.

"Time to come in," Mrs. Morcey called out to Joby, her special needs boy who swung on the front fence across the street most every evening. "Coming, Wamma," Joby said.

That was when Mercy turned and looked at me. *To* me. I guessed she was looking to me to make it easy for her. I knew I had to make it easy for her. And, really, what ease it was compared to her other mother's task? That woman had had to shove her child onto the plane, her child who was screaming and pleading with her not to. How had she been so brave? How so generous? How so stoic now?

So I breathed in deeply and exhaled, blowing kisses at our daughter. And, obviously, purposefully, I backed away. Three giant steps—may I, must I? Yes. You must. You may. Mercy smiled at me then. A full and gorgeous and knowing smile. And I smiled back brilliantly, understanding now, assuring her now, that letting her go was different from pushing her away.

Then, as smoothly as dusk folds itself into night, Mercy gave herself to the woman who had lent her to me, to us. Only then did the woman soften. She stroked and stroked our daughter's hair, kissed her face and her arms and her hands, dried her tears with the kerchief in her hand. "I have found you!" she cried. "I am here. You are mine."

I looked away, turned my back, as was only graceful and right. Let Luke and Bredice lock arms with me. Then we three walked to the cottage, where Tad had hurried to meet us. He opened and held the screen door for us so that, one by one, the four of us could go inside.

Chapter Twelve
Why Now?

The two of them walked into the cottage holding hands. It was just after ten. Mercy's eyes were red, and Thérèse's posture was more relaxed that it had been when she'd first arrived. She had found what she had been missing, after all. I had to admit, they looked right together. Had Tad not been nearby, I would have felt completely alone and abandoned.

We all re-arranged ourselves at the kitchen table so that Mercy and Thérèse could sit next to one another across from me and Tad. Luke and Bredice, at either end of the table, stood, then bustled about the kitchen wordlessly. In just minutes they placed in front of Thérèse a dressed salad of lettuce, tomato, and cucumber, a small focaccia with red peppers and shredded cheese still oozing after its brief stint in the counter top broiler, and a glass of chilled chardonnay. Then they sat again.

"Thank you," Thérèse said, and crossed herself before taking up her knife and fork.

I watched Mercy staring at her mother. Her lips were parted and little breaths emanated from her mouth the way they do from a sleeping infant's. I must have taken a long and deep one, because Tad took my hand in his and clasped it tightly beneath the table. While his doing so failed to comfort my fears of losing Mercy, his sure, strong touch at least calmed me.

"What brought you here tonight?" Luke asked. "So unexpectedly, that is."

Thérèse raised her eyebrows, then lowered them to their original placement above her eyelids. Tad adjusted himself in his chair. I could tell he was embarrassed by Luke's question.

Luke tried to recover himself.

"I'm very glad you did, of course," he continued, "because we are all here to welcome you. Had you arrived tomorrow, you would have missed Orla. She's leaving tomorrow to prepare for an exhibit in Italy."

I tried for an animated smile in response to Thérèse's pleasant facial acknowledgement of my work.

"I see," Thérèse said. "I came as soon as I was able to. And now, thanks to what you have told me, I find that I have arrived just in time."

In time for what, though? To take Mercy away? To contest her adoption? Any parental control I had, or perhaps wrongly assumed to have, seemed to be slipping away like sand in an hourglass. I know, I know, Mercy was over twenty-one and could do as she wished. But she'll always be part child to me. And I wanted the security of her adoption papers listing me as her mother.

One thing was for certain. Thérèse was very hungry. She ate her salad instantly and then took tiny, quick bites of the focaccia, patting her lips with her napkin every few moments. She sipped her wine after each pat with the napkin, and Bredice filled her glass again.

"How I wish I could have arrived much sooner," she said. "Years sooner!"

Mercy rubbed her eyes. "Why didn't you?" Her voice cracked like corrugated cardboard being crushed.

I hated watching Mercy's emotions roil, appreciated her need to know, to understand what her birth mother had and had not done.

"Well, my daughter," she began, and the lot of us—excepting Mercy, who remained at rigid attention—sat back in our chairs to listen. "Just four days after the Communists invaded Saigon, I was arrested, along with any other South Vietnamese nationals who had worked with and for the Americans. The charge against us was 'conspiring with the enemy.'"

Mercy twisted her hair with her fingers and listened with rapt attention.

"From 1975 until 1986, I was locked up in Chí Hòa Prison. The scar on my right arm came from the first day there when I did not stand to attention as quickly as the guard wanted."

As if she were a toddler examining a new toy, Mercy ran a forefinger along the scar. Thérèse appeared unperturbed. I felt like a voyeur.

"I learned to parrot the Communist sayings the 're-education' leaders forced us to commit to memory. And the fact that I was a nurse got me out of my cell from time to time when one or another of the prison administrators needed medical assistance."

"Did they beat you?" Mercy asked.

I cringed at her question and braced for Thérèse's answer.

Thérèse's eyes watered. "Sometimes," she said. She put down her knife and fork, the focaccia gone. Then she put on composure again, as if it were a coat. "But the important thing is that I finally got out. One of my childhood friends, Dinh Ngo, and I were let out the same morning. Neither of us had known the other had been there all those eleven years. And there we stood looking at one another in the jail yard, speechless. He still did not understand why his wife and son had been shot and killed right in front of his eyes while he had been spared death and dragged to a cell instead. He told me he would have preferred to have died with them instead. Nonetheless, we hugged and hugged, celebrating our survival and our long-denied freedom."

"Coffee?" Luke asked.

It seemed odd, at the very least, for him to interrupt Thérèse's story for a cup of coffee. But she did not appear to mind.

"Please," she answered, and he and Bredice got to work again.

"Then what happened?" Mercy asked.

Thérèse continued. I imagine she had had to relate the tale of her survival more than once since her release.

"That ecstasy was short-lived. I was filthy, hungry, unwell, and penniless. I hoped that a good friend who had taught chemistry at the Lycée Marie Curie years earlier still worked there. So unkempt and downtrodden was I that I dared not enter the main doors of the school. Instead I went to the custodian's entrance and asked for my friend. Her name is Hélène, after her late mother, who was French."

"And?" Mercy asked.

Thérèse smiled at Luke as he put the coffee down before her. Bredice followed him with cream and sugar. Again they took their seats.

"And," Thérèse smiled at her daughter, "Hélène took me to her apartment, fed and cleaned me, cut my hair, gave me clothing and a patch of floor on which to sleep. She had me checked by her doctor so that in a month or so, under their care, I presented well enough to be hired as a nurse at the school."

Thérèse let out a long sigh. Mercy kept staring at her. Thérèse continued her story, moving her eyes from one of us to the next.

"It took me three years to earn enough to fly to the U. S. And, fortunately, immigration restrictions for Asian nurses have been loosening over the past several years. I was able to secure a private-duty position in Washington."

Tad cleared his throat and said, "Yes, I'm aware of the lifted restrictions." He pursed his lips, then said, "You have certainly endured a very rough decade, and then some."

Thérèse nodded at him, then raised her shoulders.

"No more than anyone else who worked with Americans, as I did."

I noticed the dark rings under her eyes now. Her impeccable grooming clearly functioned as an antidote to her long suffering.

"But how did you find us tonight?" I asked.

Thérèse wrapped her hands around her coffee cup. "I flew to Washington in March, where several of my former colleagues and employers live. Once there, finding Mercy was simple. My former employer, Karl Shrove, whose late wife I cared for in Saigon before her death, works at the Department of State. He was able to trace Mercy's voyage from Tan Son Nhut Air Base to Fort Chaffee Army Base, and to New Orleans. The rest you already know."

"That is quite a story," Luke said. "And you are a persistent woman."

Therese looked askance at him. "She is my child," she said. Her voice was as soft as sand that came from rock.

Mercy stopped fingering her hair, put her right hand on her mother's scar, and asked, "Where is my father?"

My stomach tightened. Tad shifted in his seat again. Thérèse paused, then kissed the top of Mercy's head. "I do not know, Mercy," she said. "I cannot tell you."

"I want us to find him," she said. She touched her upturned nose. "We have to." Then she looked across the table at Tad. "You'll be able to find him," she said. "I know you will now that my mother can give you the information you'll need."

She turned back to Thérèse.

"What's his name? Tell Tad my father's name." She was a prosecutor badgering the accused.

I tried to control my breathing. Tad and I both knew that Hoyt Demirs, Mercy's likely father, had written in response to Tad's inquiry back in 1975 that he wanted no further involvement with Thérèse or the child she claimed was his.

Thérèse rested her hands on her lap and was silent.

"I called him 'Eagle,'" she said.

"No, his real name," pressed Mercy.

Thérèse took our daughter's two hands in hers. "That I cannot tell you," she said, and, just like that, tears fell quickly from Mercy's eyes.

Tad cleared his throat and said, "Perhaps a night cap is in order." Bredice and Luke got up to get the shot glasses and the amaretto.

Mercy kept at it. She wriggled her hands from her mother's and rubbed her fingers over and over Thérèse's scar.

"Cannot or will not?" Mercy asked. She would not be deterred.

Thérèse looked into our daughter's eyes and sat erect, as if a steel rod had just replaced her spine. "Cannot," she said, then looked down at the dregs in the bottom of her coffee cup.

Mercy's lips continued to quiver, the way they always did when she tried to stifle her crying.

"Mercy," I whispered across the table, and she reached for my hand.

Thérèse might be from the other side of the world. She might be my newest nemesis. She might engage me in a legal and/or emotional tug of war for Mercy. She might be trustworthy or not. A paragon or a lout. Regardless. She was a parent just like me. And I understood again what my own childhood had taught me: that the lies and half-truths we parents construe to try and shelter our children and ourselves from inevitable pain are as infinite as space and as particular as each snowflake that falls from the sky.

Part Two—The Past is Now

Mary Sharnick

"What's past is prologue."

— William Shakespeare, *The Tempest*

The Contessa's Easel

Dear Reader,

I interrupt the narrative here to let you know how I have decided to relate my story while residing in Italy. The Italians you will meet who spoke English with me are:

Contessa Beatrice d'Annunzio

Dottore Celestino (Tino) Bacci

Monsignore Pietro Giannini

Mina Quarto, Personal Assistant to the contessa.

With all the others I conversed in Italian. I have translated our conversations into English for your ease, slipping in an occasional Italianism, reflecting what so often occurs in one's speech when alternating between two languages in real time.

Chapter Thirteen
New Eyes

There was a three-hour delay at Rome's Fiumicino Airport, so my connecting flight didn't land in Florence until 4:45, on Tuesday afternoon, August 1st.

I thought I'd be tired, especially after the previous evening's surprise appearance by Thérèse Luong, the woman I'd previously referred to as "Mercy's birth mother." But I wasn't. To be perfectly frank, I'd slept soundly in my own bed after our little group had disbanded for the night. Thérèse had retired to the apartment upstairs, where Luke stayed when he did not sleep at Tad's place. Since there'd been no warning or prelude regarding Thérèse's arrival, none of us had had time to get worked up. Now that the ominous day had come and was already gone, the worry about it had disappeared as well. And, really, the timing could not have been better. For several months Mercy and her birth mother could plan their future relationship, without my crowding or thwarting them, in the comfort of Mercy's—and my, dear God!—home.

And yet. Yet. Crossing the Atlantic, with an overnight flight time of nine or so hours to question my apparently temperate response to their reunion, I second-guessed myself. Am I at peace with the reunion because it frees me to be solely Artist Orla Castleberry rather than Artist/Mother Orla Castleberry? Am I so smug as to think that my having raised Mercy for fourteen years trumps Thérèse Luong's having raised her from birth until Saigon was falling, and then letting her go, by God? That must have been devastating, even though it probably saved Mercy's life. Am I perhaps seeking Mercy's approval as the personification of emotional balance? Or, God help me, am I fearful that Mercy will interpret my seeming acceptance of Thérèse as signifying my less-than-perfect love? I don't, can't know.

I'd arranged for a 7 o'clock pick up in the morning. Just before the airport limousine pulled in, I'd gone to Mercy's room to say good-bye. She wasn't there. Assuming she'd gone upstairs, I made my way to the stairwell to find her. Just then, though, both she and Thérèse came down from above to send me off. Thérèse was wearing a full-length pink silk robe decorated with white swans. She handed me a square black felt box.

Mercy said, "Excuse me," and walked down two steps so that she stood between the two of us, her birth mother above her and me below.

"Thank you," Thérèse said. "Thank you for raising our beautiful daughter."

I bit my lower lip. "Thank *you*," I said. "Thank you for sending her to me."

Thérèse blinked several times. "It was the most difficult thing I have ever done."

"It had to have been," I said. "I'd be a fool to say that I can imagine how you felt."

Mercy stiffened, and I could tell she wanted our conversation to end.

"Stop talking or you'll be late," she barked at me.

Thérèse raised her eyebrows, and I could not help but wonder—not if, but how—my indulged American child and her mother from another culture would wrangle over behavioral norms.

"A bit bossy this morning, Mercy, are you?" I said.

Thérèse looked down at Mercy's face.

"Sorry," Mercy said, and leaned against Thérèse. She nudged me at the same time.

"Open it," she said.

I did.

Inside, on a silver chain, was a substantial silver medallion. It was square and etched in black with the outline of two identical women leaning toward a child between them. The child was a girl. Her eyes looked outward and she smiled.

Thérèse pointed. "Our daughter and the both of us," she said.

"Yes," I agreed.

"Help me," I said to Mercy, and I turned my back to her so that she could arrange the gift around my neck.

The chain was long enough that the medallion nestled between my breasts, the V-neck of my taupe knit dress framing it.

"I love it," I said.

Thérèse unbuttoned her robe. "I wear the same," she said.

I stepped up next to Mercy and Thérèse and hugged and kissed each of them on both cheeks.

The sound of tires on gravel announced my car. The driver beeped twice.

"Come on," Mercy said, "you're never on time. You'll miss your plane." Her voice was cheerful, teasing now.

"Look who's talking," I countered, and my daughter laughed.

The two of them saw me off.

*****

The cabin's overhead lights turning on made me squint in the first-class section of the connecting flight the contessa had generously arranged. I lifted my bag from the compartment to the left of my seat and rummaged around for my sunglasses. After I put them on, I looked for the jewelry box that had housed Thérèse's gift. When I found it, I placed it on the left armrest, then unlatched the chain around my neck. While the pilot told us how much he had enjoyed captaining the flight, I put the gift back in the box and zipped the box into an interior pocket of my bag. Then I retrieved my favorite linen-and-silk long scarf, which I'd folded into what looked like a dinner-napkin-sized square. Unfolding it gently to its full length, I twisted it and put it around my neck, knotting it just below the V of my dress. It hung just short of my knees and the dress's hem. Other than the scarf's broad-painted strokes of turquoise, lemon, orange, and blueberry, I was dressed completely in taupe. On my left wrist I wore a two-inch bangle of hammered gold, and on my right ring finger I'd placed a stack of six similarly flattened bands, alternating gold and silver. My earrings were coral teardrops. I found some lip gloss in my bag to add some shine to the coral lipstick on my lips. I was ready to get off the plane.

"Please remain in your seats with the seat belts fastened until we reach the gate," the chief flight attendant's voice said in Italian, then again in English.

The majority of us ignored her injunction, if the clicks I heard around me, including my own, were any indication.

Surprisingly soon, the plane's motors ceased and the flight crew assembled near the exit door. We were allowed to disembark. In fewer than twenty minutes my baggage and I were reunited at Carousel Number Four.

"Lady, lady, I help you!" called a porter.

I handed him a twenty-dollar U. S. bill, which, I'm pleased to tell you, he took; then he led me right through the entry authorities. The uniformed young man who stamped my passport did not even look up, just murmured, "*Buona sera, Bruno.*"

"*Permesso, permesso!*" Bruno bellowed, though it appeared that three chatting airport functionaries off to our right side were his only potential obstacles.

If Luke had been with me, he would have said that Bruno was simply earning his tip. Spectacle was all. *It is Italy, for God's sake, Orla*. Luke was talking in my head.

Once the sliding doors opened so we could exit the restricted area, Bruno stood by while I searched for Marciano. He was nowhere to be seen. I scanned the lineup of sign-holding men a second time.

"*Signorina* Castleberry," a deep voice called out, and I saw a man I didn't recognize pointing to a sign with my name scrolled on it in paint.

He was most definitely not Marciano, who had greeted me here at least three times during college. No, this man was much younger, perhaps in his late thirties or early forties, casually dressed, and a real eyeful.

I waved to him and, before I could direct Bruno to do so, he had already wheeled the cart with my baggage around the stanchions that separated the arrivals staging area from the throng of drivers, tour leaders, and families who awaited passengers. I followed.

When I reached the man with the sign, having had to scoot around a boisterous group hugging and kissing a tired toddler who sucked his thumb, he and Bruno stood talking. They appeared to be enjoying some kind of joke.

"*Signorina*," the man with the sign said. "I am Tino. I am here to drive you to the contessa."

I had to look up at him.

"Buona sera, Tino," I said.

Tino smiled broadly. And his eyes... They were honest-to-God turquoise, I tell you. There had to be a story there.... His eyes twinkled. Whether merrily or conspiratorially, I could not yet tell.

"The contessa has told me you speak Italian well. But I must implore you to let me practice my English."

I smiled back and said, "*Certo.*"

He laughed out loud—merrily, as if I had told a fine joke. Then, he pointed to my five pieces of matching luggage, stacked high on Bruno's cart.

"I see you are prepar-éd"—(Can I tell you how much I love the stress on the "-ed"?)—to stay in Italy for some time."

Now *I* laughed.

"As long as possible," I said.

He smiled again. "The contessa did not tell me that also you are wise. A brilliant artist, yes, but a wise one, I did not know."

I felt myself blushing. I was glad I had used the delay time in Rome to freshen up. I looked good. Dare I say I was aroused, too? Who was this scintillating Tino?

"Ah," I replied, "perhaps the contessa does not know me as well as she thinks she does."

I could not stop looking at his eyes.

"A moment, please," he said, and touched my shoulder.

I shivered. But the arrivals and exits area was certainly not cool.

He took the few steps to Bruno and put his arm around him. Then he whispered something to him. In fact, he whispered multiple paragraphs of somethings. "Fervently" is how I would describe whatever he was saying.

"*Si, si,*" Bruno replied to the secrets. "*Subito.*"

Then Tino handed Bruno a wad of *lire* and a business card that he took from his breast pocket. As soon as he did, Bruno and my luggage headed for the taxi stand outside.

I followed, but Tino intervened.

"No need to go with him, *Signorina,*" he said. "He will see to it that your things arrive."

I must have looked puzzled.

"You will understand in several moments."

Tino offered his left arm, and I took it with my right, glad my carry-on bag had a braided leather strap that would not slide off my other shoulder.

"We go to the car park now, *Signorina,*" he told me. "Unless you need otherwise, of course," and he pointed toward the rest rooms with his free arm.

He must have learned English from a Brit, as the contessa's daughter Gabriella had.

"Thank you," I said. "We can go,"

We walked outside and into a sultry early evening, following the signs to the parking garage. While we made our way, I tried to make my study of him subtle, though I doubt I was successful. He was bronzed, with close-cropped, dark brown hair, curls slicked down with gel that smelled like sandalwood. His white shirt, its sleeves rolled to the elbow, still told of careful ironing. His sandals were darker than his hair, and his toenails had the pleasing precision one generally finds in sculpted figures. His silvered wire sunglasses were affixed to his shirt at its third button-hole. He wore no wedding ring, only a red leather-banded watch that did not need to boast a brand name.

"And we are here," he said. "Allow me, *Signorina.*"

"Ah, now I understand," I said.

He lifted the door to the silver Lamborghini, and I did my best to lower myself into the passenger seat gracefully, then swing my legs in after.

"I see you have experience with this kind of car," Tino said.

A flatterer he was, what with the *"Signorina"* and now a testament to my grace, was it, or to my legs? I hoped it was both.

I didn't answer, instead watched him study me as I rested my carry-on on my lap.

He got in, lifted his sunglasses from their perch, put them on, and turned the key in the ignition. Then he turned to me and asked, "Are you ready?"

I looked at his pleasing, animated face, and smiled. *Why not,* I thought, and said, "Should I be?"

He laughed and laughed, then took my left hand in his right. He leaned toward it, and gently, gently, touched it with his lips. We were off!

Chapter Fourteen
The Contessa Awaits

"*Finalmente!*" the contessa cried. "I thought I would have to entertain the *monsignore* alone. But now you are here."

She had walked out onto the drive in one of the colorful caftans she favored during the summer heat. Though she gripped a walking stick—beautifully made of hickory, with a ceramic parrot for a handle—she did not hunch over it. Its length had clearly been gauged to allow for her height and admirable posture. Pure white now, her chin-length hair was coiffed and decorated with a small yellow rose close to her right ear. Her fingernails were shellacked a deep and shiny maroon, as I remembered them always. I had not visited her in nearly twenty years. I had been busy building a portfolio of American portraiture and raising a child who enjoyed summer vacations in Grand Isle. During that time the contessa had transformed from a classic beauty into a handsome woman of a certain age. Her vivid presence defined her as a personage as well as a person.

"I am so happy to see you!" I said. "Thank you for making yourself and Villa d'Annunzio available for the exhibit and Tad's book launch."

She walked to me where I stood, having just gotten out of Tino's car, and held me by the chin with the thumb and forefinger of her free hand.

"You will make the property come alive again," she said. "My orphans have all grown up, some have even grown old. I am alone here now but for those who help me and those who need my help. They come and go. During the night, there is only Mina Quarto, who last year graduated from the Institute of the Sacred Heart in Florence, my alma mater, in a room next to my apartment. You will recognize her from among the photographs I sent you. She is marvelous with the languages. While I have only my native Italian, English, and French, she also speaks Spanish and German. She is a great boon with foreign visitors who come to learn about the war time here."

The contessa let go my chin and smiled.

"I look forward to meeting her," I said. "She sounds like an accomplished young woman."

"She is," the contessa said. "One who has overcome a difficult childhood."

"Oh?" I said, wondering if the contessa would tell me more.

She lifted her cane and waved it about, dismissing my question.

"You will come to know her these next months," she replied, and swatted a mosquito away from her face. "She will at last have someone besides me and the estate keeper and his sons for steady conversation."

At that the contessa pointed her walking toward a path leading to a side service entrance to the villa. There a cab driver was handing my bags to a compact sun-browned man dressed for the fields rather than for the house.

"Thank you, Beppo!" the contessa called over to him.

Bruno had done his job.

"Your luggage has arrived safely. Mina will see to it. You will have my apartment upstairs. You can go up and refresh yourself after our first toast of the evening."

"Oh, but I couldn't possibly..." I began.

"Shh, shh" the contessa interrupted. "*Dottore* Celestino"— she pointed to my driver—"required that I update the former guest quarters on the entry level floor according to my needs." She pointed to her walking stick and made a sign of disapproval with her free hand. "As few stairs as possible, though he insists that I also must exercise my legs daily on the patios or in the gardens. And swim in the pool when the weather permits. It is the arthritis. Only one of an annoying assortment of indignities caused by my advancing age."

I looked to Tino in surprise. "Marciano has not retired, then?" I asked.

The two of them laughed.

"No," said the contessa. "He tells me he cannot bear the thought. And he is still able to drive. But his wife has suffered a stroke, so he stays with her now. I promised him that he can return at any time."

"I'm sorry to hear such news about Elisa," I said.

I had enjoyed Elisa's homemade bread sticks and bruschetta many times at the contessa's table during my college years. Elisa had baked there ever since her fourth and last child had gone off to school, over two decades before.

As if taken with a sudden need for certainty, the contessa asked, "But Elisa will recover—yes, Tino?"

"She is doing well thus far," Tino answered. "I hope her progress will continue. I will see her on Friday."

He was attentive and pleasant, even as he was evasive.

"So you are the doctor, not the chauffeur?"

Tino nodded in assent.

"It is true, *Signorina*," he said, motioning me to follow the contessa through the rotunda. "I do not have the pleasure of being *Zia* Beatrice's full-time driver. Instead I am compelled to practice medicine, both down the mountain in Florence, and here in Fiesole every Tuesday and Friday."

Once again his eyes were merry.

"I see," I said, feeling sheepish. "Well, it is always good to have a doctor in one's company."

I felt myself becoming hot around the shoulders.

Tino gave a nod that felt like a bow.

"While I do not hope any illness to beset you, *Signorina*, you may count on me to aid you if necessary," he teased, his turquoise eyes dancing. "I will even drive you to a clinic or the hospital myself."

The contessa looked at him, then at me, smiled a close-lipped, lingering smile, and said, "*Bene. Andiamo.*"

She led us through the grand frescoed rotunda into the long lounge at the villa's west-facing rear. The lounge's four sets of double French doors opened onto a marble patio, then down to a pool surrounded with large urns of rosemary plants, and a spacious lawn that ended abruptly in a steep, wooded drop. The lounge and its outdoor continuances overlooked the Etruscan amphitheater and, beyond it, acres of a forested surround. Already the sun was setting.

So you are Tino's aunt?" I asked the contessa.

The two of them laughed again.

"She is not my aunt by blood, *Signorina*, although she is my godmother." Tino grinned at the contessa.

"She is as close to blood as can be."

The contessa took my arm in hers. "I am his godmother by love, the same way I am your grandmother," she said. She let go of me and touched her throat with her free hand, staring off at something invisible to me. Then, looking back at me, she said, "How I wish your grandfather had lived to know you."

I felt a bit uncomfortable, knowing this was the woman who had stolen my grandfather from Grandmother Castleberry. She sounded so proprietary about him. Then, again, maybe Grandmother Castleberry had been as tough on her husband as she'd been on my mother. I would likely never know.

I walked several steps further into the lounge, stopping just before one of several spots where the furniture had been arranged to facilitate face-to-face conversation.

"Ah," I said, "I wish I had known him, as well." Would he have accepted me right away? Mamma seemed to think so. "So, you have known Tino since his birth?"

Tino smiled at his godmother. "Even before," he said.

"Yes, it is true," said the contessa. "His mother was one of my older orphans. A natural musician from her childhood, Aurora was trained to become a great one. You will meet her tomorrow."

I raised my eyebrows and waited for one of them to continue.

"But enough now," the contessa said. "You will have many days to talk some more, the two of you." She paused before her preferred chair, a high-backed wing chair patterned with gold lions' faces on red silk. "We must prepare for the *monsignore* now." She motioned for us to sit side by side in the two leather club chairs that faced her.

A substantial oak table with lion-claw legs rested between us. On it were set four glasses, along with bottles of gin, vermouth, and Campari—all the ingredients for Negronis, a favorite pre-dinner drink. A silver ice bucket sweated, and I could see several round cubes peeking from beneath a lid that did not fully close. A plate of blood orange wedges awaited. Cocktail napkins with the d'Annunzio crest, along with round china dishes of cashews and almonds, lay about the table. Here the contessa held court, presiding like a *maestra*.

She arranged herself on her chair, placing her walking stick across her lap. Then she looked directly at me.

"Orla, the priest you will meet, Pietro Giannini, he is my Tuesday priest."

She laughed while an amused Tino stood and prepared the drinks.

"Yes," Tino, said as he filled each glass tumbler with ice cubes, "the *monsignore* and I have a standing Tuesday evening dinner date with *Zia* Beatrice."

He handed the contessa her drink and she wrapped her hands around the glass.

"I tell the priest that Italian men have always had their Tuesday courtesans, but I have a doctor and a holy man. For several hours the two of them prevent me from unwise indulgences and limit my bodily and religious infractions to venial sins."

I laughed and accepted my drink from Tino, who quickly made one for himself.

"To Hippocrates and Jesus, then," I raised my glass.

"And to *Signorina* Orla Castleberry, who has at last arrivéd."

I smiled again, my lower regions reminding me that one's body cannot lie.

The three of us drank.

"Go now," the contessa directed, pointing her walking stick at me like her conductor's baton. "The *monsignore* always arrives promptly at 9 o'clock. You will have ample time for whatever ablutions you favor. Mina will have made the apartment ready for you. You will notice some changes to my sitting room, Orla, and there you will discover a little gift of welcome. I hope your stay will be one of productive happiness."

I crossed my hands over my heart. "Thank you for your tremendous generosity."

Tino stood as soon as I did.

"I, too, *Zia*, will prepare," Tino said. "And *Signorina* Orla, I am certain that you will prove an essential asset to our eventual and inevitable discussion with the priest."

"I will?" I asked. "How so?"

"You will, both because of your experience and your temperament."

"I'm flattered," I said, enjoying the slight breeze from the open doors that led to the patio. "But we've just met."

At that, Tino went to an antique refectory table behind the blue velvet sofa that faced the lounge's fireplace. He picked up a manila envelope, opened it, and drew out facsimiles of publicity about my AIDS exhibit in New York along with prints of my paintings.

"I have been spying on you and your work," he said. "But it is this particular work that concerns the *monsignore*."

Several more breezes continued to cool me. I nodded and waited to hear more from him.

"The *monsignore* has copies, as well. I dropped them at his residence several days ago."

"Why?" I asked.

Tino stroked his chin with his right hand.

"AIDS is rampant in Italy, as you know it is worldwide. But Donat Cattin, the former minister of health, refused to take action to educate the public. He was detested men he called 'the perverts.' Perhaps Francesco De Lorenzo, his successor, will do better."

"I see," I said. "So where do I come into this problem?"

Tino put the papers back into the envelope.

"The *monsignore* ought to learn of your relationship with the Sisters of Charity and their staff, and with Doctor Torres from St. Vincent's in New York. As you will no doubt understand tonight, the crisis has found its way directly to his purview in the seminary he heads. He is conflicted about what to do."

Tino paused a moment, considering his next words. I stood still, eager to hear them.

"He is a most decent fellow, a dedicated administrator, and a compassionate man by nature."

I nodded. "Good."

"Yes, good," Tino said, placing the envelope back on the table. "At the same time, like many others of his—our—faith,"—here Tino pointed to his heart with his right hand—"he is having difficulty reconciling theological ideals with sociological, let alone individual, realities. He is overwrought by the more and more prevalent and public suffering caused by sins of human frailty, as he would likely describe them."

Here Tino stopped again. Then he went on.

"Perhaps you can help him find a way to uphold his beliefs and respect Church doctrine while simultaneously helping AIDS sufferers. The way I have read the Sisters of Charity and their medical staff have done."

I scrunched my shoulders and, drawing my elbows to my waist, raised my palms upward.

"I don't know," I said. "I am happy to try. Though I fall short, too. Very short from theological ideals."

I felt my body and all its senses taking over my mind. A body that had enjoyed immensely a string of men not mine by sacrament or law, not even by love. A body that had held and nurtured a child, but not completely, not enough. No, I fall very short. The sacrificial love of theology has never realized itself in the sinews of my flesh or driven self-centeredness from my decisions and actions.

I was quiet for a bit, thinking of Don. I knew in this moment, even before I did so, that I was going to hurt him.

Tino said nothing, just looked at my face with kindly interest.

"You are up to the task," the contessa countered. "Your portraits are powerful and do not allow a viewer to blink."

"Thank you," I said.

She was as alive a critic as ever.

Tino looked to her. "The *monsignore* phoned me early this morning," he said. "He is most distress-éd, and for good reason. I am sure he will seek your significant help, *Zia*. He has already committed to whatever medical help I might provide. But I am still learning, still reading about this plague."

He waited for her reply, but she said nothing.

"And of course he is deeply concerned about scandal."

The contessa pursed her lips, but, again, she did not speak.

I stood watching the two of them. They clearly had a partnership going. And now they were drawing me into it. I'd need to learn how it worked, how we would work. I shouldn't have been surprised. Visiting the contessa had always been an education.

Finally, just as the great rotunda's clock struck eight bells, she said, "I will make sure we have more wine than usual." She paused. "Mainly for me."

At that, we all laughed.

Before I turned to go to my apartment, I said with a half-smile, "Silly me for thinking the exhibit would be our only project."

The contessa raised and lowered her walking stick across her lap, exercising the parrot, who stared out onto the patio.

"Ah, my dear, there is never only one project in life. It is merely at table that the food arrives in courses, in symphonies with movements, operas and plays with acts, and it is only in books where the first chapter is followed by the second, the second by the third, and so on."

I remembered hearing writer Annie Dillard speak one time at the 92nd St. Y in Manhattan.

"The only thing that art cannot tolerate is disorder," she had said. That much I knew. Life, on the other hand, birthed chaos with the same speed as cockroaches procreating. Just consider the seemingly endless collision of events that had occurred back in NOLA the past few months.

"True enough," I said.

Then she took up and pointed her baton again, this time at the two of us, once to the left, once to the right.

"Go, ready yourselves, both of you."

She put the walking stick next to the right arm of the chair, pushed herself up with one hand on each armrest, then took the cane in hand.

"I will await the *monsignore*'s arrival on the patio," she said. "Don't let me stay too long with him alone lest he renew his persistent efforts to have me confess and repent my greatest and most satisfying scandal."

I looked at her askance.

"My dear Orla, do not look so surprised. It was that very scandal, my love affair with your grandfather, a daring and generous man, that gave me the joy of our absent Gabriella and, later on, you, a virtual granddaughter to vivify my old age. I shall never repent!"

I went to her and put my arms around her slender body. She patted my back and kissed my forehead. Then we parted.

"Please," Tino said, extending his arm, and I went ahead of him into the rotunda and up the circular stairs.

Chapter Fifteen
An Unexpected Gift

The contessa's former sitting room, at the front of the villa, faced east. It connected to her bedroom through double doors. The two rooms together ran the full length of the main house. One could also enter the bed and bath chambers directly from the hallway. So eager to indulge myself with all the comforts those two rooms offered, I entered directly from the top of the stairs, saving my visit to the sitting room for after a much-desired shower and change of clothing.

Mina had certainly taken charge of my belongings. When I entered the bedroom, I saw that the floor-to-ceiling windows, their filmy summer draperies tied back, had already been shuttered against the coming darkness. Soft lights from both table and standing lamps bathed the room in a restful glow. A chaise lounge with a side table next to it held a tall glass and two bottles of water, one with bubbles, the other flat. The massive bed's flocked champagne coverlet had been turned down, revealing a set of crisp white sheets, their edging scalloped lace with tiny embroidered buttercups. A note pad and pen were ready for me on a bedside table next to a phone, and a terrycloth robe lay across the bed. My initials had been monogrammed in maroon on its left breast pocket. A pair of slippers with the family crest lay on the floor next to the bedside nearest the windows. The largest two suitcases had been emptied, their dresses and slacks and blouses hung in the wardrobe directly across from the bed. My undergarments were stacked by color in the wardrobe's drawers, each drawer left partially open for my convenience. And a table for two at the foot of the bed was topped with a bowl of fruit, some wine biscuits in a covered glass container, and an unlit candle, its fragrance of roses.

"Ah," I sighed aloud, then shed my clothing, letting it drop to the floor at the foot of the bed. All of the floor but its outer edges was covered by a plush, leopard-patterned rug. I slipped out of my shoes so my feet could luxuriate in the rug's dense softness.

My body at last freed from clothing, travel, and any other concerns, I breathed in the scent of the yellow roses in the four vases the contessa had arranged throughout the room. At the bathroom door, I turned and looked back at the thoughtful comfort she had prepared for me. I was very glad to be here. But it was not yet time to rest. A shower would refresh and quicken me for the evening ahead. So I entered the bathroom, shut the door, and turned the shower fixture to hot, *caldo*. A steamy cleanse, followed by a quick burst of cold, would invigorate and prepare me for a potentially difficult evening. In less than half an hour, I had toweled off, blown dry my hair, and applied some eye makeup meant to be suitably dramatic for an evening in a Tuscan villa with a countess. And, I must also add, to inspire a charming doctor I fancied.

"*Signorina*," a sweet voice called, accompanied by several quick knocks to the hallway door outside the bedroom.

"Yes," I answered. "Is it Mina?"

I was just buttoning the tangerine silk "man shirt" that I thought looked smashing over oatmeal-colored palazzo pants. All I needed to add were my flat leather sandals, coral drop earrings, and an enamel ring that practically shouted, THE WEARER IS AN ARTIST.

"Please, come right in," I said.

"Thank you, *Signorina*."

Mina had the look of a gamine, with cropped black hair, wide-spaced dark eyes, a red smile, and a serviceable gray skirt just to her knee. She had topped the skirt with a white camisole that dipped low in front and back. Slim-hipped as a teen-age boy, she walked with a bouncy gait, her feet in pink sneakers not unlike the kind my Mercy wore.

"Is everything to your liking, *Signorina*?" she asked.

I sat on the bed and put on my sandals.

"Beyond my liking," I said. "You've made me feel like a princess."

She smiled and bent her knees in a quasi-curtsy.

"The contessa sent me up to make sure you had not fallen asleep. I know there is a time difference of some seven hours, and the overnight flight."

"You're right."

Mina ran her hands through her cropped hair.

"It is tempting to take a nap, no?"

"It is," I replied, and looked at my own hair in the full-length mirror in the corner. Liz Murchison had given me a terrific cut.

"But I learned that lesson the first time I visited here," I said. I turned back to Mina, and continued, "Best to stay awake the first evening, so I can catch up to your time zone."

I looked at the clock on one of the night tables. It was ten minutes to nine.

"Has the *monsignore* already arrived?"

Mina grinned, her toothy smile one a dentist could be proud of.

"No, *Signorina*, but I guarantee you that when the clock strikes nine, he will emerge from his car. He is as precise as a surgeon."

My earrings in place and the ring on my finger, I said, "I will be prompt, as well. I mustn't disappoint the contessa."

"Very good, then, *Signorina*," Mina said, and turned to leave.

It was then I saw the jagged scar parallel to her spine that rose above her blouse all the way to her hairline. I shuddered, and knew that in the coming days and weeks, I would seek to learn of its origin and effects.

Since I had ten minutes, I decided to go into the sitting room before going down. Legend had it that every time one of the contessa's orphans was ready to leave the villa—had become skilled at some trade, was to marry, or go off to the military or university—she brought them into this private space and fitted them with clothing and generous sums to start them off. The "giving room" was what the Fiesolani called it. Even when their contessa—they called her *"la nostra contessa,"* as if she belonged to them—was imperious, she was beloved for her generosity, which spanned from the war years to the present day.

Pulling the double doors toward me, I saw the room had also been shuttered for the night. Feeling along the wall, first to my left, then to my right, I found a light switch, and at once the room was ablaze from the central chandelier, its translucent, swirl-patterned glass certainly blown in Murano. I blinked. Two or three times. The room had been completely transformed. It had become an artist's studio. The contessa had built a studio for me.

"My Lord," I whispered.

Never mind the canvases of many sizes that rested against one wall. Or the oils, water colors, and brushes that waited on a long, sideboard-like work table, or the open cabinets with shelving both vertical and horizontal. Several stools, two easy chairs, a rack of new towels, even a deep sink. Thick wrapped bricks of citrus-scented soap. I could go on, but I won't. For what anchored the room and demanded my attention stood under the Venetian chandelier. It was an easel, in itself an ordinary necessity for a painter. Yet leaning against this easel was no painting, but instead a black-and-white photograph eighteen by twenty-one inches, at least. A photograph of my Grandfather Castleberry and the very pregnant contessa.

I walked toward it as if to an altar, my eyes honing in on a past I'd never known. So close did I get to my grandfather's face that my nose brushed the image. It might have been a kiss.

The two of them were dressed for a relaxing day in the country, he in pleated slacks and an open-collared shirt, she in a long lace shift, cut low in front. A picnic basket lay on the grass beside her. She rested her outspread hands on her belly, accentuating her maternity. His left arm was draped over her shoulder, while his right hand remained frozen in time by the camera just as it had been about to cover her hands. They were smiling broadly, not at the photographer, but at each other. Grandfather's hair waved over his forehead like my father's does his. The contessa's tresses refused to be held back by the ribbon that nonetheless tried. They were beautiful, young, and in love.

I traced my grandfather's image with my right forefinger. I wanted to know everything. Who, for instance, was the photographer? And was he or she still alive in Fiesole?

A wall clock above the sink read five minutes to nine.

As I turned from the easel and the photograph, something sticking out from behind it caught my attention. It was the edge of an envelope. I pulled it out. *Orla* was written on it in cursive.

The Contessa's Easel

The envelope was not sealed, its glue-edged triangle only tucked in. I untucked it and read in the contessa's hand:

Dearest Orla,

Your grandfather gave me this easel after my son Paolo was murdered by the Fascists along with his father. As you can imagine, I was devastated and at a loss as to how to appreciate life. I even considered ending my own. One evening a few weeks after the tragedy, when he came by to keep me company, your grandfather carried this easel with him. "My Contessa's Easel," he called it. The day before we became lovers, he wrote to me. I have transcribed his words from his letter to me. The original, you must understand, I cannot part with.

"Beatrice,

Here is my doctor's prescription, which you must follow in order to salvage your life. Every day, look out over the garden, the ruins, the forests, and with your brush paint a single image of nature's beauty. In this way you can and will return to life."

I know you never knew your grandfather, but now you can touch what his hands touched and create beauty on wood that is much more than wood. Be like him, dearest Orla, recognize, make, and be beauty in an often ugly world.

Con molto affetto sempre,
Your (and His) Contessa

I was dumbfounded. Speechless. Shaken. Awed.

"Grandfather," I said.

I walked from the studio back to the bedroom. I stared at the bed, imagined the two of them, the married American doctor and the widowed Italian countess, huddled together against the terrors outside. Defying convention. Insisting that living and loving go on. I wished Gabriella, my half-aunt, were here so we could talk. And I wanted to see the paintings, if in fact there were any. I wanted to touch those prescribed bits of beauty that the contessa might have had the courage to acknowledge and record.

I walked back to the studio to see if perhaps they had been stored on any of the shelves. But the shelves were all empty. Like a camera filming the room, I scanned the walls, too. They were bare for now, as well.

The sound of wheels on the cobbled drive outside the studio's windows matched the rotunda's clock striking nine. I giggled. Mina had not been kidding. A car door slammed, and a series of sturdy footsteps walked around the car, stopping at the front door of the villa.

"*Buona sera, Monsignore,*" I heard Tino say.

It was time for me to leave the past for the present, if only for a little while. So I stood up straight, fluffed my hair with my fingers, smoothed my shirt, and walked down the spiral staircase that had once also withstood my grandfather's tread. If Villa d'Annunzio had once seemed exotic and unfamiliar to me, it now tantalized with the comforting promise of home.

Chapter Sixteen
The Monsignor's Request

The contessa, Tino, and the *monsignore* were already seated on the patio when I came through the adjacent lounge. The night was still, and at least a dozen candles of varying heights lit the length of the marble dining table. Wine barrel-sized clay pots of basil, rosemary, and mint lined either end of the patio, while between the patio and pool stood even bigger plant holders of hydrangeas, blue and pink and white. Flute music and bongo drums, along with a babble of festive-sounding voices wafted up the mountainside from villas and farmhouses below. A delightful summer evening was in full swing in the hills above Florence.

Both men stood as I joined them.

"*Monsignore*, I'm delighted to meet you," I said.

The *monsignore* did not look like a priest at all. He was dressed in a bright plaid sport shirt with a Ralph Lauren emblem on the breast pocket. His slacks were expertly pressed linen, the color of almonds, and his shoes the soft driving loafers favored by Luke. His close-cropped hair was more salt than pepper, and, like Tino, he had skin suited for the sun. He wore thick-lensed, square black eyeglasses.

"As am I to make your acquaintance," he said, his English clipped and precise.

He took both my hands in his and held them upright so that, during our introduction, we looked like a duet of prayer.

"Tonight, since we are all family or close friends here," he said, "you must call me only by my given name, Pietro."

He seemed more worldly than I had expected. And physically comfortable with a woman.

"Pietro, then," I said, and he let go my hands.

From the corner of my left eye, I saw that Tino was mixing another Negroni. The contessa said nothing, but only nursed her drink from her chair near the edge of the patio and watched the priest and me converse. A Siamese cat prowled among the planters of hydrangeas.

"You see," Pietro continued, even as he strolled over to the bar, retrieved the Negroni from Tino, then walked back to hand it to me, "Tino and I are second cousins from the maternal line."

Tino continued to surprise me.

"How nice." I said. "A family man of the cloth, a priest on demand, as it were."

"Most of the time," Tino laughed. "Unless he is with—how do the Americans say? —the higher ups?"

"So you party with His Holiness?" I asked.

The *monsignore* raised his eyebrows, but also smiled.

"Mainly I try to avoid His Holiness's notice."

I liked that answer. While it was humorous, it also carried a brief cautionary tale.

Tino continued, "My dear cousin, as a matter of fact, baptized me right in the contessa's chapel, just one month after I was born."

The contessa tapped her walking stick sideways on the arm of her chair and said, "And he is entertained when he hears my yearly confession during Holy Week."

The priest's eyes widened and he pretended to glare at his hostess. "Fortunately for the contessa, the seal of the confessional prevents me from sharing her more tantalizing offenses with you."

The contessa tapped the cane again. "Admit it, Pietro," she teased, "without me you would be bored silly with those penitents nervous about how many times they swore at their spouses, or put a handful of chestnuts into their pockets from the produce stand. I liven things up and compel you to invent original penances for me."

I was enjoying the banter. The three of them must find Tuesday evenings a respite—Tino and the *monsignore* from their professional duties, and the contessa from the loneliness her status and age so often exacted.

I questioned the *monsignore* further.

"So your surname is not Bacci, then?

"Correct," said the priest. "Mine is Giannini. My cousin, Tino's mother, is Aurora Giannini Bacci."

"My father," said Tino, "was Silvio Bacci. I never knew him. He was a university student from Bologna, a resister, my mother told me, a resister who could not resist her. He never return-éd to Fiesole from the war, so was presume-éd dead."

"*Dio!*" the contessa blurted.

The cat had jumped onto her lap, startling her.

"But whose animal is this?" she asked no one and everyone.

Tino made for the ice bucket. "He never knew of my mother's pregnancy, let alone of my birth," Tino continued. "My mother told me I have his eyes. Being from the north, he had some Austrian and German blood."

"I am sorry for your loss," I said.

"Thank you," Tino replied.

Then he went over to the contessa, leaned over her, and kissed her on the top of her head.

"And my godmother," he said, "this most generous contessa, saw to it that my mother, who, as *Zia* has already told you, possessed a natural gift for music, was mentor-éd in the violin."

He walked back to the bar, took up the tongs, and dropped three ice cubes into his drink.

"Then my mother was able to support me through her music. When she was not traveling to concerts after the war, she held music classes at the orphanage here, where we both live-éd until I was ready for the *liceo* and old enough to stay alone during her intermittent absences."

"Tomorrow you will meet her and her mentor, *Dottoressa* Antonella Ghiraschi, should the older woman's health allow," said the contessa. "We shall go to Antonella's home. She uses a wheelchair now, so coming here, even when Marciano helps, is taxing for her." The contessa re-arranged herself on her chair.

"Oh, yes," she continued, "you must bring along the galleys of the book."

"Of course," I said.

In my mind I was drawing family and community trees. Though certainly superior in stature and iconic for its artistic, historical, and cultural heritage, Fiesole, like quaint and homely St. Suplice, had a small-town feel. Like St. Suplice, its population formed a web of alliances. Perhaps that is how it survived a Nazi occupation. I was keen to meet those who were still alive to tell their stories from that period, as was Tad. And I was curious also to learn from them how they lived today. What were their memories? How had they gone on? Had the enemy disappeared? Or, as was the case for my late friend and Vietnam vet, Danny Cowles, had the Nazis and their occupation at Villa le Balze dug a permanent foxhole into their group and individual consciousnesses?

The contessa's walking stick fell onto the slate with a gun-shot type crack. Tino hurried over to retrieve it and placed it gently by her chair. The parrot stared at her shoulder. I sipped my drink, nudging the orange slice into the glass with my tongue.

"*Signorina* Castleberry," the *monsignore* said, "it is a pleasure to meet in life the artist I have been introduced to only recently through newspaper and magazine clippings and photocopies of your works."

I looked to Tino and smiled.

"Then you must call me 'Orla,'" I smiled. "No formalities, as you have already suggested. And we can blame Tino if my paintings were not to your taste."

When Pietro did not respond but only smiled, I knew they were not. I could only hope that the supper conversation would not be long on negativity. I would try not to be defensive.

Pietro walked over to the low table by the contessa's pillowed wrought iron chair and picked up his own drink.

"*A la salute*," he toasted. "To art, Orla."

"Cheers," I replied.

As soon as Mina arrived with the antipasti, both men helped the contessa to the table. She and the *monsignore* sat at either end, while Tino and I faced each other from across the table's length. After the *monsignore* said grace, Tino poured the wine. And for the next hour, over antipasti and drinks, one would have thought that Pietro had come by only for a deceptively simple weeknight meal. He appeared calm and relaxed and, during the pasta course, regaled me with tales of how he had been the slowest in his class to learn English when he'd studied Educational Leadership at Catholic University in the District of Columbia some twenty years earlier.

The contessa primarily listened, saying only that, "The *monsignore*'s talents, including for linguistics, are many, Orla. Do not let him fool you with his self-deprecation. And never mistake his gregariousness for malleability."

The *monsignore* did not defend himself against the contessa's words. In fact, he did not even look up from his food after her pronouncement.

"My mother would agree with that," Tino said. "She tells me my cousin here is obstinate about the types of music he allows in church. No secular tunes whatsoever."

Pietro spoke soberly. "There is the sacred, and there is the profane, Tino. One or the other. And I will have none of the other." He'd put down his utensils and made quotation marks around "other" with his fingers.

Clearly the *monsignore* and the contessa both enjoyed the authority that their ecclesiastical and social statuses conferred on them.

Smiling at our hostess across the long table, the *monsignore* said, "Contessa, though I appreciated your compliment, such as it was, I do think it better not to boast, or even admit to, one's talents."

One-upmanship appeared to be their game.

The *monsignore* pointed his knife to the ceiling, then turned to Tino.

"Do you not find, Tino, that if persons have no or low expectations for you, it is much easier to gain the upper hand when you surprise them with success?"

So the *monsignore* valued the upper hand. Hmmm. The night could prove interesting.

Tino paused and held his fork mid-air with his left hand. Then he said, "Certainly, my cousin. That is why I share the worst-case outcomes with my patients' families and my greatest hope with the patients themselves."

"You do not!" I protested.

Tino looked at me, shrugged his shoulders, and continued eating.

"This method has work-éd so far. I have many patients who have been call-éd Lazarus by their relatives."

"I refuse to believe you," I said.

He winked at me, and, I tell you, I felt like a girl again. Flustered. Truly.

I turned to the *monsignore*, hoping to regain if not an air of sophistication, at least one of mannerliness.

"So, tell me, *Monsignore*—Pietro, I mean—if you struggled with the English language so, how did you arrive at the mastery you presently demonstrate, even if you do not admit to that mastery?"

I had decided to play the game as well.

The *monsignore* chuckled, placed his napkin to the left of his pasta dish, and said, "I had to be tutored, so slow was I to learn the irregular verbs," he said. "Each past tense was a singular Germanic enemy of the simple logic and symmetry of my native Italian."

I laughed, and felt my head swimming with "swim," "swam," and "swum."

Pietro wound the *bucatini* around his fork so that the utensil became a spool of *puttanesca*-coated deliciousness. He waited to bite into the pasta. "The tutorials, you will be surprised to learn, even tempted me to reconsider my calling."

I raised my eyebrows and Tino teased, "Cousin, you are a scandal to your profession."

"You have no idea with what prescience you have spoken," Pietro replied.

Tino, as if suddenly aware of some knowledge he had forgotten, said softly, "I am so sorry, Cousin."

Allowing no pause for anyone to respond, the contessa rang the little bell by her water glass, and Mina came out onto the patio to remove the pasta plates. In short order she returned with a grilled pork tenderloin sliced into juicy medallions, accompanied by grilled zucchini, red and green peppers, and mushrooms. She served the contessa first.

"Really, Pietro?" I said. "You're kidding, right, about doubting your calling?"

Pietro wiped his mouth with his napkin, looked across the table at the contessa and to his left at Tino. Both of them waited. I wondered if they were about to hear his story for the first time or if this was part of a repertoire he repeated at function after function. Neither of their faces revealed an answer.

"Claire Wesson was her name," he said. "She was blonde, blue-eyed, svelte, and athletic."

I could tell he was seeing her while he spoke. Then he said, "Thank you, Mina," as the girl filled his plate.

He waited until all of us had been served, then continued.

"Claire was the English-language teaching assistant. Her family owned a horse farm near Fredericksburg, Virginia. And her father invited all the priests in the English-language program to a splendid outing at the place." Pietro ate with gusto as he spoke.

"Seeing that young lady ride and jump nearly made me toss my vow of chastity away. What I wouldn't have given for, excuse my vulgarity, Contessa and Orla, what the Americans refer to as a 'roll in the hay.'" Again, quotation marks around "a roll in the hay."

I opened and shut my mouth. This was not the *monsignore* I had been prepared for.

"What prevented you from leaving the priesthood?" the contessa asked. "Fear of eternal damnation or something less permanent?"

I burst out laughing and Tino's eyes danced.

The contessa was completely serious and straightforward. The cat that had jumped onto her lap earlier, then hopped down to prowl around the hydrangea urns, now curled around her ankles.

Pietro stopped talking, and downed the three medallions of pork on his plate in quick succession.

He considered for a moment, drank from his water glass twice, then said, "Guilt at first. Guilt for several months."

He played with his fork and knife, holding the former in his left hand, the latter in his right, as if they were drumsticks with which he was about to beat his plate. His face flushed red over his tan.

"More meat?" the contessa asked, her eyes twinkling.

She was toying with him as he reveled in his memory of Claire Wesson's flesh, but he did not get the joke. In fact, he was dead serious.

I tried to suppress a giggle, not at all successfully. Tino examined his bread dish and did not look at me.

"In the end, Contessa, it was grace. Grace helped me suppress my carnal desires." Pietro placed his knife and fork down on his plate.

He sounded like the ideal priest from central casting, excepting perhaps Bing Crosby in *Going My Way*. Bing's Father O'Malley had understood the wayward girl without reducing her to the status of a strumpet. *Monsignore* Giannini perhaps still held fast to the iconic madonna/whore dichotomy that identified all women as one or the other.

"How dreadful!" the contessa cried.

Tino laughed out loud this time, and I covered my mouth with my napkin.

But the *monsignore*'s demeanor was somber. He pushed the bridge of his eyeglasses higher up on his nose, then adjusted the temples so that the glasses sat firmly in place.

The contessa continued. "That sort of grace has generally eluded me."She sounded as if she were talking to herself.

Once more, Tino interjected. "So this experience has helpéd you, Cousin, when you advise your seminarians about matters of the flesh?"

He couldn't have been more pointed. Had he been an attorney I would have said he was leading the witness.

The contessa passed the *monsignore* the plate of meat and vegetables. He spooned himself several more pieces of pork.

"Perhaps you are correct, Tino," he said. "At least they know I am human, or was human at one time."

At this the contessa smiled.

Now Pietro ate quickly, wiping his plate clean.

The rest of us were quiet for a while. I sipped my wine. Tino finished his vegetables. The contessa drank glass after glass of water, leaving most of her food untouched,

All of a sudden, she became animated and jingled her bell. Mina arrived in an instant.

"We will take coffee and the *nocelli* inside," the contessa told her. "Some grapes also. In the library."

She made to rise from her chair, and Tino hurried to her assistance.

"You have a matter of importance you wish to discuss?" the contessa asked Pietro.

The *monsignore* stood.

"Yes, Contessa,"—he made a slight bow to her—"I have been dreading the discussion now for more than two weeks."

The contessa raised her eyebrows.

The Contessa's Easel

"Am I so difficult to consult?" she asked.

The *monsignore* rubbed his chin with one hand. "What I wish to discuss will be difficult, both for you and for me."

"Well, then," the contessa said, "we'd best talk and be done with it. If we are still friends at the end, we will enjoy some port." The contessa was all business now.

I stood and pushed my chair under the tabletop. "Perhaps it is time for me to go upstairs," I said.

With the contessa on one arm, Tino offered me his other. "Certainly not," he said, then looked long at his cousin. "Among us all, Cousin, Orla can offer the most insight. I have already share-éd with you the limited options medicine presently offers for what dismays and burdens you."

I slipped my arm through Tino's, and the four of us walked from the patio, through the lounge and the rotunda, then made our way to the library just beneath the contessa's former sitting room. Mina must have readied the library earlier, for it glowed with light, and two ceiling fans moved the air over us.

"Now, then," Pietro said, "I must be the *monsignore* completely."

Was he going to role-play? Perhaps "*Monsignore* Pietro" was an oxymoron. Poor guy, if it was.

I had forgotten how intimate the library was despite its significant size. The contessa had arranged six different reading spaces around its perimeter, as well as a centered discussion area, set off by two leather couches that faced each other. Between them was a long, low table that held blank note pads, a leather catchall for pens, pencils, rulers, scissors, a stapler, boxes of staples and paper clips. On the table was the manila envelope Tino had shown me earlier in the evening. Before we sat down, Mina carried in the tray of coffee, cookies, and fruit. She placed it on a refectory table that stood in front of the windows facing the drive outside.

"Please," the contessa said, motioning with her hand, and for several minutes Tino and I filled and carried small plates of treats and poured coffee for the contessa and *Monsignore* Pietro. Then we took care of ourselves.

The *monsignore* and the contessa sat on either end of the same couch, where they could lean into the sofa's comfortable pillowed corners. Tino and I sat directly across from them, next to one another in the sofa's middle. While Tino opened the envelope and arranged several photocopies of my AIDS portraits facing his cousin and the contessa, I sipped my espresso and waited to discover what I was expected to bring to the discussion.

The contessa cringed when she looked at the painting of Karl X., sitting in a wheelchair, naked from the waist up, with Kaposi sarcoma blotches all over his torso, arms, and cheeks. He was as gaunt as the Christ on the Crucifix in the villa's small chapel. The *monsignore* stared at the copy of the painting, then took up in his hands each of the six others Tino had provided. He betrayed no emotion, but his eyes lingered on each image. One by one, he placed the images back onto the table. I hoped he felt sorrow and pity for the men whose suffering I had tried to portray in an unflinching, realistic manner. I knew he had looked at all the photos before. Even if he could not appreciate them, they at least had gotten his focused attention.

When he was done considering them, the *monsignore* turned the papers one by one so that they faced Tino and me. Then he looked across at me, his face stern. Two deep lines curved downward on either side of clean-shaven cheeks, almost to his top lip. I readied myself for a scolding, not unlike the one I had experienced in high school, when Sister Martine, the principal, had reamed me for having lifted some altar wine from the convent chapel. Of course that incident bore little resemblance to tonight's gathering, but my feelings of both annoyance and dread were the same. To my way of thinking, being an unimaginative and petty thief had actually been wrong and unbecoming of me, while making art that inspired attitudinal and social change demonstrated initiative and character. My high horse had joined us in the library.

I crossed my legs in an effort to appear unperturbed, made sure my hands were motionless on my lap.

"I must be honest, Orla," the *monsignore* said, "I find it difficult to appreciate these paintings as art. Actually, I find them obscene."

I smiled a practiced smile at him across the table and responded as I had to a slew of others who had been offended by my work.

"You are not alone, *Monsignore* Giannini," I said. I took another sip of my coffee. I was now the *Encyclopedia Britannica* version of the Twentieth-century American Painter, Orla Castleberry. "But from my point of view, the degree of suffering the men in the portraits endure from AIDS is the obscenity you see."

The *monsignore* scratched his head.

"You must know my point of view," he continued, ignoring his coffee and the sweet treats, "I believe art should uplift." He paused to point at each painting, holding his fingers on sores and sunken chests, tears, and terrified eyes. "These paintings, focusing on sinful flesh, they do nothing but degrade. They cause their viewers to wallow in the consequences of human depravity."

I put down my cup. "I understand that point of view, and I do not disagree that much of art uplifts, as it is intended to. But have you heard of Spaniard Joaquin Sorolla's painting, *Triste Herencia*?"

"No, I haven't," the *monsignore* replied.

159

"It depicts a monk from Valencia's asylum hospital of San Juan de Dios taking seriously ill and disabled children to the seashore to enjoy the therapeutic salt water."

"It is most disturbing," added the contessa.

"I hope you will have a look at it," I continued. "Sorolla compels his audience to witness human suffering as it happens in real time. In his day, the disease was syphilis. Those boys were born crippled, blind, and diseased, quite literally because of 'the sins of the fathers'. Sorolla did not flinch from depicting the truth, no matter how terrible. I do the same thing."

Tino interjected, "Why did you paint these particular men, *Signorina* Orla?"

He led a different witness now.

I looked to him, then to the *monsignore. Monsignore* Giannini bent his head in a gesture of anticipation, appearing to want to hear my answer.

"I painted these men with their permission and with the enthusiastic cooperation of St. Vincent's Hospital, a Catholic hospital, where AIDS patients are treated with compassion and dignity."

I felt myself rising to the occasion. Remembered how much money my exhibition in New York had raised for AIDS research. How it was likely to do so again for Project Lazarus come next Mardi Gras in New Orleans. How research was needed to stop the deaths. How my provocative portraits might lead to a mitigation, if not a cure, for AIDS.

"*Monsignore*,"—I leaned toward him over the table—"I painted them to illustrate the truth of this illness. I painted them to jar and upset viewers. I painted them to compel researchers to work for ways to end, or at least to lessen, human suffering caused by this disease."

I felt my voice rising.

"Most of all, *Monsignore* Giannini, most of all,"—here I stifled a sob rising from my center—"I painted them so Karl and Max and Felipe and Robb and Brett and Juan and Li,"—I pointed to each man—"and 30 more in total, would know that *I saw them* as people worthy of attention and note. That I saw them as human beings, not pariahs or demons. Or simple turners of tricks."

Tino's arm draped itself over my shoulder. I welcomed its comfortable weight, its consoling hold over the roiling emotions under my skin.

The *monsignore* moved forward on the couch so that he, too, hunched over the table between the two of us. He gesticulated with his hands, raising them upward and shaking his fists. "But did they not bring their suffering upon themselves?" he asked. "Is not their suffering a direct and natural consequence of aberrant, sinful behaviors, with drugs, with homosexuality, with total disregard for the laws of God?"

Tino answered before I could open my mouth.

"Often," he said, "yes, my cousin, often it is. Though not all are agree-éd on what you consider sexual aberration."

His arm held steady on my shoulder.

"Dammit!" the *monsignore* said. He banged his fists on the table so that the plates and cups shook.

The contessa watched him with narrowed eyes, playing her fingers against one another as if practicing piano scales.

"The teachings of Holy Mother Church are clear. And they are to be followed." The *monsignore* spoke as if from the pulpit —loudly at first, then softly, though no less forcefully. "It is required of us that they be followed."

I looked at the brown swirl at the bottom of my espresso cup, then up at the *monsignore*'s face. "That is true, *Monsignore*. They are most clear. Absolute, in fact," I said.

161

The priest took several breaths, apparently trying to calm himself. "So we are in agreement, then, Orla. You recognize Church doctrine and our obligation to obey it."

I sighed and wished I had several shot glasses of sambuca in front of me so I could swallow them one by one without stopping. Instead, I continued to speak, striving for calm and offering what insights I could.

"I certainly am no theologian, *Monsignore*. All I know from my own life is that people, myself included, do not generally behave absolutely, one way or its opposite, all the time. We are more mercurial, capricious, than absolute."

I sat very still and tried to modulate my voice.

"In fact, we behave contradictorily, surprising and confusing ourselves with our all-too-human inconsistencies."

The priest locked eyes with me. "Are you a relativist?" he asked. "Do you hold all behaviors to be equally acceptable? This and that, willy-nilly, whatever you want at the moment?"

I smiled at him and offered my hand across the table, but he didn't take it.

"I am a painter, *Monsignore*. Simply a painter. With my brush strokes I interpret what I see in the physical world."

For several moments, silence loomed about us. Tino removed his arm from my shoulder.

Then the contessa turned her body on the sofa to face the *monsignore* directly. She flicked her black pearl-drop earrings, first on one ear, then on the other, as she spoke. "Surely, Pietro, you would not leave these men to die without succor?" she said, "regardless of how they contracted the disease? I know you would not."

The *monsignore* sighed deeply.

She was at once scolding and praising him. Tino and I watched and waited for him to respond. But he said nothing. Just sat and was silent.

She kept her eyes on him, her posture seemingly ignorant of her age. "I ask you, Pietro," she said, her voice authoritative now, "what kind of a Christian, let alone a consecrated one, would that make you?"

She let go of the earrings and, reaching for her coffee cup, downed her shot of espresso the way my baby brother guzzled beer on the sly so our parents wouldn't see him. Then she shook her head.

The *monsignore* put his hands together, cracking finger and wrist joints as he did. His shoulders drooped, and he spoke in a sad, resigned tone. "My problem is this." He sighed audibly and looked to each of us in turn, first to the contessa, then to me, and finally to Tino. Tino encouraged him, "Go on, Cousin. Tell *Zia*. It is for the best." Then he put the photocopies back into the manila envelope, taking his time.

The *monsignore* began.

"As you have long been aware, Contessa, and as you, Orla, are just now learning, I am the director of a residence in Via Cavour in Florence. Under my care are 24 seminarians studying for their academic, or non-theological, degrees at l'Universita degli Studi di Firenze."

"I see," I said.

"Go on," the contessa prodded him.

"Several months ago, the priest who advises the seminarians, who celebrates the Mass with them and lives among them in the dormitory, took ill. Suffice it to say, Tino treated him, as he does all in our facility."

Tino took one purple grape at a time from his plate. One by one, he chewed and swallowed at least eight before he spoke. His steady, deliberate pace had a calming effect, at least on me.

"Yes. In addition to leading the Emergency Department at Santa Maria Nuova and my little practice here in Fiesole, I am also on retainer for the diocese. I treat many seminarians, nuns, and priests. I saw the priest in question several times. And after eliminating lesser afflictions, I was force-éd to conclude that the unfortunate fellow indeed is infected with AIDS."

I nodded, while the contessa kept her eyes on Tino.

"As we three all know," he said, sweeping his right hand across the table, "with that diagnosis comes a death sentence. Not to mention intense psychological distress and, for him, in addition, heavy shame."

"I am sorry, Tino," I said. "I am sorry for the priest and for the difficult position his illness puts you in, *Monsignore*. I really am."

The *monsignore* took up his demitasse cup and drank his coffee, certainly lukewarm and murky by now. He became overtly distraught, putting his hands to the sides of his head, then slapping them onto his knees.

"It is a scandal. A disgusting scandal. And it is—it was—my job to avoid and prevent scandal. I have failed completely." He took off his glasses and wiped his eyes with the back of his hands.

"So,"—the contessa's tone was at once critical and calm—"you care more about the scandal and your job than you do about the priest." She grabbed onto her walking stick leaning against the sofa and twirled the parrot's head round and round. "You admonish yourself now the same way you have admonished me for decades about my own scandal," she stated. The contessa pulled at the fringe on the magenta linen shawl she had worn over her caftan all evening. She was like a cat scraping its claws on upholstery. "Perhaps you would have been happier if I had killed myself, committed the sin of suicide rather than love illicitly the man who saved me, who gave me a daughter for whom I wanted to live again."

The *monsignore* scowled at her and sighed deeply once more.

I motioned to him with my right hand across the table. He looked at my waving hand.

"*Monsignore*, where is the priest now?" I asked.

Tino stood up and, taking his plate with him, walked to the refectory table and piled it high with the hazelnut-filled cookies. "He is at the Ospedale Santa Maria Nuova," he said, "secluded in a private room on a unit generally reserved for clergymen and sisters whose modesty prevents their presence on a more public ward."

I nodded, waiting for him to speak some more. But he added nothing.

The contessa folded her arms across her chest and leaned toward the priest once more. "Is the priest a drug user?" she asked. "A homosexual?"

The *monsignore* put his head in his hands. Then he looked up and said, "He is the lover of one of the seminarians and God only knows who else."

"Not surprising," murmured the contessa. "There is nothing new under the sun. All one needs to do is read history and Dante."

If he heard her, the *monsignore* did not acknowledge her words.

Tino spoke. "Obviously, *Zia*, we have had to test the seminarian as well. A number of them, in fact. And some of their faculty."

The contessa looked to her godson. "And?" she deemnded.

Tino said softly, "The seminarian does not show the infection yet. Likely it will be only a matter of time. And we must find, if we are able, all former associates of both the priest-advisor and his young lover, and so on. I am not confident I know them all at this point."

The *monsignore* spoke again, rubbing his chin with his hand. "Thank God he is no longer my problem. He has been expelled and sent packing."

"Have you no shame, Pietro?" the contessa said. "He is your responsibility."

The *monsignore* shook his head vigorously and his shoulders tensed. "He is not. Was. He *was*. He is no longer worthy to ascend to the priesthood."

"And what of the older priest, the advisor?" she asked.

The *monsignore* did not reply.

Again Tino sat down beside me. "The seminarian remains my patient, *Zia*," he said. "Do not worry. I will still take care of him."

Her anger evident, the contessa rang the bell excessively for Mina. I realized then that she must have placed bells in every room of the villa.

I watched her and waited for her to speak. So, too, did the two men.

After drumming her fingers on the arm of the sofa while moving both her feet in circles at the ankles, she finally spoke. Her voice sounded impersonal, modulated, and businesslike.

"So," the contessa said, "how may I be of help to you?"

The *monsignore* looked the contessa in the eye and relaxed his tense posture. He had gotten to where he needed to be. He was the plaintiff, she the judge who would decide his case.

Oh, she was all countess now, I tell you. Pragmatic. Powerful. Condescending. And the *monsignore* appeared both cowed and relieved by her prerogative to manage his mess.

Mina came into the library.

"Port, please, Mina," said the contessa.

And, just like that, she had declared their longtime friendship intact.

"Yes, Contessa," Mina said.

166

The *monsignore* stood and walked from the sofa into the very center of the room. He stopped at the round table under the ceiling painted with *putti*. The table held a globe on an axle stand. Spinning the sphere with his right hand so that the world passed before our eyes, he said, "I would be most appreciative if you could hide the priest here."

"Of course," the contessa said, without a moment's hesitation. "But he shall be my house guest, not a prisoner in solitary confinement. He already knows his hell."

Tino stood, walked to the contessa, bent, and kissed her on her cheeks. *"Mille grazie, Zia,"* Tino said. "Thank you very much."

The contessa said, "Help me up."

The *monsignore* also went to her aid.

She raised herself between them.

"You will find a full-time nurse," she said, speaking to Tino now. "I will see to everything else."

She shook the men off her arms and, using her walking stick, walked to the refectory table and motioned for Mina, who had just arrived in the doorway, to set the port out there.

Tino filled a glass and handed it to the contessa, and did the same with a second for the *monsignore*. The third and fourth were for me and him. *Monsignore* Pietro looked old now. Tired and spent, his shame weighing on him like a heavy cloak. He had opened himself to ridicule, humbled himself to protect the consecrated priest, and failed to whitewash the besmirched façade of his Church's moral purity.

Chapter Seventeen
Good Night

As soon as the *monsignore*'s Fiat had left the drive, the contessa said, "I must go now, my children. Stay as long as you like, Tino. You will apprise me tomorrow of what needs doing."

"Yes, *Zia*." Tino made a quick bow from his waist and kissed the contessa on both cheeks.

"Oh," she said, taking both his hands in hers, "where is best to make this unfortunate man safe and comfortable?" She put one hand to her mouth, then let it drop, and said, "I will open Paolo's room and bath if that will help." She had tears in her eyes. I realized that Paolo's death was as present to her as we were.

"That is a generous offer," Tino said. "Most generous." He paced back and forth in front of the contessa, a forefinger to his lips, thinking. "So," he said, then paused, his top front teeth lightly scraping his lower lip, "I do not know if what I will suggest is possible, *Zia*."

She smiled at him and at the same time blinked her eyes several times. "We will know only if you suggest it."

"Yes," he said. He glanced at the two marble stands on either side of the rotunda's great door. On one, cigarettes stood upright in an open brass cylinder, while on the other lay a candy dish filled with individually wrapped chocolates. He chose a cigarette. His hands shook a little.

Taking a lighter from one of his pants pockets, he lit the cigarette and inhaled. Then he exhaled a slender line of smoke that curled where it left off.

"I wonder, *Zia*, if you are willing to open the infirmary of the former orphanage."

The contessa regarded him steadily. "Go on. I am listening."

Tino took a second puff of the cigarette. "If my memory has not fail-éd me, there were three rooms that made the infirmary. And they were all accessible to the outside without steps."

The contessa leaned both hands, one over the other, on the parrot's head. "Yes, you remember correctly. One room for the sick. Another for the treatments. And the third for the nurse. We made sure to have no steps, for the wheelchairs. So the children could go outside."

I recalled the many photographs of injured, sick, and orphaned children Tad had discovered when, at age twelve, he was already scouring my grandfather's diaries. I wondered if any of them other than the contessa's own Paolo had died. How many of them had lost the ability to walk? Or to learn to make the gesso statues the contessa sent to Grandmother Castleberry every holiday? Or simply to play?

"Correct," Tino said, bringing me back to the present. "Good. I have remember-éd rightly."

He drew on the cigarette. Then he snuffed it out in the glass ashtray by the cylinder.

"I had my tonsils taken out in the treatment room when my mother could not be with me." He was speaking to himself with the voice of memory. Then he looked first at the contessa, then

169

at me, and putting a hand to his chest, said, "Please forgive me, ladies. I should not have mention-éd how sad I was for so small a thing. A thing that heal-éd and was done."

I wanted to hug and console him. Instead I said, "But you were a child, and your mother was not with you." I wondered where she had been. I thought of Mercy's rage at Thérèse Luong's much longer absence. My own anger at Daddy's eleven-year desertion of me and my mother, Mamma only eighteen at the time of my birth. The lot of so many children. Their undeserved, heavy, life-draining lot.

"She was down the mountain at the cathedral, playing the violin at someone's funeral. She came as soon as she could. But I did not understand. I slapped her when she came, and made her cry."

He was quiet again, then shrugged. "Still, I do not forget how sad I was."

The contessa put her hand to his cheek. "Tell me more about the priest," she said. "We do not even know his name."

Tino scratched his left cheek. "He is call-éd Father Donato Caduto and he is thirty-three years of age."

The contessa nodded. "What do you call him?" she asked.

Tino smiled. "Since the first time I met him, he ask-éd me to call him 'Dona.'" Tino shifted his weight from one foot to another. "You will like him, *Zia*. He is sardonic."

"How well you know me." The contessa laughed.

But then Tino became serious, thoughtful. "Dona already suffers fevers, night sweats, and significant loss of weight. He will become much weaker. Opportunistic infections will plague him. His immune system will not be able to fight the infections other people will inadvertently expose him to."

The contessa nodded. "I have heard this," she said. "And I know that my house is too busy. Inside the villa will not be safe for him. Plus, the stairs would confine him."

We all stood silent for a moment. Then the contessa raised her head as she always did when she made a pronouncement or offered a toast. "Yes, the infirmary," she said. "And for as long as he is still able," she continued, "he must be afforded the chapel. He must be able to perform the sacraments as a priest."

She looked at me then and made another pronouncement. "He will not be a pariah, Orla. As at your St. Vincent's Hospital, there will be no pariahs here."

She raised her voice to a higher pitch. "He will be the d'Annunzio chaplain. I will ask him to accept this position. He will do me the service of not having to go down to the cathedral for Mass." She raised her walking stick like a crusader's sword.

Tears came into my eyes now.

"I love you, Contessa," I said.

She removed one hand from the parrot and touched my arm. "Rest well. You have earned your sleep. And you have persons to meet in just a few hours."

"Thank you," I whispered now, as if we stood in a sacred place. "You know, for everything upstairs."

"You are most welcome." She smiled a brilliant smile so that even the lines on her face looked happy. "Your grandfather would be so pleased that you are here to stay a little while."

And she left the rotunda for her new suite opposite the library just as the clock struck midnight. Despite her advancing age and the toll that arthritis was taking on her body, she remained herself—generous, handsome, imperious, but, most of all, good. I turned to Tino. "I must be going to sleep, as well," I said. "It's been nearly two days since my body has rested on a bed. I thank you for welcoming me, Tino. And I look forward to seeing you again."

Tino smiled and smiled. The clock must have ticked twenty times.

"You must be very tir-éd," he said, but even as he spoke he took my right hand and led me back through the lounge and out onto the patio. I did not resist.

"Look up," he said, pointing to the sky. "It is beautiful, no?"

I raised my eyes.

"Very."

The constellations sparkled above us. The lights, voices, and music that had earlier enlivened the mountainside had gone dark and silent. We heard instead only soft air, the gentle whirr of the night's insects, and the rustle of leaves and creatures among the trees beyond the manicured lawn.

After several moments, Tino left off looking at the sky, turning his gaze instead to me.

"I am so very glad you have come, *Signorina* Orla. *Zia* has often spoken to me about you, how you visited when you studied in Florence. But all those times I was away. At medical school, at residency in Rome, in Sardinia with the girl who abandon-éd me and our engagement for a banker with regular hours." He laughed.

"Where is she now?" I asked.

He shrugged his shoulders. "Who knows?" he said. "Who cares? You have made me forget her."

I laughed then.

"Her and all the others," he added.

I shook my head and pointed my forefinger at him like an admonishing schoolteacher. "You are a charming liar," I said. "But a liar, nonetheless."

"Sometimes," he said. "Sometimes it is true. I have lie-éd to women."

He looked into my eyes.

"But not now."

I felt bathed in loveliness.

He extended his arms either side of me. "May I?" he asked.

The Contessa's Easel

"You may," I answered.

A kaleidoscope of butterflies fluttered inside me.

He wrapped me in his embrace, and, I tell you, I kid you not, we kissed as though the sun would never rise.

Chapter Eighteen
Unlocking the Past

I woke after ten, took my time getting ready, and came downstairs to find a breakfast waiting for me on the patio. I'd dressed in a knee-length violet linen shift for the hot day predicted in yesterday's papers. A pair of twisted silver hoop earrings and an oversized fashion watch jazzed up the outfit a little. A vanilla leather carryall and deep purple Ferragamo flats finished the outfit. As always when I traveled in Italy, I tied a long scarf—today's was violet, purple, and white voile—on the carryall's strap in case I found myself in a church and needed to cover my shoulders.

"Good morning," Mina said, "I hope you slept well, *Signorina* Castleberry."

"Yes, very well," I said. "And thank you," I continued, pointing to the inviting spread, "for this delicious start to my day."

"It is my pleasure," she said, and dipped from her knees.

I liked Mina very much.

The Contessa's Easel

This morning she was dressed as the night before, but her skirt was navy blue instead of gray, and her camisole a pink that reminded me of the sand in Bermuda's Horseshoe Bay. Whatever had caused the vertical scar on her back did not appear to hamper her quick, bouncy, and accurate movements. She gamboled about the villa like a fine, unbroken filly. Though I will of course continue to call her by her given name, in my imagination she is none other than "Filly Gamine."

"Would you like some coffee?" she asked.

"Certainly," I said.

Mina filled the delicate china cup decorated with turquoise birds, first with steamed milk, then with coffee from a monogrammed silver pot. I skipped the sugar cubes, but did not hesitate to place two crescents of cantaloupe and several tissue-thin slices of *prosciutto* onto my plate.

"The contessa says that when you are ready, she wishes you to join her in the former orphanage. She waits there for you."

"Thank you, Mina. I'll make short work of breakfast, then."

I enjoyed a fruit-filled *cornetta,* licking some lemon curd from the edges of my lips. I drank two more cups of coffee that made me feel energized and alert. Deciding I mustn't keep the contessa waiting any longer, I folded my napkin and placed it on the dining table. Jet lag should prove negligible now. I was settling into Italy.

"Thank you, Mina!" I called. "See you later."

Filly Gamine came running, and I realized what an American (by that I mean democratic) gesture my farewell had been.

"Yes, may I help you, *Signorina*?" Mina asked.

All of a sudden I felt silly. Demanding as I could be about my work and annoyingly critical (so Mercy has told me many times) of family and friends, I was also at my core a girl aspirant from small-town St. Suplice.

"No, I just wanted to thank you and let you know I am going to the contessa now."

Mina smiled at me. "You are most kind to let me know, *Signorina*. Have a lovely day." Her knees dipped down once more.

I left the table and the patio, stepping out onto the pool surround. Perhaps I'd have a swim later on. It was getting very warm, though with a drier heat than in NOLA and St. Suplice. Walking away from the pool, I passed in front of the stone chapel, making the Sign of the Cross as I did. Fewer than twenty steps away from it, I stood facing the former orphanage and the brass plaque that read:

la Casa dei Bambini
1943-1964
Lovingly erected and supported by
la Contessa Beatrice d'Annunzio and il dottore Peter
Clemson Castleberry, M. D.,
and a host of international friends.
"Children are a heritage from the Lord."

I felt Grandfather Castleberry's presence again, just as I had when I'd stared at the photograph on the contessa's easel the night before in the upstairs studio. While we had never met in life, and I couldn't tell you how his cheek might have felt against mine, or if he would have made up a little-girl nickname for me, I knew, both from St. Suplice lore and my mamma's and daddy's personal stories, that he had been a nurturer. He was the kind of man my mamma had told me "always made you feel like you were paying a social call when you visited his medical office. He made you think you were doing him a personal favor by stopping by." Daddy had said he was "more open to people than your grandmother. He had a sympathy for human frailty that she found more difficult."

I ran my fingers along the plaque. It was already oven-hot in the late-morning sun. I heard men's voices from inside the long, low stone building that, from afar, looked like, and in fact was, a museum now. A place that until twenty-five years ago would have resounded with the voices of children almost grown by then, just about ready to leave the contessa's benevolent and demanding care.

While she daily hugged, painted, and sang with them—so Grandfather's wartime and post-wartime letters told—the contessa also required that her orphans study through a curriculum rich in languages, music, and math. Those who showed an aptitude for craftsmanship were instructed by Egidio, an expert gesso craftsman from Arezzo that she had hired. Those tending toward the musical practiced with the orphanage's violin and piano instructors. And so on. The teachers, among them two Poor Clare Sisters from Assisi, lived with the children, eating meals with them, comforting them when they cried during the dark nights, sitting next to them in the chapel at daily prayer. Swimming and racing with them, and playing games of tag, hide-and-seek, and soccer, all within the villa's grounds which, even during the Nazi occupation, offered a degree of safety, although still fraught with uncertainty.

"You see, Orla," the contessa had told me the first time I visited here, after my freshman year at college, "the German officers were always trying to demonstrate that they were cultured despite the brutality the Third Reich demanded of them."

We had been sitting by the pool on a languid July afternoon. A bowl of peaches and some lemon water in a glass pitcher rested on a marble table between us. We both lay on two identical iron chaise lounges pillowed in fabric with birds of paradise and jungle orchids.

"Of course, some of them were brutal men to begin with. Others were merely ensnared in a powerful movement that demanded they suppress their humanity or else be brutalized themselves."

She had played her fingers, one against another. I remembered the deep maroon nail polish I told you about earlier and the glare of her oval aquamarine ring in the sun.

"One officer," she went on, longer than I cared to listen to then, though what she told me was quite compelling, "by the name of Friedrich Klumburg, appropriated a grand piano from Villa Medici and had it carried by six grunting men, I'm told, over the alleyway to Villa le Balze so he could practice every evening. He played beautifully. I heard him on my usual evening stroll, the *passagiata*. One could hear strains of Brahms, Beethoven, even Debussy, over the walls of the villa. He had long, graceful fingers. Those same fingers wrapped themselves around an ebony truncheon by day when he traversed the Piazza Mino. He kept the truncheon at his side, switching it from left hand to right hand once he reached the end of the piazza and turned. His choreography with the potentially fatal baton was a most effective deterrent to any local uprising. Terror and beauty mixed in him like first cousins."

I must have yawned back then, because the contessa asked, in a voice brusque with sarcasm, "Am I boring you?"

How embarrassed I was. How Mamma and Grandmother Castleberry both would have reprimanded me, not to mention Tante Yvette, who had arranged for me to be the contessa's houseguest.

"Please excuse my horrible manners, Contessa. Jet lag has overtaken me," I had lied, trying to inflect my words just as Tante Yvette might have.

She must have accepted my explanation, and so she had continued. I leaned on my elbows and turned my head to face hers as she spoke.

"I sponsored weekly concerts in the piazza, where Officer Klumburg and several others performed. I even invited the full cadre of German officers to a Christmas party at the Hotel Villa Aurora—you know it, the hotel facing Piazza Mino. I flattered them, trying—successfully, much of the time—to feign a state of normalcy and to safeguard the children."

She had sighed and fingered the charms on her jangly bracelet, each charm engraved with an orphan's name. She'd had it on the previous day, when I'd arrived. In fact, I've never seen her without it.

"They knew I hated what they stood for. They knew my late husband had been a vocal anti-Fascist. But the officers and I never spoke of such matters. Instead, those who were Catholic and went to Mass on Sundays tipped their visored hats at me as I sat in the d'Annunzio pew at the cathedral. I nodded back at them, my long black mantilla purposely covering my face as well as my hair. I didn't want them to see expressions of disgust I found difficult to suppress when their own Catholic chaplain, Father Ernst Adenauer, celebrated the Mass. We all used one another."

I remembered that the contessa had had to pause to collect herself a moment back then. She had raised herself up in the lounge chair, visibly upset. But, after drinking a glass of lemon-water, she had continued.

"You see, Orla, if I could act calmly with them, so would the other Fiesolani. We both knew that. It made it much easier for them to control the townspeople. That way they didn't feel the need to resort to violence at every turn."

I remembered what the contessa had done next as if it were this morning. She stood, threw off her long caftan, dropped it onto the lounge chair she had been sitting in, and dove into the deep end of the pool. She was naked but for her deep purple bikini bottom. I'd been typically American then, too prudish for nudity in her company. So, even as I hoped that she was finished talking, I looked in dismay at the cup lines around my breasts my reticence had caused. I could have had an even tan had I been willing to sunbathe topless. Soon enough, the contessa's head emerged from the water, and she went on as if she had simply taken a break midway through her narrative.

"But that period of calm, insecure as it was, ended when they discovered the *carabinieri* were leading the resistors, feeding them information every day. The very gates of Hell were flung open then. On the 6th of August, 1944, all Fiesolani men between the ages of 17 and 45 were told to report to Piazza Mino. There the Nazi officers selected ten innocent men, imprisoning and torturing them as a deterrent to any others who might dare oppose the Reich."

I couldn't help but cringe. The contessa's voice rose as she spoke, gathering speed in her telling.

"The soldiers also bludgeoned Pepino Sarto, Franco Cucinelli, and Enrico Senzo, all in their seventies, who had offered themselves in exchange for the young men. Heads bloodied, the three managed to stagger from the piazza into the cathedral, arm in arm. There they waited until several priests from the episcopal residence came to their aid. The priests washed and bandaged them. Pepino was never the same. He slurred his words and slumped on his left side. On the other hand, Franco and Enrico became rabid instigators. The next night, in an act bordering on madness, they set several animal traps just up the alley from Villa le Balze. It is said that one of the night watch soldiers stepped right into one so that his thick boot was stuck. Legend has it that he dragged the trap, boot and foot stuck fast, back to his partner. The fellow had to cut off the boot's top so the soldier could lift his foot out. It was only the embarrassment of the watch soldiers that saved Franco and

Enrico. I believe that, for I had seen some of the officers abuse their underlings the way they did the townspeople."

The contessa had paused, her eyes filling with water as she went on.

"Encouraged by the officers, several among the lowest-ranked soldiers gang-raped widowed Mafalda, the bishop's cook, as she drew water from his courtyard's well. Another, his leashed German shepherd snarling, terrorized eighty-three-year-old Lydia Caldi, slashing her face and arms with a pocket knife and leaving her for dead by the fruit stand near the taxi park. A pair of young sisters outside the *liceo* did not escape a painful shame. The older Renata screamed for the younger Pia to run, but she was caught. Their blood streamed down their legs and reddened the cobblestones as they held each other's hands and hobbled home in unforgivable humiliation. Their mother's cries when they reached her could be heard even across the ruins. Renata entered a cloister soon after, and Pia flung herself into a precipice below the hotel the day before her fourteenth birthday. Friar Martino, the oldest monk from Convento San Francisco at the very top of the town, never returned from his doctor's visit with your grandfather in his little clinic in the Hotel Villa Aurora. It was but for a cyst on his back. Only a little cyst. Two of the soldiers played target practice when he started home, a fresh bandage on his back, and then, as he trudged up the steep hill to his convent, two bullet holes to his brain."

At that the contessa had cried. Composing herself, she then climbed out of the pool and returned to her lounge chair. She said no more, but lay back and closed her eyes.

Ashamed as I am to admit it now, at the time her painful narrative ran like an action movie in my head. It was not real to me at all, just a flash of ugly images on a big screen. There I was, 18 years old, lolling around a pool on a gorgeous estate. Oranges and lemons were hanging off the trees for me to pick at my whim. A maid made my bed, and drinks and dinner were mine like clockwork every evening. A chauffeured sedan took me anywhere I chose to go.

Even my own memories of the Klan threatening my grandmother and Reverend Makepeace in St. Suplice in 1962 did not help me identify with the despair the contessa had expressed. Scared as I had been as an eleven-year-old child, I'd never felt personally threatened or afraid I was going to die. I was white. And there had always been Mamma or the sheriff and other adults circling around me to guarantee my safety.

In fact, on that summer day with the contessa, so self-centered and devoid of common human empathy had I been, that all I could think of was how soon I could ditch the contessa and have Marciano drive me down the rolling mountain to Florence. I wanted to meet up with Nate, Zoe, and Keith, also art students from NYU, and hang out in Oltrarno, across the Ponte Vecchio on the other side of the Arno River. Sure, we'd visit the iconic Pitti Palace and Chiesa Santo Spirito so we could write the papers we had to for summer class. But, really, finding a shady hideaway above the Piazzale Michelangelo with a joint and a bottle or two of wine was my more pressing desire.

Jesus, what a louse I was. Really, there had been no excuse for it. Looking back, I was terribly and rightly ashamed of myself. I wanted to make a restitution of sorts. I wanted to use my art to let the contessa and the others know that I saw how horrific the war and Nazi occupation were for them. That I admired not only how they had survived, but also how they had prevailed (to paraphrase my favorite author, William Faulkner).

So twenty years later I was back, better schooled in the contessa's past and aware of the horrors the Fiesolani had suffered at the hands of the German soldiers. Thanks to Tad's obsessive interest in and relentless study of Grandfather Castleberry's papers and other journalistic, historical, and scholarly accounts, along with the contessa's own collection of photographs, I now wanted to discover and paint what that time period had meant to those who had lived through it and come out on the other side. Today the contessa was offering me my first chance. In preparation, I had re-read a review copy of Tad's book on the plane. I was ready to ask questions of those willing to allow my intrusion. If any of them permitted, I'd tape them so Tad would have access to some first-person histories.

"Until they arrived here," the contessa had written and Tad had quoted from a 1948 orphanage newsletter, "the children experienced not minor difficulties, but severe deprivation and cruelty. *La Casa dei Bambini* returns to them a childhood previously stolen from them. And our education promises them the skills and the chances for productive and, we hope, happy futures."

I decided to enter the orphanage through the main door to the right of the plaque. But before I even wrapped my hand around the door handle, the door swung outward. The man who had taken my luggage into the main house yesterday was wheeling out a dolly filled with outdated medical equipment.

"*Signorina,*" he said and nodded, "Welcome. I am Beppo. I am the one who has made safe your paintings that have arrived."

"Good morning, Beppo, thank you," I answered, and held the door for him.

Right after him came two more men, much younger—teenagers, really. They looked to be his sons. One looked quite similar to his father, small and square. The other was taller, but with the same deliberate walk. They rolled out, one after the other, four child-sized hospital beds. The last had a screen around it, like playpens do. I assumed it had been for the orphanage's youngest residents.

"*Signorina!*" they both called out. "Roberto," said one, showing his teeth with his smile. "Carmine," the other, his eyelashes dark as coal.

"Good morning, good morning," I said.

I waited to see if more workers would follow, but none did. So I walked in, feeling the immediate cool and hush of tile, wood, and whitewashed stone. The overhead light fixtures, equidistant inverted domes, were not lit, nor was anyone else in sight.

Across from the main door and through the long corridor, a large room beckoned. It had the same overhead light fixtures, and six round tables were each surrounded by eight chairs. At the farthest end of the room, a counter divided the dining area from the kitchen. The room was painted a cheery yellow. On one side wall were framed oil paintings done by the children, each child's name printed, written, or scrawled in black paint revealing the developmental stage of the artist. *Luigi, Clara, Tomasso, Livia, Ernesto, Tino, Elena, Tati.*

Tino.

I walked to the painting. A rabbit entering some brush. All browns, whites, greens, with several yellow flowers. I touched it.

On the opposite wall, unframed stretched canvases in oils. Here all were the same size, nine by twelves inches, spread across the wall in two straight lines. There were at least two dozen. Each canvas showed one centered subject—a hummingbird, a chestnut, a caterpillar, a twig, a cloud, a fish. The brush's touch had been light, the effect charming and bright.

"They're hers," I said out loud. "Grandfather's prescription for life."

I walked from one painting to the next, wondering. Had she thought of them as pills she had to swallow? Did she simply follow doctor's orders? Or had it been possible, did it really happen, that she began to see beauty again? Her images seemed to favor the last possibility.

At the Lazarus Project meeting I'd attended with Luke the previous week, there'd been a woman named Siobhan, and she had spoken with a brogue.

"Several board members have told me I'm foolish to spend money on planters with blooms to put outside each client's bedroom when they need clothing and socks and shoes, medicine, and therapy," she'd said.

I smiled again, hearing her brogue in my mind.

"To be sure, they do," she had gone on. "But they need beauty as well. Unless they can find beauty, they might well give up on living."

"Grandfather," I whispered, and felt his blood run in my veins.

Someone was walking on the red tile floor.

"So, there you are," the contessa said.

She was dressed in a most becoming shirtwaist dress, pure white dotted with turquoise, pink, green, and yellow circles, each the size of a dime. She wore flat, bowed shoes, and her sunglasses were perched upon waves of her hair. Even though she was groomed for our afternoon visit with violinists *Dottoressa* Antonella Ghiraschi and Aurora Bacci, Tino's mother, she carried two cans of paint, one in each hand. Her walking stick was nowhere to be seen.

"Please, let me," I said, and reached for one of the cans.

"No need," the contessa said. "Carrying strengthens my arms."

She lowered each of the cans onto the floor.

"Shall I get your walking stick?" I asked, even though I could not see it.

"The contessa waved her hands dismissively.

"I left it in the infirmary," she said. Then, somewhat conspiratorially, "When I am alone, I hardly use it, Orla. It is only when Tino is here that I must." She laughed. "Otherwise he scolds me."

"I see," I said.

"'You must not fall,' he tells me. 'You must prevent yourself from a fall.'" The contessa looked at me head on.

"But I must live, as well. I want to live until I die. If I die falling, so be it."

She flipped her right hand upward as if dismissing talk of walking sticks, falls, and her demise, and pointed down at the paint cans instead.

"You are the artist. You decide the colors."

I saw that a daub of each color brightened the cans. One daub was periwinkle blue, the other a frothy yellow.

"What are the colors for?" I asked.

"The priest's and the nurse's rooms," she said. "I see no reason why their bedrooms must be stark and clinical. It is enough that the treatment room be thus."

I must say, I agreed. Being ill was bad enough, but feeling like a specimen under bright ceiling lights in an all-white room could only add to one's distress.

"Well, how about we paint the priest's room the periwinkle, and the nurse's room the yellow?" I suggested.

"Fine," she said. "I will let Beppo and his sons know."

I pointed toward the door.

"I just met them."

The contessa nodded.

"Beppo lives in the cottage at the edge of the lawn where Gabriella's tutor used to reside. She visited St. Suplice with us soon after your grandmother died. Do you remember?"

"Yes," I said.

The tutor was British, so Gabriella had spoken English differently from those of us raised in St. Suplice. At any rate, Julia Norwich got on splendidly with my mamma, as the two of them had a passion for maple walnut ice cream. So they said, anyway. But perhaps they just wanted to get away from their obligations for a while. The entire two weeks the contessa and Gabriella were with us, Mamma and Miss Norwich had gone off "for an ice cream cone" every afternoon while the others lazed around and the contessa took to her bed for an hour or so for her *riposa*. Daddy said he thought Mamma poured glasses of bourbon for Julia and herself in Grandfather's library, where the doors could be locked from the inside. After that, smiles as wide as the open church doors before Sunday Mass, they strolled to the center of town and got their maple walnut cones, Miss Norwich's with a rainbow of sprinkles, Mamma's with chocolate sauce squirted on top.

"Contessa!" Beppo called out as he entered the foyer again with his boys. "Have you picked the colors?"

"Yes," she said, "the artist did."

Beppo bowed his head and smiled. "Roberto will paint one room, Carmine the other," he said. "I will sanitize the treatment room and await the delivery of the hospital bed and the other equipment."

As soon as Beppo left them, each boy picked up a can of paint and headed down the corridor to the infirmary, which was situated away from the common rooms and the children's sleeping quarters. One of them must have had a radio or gotten hold of the orphanage's stereo, for almost immediately Alice Cooper's *Poison* blared. I felt as if Mercy would turn up at any moment.

Mop in hand, Beppo hurried out of the treatment room as if to silence the music, but the contessa said, "Please. The music will help them paint faster."

The three of us laughed, and Beppo went back to work.

"Impressive, Contessa," I said. "Things were moving very fast, even before the music started." I raised my eyebrows and smiled a mischievous smile. "It hardly feels like Italy."

The contessa laughed out loud. She sounded like Lauren Bacall. "This is true, Orla. But, you must understand"—and with an outstretched hand she urged me to follow her to the infirmary area—"we have a holy trinity at work here—an aristocrat, an ecclesiast, and a doctor."

I nodded.

"When we work together,"—here she paused to chuckle—"a rare occurrence, we can be most efficient. Almost German."

She shuddered then, but I couldn't discern if her movement was visceral or contrived. I wondered if the war ever went away for her, if any German trait or artifact or individual could be admired.

Just as we reached the treatment room, where the contessa's parrot rested its head on the side of a doorknob, a vehicle came to a stop outside.

"Impossible," Beppo said. "Not even the Pope could get the equipment this fast."

I laughed out loud and decided I wanted to get to know Beppo. He seemed to possess the forthright and amiable personality beneficial to one who deals with bureaucracies, businesses, and the personal whims of those whom social mores define as his betters.

He had just finished mopping the floor. The white-tiled room smelled of alcohol and chlorine. Its fluorescent lights made me think of winter sun on ski slopes slick with frozen glaze.

The contessa took her walking stick in hand and, together, we walked to the side doorway and the ramp that led into the orphanage's driveway. Having put his mop to rest for a moment, Beppo followed.

The vehicle in question was not a delivery truck, but instead a silver Fiat Tipo.

"So," said the contessa, "it is Aurora."

Tino's mother, I thought, and my body quivered, recalling last night's delights with her son.

Aurora emerged from the driver's seat and waved at the two of us.

"I hope I am on time," she called out, striding around the back of the car. She carried only her keys in her hand. She wore her sixty-two years well, if my calculations were correct. She appeared fit, quick, and cheerful. Energy personified.

"I went to the villa first, but Mina said you both were here. And I dare not be late for *la dottoressa*. Though I am certain, Contessa, that you and your guest will be exempted from her wrath," Aurora laughed. "As for me, I always must be her obedient student."

She and the contessa hugged and kissed on both cheeks.

"Aurora Bacci, one of Italy's most acclaimed violinists," the contessa said, and, extending an arm my way, continued, "may I introduce Orla Castleberry, eminent American painter." The contessa's voice sounded like warmed honey.

Aurora turned away from the contessa and took several steps towards me. She extended her arms. I took her hands in mine and wrapped them in a clasp I hoped signaled the start of a friendship. I wanted to know as much as I could about her. While a hankering for her wartime story had brought me here for a work-related opportunity, now—I have to say it—my infatuation with her son made her a source of interest to me for a personal possibility, as well.

"I am honored to meet you, *Signorina* Castleberry. It is wonderful you have come to Fiesole."

Aurora spoke in a tone at once assured and unassuming. Her movements were as natural as they were graceful.

"Oh, and I want to tell you, my son thinks so, too." Her eyes were playful. "He was most enthusiastic about you on the telephone this morning. Perhaps he will stop by later and we can all enjoy a drink together."

I grinned. "He was terrifically generous with his time yesterday," I said. "And I truly enjoyed his company."

Aurora smiled broadly and I smiled back, as happy in the moment as I could be. The contessa said nothing, but winked so that the both of us saw.

Aurora had certainly given her son his smile and his bronzed skin. His turquoise eyes must have come from Signor Bacci, as Tino himself had suggested. Aurora's were as dark as roasted chestnut shells. Gone was the long braid that had reached her waist in the wartime photograph of her with the Nazi officer violinist. Instead, her amaretto-dyed hair was cut in a chin-length bob. Bangs ran straight across her forehead, trimmed so that they just brushed her eyebrows. She wore a sleeveless, loosely-bowed honey-colored blouse, the bow giving some heft and interest to her otherwise flat chest, as board-like now as it was in the four-decades old photograph. She wore a graceful, tissue-thin skirt decorated with yellow hyacinths. The skirt fell to her ankles. And her toesnails, painted cinnamon, peeked out from open-toed leather shoes with wedge heels of natural straw. She was lovely and long.

"My goodness, Contessa," Aurora said suddenly, as if she had just realized where we were standing. "I haven't been inside here since—let's see—1957 or so, when Tino and I left to move into our apartment."

Tino had told me last night that they had lived high above Piazza Mino, a short distance from his *liceo's* soccer field.

"Then let us show Orla where you stayed when you were both in residence," the contessa said. "Orla has not been here in two decades."

Again the contessa left her walking stick behind. Instead, coming between us, she hooked her left arm through my right, and her right arm through Aurora's left. We might have been the Three Musketeers off on an adventure.

We passed the infirmary and the rooms for the nurse and Father Caduto, going through the orphanage's center, with its dining hall and kitchen. Continuing on, we came upon one long room, the dormitory, with a movable divider made of wooden shutters down its center. Rows of cots were lined up, about three feet apart from one another, on either side of the shutters.

"One side for the girls, the other for the boys," the contessa explained, pointing. Simple muslin curtains were latched on hooks on either side of each cot. Metal rods that hung from the ceiling ran the length of each, as well.

"We wanted them to have the security of a group at night," the contessa said. "But also," she held her chin with thumb and forefinger, "privacy."

I stared at the spare, clean rooms, noticed a small trunk at the end of each cot, and a cloth doll or a stuffed animal on top of every pillow. The cots were covered with soft chenille spreads of pistachio. Open clerestory windows on either side of the room provided both natural light and a welcome respite from the heat today, as they surely had for the orphaned children.

"Where did you and Tino live?" I asked Aurora.

She looked to the contessa, seemingly for permission.

"Yes, please, show her," the contessa said.

Aurora led me into the corridor again, and we walked past the orphans' dormitory to a honeycomb of rooms for the staff. Each one had a door leading from a central hallway and, as I could deduce when Aurora took me into her former space, a large window that looked out onto the vegetable gardens. Aurora's room had two single beds with a nightstand between them and, folded against the far wall, a wooden playpen.

"That is where Tino slept when he was an infant."

Aurora ran her hand across the top of the playpen. The contessa smiled at her, then urged us back into the corridor.

"And there,"—she pointed opposite the honeycomb configuration of rooms—"were the classrooms that led onto the playing fields and swings."

I took a deep breath.

"It must have been quite an operation," I said. "How did you manage, Contessa?"

She laughed. "Often, I didn't. Although I was fortunate enough to have funds, first my own and then the substantial donations, especially from your grandfather and grandmother, I never expected the number of children we needed to care for at any given time."

She pointed back to the dormitory. "We were able to accommodate twenty-four children comfortably," she said, "but sometimes our numbers swelled to 40, and I had to convert the library and even several bedrooms on the second floor of the villa into a nursery for the youngest and sleeping quarters for several older children who could manage the stairs."

Aurora nodded her head in agreement. "I remember bassinet after bassinet, and how the two nuns went up and down the rows, first feeding, then changing, and, after that, thank God, holding and rocking each baby, sometimes two at a time in their arms."

The contessa started humming, at first softly. When Aurora heard her, she joined in. I recognized the tune, so sang the words:

"Hush, little baby, don't say a word,
Papa's gonna buy you a mockingbird.
And if that mockingbird won't sing,
Papa's gonna buy you a diamond ring."

Aurora looked at me and smiled. "Your grandfather taught us that song," she said.

"Yes," agreed the contessa, "he sang it the entire time he came in and checked on the infants. They came to recognize it and, more importantly, him." Her smile was as mournful as it was radiant.

"More than once," Aurora, went on, "an infant was left in a basket outside the *carabinieri* headquarters or on the altar at the cathedral. Three times at least, I believe you told me, Contessa, a piece of paper or cloth had been pinned to the child's clothing with only your name written on it."

The contessa now stood with her hands on her hips and flats pointed diagonally outwards, like an instructor of young ballerinas preparing to practice at the bar.

"You speak the truth, Aurora," the contessa said.

Then she looked back toward the dormitory.

"The two nuns, the teachers, the cooks, the day laborers, they did the yeoman's work. The children would have perished without them. All I could give was my title and the influence it brought to bear, for good or for ill."

Then the contessa looked straight into my eyes. "And your grandfather, Orla, he brought his doctor's skills, true enough. But, even more importantly, he brought his love. His love so big it could not be held within the confines of social groups or conventions. So big that your grandmother was doomed to enjoy only a portion of it."

She stood straight then and rubbed her arms. "I am truly sorry that his love for me and mine for him caused her pain. I hope you can believe that."

I wondered if the contessa knew that Grandmother had suffered a stroke and died when she learned of Gabriella, the child her husband had fathered with his Italian mistress. Or that I had watched Grandmother crumble to the floor from the hurt in her attic in St. Suplice. Or that, though I tried mightily, running for water and screaming for Mamma, I had failed to save her.

I shifted my weight from one foot to the other, remembering. And for an awkward moment I hated how just one person, any one person, can alter so many others irrevocably. Sometimes for good and for ill at the very same time.

"I believe you," I said, but my conciliatory words felt like a cruel betrayal of my complicated grandmother who, like the contessa, always made choices she thought right, no matter their repercussions on others.

No one said anything for a moment. Then the contessa turned to Aurora and continued talking about Grandfather Castleberry.

"He loved people so much he thought he could turn every bad thing into a good. But the rules most people follow had to get out of his way."

Footsteps from down the corridor made us look away from one another.

"Which is why he made a good spy," she said, as if her news were an offhand remark.

I was dumbstruck and shook my head like a wet dog. "Grandfather was a spy?" I blurted.

The contessa raised her hand to indicate a pause as Beppo ran toward us.

"Contessa," Beppo panted.

The contessa walked to meet him. "Is everything all right, Beppo?" she asked.

"Yes, yes. Just two things, Contessa," he said. "First, the equipment is here for you to approve."

He handed her a paper and a pen so she could sign, and she scribbled her initials. Then she returned the paper to him.

Beppo went on, "So the priest can come tomorrow if he wants." He fanned his face with his hand. "And, two—Mina said to tell you that *Dottoressa* Ghiraschi expects you all at 5 o'clock, rather than 1 o'clock, in her garden. She says she must rest until then."

"Thank you, Beppo," the contessa said. "Have you enough water?"

"Thank you, yes, Contessa." He bowed his head. "I am just breathing hard because the new bed is heavy, even with the help of my two sons."

"*Babbo*,"—Carmine came halfway down the corridor—"where do you want us to place the IV and the heart monitor?"

Beppo bowed again. "I go," he said.

As soon as Beppo left, the contessa turned to Aurora and me and said, a hint of annoyance in her voice, "Antonella is always changing her mind. I could have spoken already with the caterers for your exhibit." She made a face. "Well, it is done. No matter. Where were we?"

I looked at her and said, "Please, Contessa, did I hear you correctly? My grandfather was a spy?"

The contessa nodded her head up and down several times.

"Even I did not know until the first time we were intimate, when we were sure of each other."

I imagined him telling her in the middle of the big bed that I was sleeping in now. Had she believed him? Was she fearful that their lives had intertwined? How did she know he was telling her the truth? Had she voiced any concerns? Or had her body entwined with his superseded such worrisome, wearying considerations?

Aurora said, "I did not even know until after the war, when Doctor Castleberry returned to visit the orphanage, that he was from the United States instead of the Republic of Ireland. He had stopped speaking with the brogue."

"What!" I exclaimed. "He was pretending to be Irish?"

I was completely flummoxed. The things I didn't know that I didn't know.

"Let us sit down," the contessa said, and Aurora, pointing to one of the classrooms, led us in.

We each eased ourselves down onto wooden chairs sized for young children, and the contessa narrated a story I never saw coming. She might as well have begun with Once upon a Time.

Chapter Nineteen
Grandfather Castleberry, Spy

"The first time my husband and I met your grandfather, Orla, was at a summer gathering at Villa I Tatti, now owned by Harvard University, but for many years it was the home of Bernard and Mary Berenson. I expect you know more about the Berensons than I do."

What I knew about the iconic art collectors and critics was purely academic and had virtually nothing to do with what I was learning now.

"Let's see, it was after Mussolini had been removed but before the occupation of Fiesole. I understood that Dr. Castleberry was one of Mary Berenson's numerous physicians. Already by 1935 she was practically an invalid, though I was never quite sure if all her ailments were strictly physical."

I determined that I would find an encyclopedia and review the history of the American Mary Whithall Smith Costelloe Berenson. All I could recollect was that she had left her Irish barrister husband and two daughters to take up with Berenson, marrying him only after Costelloe had died. But her story was for another time.

I wrapped my arms around my knees and listened as avidly as a child hearing about octopuses for the first time. Aurora, too, listened with interest, although I am sure she already knew a large part of my grandfather's history, having lived it in real time.

"Your grandfather spoke with an indisputable brogue and regaled my husband and me with tales about his rascally childhood at the family homestead just outside of Dublin," the contessa said. "Naturally, we accepted his stories as the truth. The Republic of Ireland had declared itself neutral during the war, so persons with passports from there were allowed to remain in Italy and move about as freely as was possible, whatever their circumstances permitted."

I spoke now. "And Mary Berenson had once been married to Frank Costelloe, an Irishman."

The contessa nodded.

I continued. "So it wouldn't have been odd that she might consult an Irish doctor in Italy."

"I imagine not," the contessa said. "And while your grandfather did indeed treat Mary, he also channeled information through the various artists, scholars and hangers-on who came and went at the villa. But eventually Bernard had to go into hiding with friends in Florence. Wouldn't the Reich have loved to catch a Jew like him!"

"No doubt," I murmured. What a life my grandfather had lived. And in circles many orders of magnitude larger than those of St. Suplice.

"But Mary stayed at the villa, and your grandfather came and went in relative security all through the occupation here."

This news was quite a bit to take in. I wondered what Grandfather had told Grandmother or my father. Perhaps nothing. *I think even Tad will be surprised by this.*

Aurora spoke up. "I met your grandfather first at the Hotel Villa Aurora," she said. "He acted like a guest, but actually he was doctoring and, as I learned much later on, helping the resistors."

"He was the hotel doctor?" I asked. I felt as if my brain were being punched by an electric stapler, punch, punch, punch, one fact after another.

Aurora stretched her legs out in front of her so that her skirt fanned out over the classroom floor. "Not exactly," she said. "Am I correct, Contessa, in saying that before the orphanage came to be, the hotel allowed Doctor Castleberry to operate a little clinic there?"

"Yes," the contessa said. "He saw patients and performed whatever procedures he could manage under makeshift conditions."

"I see," I said.

Aurora continued. "And, if I remember correctly, sometimes a nun or two assisted him."

"Exactly," the contessa said, and she stood up from her little chair. "I must go now," she said. "I need to rest before we see Antonella."

Both of us stood, as if we were still students and the teacher were dismissing us.

"I will tell you more, Orla," Aurora said. "Your grandfather spoke with me every day, always asking me how my violin lessons were going."

The contessa walked toward the door of the classroom that led outside.

"Come to the villa at a quarter to five and we will go. Unless..."—she paused in dramatic fashion—"Antonella changes her mind again."

The two of us laughed.

"The prerogative of her advanced age," offered Aurora.

"Humph," the contessa grumbled. "As if I spend my day waiting for her call."

Aurora smiled, but kept her own counsel. And off the contessa went.

"Let's find a more comfortable place to sit," I said.

"Yes, let's," Aurora agreed.

And we soon found ourselves in the dining hall seated at a round table near a standing fan. Aurora plugged the fan cord into an outlet and told me more about my grandfather, to the cooling whirr that reminded me of home.

"He was so kind to me, Orla," she said. "He always asked me to play the violin after I had served him supper on the terrace. And sometimes he brought some chocolate back from the Berenson's parties."

I felt a bit jealous. Aurora had known him while I never had.

Then Aurora looked at me and asked, "Do you mind if I am quite direct?"

I shook my head in the negative and said, "Of course not. In fact, I welcome directness. It will help so much for Tad's next book and my paintings."

"All right, then," Aurora said. "I want to get the past off my chest. It has been a burden I'd rather not have borne." And she sat up straight in her chair, folded her hands on the table, and began.

"Your grandfather knew I was pregnant before anyone else, even me," she said. "He was the only one who did not call me a whore."

I must have looked shocked. Aurora just looked weary, as if the energy in her had dissipated.

"Oh, there is much I want to tell you, so much you need to know if you and your collaborator—Tad it is, correct?" I nodded. "If you are to paint us and Tad is to write our stories."

"I am happy to listen," I said. "And I shall probably want to ask many questions."

Aurora nodded. "I understand."

I lifted my head so that the fan would cool my neck.

"But do you mind if I tell you at the hotel?" she asked. "It will help me be more precise, more complete. For it was there that everything started."

"Anywhere you prefer," I said.

I stood, went over to the wall outlet, and unplugged the wire for the fan. The whirring slowed to silence.

Then I turned to Aurora and said, "Aurora, please know that I'm very grateful that you are willing to tell your story. I just want my future portraits of you—and the others—to represent who you actually are, not who I suppose you to be. But, should you find any of my questions too intrusive or jarring, please let me know."

Aurora came to stand by me. "Please," she said, her voice throaty with emotion, "I have been waiting to tell my story for almost half a century. Forty-five years is a long time to sequester the truth."

I took her hand in mine. "I will try my best to do right by you," I said.

Aurora's dark eyes flashed, as if her energy had been restored. "And I for my son," she said. "For the truth I must tell you will not be easy for him to bear."

What could I say that wouldn't be senseless or shallow? So I kept my peace. I wondered how his mother's story would explode Tino's universe. If he'd be able to locate the stars in a different cosmos.

And in that moment a voice in my brain sounded just like Mamma's quoting Flannery O'Connor, another Southern girl and Mamma's favorite author. Whenever I tried to talk myself out of some big lie I'd sworn was the truth, Mamma always stared at me straight and said, "The truth does not change according to our ability to stomach it."

You sure got that right, Flannery. No doubt about it. And that's the God's honest truth.

Chapter Twenty
The Hotel Villa Aurora

When we stopped at the villa, I told Mina where we were headed in case the contessa needed to be in touch. I also picked up my tape recorder and the four photographs from 1944 that featured Aurora. Safe in my carryall, they might prove useful if Aurora needed a visual nudge or two to recall and share her experiences. Not only was I interested in her remembrances, I was also interested in how she framed them. Was her intended audience larger than Tad, me and Tino? I'd need to study her body as she spoke, to detect the nuances of her telling that would evidence themselves physically in a shrug, a twitch, watering eyes, whispers, a shout, a looking away, or silence—especially silence. All those elements would inform my portraits, and the recordings would certainly please Tad.

"Carlo," Aurora cried to the waiter who greeted her with open arms. Then, looking at me, "Carlo played *il calcio*—what you call soccer—with Tino at school."

"Signora Bacci, it is always my pleasure to see you," Carlo said. "I saw Tino just yesterday. But for too short a time. He had time only for an espresso."

"Happy to meet you, Carlo," I said. "I hope to see you many times in this beautiful garden over the next few months." I smiled. "Might we order two Negronis?"

Carlo bowed in the way that made one understand he served as a living testament to an honored profession rather than as a lackey doing insignificant work. Like the two other waiters and the veteran barkeep tending to patrons enjoying food and libations, Carlo was quick, precise, and attentive. He was one of the reasons reservations were hard to come by at the Hotel Villa Aurora if one did not make them well in advance.

The half-covered, half-open terrace was perched above the mountainside and was reached through a short passageway from the hotel's lobby entrance facing Piazza Mino. Round wrought-iron tables were arranged in a pleasing pattern across the terrace, their center umbrellas up to protect patrons from the early afternoon sun. A delicate gesso bud vase with a single yellow rose graced each table, along with an ashtray, the usual sugar packets, and small rectangular boxes of matches with the hotel's insignia on their covers. There were no salt or pepper shakers in sight, since in these parts, as I recalled the contessa teaching me years before, they are frequently considered an affront to the chef.

The terrace was busy. The cameras and maps of three sunburned French tourists took up much of one table top. The two men appeared to be brothers with copycat noses; the frizzy-haired woman with them hung onto the arm of the blue-shirted brother rather than the red-shirted one. Neither seemed to mind. Two men in rolled-up shirtsleeves and somber ties argued vociferously about an upcoming court case, their hand gestures a veritable tutorial in bodily Italian debate. A fair-skinned young nun and an older woman in pearls and sensible shoes spoke softly and from time to time referred to a missal. Every now and then the older woman pointed to the cathedral across the piazza. The nun's blue veil fluttered a little in the hot breeze and her bare toes peeked out of leather sandals under her long habit. I marveled that there was no sweat on her brow. At the farthest edge of the terrace, a new mother, who resembled Grace Kelly before she became Princess Grace, rolled a baby stroller back and forth, back and forth, from her chair as her infant slept. She squinted out over the expanse of fields, trees, and scattered farm houses, her *cappuccino* and a half-eaten pastry on a small plate attracting the interest of a pigeon she ignored.

"Carlo lives at the hotel now," Aurora said, as he went over to the bar to order our drinks. "Just as my grandmother Rossella, my parents, Giulia and Vito, and I did when we women served as personal ladies' maids and my father tended bar. He knew everyone and kept as many secrets as a priest in a confessional."

I'd not heard about Aurora's previous jobs—or anything, in fact—about her childhood. The contessa had told me only that Aurora had been a well-regarded violinist by the time she'd reached her twenties, and had become a celebrated one since then. Like her mentor, *Dottoressa* Ghiraschi—who, before the war, had performed in Paris, Rome, Vienna, and London—Aurora was a coveted soloist who occasionally allowed herself a violin duo with members of Europe's finest orchestras.

"I've been dying to ask you, Aurora—are you by chance named after the hotel?"

Aurora laughed and nodded in the affirmative. "At last you ask," she said. "Most everyone I meet does. Yes, Orla, for I was born here, so quickly did my mother's labor turn to my birth."

Carlo placed the drinks on our table, along with a dish of mixed nuts and some cheese threads so thin they looked like angel hair pasta that had been baked in a kiln.

"Cheers," I said, and Aurora and I clinked our glasses together.

"Your mother was still working so late in her pregnancy?" I asked, incredulous.

Aurora nodded. "Yes," she said, speaking softly now, as if she were telling me something private. "Her services were greatly in demand." She sipped her drink, letting the orange slice slide into her glass like a lady easing herself into a pleasant pond.

"You see, since the nineteenth century, when the hotel first opened, it was a favorite of many noble families. They preferred to stay on the mountain top here in Fiesole rather than below, in Florence. It was cooler up here during the summer months, and the view, as you can see, is magnificent."

I couldn't dispute her observation. The view was indeed spectacular. From the garden terrace one could scan the rolling mountains that led, winding and winding, down to Florence, the orange-tiled roofs of the city, Brunelleschi's Dome, Giotto's campanile, and the Arno River running like a line of blue silk. It was all there to take in.

"Even the British Queen, Victoria herself, spent many days here," she added.

"I hadn't known."

Aurora was certainly proving herself to be a most willing and instructive link to the past.

Reaching for one of the cheese threads and holding it mid-air as she spoke, she continued, "As for my mother, one of the Belgian royal cousins, Princess Henriette, always asked for her. I think it was because my mother kept silent when she worked." With that, Aurora laughed.

"Princess Henriette wouldn't have abided me. I talk out loud to myself when I paint," I said.

Aurora looked at me, her dark eyes dancing, and said, "And I must force myself not to hum while I play in public. When I rehearse, it is another thing altogether."

She hummed as she ate another cheese stick. Then, smiling, went back to her story. *She is a delightful person*, I thought.

"So even though she was heavy and tired with child—with me—my mother came to oversee Princess Henriette's personal needs."

I was mesmerized by this story, though it was not the one I had come to hear. Isn't that the way with life, though? You follow a path to a sought-after goal and find yourself another while you're looking. Or you take a wrong turn that turns out to be the right one after all. It's like what Luke says about walking in Venice: "Just leave your hotel and stroll. If you stroll long enough, you'll eventually find yourself back where you started. But you won't be the same person you were when you began. You will have visited every place in between."

Aurora's face brightened as she recounted the peculiar circumstances of her birth. I could tell she loved telling the tale, so animated was her narration.

"I was delivered among the clean and pressed linens in the big closet at the end of the corridor near Princess Henriette's suite. The other maids had turned the folding table into a birthing bed complete with the down pillows the royal ladies preferred. Cesare, the youngest porter, had been sent running for Claudia the midwife, who lived less than a kilometer from the hotel. But by the time the two of them arrived on foot, my cries were already greeting them. My mother told me her teeth shredded one of the hotel's hand towels, so hard had she chewed on it to stifle her screams."

"Remarkable," I said.

I stirred the little straw around in my glass.

"Only when the news reached my father at the bar did the hotel guests know. Then word of the happy, if unscheduled, event spread throughout the hotel."

I leaned my elbows on the table and rested my chin between my upraised palms. "Tell me more. Please," I said.

"As you can imagine," Aurora continued, flushed with pleasure, stopping only for one sip of her Negroni, "my father bought a round of drinks for all. And then and there, he announced, 'She shall be called Aurora.'" Aurora smiled broadly then and folded her hands around her glass as if to gesture The End.

"And what did your mother think of the name?"

Now Aurora unfolded her hands and placed them flat on the table. She tried unsuccessfully to stifle a little snort. Truly.

"My mother said, or so I have been told, 'Typical. I did all the work and then he named my product.'"

I leaned back and felt sunlight on m back. "And where was Princess Henriette while your mother gave birth?"

Aurora pushed her bangs sideways with her hand. Her forehead was shiny from the heat.

"Ah, the princess was on a carriage ride to a picnic lunch."

I moved my chair a bit to get out of the sunshine that was working its way around our table.

"The event was documented in the papers both here and in Belgium," she said. "Thus was our modest family for a moment waving at fame."

I was enjoying the nuts as much as Aurora's story, I realized. The bowl was just about empty.

"And your mother is now...?" I asked.

Aurora crossed herself before speaking. "She died of stomach cancer one week after my fourteenth birthday."

"I'm sorry," I said.

At this, Aurora held out her right hand. On her ring finger was an oval sapphire, surrounded by tiny diamonds set into a thick gold band.

"She left me this, a gift from her Princess Henriette."

"How lovely."

The ring was gorgeous, and the way Aurora caressed it, then gently covered it with her left hand, revealed that its value to her was beyond what any jeweler might declare.

"And I was baptized in a Belgian linen robe that Princess Henriette sent for the occasion."

"Are there photographs?" I asked, sitting up straight in my chair.

Tad had trained me well: "Try to get primary sources whenever you can, Orla." Since he had chosen to stay with Luke until the day before his book launch and my exhibit, I needed to act as his surrogate. I didn't want to disappoint him. Nor did I want my paintings to lack the depth inherent to a subject's personal moment in the historical landscape.

"No photographs of me that I know of," Aurora said, "but I dressed Tino in the robe for his baptism. I will find you the pictures."

"That would be wonderful," I said, looking forward to seeing the infant Tino and Aurora as a young mother. Maybe the godparents and others would people the photos as well. I wondered if any photos of Signor Bacci before his mysterious end existed.

The campanile bell struck two. We had been sitting there for over an hour. But Aurora had just begun.

She went on, "After my mother died, the hotel owners asked me to learn her job. I accepted. I did not yet know my musical dream could be larger than playing the violin at church on Sundays. Our family was accustomed to imagining only small dreams."

She did not speak critically or sarcastically, just stating the way of her people. Then she ate another cheese thread.

"That is why you must get to know *la dottoressa*," she continued, sitting at attention in her chair. "She always became infuriated if I so much as uttered a word about limiting my playing. Once she even slapped me in the face."

"Goodness!" I said. "Did you tell your parents?"

Aurora looked at me as if I had lost my mind. "Certainly not," she said. "One, I did not want them to know that *la dottoressa* thought I possessed a talent for my instrument; and, two, they would have slapped me some more. You see, my teacher's authority was unquestionable and unquestioned by everyone in Fiesole. Even the German army chaplain, Padre Adenauer, was afraid of her."

I looked up in surprise.

"Wait a moment, please," I said. "I thought I had only imagined the contessa referred earlier to a German chaplain at the orphanage. You're telling me that the Nazis had a Catholic chaplain?"

Aurora nodded. "I probably should have been surprised as well. But what did I know? I was a young waitress who wanted only to become a great violinist. He was yet another man in a uniform I had to be wary of."

She toyed with the dish that held the cheese threads, then continued. "I will tell you more about him later," she said.

"All right," I said. "Let's get back to your family history."

I paused to remember where we had left off. "And your father, Aurora, is he still alive?"

At this question, Aurora stared down into her drink. Her face drooped in sadness and her energy diminished.

"I do not honestly know, Orla," she said. "After my mother died, he left the hotel to move in with Greta, a seamstress who made the table linens. They lived just two hills down in a tiny cottage." She pointed out over the terrace rail. "I think they had been lovers for a long time before my mother's illness. My father disappeared every Sunday afternoon that I can remember. And when he returned after dark, my mother always pretended to be asleep. Once I saw her spit at his face and say '*la tua putana.*'"

She sighed.

"I tried to be a good daughter, brought him and Greta palms on Palm Sunday, smelts I had prepared at home on Christmas Eve. They were kind enough when I visited. But Greta never allowed me to be alone with my father."

Her eyes watered.

"Then,"—her voice turned to a whisper; I had to lean over the table to hear her—"when I visited for my father's birthday in May of 1944, and they saw that I was expecting a child, but could not produce a husband..."

She covered her mouth with one hand.

"Then they called me a whore and told me not to come back again."

She wept in silence. The red-shirted Frenchman stared.

"I brought Tino to meet them when the Germans left, but a woman I didn't know answered the door. She told me she didn't know where they had gone or if they were alive or dead, just that they had left a pile of dirty laundry in the wash room."

I reached my hands across the table to clasp hers. For some moments we were silent together. Then Aurora raised her head, let go of my hands, and continued.

"Of course, when I was with child I had been forced to leave the hotel in disgrace."

She took a handkerchief from her purse and dabbed it under each eye. Looking around the terrace before she continued, she took two quick sips of her drink.

"Would you mind if we found a more private place so you can tape me?" she asked. "I want you to tape me now."

Carlo appeared as if by magic.

"Carlo," Aurora said, her voice having returned to an assured tone, "This lady is interviewing me about the war and occupation here in Fiesole."

Carlo nodded, holding his folded white cloth behind his back. He leaned down to listen to Aurora's words.

"Might you direct us to a private space where we will not bother anyone else?"

The French tourists stood, collected their cameras and maps, and left.

"Certainly, Signora Bacci," Carlo said, and he stood by as we gathered our belongings.

He led us inside, through the corridor that connected the hotel to the restaurant and terrace, and opened a door to a small room that offered the degree of privacy preferable for a romantic dinner or a suspect business deal.

"Thank you, Carlo," Aurora said, and the two of us sat down at a table for two adjacent to a window that afforded the same brilliant view as the terrace, but with paned glass and four sturdy walls to enclose us. The room smelled like a confessional. I realized it was. Only I could offer Aurora no absolution. A practiced sinner myself, I would only listen, my empathy for her no pretense at all, but a shared sisterhood despite our age difference.

"I will bring you another round," Carlo said, "so your mouth does not get dry as you talk, *Signora*."

Aurora smiled.

"Good idea," I said. "On my tab, please, Carlo."

The waiter bowed. As he left, he closed the door as carefully as one would so as not to wake a sleeping baby.

It wasn't only a drink I was thirsting for now. Clearly, Aurora was getting to the heart of the matter.

I reached into my carryall and took out the tape recorder. Looking to her for permission, I waited.

"Yes," she nodded. "I am ready."

Chapter Twenty-One
Beautiful Music Together

TAPE #1—Aurora Giannini Bacci,
8/2/1989, at Hotel Villa Aurora

"It was summer when the Germans came. They commandeered Villa le Balze, and we understood that they were interested in what was happening in Florence. I don't think they realized at first how many Fiesolani were active resistors, because most of their attention was focused down the mountain. It seemed as if every officer had binoculars hanging from his neck.

"As for me and the other maids, we were told to speak with the soldiers as little as possible, just serve them the food and drink they requested when they sat at the tables. We were to avoid eye contact and, above all, to be respectful—certainly not flirtatious. No small talk was allowed.

"Our normal attractive black shirtwaist uniforms trimmed in white were replaced by shapeless black smocks with long white aprons pinned over them. We were required to cover our hair under little white caps. No makeup or ornamentation was permitted. I remember feeling like a convent postulant, and I realized, even then, that was the goal. Everyone had heard stories of the horrific Wehrmacht assaults on women. If the hotel owners could have made us invisible they would have. What they did instead was to try and erase our femininity.

"I was a true innocent then, no matter my attire. My knowledge of sexual matters was limited to the grunts and groans I sometimes heard behind guest room doors. Or sheets stained with varying shades of bodily excretions. Occasionally I heard a lusty laugh or watched a happy embrace between a couple. And I knew, from the jokes made by the more experienced maids and porters, that sometimes two men or two women did together what mostly one man and one woman did.

"Most of the soldiers were handsome. Probably their uniforms made them seem more so. For the uniforms were well made, creased, with squared shoulders, glittering buttons and pins. They gave the men a look of importance. Naturally, I was curious. But my curiosity was tempered by the sight of the guns and truncheons the same Wehrmacht officers kept at their sides. I knew they could do what they wished with us, with me, and that if I could achieve it invisibility was best.

"To tell you the truth, I think it was my innocence in conjunction with my musical skills that transformed me from an inexperienced little girl into Signora Aurora Bacci. Yes, I am certain of it. Those two factors brought me both immediate shame and long-lasting joy. If only Tino and his father could know one another, I still fantasize. Then, too, I continue to speculate how or even if they could accept, let alone embrace, each other.

"You see, Orla, there never was a Signor Bacci. There was only the man ten years my senior, also a violinist, whom I came to love. *Leutnant* Dieter Ahl. I should have hated him for what he represented, for the things he did when he was not making music or love with me. But I didn't. Instead I reveled in the way our two violins filled the war-polluted air with sounds antagonistic to bombs and guns and brutality. The way our notes blended in harmony, proving that something other, something beautiful and just as true, existed. And the two of us made it happen every time we played.

"I waited eagerly for every Sunday High Mass when we joined the organist and the choir in the cathedral. I jumped for joy when *la dottoressa* said we would perform the *Grand Duo Concertante* by Beriot at the concert the contessa arranged. I knew I would try to see him, my young body pulsing with an urge I barely understood yet refused to ignore. One Sunday at Mass, I slipped a note to him. 'Meet me before the sun rises beneath the terrace. I must see you alone.' So, daring as I had never dared before or have since, just before daylight I slipped under the terrace and scurried like a rabbit to the untamed bushes and trees below. There we met, and there he named me.

"'You are not Aurora Giannini,' he said. 'You are Aurora Bacci. You are Dawn Kisses.'"

END OF TAPE.

We were both silent. Aurora stared at my face, unblinking. Calm. Perhaps even happy.

Still studying her face, I fumbled for my carryall with my left hand. When I found it, I reached in and pulled out the folder with four photographs she was pictured in. I placed the folder on the table and opened it. The one I handed her was beneath the first two.

"*Dio,*" she said, and held the picture to her chest with both hands.

I imagined her heart beating in the most perfect rhythm a human heart could achieve.

Chapter Twenty-Two
La Dottoressa's Unexpected Turn

Aurora and I made it back to Villa d'Annunzio in her Tipo just before 4:30 and found we could not enter by the rotunda's front doors. Two large gray service trucks were taking up much of the demi-lune drive, and the loud sucking noises of an industrial-sized vacuum sounded from inside. The four long sets of library shutters were opened outward and the windows they usually covered had been flung open. I stuck my head inside the window closest to me and saw two white-uniformed men moving vacuum cleaners over the frothy white foam that carpeted the library's massive rug. All the furniture had been placed against the walls. Even the big round center table that held the globe was turned on its side. As for the globe and lamps and other table decorations, who knew where they'd been placed for safe-keeping?

"The kitchen door," Aurora suggested.

Mina greeted us and said that this was just the start of preparations for the exhibition and book launch just twelve days hence.

"The contessa told me your paintings will be displayed in the library, *Signorina* Orla, and the author's books will be sold in the lounge across the way. Tomorrow Beppo and his boys will place the easels where you want. Or, if you prefer, they will hang the paintings."

That ought to be something, I thought, though I had no reason to suspect the three workmen were not up to doing a fine job. Well, time would tell.

The contessa came into the kitchen. She carried her pocketbook and a barely blue linen wrap.

"Contessa, what may I get you?" asked Mina.

"Only sparkling water, and also a lemon," she said. "Thank you."

Mina looked to Aurora and me.

"The same, thanks," I said.

"For me also," said Aurora.

The contessa did not sit, but simply continued with Mina's explanation. "Yes, I think we will bring the visitors in through the rotunda, then let them into the library through the rotunda's doorway, have them view your paintings, then exit the library through the interior doorway and cross over into the lounge. There they may purchase Tad's books. And finally they may exit onto the patio. The reception tent will be set between the pool and the chapel. The musicians will play at the far end of the tent, if that is suitable, Aurora."

Aurora nodded her head. "Perfect," she said.

As soon as the contessa took a seat at the long refectory table, Aurora and I did as well. We both faced her, and Mina brought us our drinks on a silver tray.

"Thank you for seeing to all this preparation, Contessa," I said.

"You are most welcome," replied the contessa. "We have had two hundred and thirty-two responses in the affirmative." She smiled.

"Good. Tad's book will do well."

"And," she continued, "that number does not take stock of the visitors who will come to Fiesole unannounced on that day." She sipped her water. "I shall be prepared for at least one hundred more."

Putting down her glass, the contessa motioned to the delivery area near the pantry. "Ah, yes, I meant to tell you first of all. The books arrived today, only one week later than the date I told the book shop manager we needed them."

Aurora laughed. "Business as usual," she said. "They know you will tell them an earlier date than necessary. They order when they see fit to do so. The books arrive in plenty of time. And there we are. This is the Italian way, you know, Orla, at least when only one-third of the holy trinity is at work."

The contessa raised her eyebrows and hands in what looked like heavenly supplication. "They are still in the boxes," she said. "One of Beppo's boys will move them into the lounge."

I stood. "If you don't mind, Contessa, I'd like to give Aurora a copy now."

The contessa shrugged. "They are not mine to give," she said.

Aurora looked up at me. "Thank you," she said. "I would appreciate one."

Before I could even stand, Mina left the room, taking scissors to slit the box's top, and returned with a copy of the book. I must say, it was quite handsome, both back and front of its glossy paper cover a collage of muted black-and-white photographs outlined in bright white. The Rizzoli stamp at the bottom of the spine. The title in crimson block letters, and, in green, Tad's name and the pre-publication stellar reviews (*The*

New York Times, The Times-Picayune, The Guardian, L'Osservatore Romano, La Stampa, Die Tageszeitung/Taz). The colors of Italy. Even though I had read the galleys and the reviewer copy several times, I was eager to spend an evening savoring the final result.

Aurora held out her hands and Mina gave her the tome. Then Aurora put the book onto the table, paused, and said to the contessa and me, "I will read it first, then decide when to show Tino the photograph of his father with me."

"And tomorrow," I said, "you can have a look at my painted interpretation of the same."

The contessa listened. She also watched the unspoken between us, studying both our faces. Though of course I couldn't read her mind, I imagined she might have been looking for clues about how our afternoon together at the Hotel Villa Aurora had strengthened or weakened our new relationship.

"So you have told Orla your story?" she asked Aurora.

Aurora nodded. "All except for the part that involved *la dottoressa.*"

At that, Aurora turned to me.

"*Dottoressa* Ghiraschi took me into her home and hid me from the very day I was thrown out of the hotel until one week after Tino's birth. The contessa saw to it that your grandfather treated me throughout the final months of my pregnancy. And after Tino was born, we left *Dottoressa* Ghiraschi's home to live here. I became a music instructor to the orphans. Then, after the war and when my mentor decided I was ready, I toured throughout Europe with several orchestras. The contessa made sure Tino was cared for."

I smiled even as my eyes watered. "So much goodness," I said. "And so much surprise that in our big world we should be all together now in a place at once small and so consequential."

"Orla, there is more I need to say," Aurora said, speaking directly to me. "Especially about the last few days before the liberation."

I nodded.

"If you do not mind, I would like to make another tape."

"Whenever you want to," I said.

"Perhaps tomorrow before I look at the painting."

"That sounds fine."

"Or maybe tonight."

I reached into my carryall and handed her the tape recorder.

"Here," I said. "Take it with you."

"Thank you," Aurora said. "Tonight, then."

I re-adjusted the folders and other sundry items in my carryall. Then, suddenly, as if she had just thought of something pressing, Aurora spoke again, this time as if she were making a formal address to an audience invited to the occasion.

"The actions of *la dottoressa* and the contessa were beyond kindness. They were exemplary, saint-like."

At her pronouncement, she picked up an invisible violin and held it under her chin as if she were about to play. Instead, her words were the music, and she moved the invisible bow in time with them.

"Both of them required that I continue my lessons every day. *La dottoressa* made me practice long hours, even as I grew larger and heavy with child. 'You must have a profession,' she told me every morning. 'And you must never doubt that love conceived the child. It was not rape, nor war, nor lust. It was mutual love that the music inspired.'"

Aurora stood straight the way one does when feeling accomplished and proud.

"And so I became la Signora Aurora Bacci, which at first was only my lover's name for me. After *Dottoressa* Ghiraschi's demanding and constant care, it became my identity and my pride. My violin was the weapon I wielded against shame. My music the way I accounted for myself. My mentor's faith in me, my audiences' and critics' acclaim, afforded me a satisfying life and a way to support my son like a gentlewoman's child rather than as a Nazi's bastard boy."

Aurora's face was radiant now. "Tino himself was the gift of the music."

She put down her invisible instrument and returned to a conversational tone.

"I pray that when he learns the truth Tino will be buoyed by me as deftly as you, Contessa, and *Dottoressa* Ghiraschi kept me afloat until I could eventually swim alone."

The contessa shifted in her seat and pulled on her right ear lobe. "Do not be surprised when he angers, Aurora, whether for the secrets we have kept or for the fact of his father's unquestionable complicity in the Third Reich. He may not accept that our intention was to ensure that his life would be as uncomplicated as we could make it. He will certainly feel his trust in us has been breached."

Aurora nodded. "I dread his anger," she said.

"As anyone would," replied the contessa. "But I believe eventually he will accept and understand, as we all are asked to do with life's consternations. In the end I believe he will embrace you and us once again."

Aurora bit her lip, and I thought of my own mother's lies about my paternity. It had been a long while before I'd understood that Mamma's lie had been necessary to keep me in my actual paternal grandmother Castleberry's presence all through my childhood. As the daughter of her maid, I unknowingly reminded Mrs. Castleberry every day that her absent son had fathered me. My mamma saw to it that my grandmother couldn't help but come to love me. Mamma had persisted—even when Mrs. Castleberry treated her with condescension—so that I would finally meet my father and inherit what was rightfully mine.

"I do not doubt Tino's love," Aurora said, "or his grasp of human weakness, especially in his patients. His compassion never ceases to amaze me and make me proud of him."

I had taken note of Tino's compassion when he'd spoken with *Monsignore* Giannini, and not just compassion for Father Dona and the seminarian. He had expressed the same human understanding for his cousin. He understood Pietro was ashamed of his failure to run a tight ship, ashamed of the limits of his control.

The contessa looked at the clock on the wall opposite the refectory table. Aurora followed her eyes.

"Oh, *Dio,* ten minutes to five," Aurora said. "We must be on time, or my teacher will reprimand me." And then she smiled, perhaps in a schoolgirl's memory.

The contessa stood. "Yes," she said, "let us go now, lest Antonella phone again—to disinvite us. If the phone rings, Mina," she called over to the sink, where Mina was washing some string beans, "do not answer it."

Mina giggled.

Zooming past Hotel Villa Aurora, Aurora seemed to have regained some ease. I wondered if taping her experiences had freed her from the burden secrets always impose. I wondered, too, how and when she'd decide to share the truth with her son. I felt awkward knowing important pieces of Tino's past before he did. And it did give me some pause to know that I was smitten by the son of a Nazi.

Then, again, my best girlfriend, Katie Cowles, is the daughter of a racist murderer. She had neither inherited nor adopted her daddy's traits. Heck, she actively demonstrates the very opposite of his behaviors.

Aurora parked on the narrow street.

Although *Dottoressa* Antonella Ghiraschi neither lived in a villa nor laid claim to an aristocratic title, in the way she presented herself she was just as much a member of the nobility as the contessa. Her well-appointed townhome, which one reached through an iron gate and up a rather precipitous set of twenty-five stone steps, offered yet another panoramic view of Fiesole and the surrounding Tuscan countryside. Her personal caretaker, the pink-uniformed Alessia, led the three of us through a music room that contained a grand piano, a harp, and two violins prominently displayed and ready for use. Next we passed through a dining room with two round tables large enough that, between the two of them, twenty could dine comfortably. All along the dining room walls were framed photographs of *la dottoressa* performing, taking bows, accepting flowers, and signing autographs. A large cabinet with drawers—one opened—held musical scores. From outside, on a covered patio, music played, though the sound was not of violins. Instead it was of a cello, its low, rolling refrain reminding one of resting livestock in a meadow, imparting a soft and soothing serenity.

Before us, in a wheelchair that was locked into place on a raised plinth at the edge of the patio, sat *la dottoressa*. A wooden ramp allowed for her coming and going from that relative height. She was quite thin, outfitted in a black linen dress with detachable white lace collar and cuffs, the same uniform she had worn in the wartime photographs. She wore a black veil attached to a pill-box hat, very much like the one Jackie Kennedy had worn to her martyred husband's funeral. The veil encircled her head. Her stockinged feet, despite the heat, had been slipped into silk, bowed slippers. And her hair, ebony beneath the veil, had been trimmed severely but for a wave that I could see reached her right eye. Her nails were rounded and polished in a neutral tone, and her left hand hung limply over the wheelchair's left armrest.

She raised the veil when we entered, and all three of us gasped. *Dottoressa* Ghiraschi's face was yellow. Not olive-toned, not sallow, not pasty. Yellow.

"I dressed for my final confession," she said, the left side of her mouth drooping a bit. "Friar Marcello left less than half an hour ago. Sit."

We all three did.

Alessia must have lined up the three comfortable club chairs just below the raised stage. Really, that's what it looked like. A stage for a performer or a platform from which a professor lectured her students seated below. Whatever *la dottoressa's* intentions, I knew we were in for a surprise.

Aurora made the first move.

"*Dottoressa,*" she said, and took her mentor's good hand in both of hers. She kissed the hand gently.

"Beatrice, you honor me," the *dottoressa* said, smiling a crooked smile at the contessa. "I am glad you have deigned to come down to me from your mountain top.

"Antonella," the contessa said, mincing no words, "have you seen a doctor? You look ghastly."

Dottoressa Ghiraschi laughed.

"Too many doctors," she said. "And all since Easter, when we last exchanged greetings at Mass. I have been at Santa Maria Nuova in Florence for weeks. Nothing but tests."

Evidently Tino had not known. Or, if he had, he had kept his counsel.

Aurora looked as if she were fighting back tears. The contessa's face evidenced complete horror. It seemed I was on my own.

"I am so pleased to meet you, *Dottoressa* Ghiraschi," I said.

The old woman nodded down toward me.

"Yes, you are the artist who paints in ways some do not like. You must be an honest woman."

I couldn't help but smile. She was as irascible as I had been warned, despite her obviously diminished state.

"My own mother has told me that I am sometimes impossible," I said.

Dottoressa Ghiraschi attempted a smile. "It is our duty as artists to be and attempt the impossible," she said.

At that, Alessia carried in Aperol spritzes for the four of us. Serving her patient first, she then moved from the contessa, to Aurora, and finally to me.

"To your health, *Dottoressa*," said Aurora, and the three of us raised our glasses.

Dottoressa Ghiraschi drank, and I saw that her good hand shook. After one sip, she paused, trying to hold the glass steady in her hand.

"It is too late for that. My health is gone," she said. "Perhaps to a quick and not too painful death instead."

It was as if she had dropped a boulder into a wading pool filled with lily pads.

"The doctors say I shall be dead in a few weeks' time. That is why I called you here today."

Aurora did not attempt to stop her tears.

"It is your pancreas, I presume," said the contessa.

"Yes," *Dottoressa* Ghiraschi said. "Pancreatic cancer."

I stood.

"Perhaps it would be best if I took a walk," I said. "I am intruding on your longtime relationships."

"Sit, sit," *Dottoressa* Ghiraschi said. "I insist. It is because of your paintings and the book by the historian lawyer that I decided to go forward with a desire I have ignored for a long time."

I raised my eyes as if they were question marks.

Dottoressa Ghiraschi continued, "More than a year ago, the contessa shared with me all the photographs, including the one of you, Aurora, with your *Leutnant* Dieter Ahl."

I felt as if I would explode. Now two people had referred to the man in the photograph as Tino's father. Jesus. But instead of interrupting with my usual barrage of questions, I sat, sipped my drink, and waited.

"Yes?" asked Aurora.

She left her chair, climbed up the step to her mentor's level, and sat on the floor beside *Dottoressa* Ghiraschi's better side. Her skirt cascaded over the plinth.

Dottoressa Ghiraschi handed her spritz to Aurora, spilling a few drops as she did so. Aurora placed the glass on the floor beside her. Then *la dottoressa* caressed the top of Aurora's head as if she were a child.

"I have located him," she said.

Aurora gasped and covered her mouth with both hands.

"Do not worry," *Dottoressa* Ghiraschi said. "I have not contacted him myself and will destroy the information I have if you wish me to. Or..." She removed her hand from Aurora's head and reached into her dress, removing a sealed envelope.

Aurora stared. I stretched my neck and could just make out a return address at the top left corner of the envelope. The name in the first line was written in artful script. It read: *Dieter Ahl.*

"How?" she asked.

"I phoned Kurt Masur," she said. "He has conducted both of us, and I consider him a friend."

Aurora reached for the envelope. The two of them held it at either end.

"I told him I wanted to contact a German soldier who had played for me during the occupation of Fiesole. I was ill now and wished to tell the man how much I had enjoyed working with him despite the war and our significant differences. Would he use his contacts to hunt him down, to see if he was still alive?"

Aurora stared at the envelope.

"I have no knowledge of the information inside," *Dottoressa* Ghiraschi said. "Do as you wish, my dear Aurora."

The two still held the missive between them. Then la *dottoressa* let go.

"Thank you," Aurora said, and kissed her mentor's hand again. "I must think, consider all three of us—Tino, Dieter, and myself," she said. "And, most of all, you."

The contessa shifted in her chair and pulled her ear lobe as she had earlier in the kitchen.

Again Aurora stared at the envelope. Then, with her right hand she covered the script of her lover's name.

"Dieter," she said, as if she were speaking to him, as if the three of us had disappeared.

The way she said his name left no doubt in my mind what he meant to her.

"Just so," said the old woman. "You must think. You have the time. But for me, the time is almost over."

Aurora gave in to abundant sobs. A great weight had been lifted from her and a great responsibility loomed in its stead. What would she do?

"One more thing," *Dottoressa* Ghiraschi said, and she reached once more beneath her dress.

Aurora looked up.

Another envelope, this one not sealed. From it *Dottoressa* Ghiraschi, with some difficulty, lifted a document and shook the tri-folded page open to its full size.

"Aurora, this is the second of two birth certificates. The first, also a forgery, is in the cathedral's files. But you already know that. It is the one that lists a Signor Silvio Bacci as Tino's father."

She paused as Aurora nodded silently.

"Yes, *Dottoressa*, it has allowed Tino a normal life without the stigma of the Third Reich. And for that I have you to thank."

A violinist and a forger. Well, well.

"This one, a second forged certificate, documents the truth. It is signed by *Leutnant* Dieter Ahl."

Aurora accepted the parchment from her mentor's hand and read it from top to bottom. She sighed.

"I recognize his signature, but I don't know what to say. This is a great deal all at once."

Dottoressa Ghiraschi said, "I agree. But there is still one thing more you can use or choose to ignore."

This time she did not reach under her dress, but instead pointed to the file cabinet for musical scores.

"There," she said, pointing, and Aurora stood, hopped down the step, and walked into the room adjacent to the covered porch.

"The correct drawer is already open," *la dottoressa* told her.

I turned around as Aurora approached the cabinet. Forgive me for thinking that the four of us were in Wonderland and Aurora was Alice. But, really, the analogy did not seem forced in the least. Not then, not now.

"Look for a brown envelope," *Dottoressa* Ghiraschi said. "It should be in the file folder listed as Violin Duos."

Aurora's fingers flew. "Here," she said, and held a brown envelope up so *la dottoressa* could see.

"That's it," the old woman said.

Aurora brought the envelope to her mentor.

"No, you open it," *la dottoressa* instructed Aurora.

The contessa and I both waited while Aurora loosened the envelope flap from inside. She pulled yet another parchment piece out and stared at it. Then, she let out a cry.

"A marriage certificate! With my and Dieter's signatures?"

She stared at her mentor.

"How can this be, *Dottoressa*? I never signed this."

Dottoressa Ghiraschi nodded, rubbing her stomach with both hands.

"I forged your name, my dear Aurora. But you should know this: Dieter wrote his name himself."

Was she telling the truth? How could I know?

Aurora looked dumbfounded and sat down on the chair that had initially been hers.

"How?" she asked. "When?"

La dottoressa began, her words no longer instructions, but a tale.

I stood up for a moment, interrupting.

"Aurora, *Dottoressa*, may we tape the conversation?"

Aurora rifled through her bag. "Please, for Tino, so he might learn the truth," she replied.

Dottoressa Ghiraschi looked at the tape recorder.

"Yes," she said. "For Tino's sake. I shall begin again."

TAPE #2—*Dottoressa* Antonella Ghiraschi, Aurora Bacci, Contessa Beatrice d'Annunzio, in the company of Orla Castleberry.

8/2/1989, at *Dottoressa* Ghriaschi's home

Dott.ssa Ghiraschi: "Do you remember how chaos ensued after the three *carabinieri* were martyred in the hotel garden?"

Aurora: "Yes."

Dott.ssa Ghiraschi: "And I had you hidden in the attic behind the wardrobe with my winter clothes?"

[Aurora put her arms around her chest and shuddered.]

Aurora: "I remember. It was August 12ᵗʰ, just days before the liberation on August 15ᵗʰ. The Germans were running wild. They knew that Florence, and, later, Fiesole, were going to be liberated. They wanted to wreak vengeance against us."

Dott.ssa Ghiraschi: "Correct. It was nearly midnight. I had made sure no lights were on whatsoever inside, and I was dozing on the divan out here. Earlier, when night had not yet fallen, I'd heard the screams and cries of our fellow Fiesolani and the sounds of guns going off, of boots pounding the cobblestones."

[She took a moment to catch her breath.]

"I had done all in my power to make this house invisible and silent.

[She looked to the three of us, as if we were her students listening to a story.]

"At first I thought I imagined a tapping on the door. Then I was sure of it. But before I stood to answer it, a figure in a German second lieutenant's uniform, whom I recognized by his height, whispered outside the shutters. I could see him through the slats. My eyes, you see, had gotten used to the dark.

"It was Dieter. A scarf covered his face and he whispered through it.

Aurora: [Gasp.] Contessa D'Annunzio: "I never knew."

Dott.ssa Ghiraschi: "I wondered if he had become a crazed animal, too. If he had come to kill me and you, Aurora. He put a finger to his lips, and I nodded. 'Do not be afraid. I trust she is here with you?' he whispered. I nodded again. 'Well hidden?' he asked. Again I nodded. Then he asked, 'And you are sure that she is carrying our child?' I nodded once more and told him, 'She is six months gone.' He looked around. 'I want her to have proof that we married," he said. 'Otherwise she will be ruined and our child a bastard.'"

[Aurora was shaking as if the weather had turned cold and a great wind was blowing.]

"His words seemed utterly ludicrous to me. He was our enemy, and at the same time it was clear that he loved you. Why else would he think you wanted proof, let alone evidence, that he had fathered your child? But he couldn't have been more serious. And I was afraid to anger him. 'Paper,' he said. 'I will sign, and after we go you can have your forgers do the rest. As long as my signature is real. Aurora has letters from me for proof.'

[I couldn't believe my ears, and I wondered who else would think the story possible, let alone true.]

"So that is what we did. By candlelight in the center hallway where there were no windows."

[She pointed to the file cabinet again.]

Dott.ssa Ghiraschi to Aurora: "Look up Practice Exercises.

[Sound of walking. Aurora returned to the cabinet and once more opened the drawer.]

Aurora: "Ah, the file was out of order, but here it is."

[Sound of walking. Aurora brought the file folder to *Dott.ssa* Ghiraschi. *Dott.ssa* Ghiraschi opened it and gestured for us to have a look. Sure enough, on plain white paper were all the categories of information found on a marriage certificate.]

Dott.ssa Ghiraschi: "The forger did a good job."

[Contessa D'Annunzio harrumphed like a New Orleans pol, then laughed. Aurora sat upright in a chair.]

Aurora: "So what does this mean?"

[*Dott.ssa* Ghiraschi lifted her paralyzed hand with her able one and let both hands rest on her lap.]

Dott.ssa Ghiraschi: "Congratulations, Aurora, on the occasion of your marriage to Dieter Ahl, August 13th, 1944, as witnessed and stamped with the holy seal by Giovanni Giorgis,

Bishop of Fiesole, and Padre Ernst Adenauer, Chaplain of the Third Reich."

[Aurora stared upward, then down at the floor. Then she rubbed the finger that would have worn her wedding band.]

Aurora: "But these are not their actual signatures."

Dott.ssa Ghiraschi: "Of course not."

[*Dott.ssa* Ghiraschi laughed, then grimaced in obvious pain.]

Contessa D'Annunzio: "Antonella, this is the most fantastical and disturbing thing you have ever done."

Dott.ssa Ghiraschi: "Thank you, Beatrice. But it wouldn't have happened without Dieter Ahl. You needed to know now. Between us, after all, we are Aurora's surrogate mothers. And you must remain for her after I am gone. I insist."

[*Dott.ssa* Ghiraschi twitched and grabbed at her stomach.]

Dott.ssa Ghiraschi: "Please, go now. When I take the medicine, I am at once asleep."

END OF TAPE

We all stood to leave. Aurora wobbled a bit, so I reached out and took her arm.

"I shall phone you every day, Antonella, and bring you whatever you want," said the contessa.

Dr. Ghiraschi nodded, grimacing as she did. "Sometimes I will speak with you. But what I want not even you, my beloved nemesis, can procure for me."

At that, the two of them laughed out loud. Actually guffawed. Their ability to do so seemed to me one of the few advantages of age. It was as if they were not surprised one bit by this next catastrophe. They had both already survived so many. And they knew each would do her best to meet this one with all her considerable reserves. Maybe they possessed the

233

power and the will to summon a eucatastrophe, as Tolkien liked to call his happy ending.

I thought of Sister Castor, the high school English teacher who had insisted we memorize lines she deemed important, like Tolkien's from *The Fellowship of the Ring*: "The world is indeed full of peril, and in it there are many dark places, but still there is much that is fair, and though in all lands love is now mingled with grief, it grows perhaps the greater."

"I love you and you know it," the contessa said, though she spoke curtly.

"I do," Dr. Ghiraschi said. "We came through the worst of it together. We saved some children, saw to it that a few of our oppressors were killed, and carried on long and well enough to tell the stories of our lives. Good for us. May God have mercy on our souls."

The contessa went over to the raised platform, knelt on it, wrapped her arms around the legs of her imperious friend, and bowed. Dr. Ghiraschi bent her head and rested her lips on the top of the contessa's coiffed hair. Then, after a moment as brief as the "*Ite, missa est*" at Holy Mass, both of them raised themselves up, and the contessa said, "Tomorrow."

"Perhaps," Dr. Ghiraschi replied, and grabbed her stomach again.

"Alessia, now!" she cried out, and the girl in pink came running, syringe in hand.

Chapter Twenty-Three
Night

We all three of us needed to be alone. There had been no need to discuss this decision.

When Aurora pulled into the villa's drive, she did not turn off the Tipo's ignition, but instead let the engine idle while the contessa and I gathered our things. She leaned over from her driver's seat to kiss the contessa, and, after I had gotten out of the back seat and stooped down by the driver's car door to say good-night, she squeezed my hand through her open window.

"Tomorrow I will come, Orla," she said. "I will read tonight and perhaps I will open the envelope."

"Yes," I answered. "You must do whatever you think best."

She nodded her head. "Good, better, best," she recited. "Who knows? I feel like an ignorant school girl once more."

I kissed her cheek. "You will choose well, Aurora. I am sure of it."

My new friend bit her lip, then smiled. "It feels like I have known you always," she said.

I squeezed her hand again. "Likewise," I said. "I am glad of it."

The contessa and I went into the villa through the kitchen, as the main doors had yellow tape across them in a large "X" and a sign that said, *"Ingresso vietato,"* — "Do Not Enter."

Mina greeted us.

"Individual trays," the contessa said, without preamble. Then she nodded at me once and escaped to her suite without another word.

Upstairs, I felt the need to strip and draw a bath, complete with bubbles. I leaned over the tub and lit the trio of tall, honey-colored candles along its far surround. While I waited for the water to reach a soak-worthy depth, I went into the bedroom and opened all the windows, unshuttering them in the dusk. My mind was filled with thoughts and it needed soft gray space to replace the teeming array of facts, emotions, and images that had rushed into it and swirled all day long.

Once immersed in the tub, I felt the bubbly water soothe and caress my skin. I leaned back, my head on a comfortable plastic pillow attached to the tile, and breathed deeply, in through the nose, out through the mouth. Again. Then once more.

Though I tried, I knew I could not really understand how Aurora and the contessa must feel, each in her own room, both in the solitude of former and impending loss. As they had so many times in the past, they once again would have to re-adjust, re-adapt, re-assess. Each had already proven herself as strong as Tuscan stone. Each had been able to sustain enduring love, even when the beloved other's heartbeat could no longer be heard or touched.

I closed my eyes and listened to the night sounds of nature outside the windows. The candles shimmered, and the tub water temperature dropped from as hot as I could bear to tepidness.

Three sharp knocks, and Mina entered the bedroom.

"Supper, *Signorina*," she said. "I will leave it on the table for you."

"Thank you," I called out, and I heard her close the door.

Of course, supper was beautiful. A portion of grilled salmon, blanched string beans, small roasted potatoes with rosemary, a golden pear, and two pieces of darkest chocolate. A bottle of white wine. Silver and china, the works.

I thought I wouldn't eat, but the aroma of rosemary beckoned like an anodyne. One glass of wine turned into the next, and when I rose from the chair at the table meant for two, the bottle was empty and I still had a terrycloth turban around my head, its matching robe cinched around my waist. I wiggled my toes to see if I could feel them. Since I could, I stood, let my hair loose, fluffed it out, and prepared to paint. This was not going to be a night for sleeping.

I walked into the studio, saw that the shutters were closed, and turned on all the lights. The room looked like an operating theater or a ballet studio, so bright with lights that every step or misstep could be observed. I eyed three canvases, almost double the size the contessa had used when she painted each of her "one beautiful thing" pieces. Then I went to the contessa's easel and lifted from it the photograph of Grandfather, the contessa, and the child Gabriella in her womb. I walked it to the worktable and set it down. Then I took up the three canvases and, one by one, centered them on that easel, the only easel I would ever use from that moment on.

Three images had blossomed in my mind. I sketched them first. Initially in slow motion, then quickly. I decided to paint them as outlines in black. No Blessed Mother needed tonight. The three principals were mothers themselves, though the first but to her foster child. The umbilical cord that connected the two of them had been filled with euphony rather than blood.

I named the paintings: Number One—*Dying Empress Enthroned.*

Number Two—*Pregnant Woman with Violin*

Number Three—*Nobility Pays Homage.*

I worked my brush, sometimes making its ebony oil as thin as a silk sewing thread, other moments fattening it to the rounded bulk of a caterpillar about to become a butterfly. Curves, angles, lines, purposeful smears, and several fallings off a canvas edge, until, long after the music and laughter and voices from down the mountainside had subsided, there was only deepest night. And, eventually, sleep.

Amen.

Chapter Twenty-Four
Setting Up

Morning came before I expected it. The sound of trucks on gravel wakened me.

Beppo called out to his sons below my bedroom windows, "As soon as *Signorina* Orla is ready, we willl carry her paintings to the library. You will be your most careful. You understand, you must do even better than your best."

I chuckled, deducing that Beppo was ready at the moment, and was using his voice as my alarm clock. So I showered quickly and dressed in work clothes—jeans, a purple NYU tee shirt, and a pair of paint-splattered Keds that Mercy had prevailed upon me to pack. ("So they'll remember you're American.") I tied a violet colored farmer's kerchief around my head, and, without make-up to hide my so-called beauty marks and enhance the size of my eyes, I bounded down the stairs.

The front doors to the villa were wide open now, and Mina was putting serviceable movers' rugs over the marble floors.

"Ah," said Beppo, coming from the side of the villa facing the chapel, "*Signorina* Orla, I am glad to see you. Good morning."

"Good morning," I answered.

He tipped his wide-brimmed straw hat. No ribbons around it, just plenty of wear and tear from a workaday life.

"If you wish, my sons and I are ready to arrange your paintings as you like them in the library."

"Coffee?" Mina asked.

I pivoted to answer her. "Please," I said. "No breakfast, though." Then I turned back to Beppo. "Yes, thank you, Beppo. I am at your service."

Suffice it to say that this was not Beppo's first gallery installation. After he and his boys carried each and every painting—seventeen in total—with the care one expects for vulnerable infants, the draped rectangles, both vertical and horizontal, leaned against the wall outside the library. They made a ghost-like tableau in the shadowy corridor.

I stood on the other side of the corridor so as not to be in the way.

"Okay, now," Beppo said to his sons, "we put on the white gloves."

From a cardboard box in the rotunda, Beppo produced four pairs of clean white cotton gloves, one pair for Carmine, another for Roberto, a third for himself, and the last for me.

"Thank you," I said.

Beppo made a slight bow. "This way you can adjust whatever you like."

Though the clock told me we had worked for more than two hours, the whole operation had gone smoothly. The room was spacious enough that all the paintings could rest on easels of varying sizes. Although all the library furniture had been set back against the walls and the villa's front windows, I'd decided to place the round table back in its usual place in the center of the room. Doing so allowed my four favorites to stand like North, South, East, and West. Beppo suggested we encircle those paintings with stanchions and red velvet ropes. I readily agreed.

"Then," he had said, "what do you say we place the others, spaced as you like, in front of the furniture?"

"Yes, good idea. And stanchions with the ropes again," I said.

Once we had undraped each painting, Carmine and Roberto placed it on an easel appropriate to its size and heft. I walked through the exhibit at least four times, trying to do so the way visitors would, and made a few changes. Each time, the gloved Carmine and Roberto had to lift, cradle, and set paintings in place until I was satisfied.

In the end, I decided to put the wartime *Dottoressa* Ghiraschi right opposite the entrance, as an homage to her. Then, around the table to the right, the little one-armed girl. Facing the library windows, Aurora and her German soldier with violins, and, finally, Fiesole's archbishop with the Whermacht occupiers' Roman Catholic chaplain. Each of the four were shockingly oxymoronic and compelled the viewer to look more than once. While the other thirteen paintings had more expansive backgrounds and multiple figures—at work, at play, at prayer, and in mourning in Fiesole and at La Casa dei Bambini—the four I'd painted the last couple of months in New Orleans pulled at me in as compelling and disturbing ways as the in-the-flesh *Dottoressa* Ghiraschi, the contessa, and the girl who had realized herself as the Signora Aurora Bacci.

"*Grazie, Signorina* Orla," said Beppo. "It was a pleasure to work with you."

"Likewise," I said, raising my arms and standing tiptoe in my sneakers to stretch.

I think Beppo and his boys had expected me to be a bit more difficult than I was, because I heard Roberto say to Carmine as they went back outdoors, "She is easier than the contessa." So there was that.

Meanwhile, Mina had seen to Tad's books in the lounge. They were arranged in attractive stacks on a long oak table, their glossy covers seducing anyone who entered the room. Several chairs were set behind them, as was a strongbox in which to put the cash that would certainly keep several as-yet-to-be-determined sales associates busy collecting and counting it. A smaller table, set just before the French doors to the patio, was already equipped with black pens for Tad's autographing.

When I entered the lounge, Mina asked, "Is this to your liking, *Signorina*?"

"Fine," I said, "unless Tad thinks otherwise. But he won't arrive until the 14th."

"Okay, then, I must wait," she said, and left.

But just before she walked outside she said, "The contessa wants you to know that Tino will bring the nurse this afternoon, and requests that you stop by the infirmary to see her."

"Fine," I said, but first I wanted to take a swim. I started for the rotunda stairs. "Oh, Mina," I said, and she stopped again. "Where is the contessa now?"

"Ah,"—Mina dipped from her knees—"I regret I forgot to tell you. She is at her spa where she goes for massage and hair color and nails. She will return in time for cocktails."

"Thanks," I said, and started upstairs. I paused on the fourth step before Mina disappeared. "Mina, would you like to join me for a swim since we both have a lull in the action here?"

Mina walked to the stairs. "Thank you, *Signorina* Orla, but I never go in the water. I only take a shower every night."

"Really?" I said. "Do you not know how to swim?"

Mina turned her back to me, reached her right hand over her shoulder, and pointed to the long, jagged scar. Then she sat on the bottom step and I sat where I had been standing, three steps above her.

"I will tell you because you are already close, as if you are the contessa's grand-daughter."

"Tell me what?" I asked. "Why you don't swim?"

Mina sat up straight and looked up at me. "My father left us when I was so young I do not remember him. And so, of course, my mamma had to go to work. She cleaned apartments of the rich in Florence."

I nodded and slid down the steps so I could sit beside her.

"When I was too little to stay alone, Mamma took me with her."

"I see," I said.

"Then, when I was old enough to stay alone after school, I let myself into our flat, locked the door, and never, ever answered the bell if someone came."

"Of course," I said.

Mina picked at the cuticles around her nails. "There was a man named Stefano who took Mamma out several times. He drove a cab. He wanted to move in with us, but Mamma refused him. She told me all the time, 'Never worry, Mina, as long as you live with me, there will be no man staying here.'"

I chewed on my lower lip, not looking forward to where this story was heading.

"Stefano did not like Mamma's answer. He called all the time, and banged on the door when Mamma was home at night. One night, after the third time, Mamma told him she was calling the police. And she did."

Mina wrung her hands. She looked as if she were washing them Lady Macbeth style.

"The next morning, before I left for school, he banged on the door again. Mamma had already left at seven for her first job of the day. I kept very quiet. But Stefano didn't stop banging. 'I know you're in there, Mina,' he said.'"

Taking in a long, deep breath, Mina continued. "That is when he broke down the down and came in."

Mina's breaths came faster.

"I tried to run to the fire escape, but he caught me and threw me on Mamma's bed. I kicked him in his neck and his face. That made him very angry. 'Lie back for me,' he said. 'Lie back.' He tried to push me, but I kept fighting. I spit as much as I could and I bit his hand. He let go for an instant to curse at the bite I made."

My eyes were wide open.

"That's when I grabbed the pocket knife from my uniform pocket. Mamma gave it to me to make me feel safer walking to and from school when she could not walk with me."

I put my hand to my mouth.

"And I stabbed him on his chest. Stab, stab."

Mina shook as she made stabbing motions, thrusting her right hand forward into the air. I put my arms around her. She pushed me away.

"I want to finish," she said. "I want you to know what he did."

"Tell me, Mina."

She continued. "He grabbed the pocket knife from my hand, flipped me over, and tore my uniform jacket and blouse off me. Then he dug the knife blade into my back. He made a path with the knife while I screamed and screamed."

I was crying with Mina now. Then she stopped. Little rivulets of tears reached my lips and I licked them with my tongue.

"Then he got up. He said, 'No one will ever want you to lie back for him now. Ugly bitch. Ugly bitch of a bitch, that's what you are.'"

She covered her eyes.

"My body went limp. I thought he had killed me. He lifted me up, carried me into the bathroom, turned on the water in the tub, and dropped me like a dying animal. I fell hard, so hard."

The image came alive in my brain.

Uncovering her eyes, then, Mina said, "I heard him leave, and I just stayed down in the tub. The slashes hurt so much I knew I wasn't dead. I watched the water run down from the spigot. Pretty soon my own blood seeped from either side of me. It made little ribbons of red. The ribbons flowed to the drain. I must have stayed that way until Mamma got home."

"Oh, Mina," I said, and hugged her tight.

"Then Mamma called the ambulance that took me to the hospital where Dr. Bacci, Tino, helped us." She wiped her eyes with her hands. "So that is why I do not go into pool or bathtub or lake or pond."

"I understand," I said.

"Yes," Mina said.

Dear God.

Then the lovely Filly Gamine stood up, pulled herself together, and smiled, actually smiled. "But you swim," she said. "The pool water will make you feel cool."

I had to ask her something first, though.

"And your mamma now?"

"Mamma is with a nice man since last autumn. His name is Federico. He is an electrician who likes to dance. And I am here with the contessa. So we are all right."

She rearranged her camisole and skirt, taking a look at herself in one of the matching mirrors hanging by the other side of the rotunda doors.

"And, you know, *Signorina* Orla, it is true what one of Mamma's rich apartment ladies told me when she asked the contessa to hire me. The contessa really does save people, no matter if sometimes she is demanding and brusque."

I smiled back at this amazing, resilient, wounded girl.

"You most likely save the contessa, too," I said.

Mina dipped from her knees. "Maybe just a little, from her loneliness," she said. "I hope so. She is often lonely. Especially during the parties."

Then she was gone.

Beppo and his boys were laughing uproariously outside. Carmine was telling a story that involved a hippopotamus. And, dear Lord, the last thing I wanted to do now was swim.

I must have spent an inordinate amount of time trying to imagine Mina's horror as well as her mother's when she found her daughter slashed like that. Because by the time I had showered and changed, I heard Tino's voice outside the bedroom windows. Another voice, hearty and female, chattered energetically with his.

If my disoriented memory served, Tino and I had a dinner date. So I dressed for it in a maxi-dress that swirled in tangerine and white. My usual flat leather sandals, silver drop earrings that shimmered like little chandeliers, my clunky watch with a white leather band, and a coral ring Grandmother Castleberry had left me.

Tino and the woman entered the rotunda as I came down the stairs.

"Wonderful, you are here, Orla," Tino said.

He flashed his turquoise eyes and hurried to kiss me on both cheeks. But it was the brief brush of his left hand on my neck that left me weak-kneed and wanting more.

"Marta Olivetti Lodge, may I present Orla Castleberry."

"Hi," the woman said, and extended her hand. "Pleased to meet you. I'm going to be Father Dona's nurse. I saw your AIDS exhibit in New York. It is just what people need to see." She seemed as American as apple pie.

"I'm pleased to meet you, as well, Marta. Do you live in New York?"

"Yes," Marta said, her dialect American upper-class—think National Public Radio—"at least I did until June. I finished up in Public Health Administration at Columbia. It made both sides of the family happier. My parents could not bear the thought that I was 'just a nurse.' They think nursing a demeaning profession that gets my hands too dirty. They want me to head up a hospital or a government agency instead."

I smiled, and Tino waved us into the lounge and out onto the covered patio, where we stood in a triangle.

"Parents can be a handful," I said. "My own biological father didn't even show up until I was 11."

"You are joking, yes?" Tino asked.

"Nope," I said.

He caressed my cheek with his hand.

"Well, that's a story I'd be interested to hear," said Marta.

As she spoke, Tino moved his hand to my shoulder. Then he lifted it and caressed me under my chin. He was stroking kindness onto me. I actually teared up and saw that he watched me. I blinked a few times and tried not to remember the day I first met Prout Castleberry.

"Let's sit," Marta said. "I won't be able to join you over here much once Father Dona arrives."

She chose a chair at one of the round tables.

Tino nodded. "That is true," he said. "He was running a fever this morning and his immune system is shutting down."

I looked at Tino. "May I visit him after he gets settled here?" I asked.

Tino took a seat by my side. I liked that.

"If he wants to see you," he said. "Understandably, he is quite depressed. And, of course, you must cover yourself completely so as not to introduce any infection."

"I understand," I said.

Mina appeared at that moment.

"Good afternoon. What may I be pleased to serve you?" she asked.

Marta's eyes lit up. "Do you have any beer?" she asked.

"Certainly," said Mina. "Peroni or Stella Artois?"

Marta looked at each of us.

"Let's go with Stella," I suggested. "I like the name."

"A connoisseur, I see," teased Marta.

"How can you tell?" I said, laughing.

She was going to be a lot of fun. For a moment, I really missed Tad and Luke and our cocktail hours by the pool back home. The two of them would have welcomed Marta right away.

"Stella sounds fine," Tino said.

Marta was several inches taller than Tino, and all leg. Her auburn hair was trimmed short in a sporty cut. From time to time, she blew her diagonally-trimmed bangs off her forehead. She looked like a model in an L.L. Bean catalog. Khaki canvas slacks, a pink tee shirt, boat shoes, and small gold hoops on her pierced ears. A man's watch, serviceable for taking pulses, and a school ring with the Boston College insignia on her left ring finger. I felt as if we should all be on a sailboat off the Maine coast.

"So you're a U. S. citizen?" I asked.

"I carry two passports," Marta said. "And as you can perhaps guess from my names, my Italian family owns the Olivetti manufacturing company, while my American Lodge family has long been engaged in United States government positions."

Tino laughed. "Typewriters and diplomacy," he said. Then, in a teasing tone, "Marta is very well-connected. How she ended up befriending me is one of life's great mysteries."

Marta pushed her chair away from the table and crossed her long legs. She had to be wearing the Bean's "tall" slacks.

"My bi-continental DNA," she smiled.

Mina came in with the tray holding three mugs of beer, a bowl of cashews, and a second bowl of pretzel sticks. I remembered I hadn't eaten any breakfast, but vowed to myself I would not be a glutton.

"Marta and I met at a party at the vineyards of the Baroni family near Siena. I went to medical school with the mother, Greta Raffino Baroni. So far, much to my distress, Marta has put off an offer of marriage from Greta's son, Leo Baroni."

He grinned at Marta. She stuck her tongue out at him.

"If he finally persuades her to join the family, I can keep her here. She is a superb nurse."

"Thank you, Tino," Marta said.

"And, more importantly, I shall never have to buy wine again." He raised a glass—never mind that it contained beer.

Marta picked up his conversational thread at the same time she lifted her own beer mug.

"The other man I'm putting off is my dad. He wants me to pursue a career in the foreign service."

I raised my glass now, too. "Well, cheers to Father Dona's nurse," I said. "You have chosen to be here now, no matter what anyone else wants."

And we drank.

It turned out Marta had signed on at Boston College to study history, the assumption being she'd go on to Georgetown's School of Foreign Service. But she'd transferred to BC's nursing program after doing some volunteer work in Rome the summer of 1983 with the Community of Sant 'Egidio, a lay Catholic association working for social justice. She'd graduated from BC in 1985. After earning her master's degree at Columbia, she would go on to oversee a social agency at an administrative level, or so her parents hoped.

"So you're moving in today?" I asked.

"Tomorrow," Marta said. "I want to turn over my keys in person to my friend Portia who will use my, well, actually, the Olivetti apartment in Florence for the next few months." She paused. "Or for however long Father Dona needs me."

Tino stood and finished his beer.

"You are very diplomatic, Marta," he said.

Marta nodded, her face serious. But then she giggled and said, "Do let my father know that."

Tino shook his head and smirked. Then he pointed into the lounge. "Orla," he teased, "what are you hiding in there under the sheets?"

"Oh," I said, "Mina just this morning arranged Tad's books for sale on the 15th."

He stood up. "Do you mind if I steal a look?"

I shrugged my shoulders. "Not at all," I said.

As he went in to take a book from under the sheets, Beppo came to the doorway of the lounge. Then, seeing me out on the patio, he walked over. He looked completely different; no more work clothes and battered straw hat. Now he wore fitted jeans and a button-down cotton shirt the color a salmon ought to be. His sandaled feet and clean-shaven face told me he had somewhere enjoyable to go to. He was a single man, his wife having abandoned him and her sons some three years earlier, Mina had told me.

"Excuse me, *Signorina* Orla," he said. "I wonder if I might impose on you for a moment."

"No imposition at all," I said.

I saw that behind him Tino shifted his stance.

"After you left us this morning, I made my sons come back to see your paintings because, in one of them, my parents are in the background. They have been dead for many years, and neither boy remembers them." He paused, then smiled broadly at me.

"Oh, I'm glad you discovered them," I said. I stood up. "Please, show me," I said. I looked at Marta.

"Go," she waved at us. "Take your time. I'm going to ask Mina for another beer."

I pointed to one of the contessa's ubiquitous bells. "Just jangle that," I said.

"Oh, you are a dear," Marta said. Then she reached for the bell and jangled away.

Meanwhile, Beppo and I walked past Tino. I don't think he noticed us, so intently was he staring at whatever page in Tad's book had caught his eye.

Mina crossed paths with Beppo and me in the corridor as she headed toward the patio.

"*Signorina*," Beppo said, stopping, and motioned me to enter the library-turned-gallery in front of him.

The painting he pointed to was just to the right as we entered the library. It featured six very young children sitting at a long wooden table outdoors, just outside the classrooms I had visited the day before with the contessa and Aurora. Though they all were able to sit up and play with the wooden blocks scattered about the table, they would not have been old enough to cut their own food or peddle on tricycles. Behind the children were two people, a man and a woman, both in their prime. The smiling man carried a wooden box, while the harried-looking woman held a pitcher full of water and lemons. There was a glass in front of each child.

"They are my parents," Beppo said. "Constantino and Smerelda." He seemed very pleased to see them in the painting.

Tino walked into the library. He held one of Tad's books, four of the fingers on his left hand keeping the volume opened to a page.

"My parents," Beppo told him, and Tino patted him on the back with his free hand.

I smiled at both of them.

"I remember them," Tino said. "Your father was always very kind to my mother. Every time he cut flowers for the contessa, he brought a small bunch to my mamma. She kept them on the table between our beds."

Beppo nodded vigorously. "Yes, my father thought very highly of your mother, and that was before she became known as a fine violinist." He paused. "He never told me why, but he called her a brave young woman."

Tino was quiet for a bit—then he asked, "Beppo, do I remember correctly that your mother and you and your sister moved away from the cottage here when we were five or six? But your father stayed on?"

Beppo looked at the painting again, then at Tino, and finally at me.

"Yes, you do," he said, and he sighed. "I wept. I loved it here." He laughed. "I still love it here."

We all smiled. Then Beppo looked at Tino long enough for Mina to have re-stocked her tray and made her way past the library and out onto the patio.

"Remember how you and I helped pick the tomatoes and the asparagus with my father?" he asked.

"I do," said Tino. He looked straight into Beppo's eyes. "But what happened, Beppo? Why was it that the three of you left? I never understood."

Beppo took a deep breath and looked away. Then he answered Tino.

"For a long time, I didn't know, either, Tino. And my mother would not tell me." He grabbed Tino's free hand with his. "But, when my father was failing and the contessa asked me if I would take his place here when the time came, I finally got the answer. My father told me from his death bed."

Tino and Beppo were holding hands.

"Please, tell me," Tino said. "I have to know." He stood very still and listened.

"All right, then," Beppo said, "but perhaps what I say will upset you."

Tino squeezed his friend's hand. "If it must," he said.

Beppo took a long breath and began. "One day, the contessa became enraged with my mother and told her to go, and to take me and Isa with her. I remember. It was terrible."

Tino looked surprised.

"The contessa banged open the door to the cottage and yelled at my mother. We had never seen her like that. Isa and I were so frightened that we ran into our bedroom to hide."

"But why was she so angry?" Tino asked.

Beppo released his hand from Tino's and raised it to rest on Tino's shoulders instead.

"My father said it was because the contessa heard my mother call you 'the bastard with the German eyes.'"

Tino closed his eyes.

"Jesus," I murmured in English.

Tino opened his eyes. "Thank you, Beppo," he said. "I always wondered why you had gone away. And I am so very sorry you had to." He bent his head and looked down at the floor, his eyes sad. Then, slowly, gracefully, he lifted his head so their eyes met and said, "But you are here now. And we are together again."

He and Beppo embraced.

And, my friends, I tell you true, I am awash with love for this man.

Chapter Twenty-Five
A Private Tour

Marta stepped into the library and said, "I'm going to head back down to Florence. I want to get things set up for Portia, then I'm meeting Leo later on."

Tino raised his eyebrows and leered. Then his mouth softened into its usual smile.

"What you are telling me is that I have been a terrible host— and you are correct," he said. "My apologies."

"Also guilty," I added.

Marta blew up at her bangs. "Not at all," she replied. "We're all in the middle of things we must do. Tick tock, and all that, as you frequently say, Tino."

I nodded. She even talked like a private-school girl. You know, "market" rather than "grocery store," and "New Haven" rather than "Yale." I wondered where she'd gone to prep school, and, for that matter, on what continent.

"I'll move in here tomorrow morning and be ready for Father Dona whenever his condition allows his transport. I take it he will come by ambulance? And that I'll have plenty of sterile garb?"

Tino nodded. "Yes and yes," he said, and made to escort Marta out.

"No need," she said. "Orla, I will see you very soon. And Tino, not a word about my meeting Leo should my mother be in touch with you. I know she is planning a *festa* soon, and she'll want you there. You must come too, Orla."

"Thanks," I said. "I'd like to."

And Marta sprinted out and away to her car.

Once we were alone together, Tino opened Tad's book to the page he had been drawn to.

"Look," he said, and pointed to the photograph of his mother and her German soldier.

"Yes," I said. "That was my introduction to your mother."

Tino closed the book. "Did you paint them?" he asked.

I nodded.

"The painting is here?" he asked.

"Yes," I said, and took his hand. We walked over to where it was displayed.

He stared at the painting and I watched his face for clues about how he felt.

"She is very beautiful," he said. "And they appear to be close. I wonder if she chew-éd her nails because she was afraid of being discover-éd?"

"Perhaps," I answered.

"But my father's eyes are 'clos-éd.'"

He had known as soon as he'd seen the photograph. Now he covered his own eyes with his free hand.

"There was never a Signor Bacci, then," he said, "only Aurora Bacci." He looked at my face. "You know the name means Dawn Kisses."

I nodded and touched his beautiful face that had his mother's smile and his father's eyes.

"It is not my story to tell, Tino."

He nodded gravely.

"I know," he said. "But I know that you have spoken at length with my mother, *la dottoressa*, and the contessa. I can read from your face that you know more than you say."

"That is true. I do not want to lie to you."

He wrapped his arms around my waist, his touch at once light and sure. "Do you very much mind if our dinner date waits until tomorrow?" he asked. "I must see my mother and ask her why she has kept the truth from me all these years."

I smiled and rubbed his shoulders.

"Not at all," I said.

"Thank you," he replied. "You are most understanding."

I stood on my toes and kissed him on both cheeks. "Your mother will be glad to see you," I said.

I wondered if I should speak further or not. Really, I told myself, I should say what I had observed in all of Aurora's telling. That was the only comment rightly mine. And maybe it could help Tino.

My feet flat on the floor again, I looked up at Tino and said, "You know, Tino, it is you and only you who has made your mother's secret bearable all these years. What a gift you have always been to her."

Tino smiled down at my face. "And she to me," he said. "But I wish she had told me the truth, as awful as it is."

"Yes," I answered. "It is important to know one's father."

He walked away from the painting and around the table to the library door. "I will keep the book," he said, holding it up.

"Good. Your mother has a copy, as well."

He waved and blew a kiss across the room. "Beppo's mother was right," he said.

I blew him a kiss as his went.

I stared at the painting long after his car had left the drive and zoomed away down the contessa's mountain. The love I had tried to vivify in the painting was similar to the force I felt rising from the core of myself now.

"Tino," I said, and realized I had just crossed the threshold into a view of life more expansive than I had known before meeting him.

Chapter Twenty-Six
All the News at Last

A night and a day passed with me in the studio painting at the contessa's easel.

Right after Tino's departure I'd jotted a note to the contessa and told Mina that the events of the past three days had compelled me put as much as I could on canvas as quickly as possible. So it wasn't until four in the afternoon on Friday, August 4th, that I finally emerged from my suite.

I'd left behind on the contessa's easel a portrait based on fact but conceived wholly in my imagination. It was of a very pregnant Aurora, standing sideways and playing the violin. She loomed large in a small attic space, with a wooden wardrobe behind her and trunks and boxes at her feet. Her violet maternity dress was smocked with white stitching above her enormous belly. Her feet were bare, and her one large braid trailed down the back of her dress. Her shapely lips were slightly open while her eyes were completely closed. She was a child with child. One stream of sunlight shone through a small window, its shutters opened to the light and air. A small crucifix was nailed to the right of the wardrobe, and a statue of Our Lady, as tall as a vase fit for lilacs, rested on a triangular shelf that had been nailed into a corner. The Lady smiled.

Of course I hoped Tino would keep our date, but, really, I didn't know what to expect. So I dressed as I would have for any summer evening with drinks and a dinner with the contessa, most likely outdoors. I chose the same outfit I'd worn to meet the *monsignore*. Only this time I let my hair go curly, just working some mousse into it after my shower, then shaking my head like a mane after it dried.

I came down the rotunda stairs and looked out into the drive to see what cars were there. Both Tino's and Aurora's.

"Good evening, *Signorina*," Mina said as she came around the corner from the kitchen.

"Hi," I said. "I've resurrected myself."

Mina dipped her knees and smiled. "They are waiting for you," she said, pointing to the patio. "Would you like a spritz, too?"

"Absolutely," I said. "Thank you."

Tino stood as soon as he saw me. He looked tired. I went over to the contessa and kissed her on both cheeks.

"Did you paint well?" she asked.

I shrugged. "I painted."

Then Tino came to me, took my hand, led me to the settee where his mother was sitting, and motioned for me to join her. The tape recorder was in her lap. Her face was drawn. Tino stood across from us.

"We want you to hear," Aurora said. "We've already played the tape for the contessa."

The contessa grabbed the sides of her chair to raise herself up. Tino went to her aid. Then, holding the parrot's head on her walking stick, the contessa said, "I will go to the infirmary to welcome Father Dona while you three listen. Marta said the priest has agreed to see me. I will be back shortly."

Aurora and I stood as she left. Mina returned with my drink. I took it in hand, and Aurora and I sat again. I prepared listen.

Aurora said, "On this tape I am reading Dieter's letter to *la dottoressa*."

TAPE #3—Letter from Dieter Ahl to Dottoressa Antonella Ghiraschi, postmarked 10 July 1989
—read by Aurora Bacci, recorded
8/3/1989,
at Aurora Bacci's apartment

"My dear *Dottoressa* Ghiraschi,

"How very surprised and glad I was to hear from you after 45 years and a horrible war that, most ironically, brought us together. Your willingness to let an enemy, though an unwilling one, enter your beautiful world of music saved me from utter despair during the occupation of your town.

"There is too much to tell in one missive, so here I give you a short summary:

"After I returned home to Hamburg after the war's conclusion, I received word from my sister Adele in South Africa that her husband, Hans Bauer, had been killed fighting alongside the Allies in the Italian Campaign. Can you imagine our circumstances required that we fight on opposite sides? Adele begged me to come to her and help her raise their three young sons. I did. We worked their small dairy farm until Franz, Karl, and Emmer all reached their majorities and took over. Then we stayed for the seven grandchildren that followed, six boys and one girl. The war had taken me from architecture studies, and I never returned to them. I came to enjoy the physical labor on the farm and the gratification it brought, even with its rigor and the fluctuations of nature.

"This past April, Adele and I returned to Hamburg where we plan to live out our days. We share a modest apartment in the city center. Once a year, my nephews say, they will visit their mother and me with their families and go camping near Venice, Italy. I have taken up the violin again. I attend a group class for retired people.

"I am most distressed to hear of your ill health. While I long to return to Fiesole as your friend, I dare not for two reasons:

"One, I believe that my heinous actions on the 12th of August, 1944—actions I would neither have sanctioned nor committed had I been in charge, *Dottoressa*, please believe me—will have made me forever unwelcome. And two, my presence would surely injure the reputations of my always beloved Aurora and the now middle-aged child we conceived, should he or she be alive. My shame should not become theirs.

"Three times in the first year after the war, I sent letters and funds to Aurora. I addressed the first envelope care of you, the second care of the contessa, and finally, one care of the cathedral's office. Each time, despite your fame, the letters minus the funds were returned to me with the designation: "Addressee not located." I can only assume that the postal workers were less than honest. It is even possible they recognized my name on the envelope, and deliberately intervened. Perhaps they acted to protect you and Aurora. Although how anyone would have dared to tamper with mail addressed to the contessa is harder to imagine.

"While I have enjoyed the (mostly) agreeable company of several ladies in South Africa over the years, I have never married and have no other children. I have always and only been married to Aurora. Whether or not you ever saw fit to share with her the honorably-intended, forged marriage certificate I charged you to complete, I cannot know. What I do know is that you will have certainly done what is right. For that I am eternally grateful.

"While occasionally I fantasize a fairy-tale ending of reunion, I realize such a dream is unlikely to be realized. My prayerful and more realistic desire is that Aurora and our grown child have enjoyed a good life. I can die at peace knowing that. But, oh, *Dottoressa*, to be able to play the notes with her again! To hold them both in my arms so that our hearts beat together! I try to keep my selfish desires at bay.

"As ever,

"Dieter Ahl"

The two of them were silent. Aurora's face was haggard, so that she looked a decade older than she was. Tino's agitation evidenced itself as he walked the length of the patio, back and forth, back and forth. After the recording finished playing, he stopped in front of the settee and spoke directly to me.

"My mother at last has told me the truth," he said. "She played the other tapes, as well."

Aurora looked at her lap and smoothed her long dress, this one a swirl of blues. She turned to me and said, "As you can imagine, Orla, we have not slept." Then she looked up at Tino. "For how many years will you be angry with me, Celestino?" she asked. "And at the two fairy godmothers—or perhaps you think them evil witches now—who manipulated our lives?"

Tino knelt down facing her and hugged her tight.

"You have ask-éd me over and over. And, yes, I wish you had told me the truth as soon as I could have understood it. But I realize your motivation was to protect me from pain and harm."

He pulled away from Aurora, but still knelt before her. "Yet I am so full of troubling information that I feel like a history book. My head has not spun so much since I studied for the medical boards. I feel as if my brain is screaming."

He put his hands over his ears. She caressed them with her own. Then they both let go and he stood. He paced in front of the settee, gesticulating with his hands as he did so.

"I want to be furious with you. I want to run into the night and howl like a hurt wolf."

He ran his hands through his hair, and rubbed his beautiful eyes. He faced the two of us.

"I am the son of a Nazi," he said, and looked at his hands, turning them over, studying them, as if he wondered what they could do. "I hate that. I want to hate him." Aurora made the sound of a small animal in pain. Tino knelt again and rested his hands on her lap. He looked straight into her eyes.

"But you do not," he said. "Though I do not understand why or how."

His mother took in a breath, then spoke. Her voice was calm now, and sure.

"He did not act like a Nazi with me," Aurora said. "Never with me. And he made you, Tino. For that I will always love him."

Tino was quiet and stared at his mother as if he were seeing her for the first time.

My eyes teared, and Tino kissed Aurora's cheek with a tenderness I had not thought possible. Aurora, in turn, caressed his face. I dared not move or speak.

"I have returned," said the contessa, as she came back onto the patio from outside. "Father Dona is very nice and very ill. God help him, he looks horrible. Sores all over his arms and his face gone gray and pasty."

She stopped talking when she saw Tino on his knees.

"Tino?" she said, his name a question on her lips.

"Yes, Contessa." And Tino stood, seeming to reassure her with his ready response.

"We must pray for him."

"Yes, we must," Tino replied.

Aurora stood then and took her son's arm.

"Contessa," she said, "I have one question."

"What is it?" the contessa asked.

"What 'heinous actions' did Dieter Ahl commit on the 12th of August in 1944?"

The contessa tapped her walking stick on the floor several times. She bit her lower lip and pulled at her right earlobe.

"I had hoped never to hear that question," she said. "But since you ask, I must answer." She looked to me.

Oh, no, I thought.

"Orla, please go upstairs and bring down the easel."

"Of course," I said.

Tino moved ahead of me toward the lounge.

"I will get it," he said as he went.

"Oh, Contessa," Aurora said, as Tino bounded up the stairs. "How can there be more?"

The contessa lowered herself into a straight-backed wrought iron chair. Now Aurora paced and I stood still, biting my left thumbnail. We did not talk for the several minutes that passed until Tino returned, and I wondered how Aurora and Tino could and would bear yet another troubling revelation.

"Here," Tino said, as he came through the lounge and out onto the patio.

He had collapsed the easel so that he could rest it against the marble table.

"Look at the left leg and remove the wooden stopper," the contessa directed him.

Tino knelt, then gently lowered the easel onto the patio floor. He removed the wooden stopper, put it down beside him, and looked to the contessa.

"You will find a rolled message inside," the contessa said.

Tino slid out a cylinder of faded parchment tied with a thin leather string.

"Please," the contessa said, and Tino handed her the cylinder.

The contessa untied the string, unrolled the parchment, and spread it across her lap.

"Come," she said, and the three of us gathered in front of her to read the message:

From: P. C. Castleberry, M. D., 13 August 1944
To: Matteo Sforzini, Partigiani squad leader/Fiesole
Re:German officers responsible for interrogation and execution of carabinieri Vittorio Marandola, Alberto LaRocca, Fulvio Sbarretti, evening of 12 August 1944:
Hauptmann/Rittmeister Axel Lang
Oberleutnant Ryker Hofmann
Leutnant Dieter Ahl
Leutnant Max Vogel

Tino cursed, then leapt off the patio and dove into the pool, where he thrashed about. Aurora grabbed the edge of the marble table. I went to her and led her to a chair. As soon as she was seated, I realized what had happened and cried out. I felt as if my brain had been torched, and I blurted its flaming epiphany right at the contessa's face.

"You didn't pass on the message! The *partigiani* would have killed him if they'd known. You let him live!"

The contessa's face contorted. Tino stopped thrashing and stood in the pool, water up to his neck. He looked as if he were lost at sea.

"God forgive me," the contessa said. Her parrot wobbled in her shaking grip. "I couldn't do it to Aurora."

We all stared at her—Tino now swimming to the edge of the pool closest to the patio, Aurora in her seat, her hands gripping its wrought iron arms, and me standing above the easel with my arms crossed against my chest. We all waited.

"Everyone saw the two of them together playing at Sunday High Mass in the cathedral, at the concerts in Piazza Mino. Everyone heard the beautiful music they made together." She took a breath, then another. "My friends, my fellow *partigiani* —God forgive me for abandoning them." Her breaths came more quickly. "They would have tortured Antonella mercilessly to find Aurora, then hunted her down, shaved her head and tarred and feathered her. Then they would have gone for her belly. They would have slit it, let her bleed to death, and chopped up her baby, the child conceived with the enemy."

The contessa let the parrot drop and covered her face so that her maroon nails looked like bloody arrows on her flesh.

Tino pulled himself up out of the water and sat on the edge of the pool, facing the patio. Aurora closed her eyes and bit her lower lip. I stared at the contessa and waited for more. In a few moments, she dropped her hands from her face and rolled the missive up again. Then she waved it like a weapon.

"And for what?"—she shouted now—"For vengeance, plain and simple."

She leaned over the right side of her chair and picked up her cane. She re-positioned the parrot so that its eyes faced outward, toward me. She pulled herself together again and pushed herself upright, her left hand gripping the arm of her chair, her right hand steadying herself with the parrot's head. She walked a few steps forward, towards me, then turned around so that she could address both Aurora at her left and Tino by the pool. She was all contessa again.

"I myself had lost a husband and our child," she said. "I could not let the same happen to Aurora."

None of us made a move or uttered a word until both the quarter and half hour chimed in the great rotunda. Then, the contessa said to Aurora, "Come," and the two of them retired to the contessa's private quarters. I walked over to the pool, rolled up my slacks, and sat down next to Tino. He was drenched; even his shoes were sopping wet.

"Tino," I said, and let my feet play with the water.

"But how can you be with me now?" he asked. "I understand if you will not want to."

I caressed his cheek. "You are wrong," I said. "You are not your father."

He looked at his hands again and held them up, palms facing me. "But what if I am?"

I took both his hands in mine.

"In the Emergency Department, do you not treat and try to save even the abusive husband whose battered wife has at last had enough and shot him in the chest? The young girl who has filled her stomach with pills because she cannot bear the thought of a rapist's child? The men who purposely infect others with the deadly virus?"

"Yes," he said. "I do."

I ran my hand over his wet hair.

"You do not murder. You save. You try to do no harm."

He was quiet and the pool water played over my feet.

"I very much want to be with you. And whether tonight or some other night, or however long I must wait, you have promised me a date."

Tino stood up then and stayed still long enough for me to watch a dragonfly touch down on the water, then fly up into the air again.

"Wait here, please, *Signorina* Orla, while I see if my mother is well enough for me to leave her with the contessa tonight." He sounded as serious as death.

Then he went to the towel bin, wrapped a beach towel around himself, and walked inside.

My God, what they'd all been through. Some of it done to them, some of it done by them, each action connected, every action with consequences far beyond its initial moment. And yet, today's sky was blue. The birds still flitted about the trees. The sun had risen this morning and would do so again tomorrow.

Tino returned.

"My mother will stay with the contessa tonight," he said. "And I must go to the place where I rest, the place where I forget my troubles, and pray."

I reached up my hand. He helped me to stand.

"Go, then," I said. "Do as you must. But take care, okay? Please take care."

He looked down at my face with a look of surprise.

"But perhaps you will come with me?" he asked. "If you are not afraid of a Nazi's bastard son."

I leaned my forehead on his right shoulder.

"What do I need to bring?"

He held my head to him in a grip that startled me. Then, quickly, he took his hand away and lifted my chin gently, carefully, so I could see his eyes.

"Only what you need for one night," he answered.

"Wait here," I said. I ran my hand down his chest. "And maybe find some dry clothes."

He almost smiled.

Chapter Twenty-Seven
An Idyll

I came down the stairs just as Tino, drier now, hung up the foyer phone. We walked to his car, and he deposited my overnight bag in the holding compartment behind our seats.

"We are suppose-éd to take two hours and a bit longer to get where we are going, but I want you to see the sunset. So I will go too fast."

He lowered his sunglasses from the top of his head to cover his eyes.

I untied my ever-ready scarf from my pocketbook's strap, made a triangle of it, and tied it under my chin. I put the bag on the floor, my ankles holding it against the underpinnings of my seat.

"Should I be afraid?" I asked.

Tino shrugged his shoulders. "If you want," he said. "But I suggest you enjoy the scenery instead."

"Okay." I fastened my seatbelt. "Where are we going?" I asked, as he turned the key in the ignition.

"A surprise."

Now it was my turn to shrug.

Once out of the drive, we careened down the mountain into Florence, then onto the autostrada. We whizzed from town to town, passed olive groves and train tracks, hay bales and sunflowers. Suburban gated homes with in-ground swimming pools. Walled hill towns up and away, the steeples of their medieval churches straining toward heaven. Food and appliance trucks, campers with license plates from Germany and France, towering tour buses, motor scooters with helmeted drivers, some in dresses under their leather jackets. The sky was a cobalt canvas, with cumulous clouds of white and mottled gray.

We did not speak or even look at each other. It seemed we were flying, away from the past, beyond the quotidian, to somewhere other, not yet named. Where, I didn't know. But I was willing. And I was eager. So when we exited the autostrada just after the sign that said *Assisi*, I felt certain that wherever Tino was taking me was destined to be good.

He brought the car to a stop below the *centro storico* of St. Francis's home. On either side of us were fields of sunflowers in full bloom. Scarecrows scattered the fields, rising above the yellow and brown blossoms. The air smelled of fertility.

"We will be just in time," he said. Then, "Look. We go up, slowly now."

The road ahead of us wound up and up and up to the town proper where the massive structure of Francis's monastery, St. Clare's church, and the Temple of Minerva all stood. Steep warrens of walkways, alley-like with multi-level stone apartments either side of them, awaited as well. Some of the passageways were off limits to cars. At the very top of the town, the fortress called Rocca Maggiore commanded a view of the valley. This was a place of history and substance. A place that had outlasted plagues and wars. A place of belief. And, although sitting on a fault line that several times would cleave the town in half, crushing its edifices and the bodies of those who lived and prayed in them, Assisi, its people, and its pilgrims had not lost faith. They rose each day as the sun did and looked to Francis's example for hope and guidance.

"We must park the car here," Tino said.

We pulled into a parking space outside a small shop along a row of other small shops, just before the archway announcing the center of town. The shop directly to the right of the car featured handmade table linens. Next to it another advertised colorful ceramic dinnerware. A third displayed all manner of Franciscan memorabilia and religious articles.

Tino got out, came around, and lifted the passenger door. I took his hand and stood. He reached into the storage area in the back of the car for his navy backpack with the *Ospedale Santa Maria Nuova* insignia on it and grabbed my soft carryall, which I had filled hurriedly.

"Just a short walk," he said. "I will carry both."

"Thank you, Tino. Let's go, then," I said.

The scarf was still on my head. A steeple's bells clanged 7:30.

We walked to the center of town, the Piazza del Comune, with its flowing fountain. Several groups of people—locals, by the look of them—sat under umbrellas at a casual outdoor bar.

"*Buona sera, Dottore,*" a middle-aged aproned woman called out. "I will leave what you have ordered until after the sun has set."

She appeared to be the proprietor, or maybe the cook. *She must be the person Tino phoned*, I thought.

"Thank you, Angelina. Please meet my friend, the painter I told you about. Her name is Orla Castleberry."

"The American," Angelina said.

I waved at her and she blew me back a kiss. Under her serviceable apron, she wore a soft dress with a tiny rosebud print. Religious totems hung from a long chain around her neck. Her graying hair was in a bun.

"Where are all the tourists?" I asked.

"Aha!" Tino said as we walked around the bar and made a sharp turn right and up a narrow stony road. "You recognize something important, *Signorina* Orla."

"I do?" I said.

"Yes."

We came to a stop.

"Now we walk up the stairs."

I started up with a combination of curiosity and dread. A narrow stairway hewn directly out of the rock loomed to our left. Outer apartment walls stood each side of it, their iron balconies and wooden window boxes filled with profusions of potted red geraniums. Delicious aromas wafted out of open kitchen windows—garlic, rosemary, grilled lamb, basil-laced tomato sauces. I was ravenous, and panting. I had counted fifty-two steps so far.

"The tourists flock here by day," Tino said. He paused. I'm certain it was out of pity for the American woman who thought she had gotten into shape.

"The big buses come, thousands of people, all to see what St. Francis created."

"I can see why. The place is stunning."

A tawny cat slunk down the steps past us, as close to the rock wall as it could get.

"Just twenty-three more." He smiled.

I loosened my head scarf and tucked it into the top of my blouse so that it nestled in my brassiere between my breasts. We walked again.

"From 8 o'clock in the morning until 5 o'clock in the afternoon every day. They are mostly pilgrims."

He stopped again. "But I avoid them," he continued. "I come and go only at night or at dawn. I stroll about the town when the tourists leave and before they arrive. The town is a balm that way. A balm is how I you call it, yes? A restorative, like a lotion that calms the itchy skin."

"Yes," I said. "That is exactly what you call it."

The step climbing felt nothing like a balm, more like a punishing session of high school basketball practice after a team member had displeased the coach.

Tino put both backpack and carryall down and took a key from his breast pocket. It was old-fashioned. Iron, weighty, and unwieldy. But beautiful just the same. Form and function crafted to last long beyond the twelfth century.

He unlocked the wooden door, which opened inward, and said, "Please."

As soon as I went in, I knew I wanted to stay.

Never mind the interior. I'll tell you about that later. It was the seductive, eye-popping view straight through the apartment that made you feel as if you'd walked right into heaven. I nearly ran to the balcony. Tino followed, letting the bags fall to the floor behind him.

The valley below Monte Subasio's slopes unraveled, carpet-like, before us. Fields of yellow, mustard, green, brown, pink, and violet spread their vibrant bounty row by row, field by field, farm by farm. Now, with night coming on, birds and bats swooped and circled in the air. The sky seemed to undulate, its palette as fluid as running water. Blood orange, crimson, salmon, purple, violet, pink, silver, charcoal, and, finally, deepest black.

"Good God!" I cried.

"Yes," Tino said.

I turned to face him.

He pressed me to him and kissed me hard. My lips smarted, absorbing the force of his— what shall I call it? Not lust exactly. And not yet eternal love. Assurance, perhaps, maybe even certainty, that love could and might happen. I hoped so. Nazi father or not. I was already a goner, as you know. I clenched his hands in mine.

Only when darkness had fallen completely and quiet seemed the only sound, did we part, turn, and go in.

Someone knocked at the door. Tino went to answer, but no one was there when he did. Instead, a wooden crate rested on the stone stoop, and footsteps hurried down the stone steps. Tino lifted the crate up and brought it in, resting it on the marble island that separated the galley kitchen from the gathering room. Its contents were covered with a white linen cloth.

"Dinner," he said.

"And brought by an invisible heavenly spirit, I see."

He laughed and got busy unloading the crate while I stood and watched, a bit stupidly, I think.

Then, leaving the balcony doors open, he drew from either side of them louvered wooden shutters. Adjusting the louvers, he let air in while providing privacy at the same time. Then he turned on a standing, tri-leveled trio of lights by a sleek, black leather couch that hugged one wall. Two taupe leather and slatted chrome chairs faced it. Between them stood a coffee table with a glass top and a marble base. Medical journals were stacked one side of a Murano bowl decorated with circles of red, white, and black. The bowl was filled with lemons and limes. On the other side were cocktail napkins and a small tray with two shot glasses on it.

"May I help?" I finally asked.

"Yes," he smiled. "Please flip the switch by the front door."

I did, and the pocket lights over the kitchen lit up navy blue, white, and red rooster-patterned wall tiles, a white marble counter streaked with blues, and a red and black Oriental rug running from doorway to balcony.

"Tino," I said, "may I ask where the bathroom is?" I picked up my carry-all.

Tino beckoned, and I followed him to the right of the doorway. He turned on the bathroom lights and, before I went in, I looked to either side of the hallway. The light from within the bathroom was bright enough that I could see the room to the left was a bedroom and the room to the right an office. The bed, dressed in a thick white comforter, took up most of the room. A desk, a small television on a black stand, and two red-and-white-striped club chairs filled the office.

"I'll be right out," I said.

"Please, take your time. I will be here."

I was glad of the chance to freshen up. Although the bathroom was small, it lacked nothing. Like the kitchen, it was mostly tile and marble. Its color scheme was black and white. The towels, blood red, were plentiful and fluffy. A black terry robe hung on one chrome hook on the back of the door. The other hook was empty.

"Dinner, *Signorina*," Tino said, as I re-entered the main room.

He had lit a thick honey-colored candle and placed painted ceramic platters on either side of the island. Spread from one end to the other, platters and bread boards offered up their delights: antipasti, an asparagus frittata, and slices of hard-crusted, sesame-topped bread, along with a small dish of garlic, oil, and oregano for dipping. Two red goblets waited next to a bottle of chilled *pinot grigio*.

"*Buon appetito*," Tino said.

Suffice it to say we made appreciative work of the feast, and by 10 o'clock we were cozied up on the couch.

"So, do you rent this wonderful apartment?" I asked Tino.

He stroked my hair. His fingers were sure and soothing.

"No, I bought it ten years ago."

"And you come here often?" "Yes, after almost every three-day shift in the Emergency Department. And after last night's and today's revelations—my God! It is my escape."

I sat up and looked at him. "But you work for the diocese, too, and in Fiesole, you said."

He nodded. "I do. They are my second and third obligations, and, until Father Dona's troubles, my easier jobs. By appointment only, most of the time." He moved his arm from around me. "It is emergency medicine that I really love. It requires that I be quick-thinking, innovative, and on my toes."

"Ah," I said. I understood. Sometimes, painting is like that.

He leaned forward and put his elbows on his knees. "The only thing I have trouble dealing with are the cases involving deliberate cruelty. Those are the cases that make it necessary for me to come here."

I leaned forward now, as well. "A case like Mina's, is that what you mean?"

Tino looked at me. "She told you?" he asked.

"Yes," I said, "when I asked her if she'd like to join me in the pool for a swim."

Tino relaxed his shoulders. "Yes, her case is a good example. The brute slice-éd her back as if he were de-boning a fish."

I looked him in the eye. "But she has made a good recovery, right?" I asked.

He pursed his lips. "Physically, yes, except, of course, for the scar." He paused. "But she is fragile. She does not want to be isolated again, whether in water or in an apartment."

I sighed. "So much suffering." I spoke to the air.

Tino put his arm around me again and I rested my head on his shoulder.

"That is why I look for peace," he said. "And if I am very, very lucky, maybe I even find some joy."

I didn't answer, but nestled closer to his chin.

We were quiet and still for some time, and I heard, if only faintly, music and laughter coming from far down in the piazza.

All of a sudden, Tino said, "Until last evening, you knew more about my life than even I did, and not even a week since you have arrive-éd."

I laughed. "Hardly," I smiled. "I just know some things that happened. Not how you feel about them. At least not until this afternoon."

He shifted in his seat. "I will tell you."

I smiled and waited for him to speak. When he did, it was almost a whisper, albeit an animated one.

"I feel that what happens to each of us is like the clock ticking. Tick, something happens; tock, another thing happens. Sometimes more than one thing happens at the same time, and the ticks and tocks fill our heads and sound too loud."

He held his head, then rubbed his arms with his hands. "But how we respond to the ticks and the tocks, that is who we are. We feel how we feel. We cannot help that. But I always think, *Signorina* Orla, that I must transform whatever I feel into an action that proves more meaningful than just another tick and another tock."

I looked into his earnest face. "I think I understand," I said.

Tino stopped rubbing his arms.

"Or else I have completely confuse-éd you."

We both chuckled and sat closer together.

"Will you tell me your life now, *Signorina* Orla? I want to know how you have come to me at last."

I admit it, his saying that made me feel all fluttery inside. I didn't know if his words were a tick or a tock, a combination of both, or something entirely different.

I sat up, lifted my legs off the floor, and pulled my knees to my chin.

"So," I began. Then I told him everything. His eyes never left my face. He didn't interrupt. Only, from time to time, he nodded or uttered small sounds of wonder, compassion, surprise, or concern. He listened so intently and without flagging that I felt I wanted to be in his company for the rest of my life.

Then I was dreaming of roosters. They were cock-a-doodle-do-ing. Forcing my eyes to open, I realized I wasn't dreaming at all.

I stood up and stretched. Tino was still sleeping. He leaned back against the soft pillows, his hands folded on his lap and his feet resting on the coffee table. I tiptoed to the louvered shutters, opened them wide enough for me to go through and out onto the balcony. A chorus of roosters greeted me and, with me, the dawn.

A light green-gray mist hung over the valley. Houses and farm equipment looked ghostly under its cover. But the roosters persisted. Easily fifteen or twenty of them.

As if kowtowing to the fowls' insistent calls, the mist rose like a theater scrim. Slowly, steadily, soundlessly it rose until it had disappeared and in its place appeared shafts of yellow light.

"It is beautiful, no?" Tino said.

I had not even heard him approaching.

He came out onto the balcony to join me. We were both barefoot and disheveled, greeting the morning together.

"Too bad," Tino said, and turned to go in. "The buses with the pilgrims will come soon, and Assisi will become noisy and crowded."

I walked in, too, and eased the shuttered louvers together.

He looked at me and smiled. "So I would like to go to bed now," he said. "With you, if you think this is a good idea."

I took his hand. "It is a very good idea," I said.

"For that I am most relieve-éd. Even though I am the son of a Nazi war criminal and a mother who all her life has lie-éd to me?"

"And I the daughter of two fathers and a mother who married the one she didn't love so I would not be called a whore's child?"

My neck felt hot as he smiled and kissed me on the forehead.

"I will be just a few moments," I said.

When I came out of the bathroom, I was wearing a mauve silk robe I had flung into my carryall. Tino, standing just outside the bedroom door, had cinched a red bath towel around his waist.

"You will wait for me?" he smiled.

"Yes," I said.

I went into the kitchen, pulled a tall glass from an open shelf, poured myself some Pellegrino, and drank. Tino appeared again.

"Would you like some?" I asked.

"Sure," he answered, and he, too, drank.

When he was done, he put his glass into the sink, turned, and kissed me on the forehead again.

"You are sure, *Signorina* Orla?" he asked.

"I am sure, *Dottore* Tino," I said.

He grinned and ran his hands over the sleeves of my robe. "Maybe we will even sleep a little," he teased.

I laughed out loud.

Then, I kid you not, I'm telling you true, Tino picked me up and, the both of us laughing and crying at nothing and everything, carried me to his bed.

It was afternoon when I opened my eyes, my watch showing 3 o'clock. Before Tino woke up I had already showered and slipped on a pair of jeans, an NYU tee shirt, and tied my sneakers. I was ravenous, happy, and sore.

"Good morning," I teased, as bells in multiple steeples chimed 4 o'clock.

Tino came over to me and kissed me on the cheek.

"May I rifle through your larder?" I asked, already opening a cabinet door.

"Of course," he said, "whatever that means."

I laughed. "It means I will find something to cook."

He raised his eyebrows. "You do not have to," he said.

I took a box of angel hair pasta from one of the cabinets. Opening another I found a glass container of olive oil, and from the refrigerator I took several cloves of garlic. Then I walked out onto the patio and pulled some basil, oregano, and rosemary from the pots that stood in a row against the iron railing.

"If you are looking for a pot, there is a large one in the cabinet under the island."

"And the colander?" I asked.

He was grinning now. "Just next to it."

I waved him off and he headed toward the bathroom.

"Go, I want to surprise you," I said.

He stopped at the edge of the gathering room.

"You already have, *Signorina* Orla. Several times."

I bit my lower lip.

The *aglio e olio* was steaming in a bowl when he came out of the shower. He, too, was wearing jeans, but with a button-down shirt that matched his eyes. Sleeves rolled, feet still bare.

Between us we finished the entire bowl of pasta and wiped the extra herbs and oil with last night's leftover bread.

"Delicious," Tino said. "Now we go. I must check on Father Dona tonight."

I soaped and rinsed everything, while Tino went from room to room, filling a plastic trash bag.

Going to get my carryall from the bedroom, I wondered about the sheets.

"Tino," I called, and he came in and read my mind.

"Angelina takes care of the apartment," he said.

"Nonetheless," I answered, and stripped the bed.

He helped me, smiling all the while. "Next time, I will show you also what is outside."

"Oh, Tino," I said.

He came from the other side of the bed and took my hands in his.

"I do not want to scare you off, *Signorina* Orla, because it is so quick between us and with so many horrible surprises."

He sat on the stripped bed and patted the mattress for me to sit by him. I sat down. He turned to me and spoke, his hand over his heart.

"But I must tell you that with you I am finding the joy."

I put my hand over his.

"As am I, Tino."

Chapter Twenty-Eight
Two Messages

The sound of a newscaster talking from the television in the contessa's room sounded out the window as Tino pulled into the drive. Our ride home from Assisi had taken longer than our ride there, perhaps because Tino so often rested one hand on mine along the way.

He hopped out of the driver's seat and came around to help me out. Then he reached into the storage compartment in back to get my carryall. My pocketbook over my shoulder and my hair mussed from the wind, I was glad we'd arrived early enough so I could check in with Mercy back home between her work with the children over at Catholic Charities and the evening, when I assumed she'd be spending her time with Thérèse. If I phoned her at eleven from here, it would be just 6 o'clock in the evening in New Orleans.

Tino pecked me on the cheek.

"I see that the lights are on at the infirmary, so I will go there now."

"Okay," I said.

284

"Tomorrow is a Sunday I must work during the day in the Emergency Department. May I see you in the evening, *Signorina* Orla?"

I rubbed his cheek. "Of course," I said. "I will be here." Then I took his hands in mine. "Do you think the '*Signorina*' is necessary anymore?" I asked.

He pretended to ponder. "Only when I introduce you as my girlfriend to someone new."

I grinned. "Deal," I said.

"Deal, as you say, then," he replied, and jogged to the infirmary while I walked into the rotunda where Mina stood waiting.

She spoke quickly, not even bothering to dip her knees. "*Signorina*, your friend named Don called. He asked me to tell you that he is in Ireland with his daughter. He gave me this number. It is the number at a hospital."

I caught myself gasping.

She handed me a piece of note paper with Ireland's international code on it. I stared at it as if I'd never seen something like it before.

"A hospital. In Dublin," I said. "Yes, I see. But why?"

Mina's eyes opened wide as she spoke. "He wants you to know that his daughter fell off the horse in a jumping competition and she has broken her back."

"My God!" I said.

I imagined Lily on the ground, terrified, in tremendous pain. And Don, if he had been nearby, running, running, and dropping down to be beside her.

"That's horrible," I said, stating the obvious.

"Yes, it is horrible," Mina replied.

I wanted to help. But what to do? What to do? Well, the first thing I needed to do was call him. I hoped he wasn't alone, that he was with at least an acquaintance who also had children who rode. Who would understand the situation and could take him in hand.

I realized Mina was still in front of me, waiting for whatever I might say and do. I looked up from the piece of paper she had handed me.

"Thank you, Mina. I'll call him right away."

Now the girl's knees could and did dip again. "And also, *Signorina*, I have left an airmail overnight express envelope for you upstairs. It arrived by carrier this morning."

Assisi's peace had fled.

"Do you know who it's from?" I asked.

Mina tilted her head. "Maybe from a nun or a priest," she said. "On the return address is the holy name 'Mercy.'"

"Jesus," I said out loud. "I hope nothing's happened to her."

Mina looked perplexed.

I ran up the rotunda steps two at a time. When I got into my bedroom, I realized I hadn't even knocked on the contessa's door. I wondered if she knew about Don's news or had seen the envelope from home. It didn't much matter. And maybe she didn't expect me to stop by her suite either. If she had, I told myself, she would have left the door open.

I tried to be careful of the tissue-thin airmail paper, but I tore the envelope, so hasty was I to read what Mercy had written. I read aloud to prevent myself from simply scanning.

Dear Mamma,

I hope you are well and doing fine in Fiesole. Tad and Luke will see you on the 14th, as planned, but there has been a change of plans for me.

My mother and I are flying to Ho Chi Minh City on Saturday so I can meet Binh, my uncle, my birth mother's brother, and his wife. He is the only blood relative we have left. We are going to be staying with them for two weeks so I can be back in time to start my internship in Washington, D.C. I am very excited to visit my original home when it will not be frightening.

Please do not be too angry with me. You and I have been together for a long time, and I barely remember what life was like where I came from. Plus, I have seen your paintings already. And Tad and Luke will keep you company. You will hardly miss me!

Sending hugs to you,
Mercy

I sat on the edge of the bed and wailed. Not for her, but for me. Me. Me. Me. I hated myself.

I looked at the clock on the night table. I had been wallowing in my pitiable mess for at least an hour. Tino's car was leaving the drive. I went to one of the windows on the right side of my bed and saw one, two, three lights go out over at the infirmary. I needed to call Don, to see what I could do to help him with Lily. The rest he needn't—couldn't—yet know. Not about Mercy and Thérèse, and not about Tino and me. Mercy's choice to visit Saigon with her birth mother instead of joining me in Fiesole, whether a result of my own maternal failings or a logical consequence of adoption, was mine to ponder alone. And now was no time to ditch Don, that was for sure.

I turned away from the window, picked up the piece of notepaper from the table near the settee, and dialed. Lily and only Lily would be the topic of our conversation.

Chapter Twenty-Nine
Regret Is Not Contrition

The contessa was spending Sunday with Dr. Ghiraschi, Mina said, when I came down to the patio for breakfast. I was dressed in beige linen slacks and a white tunic. Instead of my usual sandals, I'd put on rubber-soled walking shoes. I was restless and needed a ramble long enough for me to work through the muddle in my mind. How to manage my anger with Mercy so as to avoid a permanent rift. When to tell Don that I'd just bailed on our no-strings-attached arrangement. The easy part was sending flowers to Lily and seeing to it that their flight home from Dublin, whenever the doctors decided that Lily was fit to fly, would be by private jet. Might as well dip into some of my inheritance from Grandmother Castleberry. Still, I was filled with self-loathing. Don and I had gotten used to one another. Been present for each other. And now I was about to pull a rug out from under him.

"They have been friends for a long time," Mina said. "I can see that the contessa is very sad."

"Yes," I said, "it is quite understandable. They have been through a great deal together. And, from what I've learned, they made a formidable team."

Mina nodded her head in assent while she poured me coffee. She left for a moment, then returned from the kitchen with a tray of fruit, a *cornetta,* and some lemon yogurt. I played with the food, eating little of it. Then I stood and decided to walk to every corner of the villa's extensive grounds.

Instead of following my usual route from the pool past the entrance to the chapel and then on to the former orphanage, I started in the other direction. The opposite side of the villa offered an expanse of grounds conducive to solitude and contemplation. I followed a narrow gravel path that veered off the drive and continued farther and farther away from the villa until it ended at the edge of a precipitous cliff. Just about two feet before the flat ground ended, and a calamitous end to anyone who slipped off its edge, was a wooden bench. I sat on it, stretched forward from my waist, and looked down.

A tangle of branches, numerous ferns, and trees growing sideways out from the steep ledge filled the canyon. The natural wall of its opposite side, which I could only see by squinting, was topped by a dense forest. This was the forest the *partigiani* had climbed out of and slipped back into when they carried missives to and from the contessa's easel. Tad had told me they'd used rock-climbing stakes and ropes for their night stealth operations. How many of them had been hurt and killed from naturally occurring accidents was a number deemed inconclusive by the historians, he'd said. A fall from a slippery rock, a gouge to the eye from a pointed branch, an entanglement in plant growth that required the cutting of a saving rope in order to escape. The physical terrain itself, let alone the possibility of capture, torture, and execution, told me that the men and women of the resistance indeed had valued freedom from their occupiers more than they did their own lives. They worked alone but together, their personal values communal, tribal ones as well. This is what Tad's book and my paintings were to honor. This is what I had garnered from the personalities and acts of the contessa and *la dottoressa*, from my Grandfather Castleberry, from the three young *carabinieri* who had sacrificed themselves to the Nazi occupiers so that their fellows would be set free.

As I sat before the precipice they had claimed and protected, I asked myself what I value? Freedom, certainly. But not in the generous, sacrificial way they had. I use my freedom to paint, plain and simple. To become the best artist I can be. I'd given only part of myself to Mercy, setting all those alarm clocks that limited my time with her all through her childhood. One half hour for a Brownie ceremony, fifteen minutes at a tennis match, two hours—too much, I had complained—for the birthday party of a little friend. Did I think Daddy's abandonment entitled me to not really being present for my own child? Dr. Ghiraschi, neither mother nor blood relative to Aurora, had made her protégé her life's imperative.

A hawk swooped into the canyon, startling me as it dove deep, then rose upward again, a brown-and-white rabbit struggling in its talons. The hawk felt like a messenger or an emblem.

I, too, took what I wanted. Pouted at whatever was disallowed me. Appreciated the heart-beating beauty of others, the rabbit in the hawk's grip, for instance. But only as a vessel for my brush's interpretation. Never as a singular entity, the very essence, itself. To be seen, marveled at, and loved for itself and its one, precious life.

I shuddered. Why? There'd been no thunderous crash or an ice blade to my back. I was not ill or frightened.

A grass snake slithered up and over the ledge toward me. I watched it, lifting my feet as it undulated under the bench and into the bushes on the left side of the path.

An epiphany inched into my cognition as naturally and as steadily as the snake had. A gentle precursor to intentional thought, it achieved its aha moment when, as genuine and as forthright as an innocent child, I blurted to the canyon, "Tino is the only person I've not wanted to paint."

I stood and went to find the priest.

Father Dona was in a wheelchair pushed by Marta. They were near the chapel. I waved. He lifted his left arm, then let it fall onto his lap.

"Hi, there," Marta called to me.

I stopped at the edge of the pool, not wanting to approach if Father Dona didn't want company.

"Do you mind if I join you?" I asked. "I'm Orla Castleberry, a guest of the contessa."

Marta stooped down and said something to the priest.

"Come, come," he said, croaking like a toad. "You are the painter Marta has been telling me about."

"Wait a moment," Marta said. "I'll get you a gown and a mask." She was gone swiftly and back in less than a minute.

Father Dona's black hair was stringy, parted and combed to the side. His face looked gaunt and was as craggy as a cliff. No doubt he had been very handsome once. Like a rogue. *Jane Eyre*'s Rochester after he had fallen off his horse.

"Shall we get out of the sun?" Marta asked.

"Yes," Father Dona said. "Let's go into the chapel. Will you join us, Miss Castleberry?"

"My pleasure," I said. I hoped he could imagine a smile under my mask.

I walked from the pool's edge and opened the chapel door, holding it so Marta could wheel him in.

It was dark and cool inside, and our eyes had to adjust.We settled ourselves just feet from the door. Marta locked the priest's wheelchair so that it faced the altar, and she and I sat down on two backless benches either side of him. Marta was wearing green scrubs, and the priest wore a grey sweat suit and flip-flops. His wide-set hazel eyes looked the essence of sadness.

We made small talk for a while. You know—the weather, the infirmary's upgrades, the photogenic meals that Mina carried over for both of them. Then I told the priest what I'd come for.

"Father," I said, "I want to go to confession."

He looked at me with a mix of surprise and wonder, as if he'd not been expecting me to treat him as a priest now. He was quiet for several moments, just long enough for me to take a look at the single white dove with its olive branch in the center of the round stained-glass window above the simple stone altar.

"All right," he said. "You'll have to forgive the absence of a stole. I didn't expect to need my sacramental garb."

I was silent for a bit, then decided, *Why not?*

"Will it still count, or do we get points off for ignoring the dress code?"

Marta covered her mask with her hand and the priest's croak turned into full-fledged laughter. I knew then he and I could get along.

Marta stood, gave me the thumbs-up sign from behind the wheelchair, and said, "Just let me know when you need me again." Then she crossed herself and left the chapel.

I moved to the edge of the bench so I would be face to face with the priest. He bent down and unlatched the wheelchair's locks.

"Sometimes I need to spin," he said, and cracked a smile.

It was an easy smile. And his fingers were long and slender. A pianist's hands.

"Thank you, Father," I said.

He pushed his wheelchair closer and turned it so that his right ear was close to my face.

"So I can hear you better," he said. "I'm going deaf, too." He folded his hands in his lap.

I crossed myself and began. At first my confession consisted of a litany of faults and failings. Then, almost without my noticing, it turned into a conversation. Father Dona listened, asked questions, wondered aloud, and, from time to time, sat silently, as did I.

"Are you sorry for all you have confessed?" he finally asked. "And do you promise to sin no more?"The traditional questions before the Absolution, stole or no stole.

I put my head in my hands, then lifted it and sat up straight. His hands rested on the arms or the wheelchair.

"Father," I said. "I regret much and have much to regret." This was hard. Honest and hard. "But I am not penitent. I love my daughter. I would adopt her again. But even with a second chance, I would not give up my art. I am sorry I am not as generous as I should be."

The priest again folded his hands on his lap. "We share this guilt of ego," he said. "I am sorry, too, and I deeply regret that my personal choices will cost me and likely others our lives." He looked to the altar and crossed himself. "But I am as poor a penitent as you, Orla."

I stared at him and wondered if he had shared his thoughts with the *monsignore*. And if he had, how his superior had responded.

"Then what must we do?" I asked him.

He licked his lips. They were dry and cracked. He closed his eyes and said, "We must pray that with the grace of God our selfishness diminishes and we learn to love more generously."

"So you cannot absolve me?" I asked.

"Correct," he said. "Nor can *I* receive absolution. At least not yet," he continued.

I stood up. "Then what do we do instead?"

The priest took hold of the wheels of his chair and rolled himself to the altar. I followed him and stood by his right side.

"We make our very imperfect acts of contrition," he said.

We faced the altar and prayed aloud. Compromised flesh beside compromised flesh.

When we were done, I asked if I could wheel him back to the infirmary. He said I could. Marta was waiting.

"I would like to rest," Father Dona told her. "My new friend has made me very tired."

"No surprise to me," Marta joked.

She should know.

The priest smiled and said, "Please, Miss Castleberry, or Orla—may I call you Orla?—I would be glad of your company again."

"I will visit. I promise."

"My name is Donato. Dona to my friends. Please call me that."

I leaned down and let my mask brush his cheek. When I stood up, I could see that his face had gone clammy, dirt-basement moist, catacomb damp.

"Rest well, Dona," I said.

I made my way back to the other side of the villa grounds again. This time I walked into the labyrinth so beautifully landscaped by Beppo. Round and round I traipsed, coming up against one obstacle or another that impeded my way out. Eventually frustrated, I lifted my pant legs and stepped onto and across several neat rows of low-lying succulents and clusters of heather. Though I tried not to botch the symmetry and precision of the paths or disturb the soil that had been raked to virtual perfection, of course I did. Standing outside of the labyrinth, I looked back in and saw the imprints of my treading. As if I needed a reminder that I didn't belong in Eden.

Chapter Thirty
Death

Dottoressa Ghiraschi died in her sleep on Monday, August 7th, 1989, at 6 o'clock in the morning. Within the hour, Alessia had delivered the news in person to the contessa, who was still in her dressing gown in her suite when *la dottoressa*'s assistant arrived. The contessa ordered all the mirrors in the villa's public rooms to be draped in black cloth. She also stopped the clock in the rotunda so that its consoling chimes no longer assured one of the steady orderliness of the household. By 9 o'clock, when the contessa emerged from her suite dressed in black and holding the envelope *Dottoressa* Ghiraschi had given her during their last visit together, Fiesole was abuzz with the news. *Dottoressa* Ghiraschi had willed her home and all of its contents to Aurora and left detailed instructions for her funeral and burial. By early afternoon, numerous news outlets, including the Associated Press, had released her obituary. Both print and televised versions included a quote from the contessa, who had taken a reporter's call soon after Alessia had left the villa.

Internationally acclaimed violin soloist and maestra, *Dottoressa* Antonella Consuela Ghiraschi, of Fiesole, Italy, died in her sleep at home on 7 August 1989 after a brief battle against pancreatic cancer. She was 89 years old.

The daughter of pianist Consuela Maria Centro and composer Antonio Ernesto Ghiraschi, both also late of Fiesole, *Dottoressa* Ghiraschi was an only child who demonstrated musical talent at a young age. At the age of 16 she enrolled in Liceo Musicale di Bologna, where she focused her studies on the violin. By the time she was in her twenties she was frequently a guest soloist in concert and ecclesiastical venues throughout Europe. She was a demanding and generous teacher who followed her students' lives and careers. Every November 22nd, on the Feast Day of St. Cecilia, the patron saint of music, *Dottoressa* Ghiraschi hosted a reception in her home, to which each of her former students was invited, and throngs of them attended.

During the Second World War, *Dottoressa* Ghiraschi sided with the *partigiani*, whose resistance against Nazi oppression is well documented in Fiesole. It is said that she frequently carried classified documents about the enemy's planned movements in her violin case, slipping the documents to fellow resisters on her way to and from music lessons and religious services.

According to Contessa Beatrice d'Annunzio, herself an anti-Fascist and lifelong friend of the deceased, "While *Dottoressa* Ghiraschi always accessorized her dresses with delicate lace collars and cuffs, she wore her resolve like steel. Even the Nazi occupiers of Fiesole respected her."

Dottoressa Ghiraschi never married and leaves no known relatives. Her noted protégé, violinist Aurora Bacci, will offer a musical tribute to her mentor immediately following a funeral Mass to be celebrated Friday, 11 August, at 10 o'clock in the morning, in the Cathedral of San Romolo in Fiesole. Burial will be on the chapel grounds at Villa d'Annunzio.

As you can imagine, the contessa's Tuesday evening supper with Tino, the *monsignore*, and me consisted mostly of personal remembrances about *la dottoressa*. The stories, whether somber or humorous, appeared to be a balm to the contessa's understandably low spirits. Laughter and grief mixed effortlessly, like a pair of old friends. The contessa asked the *monsignore* to say a monthly Mass in *la dottoressa's* honor. He agreed, and seemed even more amenable when the contessa sealed her request with what Monsignore Giannini called an "unusually generous honorarium."

After Sunday and my less-than-illustrious confession, visiting Father Dona became part of my morning routine. He asked me to push him around the villa grounds and we talked. He favored the shade of the cypress grove at the other side of the main house, farthest from the infirmary. The cicadas serenaded us, and I believed that our shared feelings of unworthiness were leading to a genuine friendship. He told me he took comfort in the words of Dante. "For instance," he said, quoting his fellow Florentine, "'Love insists the beloved loves back,' and 'There is no greater sorrow than to recall in misery the time when we were happy.'" Every day I looked forward to seeing him.

Aurora was heartbroken over her mentor's demise and, at the same time, "relieved she is not suffering any longer." She asked me to go to *la dottoressa's* house with her on Wednesday afternoon. She wanted to rehearse Vaughan Williams' *The Lark*

Ascending, the violin solo she was to play in the cathedral right after the funeral Mass, and she did not yet want to be alone in the home that now belonged to her.

With the exception of Tuesday evening, Tino was working all the time so he could take Friday off for the funeral. After he finished his shifts in the Emergency Department, he drove up to Fiesole to check in on Father Dona. Then he went back to Florence to his mother's apartment across from the Accademia to be with her and do whatever she asked. We spoke by phone every night. It was generally close to midnight by the time we talked.

"I think by Saturday we will be able to stay together again," he said, during Thursday evening's call. "If you are free."

I laughed. "I think I can make myself available."

"Good," he said.

"Will we go to Assisi?" I had asked.

"Closer," he said, "so I do not have to wait so long for you again."

"Yes, please!" I'd answered, and slept undisturbed for the first time since Mercy's telegram had arrived.

On Friday, I woke at six to the sound of my alarm. It was time to get ready for *la dottoressa*'s funeral. By 9 o'clock we were lining up in front of the gate to her house.

An honor guard of *carabinieri* from Florence lined both sides of the steep, narrow road that led downhill from Dr. Ghiraschi's house; past the fork in the town center they made a pathway through the piazza to the cathedral. I counted 40 men in total. Franciscan Friar Martino, *la dottoressa*'s longtime confessor, himself a survivor of the German occupation, was to celebrate the Mass. Two acolytes walked ahead of him, the first carrying a gold processional cross, the second swinging a thurible from side to side so that the fragrance of myrrh sweetened the air. Friar Martino's hands were folded, and he stared straight ahead. He did turn once, waving back at little twin girls who peeked from behind one of the *carabinieri* and called his name.

Six *carabinieri* of Fiesole proper served as pallbearers. Three of them were descendants, respectively, of Vittorio Marandola, Alberto LaRocca, and Fulvio Sbarretti. In a moving nod to *la dottoressa*, these men had pinned above the left pocket of their dress uniforms a ribbon of white lace. A very old man holding onto a walker wept openly as the casket passed. The casket was remarkably simple, unadorned but for a spray of heather across its lid.

Our group followed right behind, the black-gloved contessa first, in a knee-length black crepe dress, black stockings, and bowed flat shoes. Her black lace mantilla, held in place by two pearl combs, one above each ear, reached to her waist. The parrot walking stick was nowhere to be seen. Instead, her chauffeur Marciano, having left his sick wife in the care of a neighbor, escorted her, outfitted in his formal uniform and high black boots polished to shining.

Tino walked with Aurora. Her fitted dress was made completely of black lace. It had a scalloped hem. She, too, wore black stockings. The heels of her pumps click-clacked on the cobblestones. She clenched her son's right hand. His suit had been expertly fitted, and his tie matched the heather on top of the casket. He, too, wore the white lace ribbon on his left lapel.

Aurora had asked that I escort Alessia, who had served *la dottoressa* for the last four years. She was inconsolable and covered her nose and mouth with a cloth handkerchief during the entire walk. I took her hand in mine as we approached the crowd lining the perimeter of the piazza. "*Grazie*," she said, and didn't let go until we were seated inside the cathedral.

I tried to be as unobtrusive as possible, having only days ago become a tiny part of *la dottoressa*'s exceptional life. The saleswoman in the little shop where Aurora bought her concert clothes had been wonderful, outfitting me in a cap-sleeved black crepe dress that flounced at the hem. She even called over to a shoe store one block away where a just-right pair of heeled sandals awaited me.

Dottoressa Ghiraschi's immediate neighbors and at least a dozen of her former students walked behind us, as did a group of older women reciting the Rosary together. Inside, the cathedral was full, the left side in front of the altar reserved for notables from the music world, the right side saved for those who knew *la dottoressa* more intimately.

After the Mass and Aurora's wrenching tribute, the pallbearers and coffin were met by a hearse. Several cars had also been arranged for us principals. Two shiny tour buses took in the rest of the congregation. And led by a police car, its lights flashing, we were brought up and up to Villa d'Annunzio.

A white tent with seats for us had been raised just in back of the small cemetery behind the chapel. Already buried there were the contessa's in-laws, her late husband, and their son Paolo. Beppo and his two sons had dug *la dottoressa's* grave the day before. Upon our arrival, the pallbearers eased *Dottoressa* Ghiraschi's casket from the hearse and carried it to the slatted plinth above the grave. It took several trips to the hearse and back for them to move the flowers. When the baskets and wreaths had been arranged to the satisfaction of the funeral director and the contessa, the pallbearers took their positions so that mourners would pass single file between them and pay their respects at the gravesite. Their uniforms and rigid postures enhanced the proceedings with a military precision.

Mina came out of the main house as soon as we went to our seats under the tent. She carried bottles of water and placed them on a small table that held enough glasses for all of us. Tino made sure the contessa and his mother drank.

For well over an hour the mourners filed by. They were quiet and respectful, some of them nodding our way; others placing a bouquet or a prayer note on top of the casket. The *carabinieri* stood at attention throughout. I couldn't help but think of the Tomb of the Unknown Soldier back in Washington, D. C. When at last it appeared there were no more mourners in sight, the pallbearers turned in response to a loud cue, walked as a unit to the tent, saluted, and turned on their heels again. Mina stood ready.

"Mina," the contessa said to her, "please see that these men are taken care of."

And the men followed Mina inside two by two. The contessa had dressed her in a black uniform, white apron and cap, and low-heeled black pumps.

Alessia went to the grave first. She knelt, then leaned in to put her lips to the casket. Then she stood and walked toward the main house. The contessa accepted the offer of my arm. She crossed herself in front of the casket, bowed, and blew a kiss. I stood behind her. When she turned to take my arm again, her eyes were full of tears. Last of all, Tino and Aurora said their good-byes. Only upon reaching the grave did Aurora's emotions break free. Her sobs were audible and her body shook so that Tino held her by the waist lest she fall. Standing at the casket, she said, "Thank you, thank you." Tino did not rush her. When she nodded that she was ready, he kissed and kissed her on her cheeks until she looked at him and smiled.

Beppo and his sons had been standing off to the side for some time. Now Beppo came to the contessa, who was waiting for Aurora and Tino, and spoke to her softly.

"Yes," she said. "We are done."

After we had all stepped up onto the patio, Beppo and his sons took up their shovels. While the others went on ahead into the lounge, I stayed on the patio and turned to watch. The three did not speak, but the sound of their shovels lifting and dropping fresh earth onto *la dottoressa*'s casket made me shiver even in the August heat. When they were done, they all three knelt and crossed themselves at the foot of her grave, then turned and went toward the service garage.

I was about to go inside when I saw Marta pushing Dona in his wheelchair to the little cemetery. When they got to it, Marta helped the priest stand. With great difficulty, he knelt at *la dottoressa*'s grave. He made the Sign of the Cross above it. Then, struggling to keep his balance, he kissed the ground that years ago *la dottoressa* had helped ensure would remain Fiesole's.

Chapter Thirty-One
In the Middle of My Life

I didn't see or hear from Aurora or Tino until the next day, around 3 o'clock Saturday afternoon.

I'd spent most of Friday evening alone in my suite trying to find a way to get in touch with Mercy. I phoned Tad. Neither he nor Luke knew where she and Thérèse were staying in Ho Chi Minh City, or even if they had planned to stay in the city. They could only tell me that Mercy's return flight was to land at Dulles International Airport the Sunday before her internship began. She'd left a phone message for the two of them at the shotgun house and let them know that she had stopped in at the Segreti cottage to say good-bye to Bredice, Favorly, and her brothers. Thanks in part to Father Dona's counsel, I'd calmed down enough to try and act like a grown-up, and wanted to tell her to enjoy her visit and her birth family. I told Tad and Luke the terrible news about Lily's fall from her horse and let them know that I'd been speaking with Don at his hotel in Dublin every evening to get updates. He had been assured that Lily would recover, but months-long and arduous physical therapy would consume the bulk of her days. She would have to put off any post-college plans for quite some time.

Just that day Tad and Luke had phoned me at dawn, their time—about noon in Fiesole. Tad said he had ditched his Saturday-morning-at-the-office routine so he could pack for their flight on Sunday. He also wanted to prepare some remarks for the official launch of his book. I must say I was both surprised and happy to learn they were together in the house. Whether that was as lovers again, I wasn't about to ask or assume. Certainly both of them would have needed to test negative for the virus before Tad took Luke into their bed again. But at least they were talking and acting like a couple. When I told them I had a surprise for them, Luke asked, "Animal, vegetable, or mineral?" "Animal," I told him, and he had growled.

Since we'd hung up, I'd been reading Dante. Father Dona had recommended I do so, and I was reciting the poet's words aloud, reveling in the Italian language in its most sublime expression. In my Saturday morning uniform of jeans and a tee shirt, sneakers by the side of the bed, I lay stomach down on the spread, mesmerized by the opening passage of Canto One of *The Inferno*:

> *Nel mezzo del cammin di nostra vita*
> *me ritrovai per una selva oscura*
> *che la dirittta via era smarrita.*

Translated into English:

> In the middle of the journey of our life
> I found myself within a dark wood
> where the straight way was lost.

A knock at the door.

"Come in, Mina," I said.

Lovely Filly Gamine always showed up with coffee and a tray if I hadn't gone downstairs by one o'clock. Today I had not only skipped breakfast, but I'd also called over to Marta that I wasn't able to join Father Dona, either. "It's just as well," she'd said. "He's running a rather high fever, and I'm waiting for Tino to examine him."

The door opened, but it was Tino rather than Mina who was carrying the tray.

"Oh, Tino." I let the book go, turned over, and got off the bed. "I'm so glad to see you. How are you?"

He put the tray down on the table for two at the end of the bed.

"Are you expecting me now?" he asked. "Or must I wait until this evening?"

I smiled, walked over to him, took his hands in mine, and waited.

He looked down at me and kissed the top of my head. "I am good. Still much surprise-éd and shock-éd, about the truth of my father. But also good."

"I'm very glad," I said.

He motioned to the two chairs. "Do you mind if we sit down? Mamma and I stay-éd awake all night at *la dottoressa*'s house. I only an hour ago went to my apartment to shower and change." He, too, was wearing jeans, along with a button-down sport shirt that matched his eyes. "My mother is with the contessa now."

"Good," I said. I sat, and poured two cups of coffee. "And how is she?"

He took a sip of the coffee, then placed the cup in its saucer. Then he tilted his head.

"You know, Orla, she still loves him. She hates what he did and does not try to deny the cruelty of his actions, but the love is still there. I see it in her eyes, hear it in her voice."

Tino tapped one knee with his fingers, then spoke again. "What is most strange for me," he said, "is not that I want to hate him, to hurt him, to see him brought to justice." He sighed. "That is expected and obvious." He looked directly into my eyes. "What is most strange is that I cannot allow myself the indulgence of revenge if I am to honor my mother's feelings."

"Hmmm."

I handed him the basket holding two *cornette*. He took one, broke it in half with his hands, and took two quick bites before speaking again. "Dieter Ahl is seventy-two years of age. I am almost forty-five. He and I are connected by DNA. But he and my mother are still somehow connected by the love their music inspired."

He put the uneaten half of the *cornetta* down on the tray.

I picked up the other *cornetta* and held it, speaking before I took a bite. "What will you do?"

"I knew you would ask me that. I knew from what you told me about meeting your own father when we were in Assisi. And I ask-éd myself."

I tasted the flaky sweetness. "And?" I said. I finished the *cornetta*.

"I sent him a letter. And I made a copy to read to you." He took from his breast pocket a paper folded like a *quarto*. "May I read?" he asked.

"I'm all ears," I said, and sat up like an attentive student.

"Father,

I thank you for giving me life and for loving my mother and her music. Our Aurora Bacci, who does not know I am writing to you, thinks the same. Neither of us can condone what you yourself described as your "heinous actions" during wartime. Nor can we ever recover almost half a century during which you have abandoned us. While I thought I would hate you, and while I sometimes believe as a native Fiesolano I ought to hate you, I cannot, out of regard for my mother's love for you that has never wavered. What happens next, Father, is up to you.

Your son,
Celestino Bacci,
Director of Emergency Medicine,
Ospedale Santa Maria Nuova, Firenze, Italia

He folded the copy and put it back into his pocket. Then he took and ate the other half of his *cornetta*. "What do you think?"

"I think you did as you needed to. No intermediaries, no one's words but yours."

He nodded. "The lives of all three of us, my mother, Dieter, and myself, have turn-éd out differently from what any of us anticipated or could even imagine."

He was convincing me now, rolling out his argument. Sort of the way Tad did. But differently. Not with formal logic or legal principles. With personal speculation, anecdotal experience. Less rational, more intuitive. The way he had told me he had learned in the Emergency Department. Facts, yes. Medical knowledge, yes. But the idiosyncratic must not be ignored. An individual patient could always surprise.

"But I think many others experience—have experience-éd—the same, no?"

I nodded, and he went on.

"You, for example, the contessa, your grandfather, your parents, Father Dona, his lovers, Mina, and how many others?"

"I don't know," I said.

He shrugged his shoulders. "Maybe most. Maybe everyone."

I stood now, went behind him, and leaned my chin on the top of his head. He got up, faced me, and wrapped his arms around my waist, lightly, as he had the first night I arrived at the Villa d'Annunzio, so recently and so long ago.

"You remember what I told you about the tick and the tock in Assisi?"

"I do."

He pecked me on the nose. "I think that the ticks and the tocks, the things that happen to us and that we make happen, as momentous and unsettling as they can be, are actually background—catalysts, my science calls them—that propel us to decide our lives. Like the backgrounds in some of your paintings, Orla. For instance, in the one with Beppo's parents. Where their figures in space act and move in interesting ways, yet are not the principals or the focus of the painting."

"Okay," I said. I was loving how he understood. It was if he were living in my brain. Seeing how I see. Feeling what I sense.

He adjusted his arms, wrapping one firmly around my waist, and raising the other so that our two hands clasped. Suddenly we were waltzing. One, two, three—one, two, three—one, two, three.

He hummed *The Blue Danube* now, and we danced, or, more honestly, pranced, from the bedroom into the studio, around the contessa's easel, and back to the bedroom and table again.

"Does that theory make you happy?" I asked.

He bowed from his waist and said, "Of course."

I curtsied. "I am glad then."

He took a long, deep breath. "Orla," he said, "as I mention-éd earlier, my mother is downstairs with the contessa. I would like the two of them to meet you."

"Meet me?" I laughed. "But they already know me."

"Yes," he said, his face looking serious and proud. "They do. But not as the woman I ask, I pray, will agree to become my wife."

He got down on one knee.

I hadn't seen it coming.

He looked up into my eyes and waited. Life as I had known it took a bow and walked off the dance floor. Tick. A future beckoned and I could decide. Tock. I hadn't sought it, coveted it, filched it, or earned it. And yet, here it was.

"Tino!' I said, and took a step back.

He smiled and waited some more.

"You are surprise-éd?"

I nodded my head up and down.

"Take your time."

I felt flooded with loveliness, with calm, with hope. What grace must be. Grace in this man. Tino.

"Yes," I said. "I would be honored, Tino."

And I stood very still.

Only then did he lift the ring from his other breast pocket, the one without the letter. A circle of turquoise set in gold. Bright. Clean. Bold.

"The color of your eyes," I said.

"The shape of the world," he answered, standing up again.

I held out my hand so he could slip it on.

We kissed with a tenderness I had not yet known except to paint it. Then we went downstairs together. As we were. As we wanted to be.

Chapter Thirty-Two
Suffer the Children

After Tino popped the champagne out on the patio, the contessa and Aurora toasted us and in short order asked if we would enjoy making our news public at the reception on Tuesday, the 15th. We agreed, and Tino and I decided we would phone my parents very late in the evening, or perhaps even after the midnight hour. I knew they'd be watching my brother on a soccer field somewhere during the afternoon and probably go out in the evening. Best to get ahold of them after 11, their time. I couldn't imagine they'd be anywhere but home after that. It's not as if St. Suplice has any bistros, or even joints, for late-night pub crawls. Mamma and Daddy's house and veranda might be the closest thing to them.

Next to tell would be Tad and Luke. If I could count on my folks not to squeal, we might be able to share our engagement with them in person on Monday evening. I'd already reserved a table on the terrace at the Hotel Villa Aurora, where they would be staying, and I could foresee a fun and festive night. It would be a treat to watch Luke get everyone on the terrace interacting, and I hoped Tino and I would ask the two of them to be my "men of honor." We hadn't even decided on a ceremony yet, so I was getting ahead of myself.

But what I really needed to do most urgently was to find Mercy and let her know, and have Tino say hello to her, tell her how eager he was to meet her. It would be cruel to let her learn the news from someone other than me. Maybe she'd phone me from Vietnam. Or... I wondered if she might have dropped a hotel name to Bredice when she'd stopped by the cottage. I thought I really should call Bredice myself about the engagement, anyway. I knew she would be glad.

And then there was sweet, reliable, trustworthy Don, carrying his ever-present burden of an institutionalized wife, and now, his newest load, Lily's broken back. What would I say? "Thanks for the sex we enjoyed along with our friendship for the last eight years. Oh, and by the way, there will be no more of us bedding. But, hey, let's still be friends anyway. I've moved on to the real thing, with a husband and all, you know. But don't let that disturb you."

Sorry and *thank you* were the words alternating in my brain like a door closing and opening, closing and opening. But they were certainly not enough. And I would just be lying to myself if I said that I was contrite.

"Really," I heard Tino say. He was standing on the other side of the pool. "Yes, it's true."

I turned to see who was with him. It was Beppo, who looked like he had been neatening up the area around *la dottoressa*'s fresh grave. The two of them came to me, Beppo with his rake in one hand and now with a glass of champagne in the other.

"*Auguri!*" Beppo said. "I am most happy for you both. And," —he paused to raise his glass—"for us, as well, so we can see you all the time and not just when you visit now and again."

"Thank you," I said. "I think I am as surprised by our engagement as you are."

I beamed at Tino and, at the same time thought how interesting it would be to figure out our living arrangements. We both called multiple dwellings home, and several of them happen to be divided by an ocean.

"I will see you Tuesday!" Aurora called out to us from the lounge, where she and the contessa had gone to plan whatever it was they wanted to do for us. "I need to get some sleep!"

That was for sure. Aurora's emotions had certainly taken a beating.

"Do you need anything?" the contessa asked.

Aurora kissed her on both cheeks. "Thank you, but no," she said. "Alessia has taken care of everything. I will call again tomorrow, if that is all right with you."

The contessa smiled. "Of course. Come to supper. Those two"—she pointed at us—"must go elsewhere so we can plot their future without any interference."

We all laughed, but I knew better than to believe the contessa's words were simply small talk. Remember, I was Grandmother Castleberry's progeny. And, like the contessa, she had been a woman who took the long view of life's events, or tick tocks, as Tino called them. Those of you who've read my first two narratives know that with her will she transformed Mamma and me from the working poor into heiresses in an instant. But until the reading of the will, neither of us had known that that had been her plan all along. And that my mamma had put up with Grandmother's cold condescension while working for her just to make sure that Grandmother, a difficult yet good woman, would come to love me. Which she had. And I her. So you can't be surprised that I'm wondering what the contessa had up her sleeve.

The Contessa's Easel

At any rate, Tino and I went in to see Aurora off in her car. We strolled through the lounge and into the rotunda. Then, amid more congratulatory hugs and kisses, we said our good-byes. It was gratifying to see Aurora smile. She was going to be a terrific mother-in-law.

After she'd left the drive with a series of beeps and waves, Tino said, "If you ladies do not mind, I must check on Father Dona again. We cannot seem to get his fever down, and I'm afraid he is failing much faster than I expected. If pneumonia sets in, death will come sooner rather than later."

I leaned against the banister and sighed. "His body seems to be deteriorating very quickly."

Tino put a hand to his chin. "He avoided seeing me for at least a month after the first symptoms appeared. Even before his test results came in, I had no doubt it was this horrible virus that had gripped him."

I ran my hand up and down the banister. "Were you able to do anything to alleviate his symptoms?" I asked.

Tino removed his hand from under his chin and clasped both hands behind his back. "The drugs we can offer are as brutal, sometimes more brutal, than the symptoms of the virus." He pulled his shoulders back tightly, then released them. "So the honest answer is, no—I am unable to relieve his suffering. And I am seeing three or four cases like his coming into the Emergency Department every week."

The contessa rested both hands on the parrot's head. She had begun using her walking stick again on Friday, as soon as the crowd of mourners had gone and there were no more photographs being taken.

"I am very sorry for his suffering," she said to Tino. "Please let me know if there is anything I might do to help."

Tino put a hand over the contessa's. "He is here, *Zia*. You have given him a home and a place to die with dignity."

313

I watched the two of them. They shared a partnership of sorts, not of blood, but of trust. They were the kind of people Grandmother Castleberry had admired, people who, as she would often say, "got things done."

"I hope he feels that he is treated well," the contessa said.

"There is no doubt he does," Tino answered.

The contessa pivoted on her cane. "Since Tino must leave us, this is a good time for me to tell you my part of the story in the continuing history of Fiesole you came to learn, Orla."

I raised my eyebrows. I'd had no idea the contessa had more to say. And, truth be told, I thought I might have already heard enough.

"Tino already has been privy to it. And now that you are to marry him, you must know it, as well."

Oh, boy, I thought, *here it comes.*

Tino kissed my cheek and said, "I will be back in an hour or so. Can you have your overnight bag packed by then?"

I grinned and the contessa's eyes crinkled.

"Well, since you've given me notice."

The contessa grabbed her parrot firmly with her right hand and, with her left, pointed to the door leading to her private suite. She opened it and went in, and I followed.

The sitting room had been decorated for restfulness, that was clear. Sage green paint covered the walls. The furniture fabrics in shades of champagne, melon, and softest yellow. The wooden pieces were a pleasing combination of blonde and oak. And the draperies fell gracefully, their hems spreading onto the parquet floor like the imprint of waves that had come and gone from the sand.

"Please," the contessa said, and we both sat down on comfortable, high-backed chairs. Across from them, on the farthest wall, over a massive oak desk, were two photographs, one of the deceased Paolo in what looked to be a First

Communion outfit, the other of Gabriella as a toddler in a party dress cinched at the waist with a thick bow. A formal portrait of the Conte and Contessa d'Annunzio in their wedding attire was hung on the adjacent wall over a round table that held bottles of water and liqueurs with the appropriate glasses for each. A chaise lounge faced a television on the same wall. Next to it was a small side table with a television guide, a pair of eyeglasses, and a small, stand-up frame with a photograph of my grandfather in his doctor's coat. A phone and one of the ubiquitous bells that summoned Mina rested on a square table between our chairs. Two long windows opposite the television and to our left had their diaphanous raw silk curtains drawn against the sun.

"I want to tell you about Gabriella," the contessa began, and she sat up straight in her chair.

"I see," I said, rubbing my hand on the soft chintz arm of the chair. "I don't think I've been in her company since she came to St. Suplice with you that Christmas time when I was 11. She must have been 18."

"You are correct," the contessa said. "A long time ago, I'm afraid."

"Yes," I rattled on, "she was always away, at riding camp, or, one time, touring in Morocco, when I visited during my college years."

"Yes," the contessa replied. "She liked getting away as often as possible."

The contessa's voice sounded wistful.

I must say that I felt a bit excited at the prospect of re-connecting with Gabriella and speaking with her, to understand what her childhood had been like here. She'd been rather an icon to me during those two weeks in St. Suplice, as I remembered. You know, an older, worldly young woman compared to my small-town self. She wore perfume and smoked cigarettes, used tampons instead of pads, and didn't care what others said about her after she left a room.

"Will she be here on Tuesday for the festivities? I'd really enjoy catching up with her." I was already concocting questions to ask her.

"No," the contessa continued, "she has not been here since five years ago, when we celebrated her fortieth birthday."

I lifted my head in shock.

"You're kidding, right?" I asked.

The contessa shook her head and pursed her lips. "It was a disaster," the contessa continued. "Since then she refuses to see me and will not let me see my grandchildren, either. They are all of age now, but dare not anger their mother by visiting. We exchange only cards with one another. And, of course, I send gifts on their birthdays."

I sat practically sideways in my chair so I could face her. "I am so sorry, Contessa," I said. "Why? What happened?"

The contessa sat with the back of her legs resting diagonally against her chair. For a moment she reminded me of Grandmother Castleberry.

"I will share with you the letter Tino has already seen. So you will understand Gabriella's point of view."

She got up, walked over to the desk, and picked up a manila envelope. She walked back, gave the envelope to me, and said, "Read it, please. Then we can speak."

Then the contessa sat down again, laid her head back, crossed her legs, and closed her eyes.

I took the letter out of the envelope. It was typed, as if it were a business document rather than a personal note.

20 August 1984
Mother,

The Contessa's Easel

Clearly you went to a great deal of trouble to acknowledge my fortieth birthday last week. As all have come to expect, the food, the drinks, and the musical entertainment were exemplary. Even my husband, whose standards are painfully high, as you know, was impressed with the execution of the event. Your grandchildren, though they would have preferred being at home in Lucerne with friends, or in Sardinia, for the entirety of their vacation period, as has been the norm for them, certainly enjoyed the treats and activities you had arranged on their behalf. They went so far as to tell me that they were glad you did not treat them as children, but rather as the teenagers they are. They especially enjoyed the motor scooters you provided and the opportunity to explore the countryside without any interference from you or their parents.

All the above noted, Mother, the fête, like every single one before it in my lifetime, was less about the birthday girl and more about you, the secular Mother Teresa of Fiesole. One after another, each guest paid homage to you the way his beneficiaries do to the Godfather in your friend Francis's films. Your pride in their doing so is as obvious as the charm you exude when you reach out your hand to be kissed.

I cannot help that I was born on 15 August 1944. Nor can I help that my father, who I met only five times in my life after the war ended, died. But over the years since my birth and his death, you might have put that time aside and focused instead on the here and now, on your daughter. Not your daughter, the love child of the dashing spy/doctor and his grieving mistress. Just your daughter, Gabriella, who craved comfort in your arms and the bulk of your attention. I have tried to be that kind of mother to my own three children, putting aside any career or social enterprises that would distance me from them.

I was not martyred like Paolo, whose horrible and untimely death guaranteed his perfection. And I did not enjoy being forced to associate every single day with the bedraggled orphans who intrigued you so and enhanced your stature. I did not care to hear the help whisper and sneer, as if I could not hear them, that the only difference between you and Aurora Bacci, 'the other putana,' they called her, was that she was a child and poor, and you were a woman both rich and titled. And isn't that true, Mother? You never married my father, never even asked him to divorce his wife. So I remain an illegitimate child.

I know you believe you have loved me. But I have never felt loved. Instead, I have been just one more little girl raised in a gilded orphanage by the worldly beneficence of someone who needed to justify a relationship brought about by a wartime misalliance and nothing else.

I am sorry that my words will hurt you. But I am not sorry for the words themselves. You can be certain that I have shared them only with my husband and with you. They will go no further.

Please know, Mother, that I want no further connection to the war, the orphanage, the villa, or Fiesole. If you were planning to leave the estate to me, please do otherwise. I am certain the town would gladly accept it, and even in the afterlife you will enjoy the appellation of "la nostra Contessa" from the Fiesolani.

I close in wishing you no ill, Mother. I seek only peace for myself as myself—wife and mother to my precious children.

The Contessa's Easel

Gabriella

I took several deep breaths in through the nose, out through the mouth, to slow down my beating heart and buy myself time before I spoke. And, really, what was there to say? I put the letter back into the envelope, placed the envelope on the tabletop, and said to the contessa, "I am so very sorry."

The contessa opened her eyes and sat up straight in her chair. "I am not without blame," she said. "I was not the kind of mother Gabriella needed. Her letter made that clear."

Was she made of steel? Then, again, the letter was five years old. She certainly had had plenty of time to think about Gabriella's words. But they were brutal, just brutal.

She rang the bell and we waited.

"Yes, Contessa?" Mina came in and dipped her knees.

"Spritzes for both of us," she said.

"Yes, Contessa," the girl said, and left to prepare the drinks.

The contessa folded her hands on her lap. Her maroon fingernail polish contrasted violently with the peacefulness of the room's décor.

"You see, Orla, my own mother died when I was ten. She had always suffered from coughs and colds, you understand, respiratory problems. And then she fought against a pneumonia that finished her. My father was a noted doctor, as you know. He lectured at Bologna and paid house calls to the nobility. But neither he nor his gifted colleagues were able to save her."

Mina came in and placed a tray between us.

"To us," the contessa said, and we clicked glasses.

"So I was sent to a convent boarding school," she continued, "where I lived, but for holidays at home near the university and summers in Amalfi with a governess. There, my father and his mistress of the moment came to stay the weekends and all of August."

She paused to sip her drink, then continued. I wished I had my tape recorder.

"I know many hear horror stories about such places. But I adjusted to the convent just fine. The sisters were not harsh or cruel. I would say they were simply matter-of-fact. We followed a routine that became second nature to me. They saw to it that our custodial and educational needs were met. We were sent to play in the fresh air every day. And on Sunday after Mass we carried loaves of bread to the poor. In the late afternoon, my father visited and took me out to dinner. We always enjoyed gelato for dessert."

I sipped my own drink and wondered why the contessa had not become a nun herself.

"Did you miss the physical contact with your own mother and father?"

The contessa smiled. "My mother stayed in her room most of the time. She did needlework. I saw her after my nursemaid had dressed me in the morning, then again after the *riposa* in the afternoon. Her touches were correct, but not spontaneous."

"I see," I said. "And your father?"

The contessa smiled again. "He was a gregarious man. Until I became too big for him to do so, he would barge into my nursery, swoop down, and pick me up. He flew me about the room as if I were a very large bird. He felt like joy."

The contessa held her hands together, palm to palm.

"That was what drew you to my grandfather," I said.

She smiled at me now. "Exactly." Then she crossed herself. "That is who I needed to be for Gabriella. But I was not." She took the envelope in her hand. "I failed her. Not purposely. Yet I did."

"Oh, Contessa," I said and reached across the table to take her hand. She let me touch it, but did not grasp my hand in return. Instead, she pointed at the wedding photograph of herself and Conte d'Annunzio.

"The convent prepared me well for my marriage. My father arranged it soon after the conte had remarked favorably about me at the coming-out ball when I turned eighteen."

"Yes?" I wanted to hear more.

The contessa held her glass with both hands. "It was not a love match, but a practical one. I moved up in society, and my father had secured both my status and my financial security. My husband and I lived a perfectly routine life of the upper-class landed gentry."

The contessa sipped and continued. I was mesmerized by her telling.

"The conte was refined, generous, and kind. I had learned what my duty was to him several days before our marriage, from a midwife my father respected. The conte required a son and my body gave him one. For pleasure he kept a woman in an apartment in the city, as was customary. He and I enjoyed true intimacy only after I delivered him the boy. Not sexual intimacy, you understand. But the realization that together we had created our Paolo."

Here she put down her glass and covered her heart with her hands. "Then they were both murdered."

The depth of sadness in her voice was astounding.

She took her hands from her chest and rested them flat on the arms of her chair. "Your grandfather awakened me in a way a woman dreams of."

She smiled, not at me, but at his photograph by the chaise lounge. "You saw how we were in the photograph I left on the easel he gave me."

"Yes," I said. "When you were expecting Gabriella."

She nodded. "But," she said, "I understand Gabriella's anger, even though it pains me."

My eyes opened wide. "You do?" I said.

"Yes," the contessa replied. She took up her glass again. "She never enjoyed a home life with her two parents who showed her we were glad of her existence, or that she was our hearts' desire." She worked her right forefinger around the glass's rim. "And the passion I had shared with your grandfather I gave to the orphanage we had founded together. I let it go outward, to other people's children, when I should have spent it on Gabriella, the child of my womb."

I realized once again that I am not the only mother who has neglected her child even as she lives with her, supports her, and sees to her schooling and vaccination schedule. Celebrates her birthdays, teaches her manners, how to dress, which fork to use and when, and so on and so on and so on. This contessa, this woman who appeared to have—pardon my expression, her shit together—this woman, too, had screwed up royally. Well, shame on the two of us. Admired by strangers, renown for furthering a cause or two, we'd been at the same time pretty inept at the most important job in the world.

One, two, three, four, the rotunda clock was striking. The contessa put down her glass and cupped her ears with her hands.

"I hear the time. That is enough for now," she said. "You must pack your bag and be ready for your fiancé." She squeezed my hand. "Go, now," she said, and waved me off.

I had been dismissed. There was no other word to describe her sending me away. The brusqueness of it grated on me, and I wasn't even her daughter.

I put aside my annoyance and instead wondered about the contessa's motive or motives. *Why had she aired family dirty laundry? Why did I need to know about it? Perhaps Tino knew and would tell me tonight.*

Chapter Thirty-Three
A New Arrival

I came down the rotunda stairs with my overnight bag and was on my way to the kitchen to pick up a couple of peaches and maybe some grapes for Tino and me. I hadn't eaten or drunk anything all day but for a *cornetta*, one cup of coffee, and, in the last hour, a spritz with the contessa. And I didn't actually know where we were going, only that it was closer to Fiesole than Assisi. I'd munch in the car.

Mina filled a grocer's bag with what I asked for, and added some bananas and oranges as well. The doorbell rang just as she was about to start chopping vegetables for the contessa's supper.

I grabbed the bag and the two of us walked to the rotunda. My intention was to stop by her suite and say good-night to the contessa. I knocked while Mina went to the front doors. Just as she opened them, Tino, his doctor's bag in hand, emerged from the contessa's suite.

"I'm ready when you are," Tino said. He kissed me on both cheeks.

"How's Father Dona?" I asked.

Tino paused, then said, "His temperature is high and he is very weak. We're keeping him hydrated and trying to prevent pneumonia from setting in."

I asked, "Do you think I can drop by to see him before we go?"

Tino smiled. "Of course, Orla. He ask-éd for you, and I know he will be glad to see you."

Just then Mina said, "Please," and let both doors remain open as she invited a middle-aged man wearing a seersucker sports coat and khaki slacks into the foyer. The clothes were too big for him. The slacks hung below his ankles and the seamed shoulders of the sports coat drooped over his upper arms. Only his leather moccasins fit properly.

He looked as if he had arrived for an appointment despite feeling unwell. A cab, its engine running, waited in the drive.

The man carried a black suitcase that had seen a fair amount of travel, and he had a well-worn honey leather monogrammed briefcase strapped crosswise over one shoulder. The monogram read *CDM*. He was blond, as tall as Tino, and so thin that his Adam's apple was more prominent than his eyes. His face, one that would have been called handsome a long time ago, was bathed in sweat, and he appeared exhausted, though he had walked only a few yards from the cab.

"Good afternoon," he said to all of us. Then, pointing to Tino's doctor's bag, "Good. I must be in the right place."

He was an American, straightforward and intent.

We all waited.

He continued, "I'm Clark Dawson, originally from Kansas City, Missouri, a friend and colleague of Father Donato Caduto. I was told he is living here at the AIDS hospice. And I,"—he took a breath, then another—"and I..."—he paused, then found his voice again—"I want to check in."

He placed his suitcase upright on the floor and, removing the briefcase's strap from his shoulder, let the briefcase rest flat, back side down, next to it.

"Come in, Mr. Dawson," Tino said, and, assisting him with an arm around the man's waist, led him to one of the formal straight-back chairs that lined the rotunda, each spaced evenly between tables where the contessa's Boehm porcelains were displayed. Tino put his doctor's bag by the side of the chair. "Please, sit down." He had just re-purposed the rotunda as his Emergency Department.

Making sure Mr. Dawson could remain upright in the chair, Tino bent down on one knee so he was face to face with the man. He looked into Mr. Dawson's eyes and said, "I will be right with you. Don't move."

"I'll get some water," Mina said, and she hurried away.

Tino walked outside and paid the cab driver. The cab sped away.

The contessa walked from the doorway of her suite and took a seat across the rotunda from Mr. Dawson. Mina returned with a glass filled with water. I took it from her, knelt by the man, and offered it to him. He held the glass with both hands and drank all the water in a few gulps. It looked as if his throat hurt when he swallowed.

"Thank you," he said, and managed a quick smile as he gave me the glass again. Then, quickly, he added, "I am so sorry for my unexpected arrival."

Tino moved in, so I got up and backed away, going to stand by the banister. I could see Tino was assessing the man's condition even as he was making conversation with him. He opened the doctor's bag as he spoke, took out a miniature notebook with a pen jutting out from the top of the cavity the spirals made, and put on a mask he pulled from a plastic bag that could have held a sandwich. He lifted a pair of rubber gloves from a cardboard box with an opening before motioning for the man to open his mouth wide. Then he gazed in, moving his head up, down, and sideways. With a piece of gauze, he manipulated the man's tongue. His doctor's bag appeared to be bottomless, and I wouldn't have been surprised if he had pulled a live bunny rabbit out of it.

"So," Tino said, "I am Doctor Bacci, and you are a friend and colleague of Father Caduto?"

The man nodded. Tino held a hand to the man's forehead.

"Yes," the man replied. "We co-lead the consortium in Florence of colleges with populations of non-Florentine students. And I am an associate professor of literature at Gonzaga University's study abroad program for North American students."

"Ah" said Tino, taking the man's pulse at the same time. He wrote in his notebook. Taking out a stethoscope and listening to the man's heart, he asked, "What is your specialty?"

The man smiled, relaxing a bit now. He was in charge of this territory. "Dante," he said. "That is how Dona—Father Caduto— and I first met. He audited my introductory course three years ago and became an aficionado like me."

I wanted to chime in about my newfound interest in Dante, but thought better of it.

Tino must have read my mind, because he said, "My fiancée, here,"—he turned his head my way as he put a blood pressure cuff on Professor Dawson—"has just today begun reading Dante. She tells me it was Father Caduto who recommended she do so."

Professor Dawson looked at me. "You will not be disappointed," he said, and I smiled.

Tino made some more notes, then stood. He put his hand on Professor Dawson's shoulder. "So, Professor," he said, "I am curious. Who told you Father Caduto was here?"

"Oh, the housekeeper at his residence, Anna Pasquino, when I went to call on him this morning."

"I see,' said Tino, removing his gloves and dropping them onto the floor beside his bag. He lifted his mask off as well, so that it folded onto his neck. "And you have come to visit Father Caduto today?"

Professor Dawson nodded. He looked up at Tino with haunted eyes and just about whispered, "I would like to admit myself to the hospice also."

'I see," Tino said. "You have tested positive for the virus?" he asked.

"Yes," Professor Dawson said. He stood up, walked to his briefcase, stooped to take it in hand, and opened it. Turning to walk back to his chair, he pulled out a file and handed it to Tino. "My medical records," he said. "My doctor for the decade I have lived here is Arturo Casabianca."

Thank you," said Tino, and he read the records, not commenting as he did so, but moving his right forefinger over each line.

"Do you know him?" Professor Dawson asked.

Tino looked up from his reading and said, "Yes, I know Arturo," he replied, revealing no opinion one way or another about the other doctor.

Professor Dawson sat up in his chair and placed his hands on his knees. "He told me Wednesday that I should resign my position, pack up my apartment, and go back home to Missouri." He teared up as he spoke. But he remained in control of himself. If you ask me, Tino—calm, deliberate, personal, and non-judgmental—had gained his trust right away.

"But there is no one there for me anymore. My parents are dead. And my one brother, Jim, disowned me when I first came out in college." He stood. "I can pay, Doctor. I have excellent insurance." He reached into his briefcase again and pulled out an envelope thick with documents.

Tino nodded and moved his right hand from side to side, as if to indicate he didn't need the information at the moment.

"And my real home is here. Near Dona, near Father Caduto."

Jesus, I thought, *Father Dona really gets around. How many other men was he leading to their graves? Did this guy even know about the former seminarian and whoever else?*

Professor Dawson bit his lip and waited. Tino glanced at the contessa. She nodded, almost imperceptibly. He nodded back. I loved them both from a place as deep and as true as my painting. And I realized that when I had said yes to Tino I had joined an enterprise larger than the two of us.

"A moment, please," Tino said. "Contessa, may I use the phone to speak with Marta?"

"Of course," the contessa said, and motioned for Tino to enter her suite. Then she stood and walked over to the professor. "I am Contessa d'Annunzio. I live here," she said. Indicating me, she said, "May I introduce you to Orla Castleberry."

"I am pleased to meet you—the artist?"

"Yes," I answered. "Guilty as charged."

"And you're engaged to the doctor?"

I laughed out loud. "Guilty again!"

Professor Dawson became animated. "I've read about your work. You created quite an uproar at your last exhibit in New York." He paused, then continued, "Good for you. Unless people demand it, there will never be a cure."

"I agree," I said, and moved closer to his chair.

Professor Dawson dug his top teeth into his lower lip. "Too late for Dona and me, though," he said.

"I'm very sorry," I whispered.

He didn't answer.

Tino returned.

"Well, Professor Dawson, let us go over to the infirmary now. You will meet Marta, the nurse in charge, and—if he is awake—you may speak with Father Caduto."

I looked at Tino. "Shall I wait here?" I asked.

Tino motioned for me to join them. "Come with us," he said, and took Professor Dawson by the arm. "We can gather our bags later."

I picked up the professor's suitcase, the contessa returned to her suite, and Tino, Professor Dawson, and I walked over to the infirmary, where Marta stood waiting at the door.

"Welcome, Professor Dawson," she said, and invited us into the office. "There is someone who is looking forward to seeing you."

She walked us to Father Dona's room. He was lying in the hospital bed with several pillows behind his back bolstering him to an almost upright position. An IV drip led to his left arm. His skin had gone alabaster and his eyes were closed. Marta motioned for Professor Dawson to go in while the three of us stood outside the doorway.

"Dona," Professor Dawson said, leaning close to the priest's right ear.

Father Dona opened his eyes. He blinked several times, then managed a smile. "Chuck," he croaked.

Professor Dawson kissed the priest on his forehead, and Marta, Tino, and I went back to Marta's office where we said our goodnights.

Before we walked outside, Tino said, "Remember, Marta, the choice of an assistant is yours, and I assure you that you will receive whatever else you need. You have my number at the apartment?"

Marta put her thumbs to her fingers and gestured back and forth playfully. "I told you this would happen," she said, making an exaggerated grin, and putting her hands on her hips.

"I know you did," said Tino. "I just want to be sure I do not take advantage of you."

Marta pretended to be annoyed. "Since when have I let anyone do that?" she asked.

Tino saluted her, smiled, and said, "As you say, then, Marta."

"Go," she replied. "And I will see you tomorrow morning. The three of us will manage just fine."

Tino and I strolled back to the villa without speaking. We picked up what we needed, then got into his car, and drove down into Florence and his apartment a block from the hospital.

It was one spacious room, an efficiency, with furniture identical to and arranged exactly as in his Assisi home. Even the kitchen and bathroom tiles matched. But whereas in Assisi a view spread from beyond the farthest wall, here a floor-to-ceiling bookcase commanded the room. And on the coffee table between the black leather couch and the leather-slatted chairs were stacks of photocopied articles about AIDS. I rifled through them, recognizing the name Anthony Fauci as the lead researcher on several.

"He is an American, you know," I said. "The people at St. Vincent's in New York adore him. And the activists are pushing him all the time."

Tino smiled and said, "An Italian-American. Yes, he is very good. And I do not know nearly enough yet." He pointed to his head. "I have much to learn. And I am afraid more men will turn up at the infirmary."

I nodded in agreement. "No doubt," I said. "I am very sure of that. The cat, as we say, is out of the bag."

Tino walked around the island separating the gathering space from the kitchen appliances. He washed his hands at the kitchen sink, then came into the gathering space and put his arms around me.

"No more talk of work now," he said. "This time, I will cook for you. I do not want you to think I am only a doctor."

"Okay, that sounds good," I said.

Morning arrived too soon. I had set the clock for five, when it would still be night time in New Orleans, 10 p.m., to be exact. It was time to make some phone calls.

Chapter Thirty-Four
Long Distances

Mamma picked up on the second ring. I could hardly hear her. Daddy and Arthur were carrying on in the background, Daddy laughing uproariously.

"I'm going to put you on speaker," I yelled into the phone. "I want to introduce you to your future son-in-law."

"Hold on just a minute, Orla," she said.

She hadn't heard a word I'd said.

Then, "Shush, you two. It's Orla, and I can't hear her."

The other two lowered their volume somewhat as Mamma clunked the phone onto the counter. Water was running in the sink, and the refrigerator door opened and closed.

"We just got home from the summer traveling team's dinner," Mamma said. "Your brother got the MVP award."

I pushed the speaker button.

"Okay," I said, "can you all hear me?"

"Orla,"—Daddy was speaking louder than he needed to—"good to hear from you. How's Italy?"

"Hey, Sis!" shouted Arthur.

"More proof you are the most valuable," I said, not too snarkily. "Congratulations. Did you get a trophy?"

"Yeah, a solid aluminum one, only the best."

We both laughed.

Tino wrapped his arm around my shoulder. We were both sitting on the high stools at the kitchen island, a coffee cup in front of each of us.

"I want to introduce you to someone."

"What time is it there, anyway?" asked Arthur.

"My family," I whispered to Tino, and he shrugged.

"It's tomorrow morning, just after 5," I said.

"Jesus," Arthur said, "and you already have company. Are you going golfing or something?"

I sat up on my stool and proclaimed, "No, I'm getting married to Doctor Celestino Bacci, Director of Emergency Medicine at Ospedale Santa Maria Nuova in Florence."

Silence.

Then, "No, really," Arthur said.

"Orla, are you serious?" Mamma asked. "Did you say you're getting married today?"

"Not today," I laughed. "But soon, very soon, I hope."

Tino nodded and winked.

I realized we hadn't picked a date or a place or settled on—much less discussed—any particulars. They didn't seem to matter in the least.

"Oh, Orla, how wonderful," Mamma said. "Tell me about him."

I heard her sniffling.

"He's right here," I said. "He wants to say hello."

Tino leaned close to the phone even though he didn't need to.

"Hello, Doctor and Mrs. Castleberry and Arthur." He squeezed me tight. "I am very please-éd to speak with you, but I will be happier to greet you in person as soon as possible. I am in love with your Orla and I wish to formally ask for her hand in marriage, Doctor."

"Jesus!" Arthur said. "Somebody actually wants to marry you."

"Crazy, aren't they?" I whispered to Tino.

"Yes, Arthur, I wish to marry your sister. She has strike-éd me like a bolt of lightning since she walked off the plane two weeks ago. Of course, I read about her work before that and heard much about her from Contessa d'Annunzio."

"Well, good luck to you, Doctor," Arthur said. "You'll need it. She's a bolt, all right."

"Arthur!" Mamma said, and in the background my brother made crashing noises and said, "Lightning strikes!"

The refrigerator door opened and closed again.

"Hello, Doctor Bacci," Mamma and Daddy chimed in unison.

I could hear Daddy breathing, he was so close to the phone.

"Tino, I am Tino."

Daddy breathed into the speaker. "Tino, then. Orla, honey," Daddy said. "Is Tino the one?"

I looked at Tino's smiling eyes, his unshaven face, his mess of morning hair, and thought of his sense of justice and the way he treated people, no matter their status and their proclivities. "Yes, Daddy, he is. He is my one and only."

A momentary pause, then Mamma's shoes pit-patting on the kitchen floor.

"Then let's blast it to the heavens, you have not only my permission, Tino, but my blessings and joy, to boot," said Daddy. "Many congratulations."

"Thank you," Tino said. "Thank you very much, Doctor."

Something popped right next to the speaker.

"A champagne toast," Mamma said. "We'll have another the moment we can be together."

I smiled and said, "Yes, good. We both look forward to it."

"Here's your brother, again," Mamma said.

"Thanks, Sis, I usually have to do my drinking on the sly."

"Oh, you!" Mamma said.

I leaned my elbows on the island top and grinned at the phone.

"Do you play soccer, Tino?" Arthur asked.

Tino laughed and took a sip of coffee. "Only in school did I play the football. But I follow-éd Tardelli all the time. I like-éd him."

"Okay, we can talk ball when we meet, then," Arthur said. "It's my life."

"You've gotten Arthur's approval," I whispered in Tino's ear.

"How did Mercy react?" Daddy asked.

I shrugged my shoulders and raised my eyebrows at Tino.

"I have to find out where she's staying and call her," I said.

"Isn't she home?" Mamma asked.

Tino walked around the island and poured himself another cup of coffee, adding steamed milk and three packets of sugar to his cup.

"Oh, I forgot to tell you," Arthur said. "She called to say she and her mother—you know, Sis, I mean her biological mother—were going to visit her uncle and his wife in Vietnam."

"And you forgot to tell us!" Daddy said.

"It slipped my mind, I guess," Arthur said. "She said her mother kept referring to Ho Chi Minh city as Saigon. She really hates the Commies, I guess."

"Oh, Orla," Mamma said, "what a lot of changes for you, and so fast. First her mother shows up, then you leave for one

335

continent and they go off to another, and now you're getting married!"

"Calm down, Mamma," I said. "I admit it's a lot to take in, but,"—I tried to be politic and humorous at the same time—"I'm thirty-eight years old, and time waits for no woman," I said.

"As long as you can cope," she said. "Are you coping?"

She should know what Tino and his mother had just been through. Let alone Tino's having a Nazi father. But that story was for another day.

Tino chimed in, "I will take good care of her, Mrs. Castleberry. I promise you. She is a strong woman. Like you, she has told me."

"Thank you," Mamma said. "Orla has certainly known some strong women."

"Back to Mercy, Arthur," I cut in, "did she mention where she and Thérèse would be staying?"

"Another glass, Dad, for the brother-in-law?" Arthur asked.

"Since it's a special occasion," Daddy said.

"I think the word 'majestic' was in it," Arthur said. "And I know it was in Ho Chi Minh City, you know, because Thérèse refuses to call it that and Mercy insisted on the present name. She can be so annoying."

"Unlike yourself, of course. Well, that's something to start with," I said. "I've got to let her know, Mamma. I don't want her hearing from anybody but me."

"Who else have you called?" Mamma asked. "Did you tell Don yet?"

"Just you," I said. "Tad and Luke will be arriving tomorrow, so we'll tell them in person. And I'll phone Tante Yvette right away."

"She'll be thrilled, I'm sure," Mamma said.

"And of course I need to speak with Don."

Tino had come back around the island to me and was stroking my hair. "Poor Don," he whispered in my ear.

He wasn't even being sarcastic. Probably just sympathetic, given what he had told me about his broken engagement. And he knew all about me, that's for sure. I had recited a litany of my former trysts, intrigues, and alliances to him during our night-long conversation in Assisi. Seriously, you can't expect a pair of middle-aged people not to have significant pasts. If they've been living and not hiding, that is.

"It's terrible about Lily," Daddy said.

"I speak with both of them every couple of days. They're still in Dublin. I'm arranging for their transport home whenever Lily gets the okay to fly."

"Good of you," Mamma said.

"It's the least I can do," I replied.

It was time to end the call.

"I'm so glad you were all home at the same time," I said. "Tino's got to go to work, and I've got to make sure everything is a go for Tuesday's festivities. I'll call again soon, when we've decided on particulars."

"Okay," Mamma said.

"And, Mamma," I continued, "thanks for not asking for details. We haven't decided any yet. All I've said is 'Yes.'"

Tino chimed in, "And that is all I wanted to hear."

"All right, then," Daddy said. "We're so glad you phoned."

"Thank you," Tino said. "We will see you soon, on whichever continent makes no difference. Only that Orla and I are together and I meet her family."

"Love you," I said.

"Love you back," Mamma and Daddy replied.

"Arthur," Daddy said, his voice a bit distant as he turned away from the speaker.

"Me, too," Arthur said. "Go easy on Tino, Sis," he added. "We don't want him changing his mind."

Tino laughed out loud.

"On three," I said.

We all counted, and the conversation was over.

Chapter Thirty-Five
Sunday Solitude and Two More Calls

We both cleaned up, Tino dressing in his scrubs and carrying his doctor's bag and white coat with him as he walked out of the apartment for the hospital. I was in my out-and-about daytime uniform of linen slacks and tunic, leather sandals, scarf, and shoulder bag.

"*Ciao*, Orla," he'd said, pecking me on the cheek at the door.

"I'm going to Mass at the Duomo, then make my way back to the villa. May I do anything for you?"

He paused before going and grinned. "We are domesticated now," he said. "I cannot believe this."

I nodded in assent. "The doctor's wife," I said.

"The artist's husband," he answered.

Antiphony, I thought, and it seemed a synonym for happiness.

"We have surprised ourselves," I said, knowing it was true.

I blew him a kiss as he went, then locked the apartment door after him.

There was a noon Mass in one of the side chapels, I remembered from when I had come to the Duomo as a college student. Then it was the architecture that drew me; today it was what I can only describe as the miraculous goings-on in my life. Sadness and happiness, shock and surprise, ugliness and beauty flung together. And always hope thrown into the mix, even when despair felt a more likely reality.

"And that, Orla, is history," Tad has been saying to me for years.

I guess he's right. It's never just one event or one point of view. At least that's what I was learning here in Fiesole. Sure, sometimes a cataclysmic occurrence will jump start subsequent realities. For instance, the Nazi occupation. But, personal or societal, one event and another drop like stones into water, stirring things up. Plop, plop, plop. Tad's version of Tino's ticks and tocks, I guess.

After Mass, I strolled a bit in the *centro storico*, stopping in a bookshop to browse. I found a volume of letters between Abigail and John Adams translated into Italian. It seemed like a nice little gift for Tino. An American love story. And I got a gelato—hazelnut, my favorite—in a small cup. I stood and watched a little girl dressed from head to toe in pink dance in the square while a white-haired street musician played his accordion. I followed several old couples, all decked out for Sunday, holding onto each other to navigate the uneven cobblestones. The *carabinieri* scanned the streets for pickpockets and temporarily lost children. They waved itinerant beggars off one set of stairs and sent them scrambling for another. Street vendors were relentless in their efforts to have me buy a balloon, or bouquet, or mechanical Pinocchio. When I had had my fill of "Sunday-in-the-Piazza-with-Orla," I walked to the taxi stand and got a cab back up to Fiesole.

Mina came running as soon as I rang the doorbell. "*Signorina* Orla! Something beautiful has been delivered for you. Look!"

She pointed into the lounge where an enormous clay pot filled with purple and white orchids sat in the middle of the coffee table. The flowers were stunning. Tall and graceful.

"Who sent them?" I asked.

She pointed to a card next to the pot.

The envelope read "Posies International." Inside was a card:

Dear Mamma,
Congratulations on your exhibit. My mother and I are sorry we cannot be there in person, but hope to see you very soon,
With love,
Mercy and Thérèse

"How nice," I said, and realized this gift was a tiny miracle providing the pathway to Mercy.

"Thank you, Mina. They are from my daughter."

"Beautiful," she said, dipped her knees, and went.

I assumed the contessa was resting, so I took the envelope and went upstairs. I sat at the table for two, pen and note pad at the ready, and phoned the number listed on the envelope. Much to my surprise and delight, the voice at "Posies International" was able to track the purchase to the Hotel Majestic Saigon. (Yes, Saigon—even the Communists understood that a Ho Chi Minh moniker did not help future guests envision luxury.) In less than 20 minutes, Thérèse Luong answered the phone in Room #718. It was 3 o'clock in Fiesole and 8 in the evening in Ho Chi Minh City.

"Hello, Thérèse. It's Orla. I'm calling to thank you and Mercy for the beautiful orchids."

"Orla, I am so glad to hear your voice." Her own voice wavered. "I have made a terrible mistake."

And she began to cry.

"What happened?" I jumped up and put a hand on my head. "Where is Mercy? Is she okay?"

I was terrified and my heart was racing.

"She is healthy, but she is angry and sad. And—so you will know the whole truth, Orla—so am I."

"Is Mercy with you now?" I asked.

"She is having a shower."

Thank God. I could try and control my breathing now.

"We were to have dinner at my brother's home. But the moment we went in and he and his wife looked at her, they became ogres. They acted unforgivably. They shouted at me, in Vietnamese, berating me for having 'consorted with the enemy and birthing a half-breed.'"

"Oh my God," I said. "How horrible. For both of you, Thérèse."

She spoke through her crying. "They are both active in the Party. They saw right away that Mercy's father is an American. Her upturned nose and her freckles tell the story. But Mercy did not have to understand their words to know their feelings."

"Oh, Thérèse," I said, "I am so sorry."

"So our daughter ran crying from the house in her beautiful dress, still holding the bouquet meant for them," Thérèse continued. "And I followed her. We returned to the hotel just an hour ago. We will not go back."

I didn't speak for a split second. Then I said, "Thérèse, come here, both of you. Come to Fiesole where everyone will be thrilled to meet you."

Thérèse paused, then said. "Here is Mercy now. I will put her on. You can hear what she says."

"Yes," I heard Thérèse say. "It is Orla."

"Mamma?" Mercy asked, as if she couldn't believe I had called.

"Yes, Mercy. It's Mamma."

She started crying immediately. But just hearing her voice, never mind how sad it sounded, allowed me to sit down again. My heart was returning to a normal rate. I felt it thump, thump against my chest, but not as it had just moments ago. I needed to be calm, to reassure her.

"Mercy," I said, "Thérèse just told me what happened. I am so sorry, my Mercy."

"Mamma," Mercy cried, "they hated me and they hated my mother, too."

She was bereft.

"I know, and that is horrible, Mercy. Just horrible."

"Yes," she sniffled. "It is."

I heard her blow her nose. Then I said, "Please, Mercy, come here, come with Thérèse to Fiesole. I promise you both will be very welcome. Tad and Uncle Luke arrive tomorrow, so they'll be waiting for you, as well. The contessa and my new friend Aurora are eager to meet you. You can relax."

"But our tickets!" she cried. "Everything is a mess. And then my internship starts right after Labor Day."

I had to be all mother now.

"Forget the tickets. They don't matter, Mercy. You are all that matters. You have my credit card, right?"

"Yes" she said. She blew her nose again.

"Okay, go to the concierge and say you both need to get to Florence, Italy. Use my card. Both of you come as soon as you can. You can relax a bit here, then get to your internship on time with no worries whatsoever."

There was a long pause.

"Are you there, Mercy?"

"Yes, I'm here." She paused again. "So you're not angry that I left with her?"

"No, Mercy, she is your mother as well. Lucky or unlucky for you, you've got two mothers instead of one to contend with."

At this Mercy laughed, and so did I. "Can you do that?" I asked.

"What, have two mothers, or go to the concierge?" Mercy asked.

"Yes," I said, "both. First, check with Thérèse. See if she thinks coming here is a good idea. I'll hold on. Take your time."

I stood up again and walked pace by single pace around the table, making sure not to tangle the phone line as I did. Thérèse and Mercy talked in the background, their voices high-pitched, but not angry. Outside my open bedroom windows I heard Marta talking with Professor Dawson and wondered how Father Dona was doing this afternoon. I'd check later.

"Yes," the two of them spoke into their phone.

"You will come, then?" I asked. "Both of you, right?"

"If it is not an imposition," Thérèse said.

"Not at all. It will be wonderful," I said. "You know, Mercy, there is someone here who has suffered just like you have. His name is Tino. And though the war was a different one, he will understand your suffering much better than I can. Your and your mother's terrible suffering."

"How do you know him?" my daughter asked.

I paused now.

"The contessa introduced us, Mercy. He loves me. He wants me to marry him. I called to thank you for the flowers and to tell you that he has proposed."

"Mamma!" Mercy screamed.

"Does that scream mean you are glad or angry, or I don't know what?"

"Surprised, Mamma. Really surprised."

She yelled to Thérèse, who evidently had moved away from the phone. "Somebody named Tino wants to marry Mamma," I hear her say, then, "Sorry, Mamma, I needed to let her know why I screamed." Then, "Have you told Don?"

I thought quickly. Tried to keep my voice light.

"I'll tell you all about our conversation after you get here. And all about Lily's summer, too."

"All right. Here's my mother. Both of us can listen together."

I was getting used to being one of two or two of two, whatever circumstances demanded.

"Congratulations, Orla," Thérèse said.

"Thank you, Thérèse."

I made my way back to the table and took a seat in the chair nearer the bed. "One more thing, Mercy," I said.

"What's that?" Mercy asked.

"Would you do me the honor of being my maid of honor?"

"Oh, Mamma, do you really want me?"

"Oh, Mercy," I said, "I do. I really want you."

"Okay, then. I'll do it."

"I'm glad. Thank you."

"What shall I wear?" she asked.

Thérèse and I laughed.

"We'll figure it out later. I don't know what I'm wearing yet, nor have we settled on a date."

"I guess we can do all that in Fiesole," said Mercy.

"Yes."

I let out a long sigh of relief, knowing they would be coming.

"Just have the concierge contact me with all the flight information. I will pick you up the moment your plane lands in Florence."

"Will do," Mercy said. "I'll go right now," and Thérèse took the phone.

"Thank you, Orla," she said. "I am very sorry to have caused our daughter more pain."

"No worries, Thérèse," I said. "She knows we do our best even when things go awry."

"I imagine so," Thérèse said. "But I never expected this from my own flesh and blood."

"Thérèse, you and I must trade stories after you arrive. So many of us have suffered so much in the service of flesh and blood."

"I am grateful, Orla," Thérèse said.

"Stay in touch, and safe travels. I will see you both very soon."

As soon as the call ended, I blurted out, "Thank you, Lord!" and hoped that their journey would be uneventful, and maybe even joyful.

I went downstairs and into the kitchen for some Pellegrino and a piece of fruit. Carmine and Mina were standing close together at the sink, and I got the impression I had interrupted an intimate moment.

"*Signorina* Orla," Mina said. "May I help you?"

"Excuse me, *Signorina*," Carmine said, and practically ran out the kitchen door.

Mina giggled at him.

"No, I'm all set," I answered, and made off with a tall bottle of the seltzer water and a ripe peach that was shaped like the breast of a nubile girl.

As you might imagine, Tante Yvette was thrilled, even after I told her about Tino's storied conception (really) and his present life and generosity. She did declare herself "too decrepit" to travel far, but asked me to write her with all pertinent plans. She hoped I would bring Tino to Manhattan so she could give him a proper welcome. I would, it went without saying.

I had drunk half the bottle of Pellegrino while speaking with her. Now I kicked off my sandals and lay down on the bed, taking the phone with me. Its wire snaked from the three pillows under my neck all the way to the table. *That's just what I'm going to be now*, I thought, *the snake in an eight-year-old garden I've rambled through with Don.*

"Lily can go home next week," he announced first thing.

"Great!" I said. "Tell me when, and I'll have the transport people phone you."

"You don't have to do this, you know, Orla."

"I know," I said. "But think what you've done for me all these years. Kept our daughters together with some semblance of normalcy for the both of them, while we had lots of good times together. I owe you big time."

"Owe me. Don't be ridiculous."

I didn't say anything. Neither did he. The silence was long and awkward.

"Let me see if I'm hearing your tone right, Orla," he said, "Your words sound elegiac, if that's the word. As if we are done."

I didn't respond right away. Instead I looked at my hands. They were quivering just a little, as if they were trying to shake off an icky substance.

Don's voice went deeper, slower. "Are you trying to tell me we're done? It sure sounds like it."

I crossed my right leg over my left. I was lying right in the center of the spacious bed for two, the "*letto matrimoniale*," as the Italians call it. And Don already knew that I was going to tell him we wouldn't be sharing a mattress anymore.

I finally spoke, my voice sounding water-logged and sluggish. "I've met someone, Don. Someone who wants to marry me."

"I see," he said, and waited.

347

"I didn't expect it. And, believe me, I wasn't looking to change a thing. I liked us. I'll always like us."

"But," and he paused.

"But," I answered.

More silence. I heard a motor scooter climb the mountain in the distance.

"I'm very sorry to hurt you, Don," I said. "I can hear that I have hurt you. And I am truly sorry."

He banged a hand on something hard. "It hurts like hell, Orla!" he continued. "I pretended we could be buddies like we were when we started. But somewhere along the way, I crossed the line. My feelings for you got deeper. I counted on you. And I thought you counted on me, too. I thought you felt the same. Shame on me for not seeing you were just using me because I was convenient. Shame on you. Damn right, it hurts!"

He was right. I hadn't even had to try in the relationship. It was easy for me to take it as it was. Convenient. Comfortable. Pleasant. Useful to Mercy. Too damn easy.

"I'm sorry, Don. I really am."

He laughed the kind of laugh of someone realizing you are not worth his time. "Well, good luck to you, Orla. And don't bother sending a plane."

"Don!" I said.

Another long pause.

"I hope you will be very happy." His voice modulated some. "I really do. Good luck to the two of you."

He was managing to be gracious, as he always had been.

"Thank you," I said. "Those are generous words. And I'll introduce Tino to you and Lily as soon as we can get together back home."

"Probably not, Orla," he said. "I don't think I could stand it. Maybe never. Or at least not for a very long time."

He hung up right away, and the receiver's monotone sounded. All I could think of was a heart monitor confirming a patient's death. I bit my lip till it bled. Then I finally hung up, too. I rolled off the bed, sat up, put on my sandals, and went over to the infirmary.

"He says he'll see you," Marta said.

For the second time, I asked Father Dona to hear my confession. But, honestly, I only confessed so to make myself feel better. I knew that deep down I was just going through the motions, taking some undeserved consolation in the familiar sounds and gestures of the ritual. What really made me sorry was the slight gurgling in the priest's voice when we recited our imperfect Confiteor together.

Chapter Thirty-Six
Making Plans

It was just about 5 that Sunday evening when I decided I needed to dive into the pool. Given what I told you at the beginning of the story, you probably think I wanted to exercise or at least thought I *ought* to want to exercise. Not true. What I really was seeking was the kind of cleansing effect English professors always rattle on about when they analyze novels in their classes. You know, they say things like, "Every time a character goes under water and comes up again, the action represents a baptism, or a renewal of life." Like the Lady of the Lake bringing back King Arthur's Excalibur. Or, if a tumultuous event is about to occur, they say, "The thunderstorm is a foreshadowing of the particular evil to come." Think *Macbeth* and *Wuthering Heights*. Then there is the old change-of-clothes trope. You know, when Portia ditches her woman's gown and dons male judicial attire to do a job on old Shylock in *The Merchant of Venice*. Well, I felt as if all those literary devices were applicable to me that night. I'd done a bunch of stuff—announced a life change, resurrected Mercy and Thérèse, and hurt a good man who had done me and my daughter no harm. And my phone transcripts could prove it. At any rate, I rifled through the drawer I'd decided was for intimates and found the red one-piece that screamed ORLA-AFTER-SHE'S-SLIMMED DOWN.

To tell you the truth, I didn't even realize the contessa had joined me outdoors, so much time did I spend diving underwater, then popping up again. I needed to be better, to practice goodness. I wanted to. Really. And didn't I recall a childhood religion class in St. Suplice where Sister Rosette Anne said Baptism and Confession of Desire were enough? Maybe not. I was probably interpreting to my own advantage. Rationalizing. Be that as it may, when I emerged from my last underwater swim from one end of the pool to the other, there the contessa was, in a caftan as loud as my bathing suit and a wide-brimmed straw hat hanging low over her forehead.

"Oh, to be able to do more than a simple breast stroke," she lamented. "You are quite proficient."

I swam over to the edge of the pool and rested my arms on the pool surround.

"Thank you for thinking so, Contessa. Actually, I was simply trying to cleanse myself of the better part of the afternoon," I said. "It was full of messes, unlike the morning."

She took off her hat and placed it on her lap.

"Why?" she asked.

I told her everything, lingering more on Mercy's suffering than on my letting Don down. When I was done, and my skin prune-like from being in the water for so long, she said, "This calls for a stiff drink. Perhaps two."

I laughed. "I wish a stiff drink could take away everyone's pain and disappointment," I said.

"It can't," the contessa said, "but having a drink together is a common excuse for making a toast to moving on."

"A sound philosophical statement, if I do say so," I replied.

The contessa jangled the bell on the table beside her. But it was Tino who arrived before Mina.

"Ladies," he said. He was still in his scrubs. "I went to check on Father Dona right after work. He has pneumonia."

I leaned on my arms. "I thought so," I said. "I dropped by to see him this afternoon and he gurgled some when he talked."

Tino went over to his godmother, bent, and kissed her on both cheeks. He was carrying not only his doctor's bag, but his backpack as well. I wondered if he planned to stay the night.

I know it probably sounds kind of ridiculous to you, given my and my fiancé's middle-aged and less-than-virginal states, not to mention the contessa's own past, but I felt kind of funny about Tino and me sleeping together here. What *he* thought, I'd yet to discover.

"It looks like you've packed to stick around," I said. I pulled myself up, turned, and sat down on the pool's edge. Tino put down his bags, then came over and offered his hand to help me stand up. He rubbed my wet back. "The cool feels good," he said, then let his hands drop to his sides. "Yes, I will spend the night at the infirmary so Marta can get some sleep. She phone-éd me at the Emergency Department. Father Dona must be move-éd often and his lungs clear-éd as much as possible. Her assistant will not arrive until the end of the week. He is a young man who volunteers with the St. Egidio group. A former medic with the military."

The contessa stirred. "Tino, let's you and Marta meet with me soon, perhaps as soon as tomorrow morning. I can tell you will need more resources than you have at present. And probably more patient rooms modernized."

Tino knelt by his godmother again.

"Thank you, *Zia*," he said. "I will let Marta know. Perhaps I can bring you over there so we can keep watch on Father Dona.

Professor Dawson is stable, at least physically, for this moment. I do not want to leave them alone."

Mina's steps sounded on the patio.

"That will be fine," the contessa said.

Mina arrived and asked, "What may I serve you, Contessa?"

She stood waiting, hands behind her back, her knees not yet dipping.

The contessa looked at me, then at Tino, and finally said to Mina, "A moment, please."

"No hurry," Mina answered, and the dip happened. It had become a motion I could count on. And for some reason or another, I found that consoling.

"And how was your day at the hospital?" she asked. "We'll let you hear about Orla's afternoon later."

Tino raised his eyebrows and asked, "It was bad? But you are fine, Orla, yes?"

I went and sat on the pool's ladder.

"Yes, Tino," I said. "I am fine."

He came over, bent down and whispered in my ear, "And you look beautiful," as he nuzzled my neck with his chin.

Then he walked away and sat down on the lounge the other side of the table from the contessa.

"The day was very difficult for the staff," he said. "We were unable to save an infant who came in with a fractured skull. The mother's boyfriend had battered him."

"Oh, Tino," I said, "I'm very sorry."

"So were we all. He was a boy just two months old. The boyfriend must be a beast. He used a hammer."

Tino crossed himself, and the contessa and I followed suit.

Mina still waited. Obviously, she had heard what Tino had just said. I don't think she even realized what she did as he spoke, but she reached her right arm around to the scar on her back and touched it. Then, all of sudden, she remembered herself and scratched an itch, real or pretended.

"Mina, this evening requires Scotch. Please bring a bottle, three glasses, some ice cubes in the small silver bucket, and lemon slices. Thank you."

By the time we had all downed our drinks—rather quickly, I must say—I knew the three of us were about to hatch a plan.

I told them that the concierge at the hotel in Ho Chi Minh City had arranged a three-connections flight for Mercy and Thérèse. They'd be arriving in Florence the following Friday, August 18th. *Mercy really must want to get out of there*, I thought. *And Thérèse has to be heartbroken.*

"So I'm going to see if I can book them at Hotel Villa Aurora," I said.

"Nonsense," said the contessa. "They will stay here. I have numerous rooms upstairs not being used. In fact, they have not been used for too long a time."

Tino had been circling the pool for some time as we had talked. Now he stopped by the contessa's chair, knelt on one knee, and said, "*Zia*, I have a thought."

"Do tell," I said, comfortable on my perch on the pool's ladder, my feet dangling in the water.

He stood up, came over to me, and knelt on one knee again. He glanced at his godmother, then said to me, "Orla, I think we should get married when they are here."

"You do?" I was getting excited.

"I do," he said, standing up and pacing again, this time from the pool's edge to the patio and back. "Yes. We have here already my mother, your dearest friends Tad and Luke come tomorrow, and your daughter and Thérèse arrive on Friday. All we need are your parents and your brother. I will invite them. At this moment."

I nodded and nodded. Then I stood up and spun. Believe me, I'm no ballerina, but I felt like a prima donna. Tino caught me on the third go-around. If I was dizzy, it was with delight.

"I will phone them now," I said. "May I use your phone, Contessa?"

The contessa was getting out of the lounge chair. I helped her as much as she would allow, holding her walking stick at the ready.

"I want to speak with them, as well, and offer them lodging here, too," she replied.

"Are you sure?" I asked. "The villa will be a hotel."

At my words, the contessa literally took the two of us in hand. She gripped Tino's right and my left.

"Do not pity me, please, for I cannot tolerate your doing so." She took the walking stick and turned the parrot's head in her hands. "But often I am very lonely," she said. "It is true that people come and go here every day. People serve me, ask things of me. And the fortune I have inherited allows me to help them and to live in great comfort. But money does not take away loneliness. And my best friend has just died."

"*Zia*," Tino said, and kissed his godmother on her cheek.

The contessa went on, "You both would do me a great favor if you filled the villa. It will feel like a home then. And, if you agree, I would like to offer the chapel and grounds as well, for the wedding of my dear godson and my step-granddaughter whom both he and I love."

It felt as if she had married us already.

Suffice it to say, all involved were grateful for the contessa's kindness and largesse. My family would stay at the Villa d'Annunzio. On the phone, even baby brother King Arthur told her he was looking forward to seeing where his grandfather had carried out his forays as a spy. The three of them were to arrive in Florence on Saturday. So in three weeks' time, the contessa would have overseen a funeral, a book launch and art exhibit, and a wedding. She might actually crave some solitude after that. (I know, I know—solitude is not the same as loneliness.) Maybe Tino and I would go on a honeymoon. Or maybe not, given his duties at the hospital and the infirmary. After all, we'd given virtually no notice about our wedding to anyone. Heck, our upcoming merger was rather a surprise even to ourselves.

The contessa's voice interrupted my musings.

"Tino, please ask your mother to join us for dessert this evening at ten. You can all decide how you want your affair to look. Then, tomorrow, after the infirmary meeting, I will sit with Mina, Beppo, Carmine, and Roberto to organize your plans. I shall ask my usual caterer to handle the food and drink. And the rest you can decide later tonight."

"Certainly, *Zia*," replied Tino.

I realized that I was glad I was not a young bride. Had I been, I would no doubt be mistaking the contessa's generosity for interference and manipulation. Perhaps a bit like Gabriella had seen her mother's machinations. But all I wanted to do was share the rest of my life with Tino. The contessa was making the road to that commitment as smooth as she could, and I was nothing but grateful.

She started toward the patio, her right hand grasping the parrot's head, and walked straight into the lounge. We followed.

"I must rest until ten," she said. "You will not mind going somewhere to have supper by yourselves?" she asked.

"Of course not," I answered, and I excused myself to go upstairs and get changed.

"Wait, please," Tino chimed in, "I must change, as well."

He ran back to the pool surround, picked up his bags, and joined me on the stairs.

"We will get ready to go on a date, *Zia*," he said.

The contessa opened the door to her suite and waved.

We did have our date—after testing the bed and shower.

We decided on the tiny bar just up from the cathedral, across from the Hotel Villa Aurora. After the waiter took our order, Tino described in precise detail how he had held the infant's mother in his arms as she rocked her dying baby.

"'My fault, my fault' she cried. And both she and I knew that it was true in part," he told me. "But," he continued, "after the police arrive-éd and questioned the mother, they left to find the murderer. I trust he will be lock-éd away for many years. But no matter his sentence, the innocent one is gone and two lives are broken."

"For certain," I said, and sighed. In turn, I railed against the dismissive treatment Mercy had received from her maternal uncle and his wife. "Pure hatred based on race and politics," I said, "with not a shred of compassion for his sister and his niece."

Tino nodded and added, "As is frequently the case."

Then I told him I had hurt Don so much that he didn't want to see me again, and that I no doubt had damaged Mercy's relationship with Lily. We each wondered aloud why love, or what we humans construe to be love, so often goes dreadfully wrong.

"There is no answer I can find," Tino said, "other than that the wrongs encourage me to try and alleviate suffering."

I looked at him for a long time after he said that. He had spoken so simply, so directly. No fanfare from this man. No drama. I wanted to be worthy of him. I pray I am worthy.

Dinner was served. And it baffled me that, amid so much suffering, past and present, we still sat at a wooden table for two outside a restaurant on a most pleasant evening in the lovely hill town of Fiesole. We ate delicate scallion and gouda omelets, dipped crusty pieces of bread in rosemary-laced olive oil, and drank several very cold beers. All in all a most satisfying supper. Only yards away from us, a black man in a striped dashiki played his guitar in the piazza. Teenagers smoked, drank Cokes from the bottle, and teased one another by the fountain. Little white lights strung along the Hotel Villa Aurora's terrace glittered. And a very old man walking a white poodle on a leash stopped to listen to the music, then waved goodnight to the guitarist. Tino and I decided we'd alternate between his apartments by the hospital in Florence and in beautiful Assisi. I'd ask the contessa if I might rent the gallery she'd arranged for me during this visit so I could continue painting. And I would be sure to spend a day with her every week so she wouldn't be so lonely. I'd fly wherever I needed to go as my work required and as Mercy requested. When he could, Tino would join me.

And the dress. I told him I would buy a wedding dress on Wednesday, the day after the book launch/art exhibit and the liberation anniversary. "I will wear a tuxedo," Tino said. "Like James Bond." Then he reached for my hand and smiled.

Those were our thoughts and our plans, anyway.

But neither of us was young or stupid enough to be fooled.

We knew we couldn't know how our life together would actually transpire. But we had agreed to promise that, whatever happened, we would enjoy and endure it together. Celestino Bacci, physician, and Orla Castleberry, artist. Each a child of secret, forbidden love. Surprised with a union neither of us had anticipated. Eager to proclaim our commitment in the bright light of a public wedding day.

Chapter Thirty-Seven
Tad and Luke Arrive

"At last!" Luke called out over the terrace railing, as Tino and I emerged from the car and walked up to the Hotel Villa Aurora's open-air restaurant. He and Tad had already been seated at the table I'd reserved for the four of us. Now they both stood.

It was 8 o'clock in the evening, the night before our book launch and exhibit, and still scorching hot. I had made sure to order an ice bucket filled with crushed ice to hold the half dozen bottles of Pellegrino we would need to combat the heat and to keep Luke from imbibing other refreshments. I was relieved to see that the bucket had been placed on a small serving table pushed right up against the main table.

Luke and Tad looked like a couple again, with Luke's hand on Tad's shoulder. Tonight Luke was a jaunty vision in lime green, navy, and white, much as he had been the first night I'd met him almost sixteen years before, only more restrained in his chosen color palette, Tad wore a new suit of polished beige cotton, though he did bring a bit of flash to the table with a pink bow tie decorated with palm trees. God, I had missed them.

Tino and I had dressed for a party, he in a fitted white linen shirt and raw silk jacket, taupe slacks, and driving loafers to die for, and I in a gauzy turquoise and white sleeveless gown that dipped to a low V in front. I wore only my engagement ring, a pearl-decorated gold bangle on my right arm, and the pearl teardrop earrings Tante Yvette had given me for my last birthday. I'd gone to the contessa's spa with her earlier. *And I definitely will be going again*, I thought. My skin felt taut after a facial, and my arms and legs were smooth and glowing with a lotion that felt like silk against my flesh. My pedicure had been, suffice it to say, a triumph. I know, I know, I sound completely superficial, but we do live and think and dream and pray in our bodies.

"Gentlemen," I began, "may I present Doctor Celestino Bacci, my fiancé."

Tad's eyes opened wide and Luke said, "Jesus, girl, you do know how to make an entrance!"

After much kissing on both cheeks (everyone), back-slapping (the two American men), and draping arms over shoulders (the Italian fellow), Tino pulled my chair away from the table, and we all sat down. We might have been in one of Hemingway's ex-pat scenes.

Luke led the question-and-answer part of the program, as he always did, with Tad and Tino observing and taking in as much as they could. I could tell Tad was assessing the two of us and that he understood Tino and I were easy together. And I couldn't believe that my former fantasies about my gay, never-could-be-married-to Tad had been replaced by an actual husband-to-be whom I loved and desired as much as I had Tad, but in an entirely different way.

When we had all calmed down and the antipasti course had been removed, Tad asked, "When do you need us there tomorrow?"

"The festivities will kick off at two," I said, "when visitors will arrive."

Four plates of *fusilli* with fresh tomatoes, basil, garlic, and olive oil arrived at our table.

"So why don't you plan to come up by noon so you can get the lay of the land?" I said.

"I will pick you up," Tino said.

"Thanks," Tad replied.

"Tad," I said, excited for the both of us, "you can't imagine how gracious and open people have been with their wartime stories. I've made some tapes for you and, more importantly, you'll meet the principals tomorrow."

"Thanks for doing that, Orla," Tad said. "Do you think we have enough for a second book?"

The waiter cleared the pasta course.

"Absolutely," I said. "For example, my grandfather's diaries you used for the first book reveal what the U. S. government wanted us to believe about his whereabouts and function. What I've learned here—mostly from the contessa—is what really happened."

Tad smiled and said, "I'm very eager to speak with her."

"And there is so much more for me to paint."

Tino put his hand on mine and said, "Perhaps you will allow me to tour you around the town the day after tomorrow, Tad? To follow the history in the geography."

"I would really enjoy that. Thank you, yes, let's do it."

"It will be my pleasure," Tino said. "And you can tell me everything about Orla you think I do not yet know but need to."

Luke allowed a belly laugh. Really, that's what it was.

Tad smiled and pushed himself away from the table as the waiter returned with slices of grilled *porchetta* smothered in mushrooms and rosemary, with roasted fingerling potatoes on the side.

"And Luke, while Tad and Tino search out historical venues and artifacts and tell tales out of school," I said, "the contessa, you, and I can have a look at the former Berenson home and see some artwork and gardens you might find interesting."

The waiter arrived once more with knives that looked like weapons. All part of the spectacle, I guessed, as the pork was tender enough to be cut by the side of the fork alone.

We each spoke of our most recent enterprises—Luke's with Lazarus House and his "better health" regimen; Tad's with an immigration case involving a fractious family with some members Christian, other members Muslim; Tino's concern that the contessa's favor to her *monsignore* friend was going to result in a wholesale transformation of the former orphanage into an AIDS hospice; and my playing with black and white line portraits and miniatures. It felt as if we all had been friends for a long time.

We were about sated when Luke eyed the last piece of bread and, motioning to it, silently looked for a taker. When we all shook our heads, he took up the bread, the end piece the Italians call the *scarpetta,* the little shoe, and dragged it over the delectable juices still on his plate. He bit into it with palpable pleasure, then, all of a sudden, he flinched. He put the remaining segment of the bread onto his plate and drew his napkin to his mouth. After patting his lips and placing his napkin down on the table, he and the rest of us all saw a small blot of blood on it.

"I must have bitten my tongue," Luke said.

But I could see he was upset. And while we waited for dessert and espresso, he kept running his tongue along his upper left gum.

The evening's musical combo took to the small stage by the bar and started with a cha-cha. Several couples got up to dance, and I motioned to Luke.

"May I?" he asked Tino.

"But of course," Tino said.

Both he and Tad stood as Luke and I walked over to the dance floor.

"What's going on?" I asked, as the two of us cha-cha-ed our way farther away from the table and closer to the bar.

Luke held both my hands and I kept smiling.

"Tad insisted we both get tested for the virus, Orla, just a couple of days after I tried to off myself."

"Good," I said.

Luke shifted our direction with a graceful spin, so I was facing outward toward Tad and Tino and he was facing inward toward the hotel's interior wall.

"Both tests came back negative," he said.

"Thank God," I said. "So you and Tad are together again. Intimately, I mean."

He nodded, "Yes, we have been."

The cha-cha ended to light applause, and Elvis's *Can't Help Falling in Love* began.

More couples joined us on the dance floor.

"Yes," Luke said. "But I think my test was a false negative."

"Why do you think that?" I asked.

Tad arrived and tapped Luke on the shoulder.

"May I have the pleasure of dancing with you, Orla?" he asked.

"My first love," I said.

I rested my head on his shoulder and he whispered, "I am truly happy for you, Orla. Really and truly happy."

"I'm glad, Tad," I said, and we danced smoothly, like the soul mates we are. "His father was a Nazi," I whispered into

Tad's left ear, and he drew back and looked at my face, wide-eyed. "Between us for just a while, please," I said, and he nodded.

I wonder if Luke had told him of his fear. The story was his to tell. But, my God, what if he hadn't?

When the song was over and Tad and I returned to our places, the waiter was just bringing out Cherries Jubilee. When he lit the confection, a blue-tinged flame rose between us in the center of the table. The flame hadn't yet subsided when the bartender arrived with a bottle of chilled Dom Perignon and four champagne glasses.

"From this gentleman," the bartender said, nodding his head in Luke's direction.

He popped the cork and poured the bubbly into each glass. Then Luke and Tad stood and together proposed a toast, "To Orla and Tino!"

Tino stood now, too.

"Thank you," he said. "I know that Orla loves you both very much, and now I love her very much, as well." He raised his glass. "May our friendships last the rest of our lives."

"Hear, hear!" we chanted like a chorus, and the others on the terrace applauded.

May we not be the chorus in a Greek tragedy, I prayed.

Then all of us, Luke included, drank.

Uh, oh. I hoped he wouldn't spiral out of control again.

As we were saying our good-byes, I whispered to him, "I won't say a word to Tino tonight. But promise me you'll ask him to have a look at you tomorrow."

He nodded, then brought me close to his face. "What if I've already killed Tad, Orla?" he said, his hands gripping my neck. "How can I live with that? You tell me, Orla. How?"

I kissed him hard on his cheek. "See Tino tomorrow. He will help you."

Chapter Thirty-Eight
45th Anniversary

Once at Tino's apartment, we went directly to bed, few words needed between us, just close comfort through the night. When morning came, Tino left for the hospital before 6 and had already returned by 8. I was just coming out of the shower. I didn't plan on dressing for the festivities until later, so I just threw on a pair of jeans and a tee shirt. He was in his scrubs.

"Vacation has begun," he said. "I am all yours for the next two weeks."

Then the phone rang and Marta asked him to come to Father Dona right away. Tino didn't even bother to change.

We arrived in less than 30 minutes. I stood outside Father Dona's room while Tino put on gown, mask and gloves, and went in to join Marta there. Through the open door I saw that an IV drip was in place, and that Father Dona was receiving oxygen.

Tino said, "We want to make you as comfortable as possible, Father Dona. Squeeze my hand if you are in pain." Then he nodded to Marta.

She went to the treatment room. When she returned she was carrying a syringe and a vial containing morphine.

I turned away and walked over to a chair in the office. I sat down and recited the Rosary, using my fingers as the beads. Music—Bach, I think it was—emanated from someplace down the hallway. I learned later that Professor Dawson had created an office space at one of the tables in the refectory. Marta had encouraged him to spend his mornings writing, having found someone to retrieve his word processor and CD player from his apartment and bring them to the hospice.

"I just want to keep him from utter despair," she told me very late at night, after the fireworks celebrating the anniversary of the liberation had come to their blazing and thunderous end. It was then that Tino had left the patio to take her place in the infirmary overnight and she joined me in the dark by the pool.

Half a day before then, around 11:30 that morning, in fact, I had phoned Tad and Luke at the hotel and told them they would need to take a cab, that Tino was with a dying patient. When they arrived, the contessa greeted them warmly and offered them free range of the villa's offerings.

Tad went right into the lounge, and I removed the covering over his books.

"You'll sign them here by the doors to the patio," I said. "Starting at 2 o'clock, visitors will enter through the front doors, go directly to my exhibit in the library, then out through the corridor door and cross over to you in the lounge. From there they will be directed out onto the patio, to a tent set up with refreshments. Several musicians, one of them Tino's violinist mother, will play. At 4 o'clock, the contessa will say a few words. She wants the two of us to join her on the small dais."

Tad smiled. "I see this is not the contessa's first event," he said, and he cradled one of his books in his hands.

Rizzoli had sent over a representative to handle the money so Tad would be free to sign and chat. The young fellow's name was Franco, and he was all business until Luke came by and, at his onstage best, regaled him with stories about his summer escapades in Florence back in 1960 when he and "another rogue," he said, stole several loaves of just-baked bread from a bakery. "It was dawn, you see," he told Franco, "the two of us were hungry, and we pretended to be picking up the loaves for some hoity-toity name we made up. We assured the baker that the lady kept a tab going at the shop."

Soon after they had arrived, Luke excused the two of us from the contessa and Tad and pulled me into the library under the pretext of making sure he liked the arrangement of my paintings. Once in there, he opened his mouth wide.

"Look," he said, though it sounded more like "Gwook." He lifted his head back so that I could see his upper left gum.

I gasped when I saw the purplish-red sore the size of a dime above his eyetooth.

"This is bad, Orla," he said. "This is one of the signs. Jesus."

I took a deep breath. I knew he was right. But I couldn't let him upset Tad just now. Though I have to wonder how Tad could not know. Maybe he did know, but couldn't yet deal with knowing. What I certainly knew was that I was afraid for both of them.

"Listen," I said, "right after the party, I'm taking you to see Tino. He'll arrange for another test."

The contessa saw to it that both Tad and I shone. The visitors numbered 327 in total. Tad ran out of books (every author's dream) and Franco had to take orders from the unhappy would-be customers who were unable to take a tome home with them. When a fair-haired lady with a lovely floral cape over one shoulder stopped to compliment me on the painting of the one-armed girl, I thanked her, and she lifted her cape. "It is you?" I whispered. "Yes," she said, kissed me on the cheek, and put a finger to her lips.

When the contessa was ready, Tad and I stood on either side of her and she offered her gratitude "to two people who have assured us all that the historic realities of our beloved Fiesole will not be forgotten, but rather remain vivid to those who read Tad Charbonneau's words and gaze at Orla Castleberry's paintings."

Tino was nowhere to be seen, nor was *Monsignore* Giannini. I hadn't noticed that Carmine had slipped into the tent and whispered into the *monsignore*'s ear that he was needed right away in the infirmary to perform the last rites over Father Dona. It was the contessa herself who let me know, as Tad and I each held one of her arms and helped her step down from the dais.

"I cannot announce an engagement, given the sad circumstances at present," she said. "I am sorry to say that your companion in Dante will soon, if he has not already, joined the poet in eternal life."

"May he rest in peace," I said, as I wondered what his Day of Judgment would bring him.

"Yes," she said. I shivered at her apparent nonchalance.

The musicians, Aurora with her violin, a pianist, and a flautist, entertained all afternoon, their musical choices both lively and soothing. As I conversed with visitors about my paintings, I could hear strains of Vivaldi's *Four Seasons*, Pachelbel's *Canon in D Major*, and Beethoven's *Violin Sonata No. 9 in A Major*.

The contessa stopped in at the library to mingle with the visitors just as the pianist began Debussy's *Clair de lune*. "Every evening when the orphans were tucked into bed after their prayers," the contessa said, "I had one of the sisters—a fine pianist she was—play soothing pieces to help them sleep."

The Contessa's Easel

After the last visitor had left the library, I joined Tad.

Tad and I mixed with those who had come to see our work. If they had lived through the occupation themselves, they had stories to tell, and Tad wrote in a little notebook he kept in his suit jacket pocket, getting addresses and phone numbers if they wished to speak further with him, and jotting down words and ideas he wanted to pursue himself. Several people told me they enjoyed the realism of my paintings. Others regretted the experience of enjoying the composition while detesting the subject matter. I must say those comments pleased me greatly.

By six o'clock, Mina and Alessia, who had come to help, had cleared the tables of food and drink. Aurora put her violin in its case and bade farewell to the contessa. Beppo and his sons struck the set, such as it was, folding the white chairs and stacking them, then rolling the round tables turned sideways to the storage barn once Mina and Alessia had taken the tablecloths away.

The contessa took to her suite, Tad and Luke loosened their ties, and I removed my high-heeled shoes. We sat on the patio together and, if I closed my eyes, I could imagine we were in NOLA, just as we had been at the start of the summer. But plenty had changed since then.

Tino and *Monsignore* Giannini stepped onto the patio from the lounge.

I stood up, went over to Tino, and stroked his unshaven cheeks. He was tired, and he would have to contend with Professor Dawson's grief, not to mention his physical distress, overnight.

"He died peacefully, if not at peace," Tino said.

The three of us crossed ourselves.

"I will never understand," the *monsignore* said. He sat down next to Tad and removed his clerical collar from around his neck. "But perhaps I am not meant to."

Pietro surprised me, then, with his expression of humility. He really did. So maybe there was still hope for me.

"Let me get you both something to drink," said Tad, and he left for the kitchen and Mina's assistance.

"I need to borrow Luke a moment," I told the two of them. "Tino and I want to show him something in the library."

I hoped Tino could read the seriousness in my eyes.

Luke took my arm and Tino followed. We went into the library and I closed the door.

"Yes," Tino said to Luke, a few minutes later. He placed a hand on Luke's shoulder and spoke directly to him, his eyes focused and kind. "I will not lie to you. This is worrisome. We must make the test again for you, and for Tad."

I noticed that Tino, without his sterile gloves, had not touched Luke's mouth, but just crouched underneath it, looking in, after directing Luke to bite down and raise his own upper lip.

Luke's tears made a steady stream down his cheeks. He looked defeated.

Then Tino looked to me, his face showing he recognized my own pained expression.

"*Cara*," he said, and kissed me on the cheek.

And in that moment I understood this would always be his private name for me.

"After the *monsignore* and Tad are done, please bring Tad to me, also," he said. "Luke and I will wait for you."

Again, another past and present were united.

Chapter Thirty-Nine
Wedding Announcement

Noted American Painter Marries Italian Physician at Famed Villa in Fiesole
—Associated Press, 20 August 1989

Orla Castleberry of New Orleans, Louisiana, and Celestino Bacci, of Florence, Italy, were married Sunday, 20 August 1989, during a Roman Catholic Mass in the private chapel on the grounds of Villa d'Annunzio, in Fiesole, Italy, at 5 o'clock in the evening. Monsignore Pietro Giannini, a cousin of the groom, officiated. Dinner and dancing followed on the estate.

Ms. Castleberry is the daughter of Doctor Prout Castleberry, a family physician, and Minerva Castleberry, a bridal-wear designer, both of St. Suplice, Louisiana. She is the granddaughter of the late Belle DuBois Castleberry, a Civil Rights activist, and the late Doctor Peter Clemson Castleberry, a physician in Fiesole during the Second World War, where he operated as an

Allied spy working with the partisans against their Nazi occupiers. Ms. Castleberry has one daughter, Mercy Castleberry, a recent graduate of Georgetown University, whom she adopted after the girl had been airlifted from Vietnam before Saigon fell to the Communist regime.

Doctor Bacci is the son of Aurora Bacci of Fiesole. Ms. Bacci, the acclaimed violinist, still performs internationally.

Ms. Castleberry's works, among them collections focused on the Vietnam war, the AIDS crisis, and, most recently, the Nazi occupation of Fiesole, Italy, are said to "both delight the eye and disturb the soul," according to her agent, Luke Segreti, of New Orleans.

Doctor Bacci is Director of Emergency Medicine at Ospedale Santa Maria Nuova in Florence. He is also the recent founder of an AIDS hospice housed in a building that formerly hosted World War II orphans on the grounds of Villa d'Annunzio. The orphanage was established by the Contessa Beatrice d'Annunzio and the bride's paternal grandfather.

The couple will divide their time between Florence/ Fiesole and Assisi, where the groom owns a second home. Ms. Castleberry has relocated her studio from New Orleans to Villa d'Annunzio at the Contessa d'Annunzio's invitation.

I read the wedding announcement many times over. Every word of it was true. But it didn't, couldn't, begin to tell my story. Facts never do that. It's not their job. What facts do instead is a kind of strip tease without the come-on of music or images. They're reductive and lack sentiment and point of view. They leave it to their readers to dress them, to apply and infer meaning and nuance.

The Contessa's Easel

Story is something else entirely. Story seduces, makes us readers forget our own lives and inhabit different ones for a while as they reveal themselves in imagined worlds. Story is the riotous parrot you grasp at the top of a cane to keep from losing balance and falling. It is the violin tucked under your chin whose music is the voice of the assassin you nonetheless love. It is the jagged scar down your back that keeps you from pools of water, the impossible turquoise of your eyes that reminds of secrets in the blood. It is the delicate lace that covers your iron resolve. It is sinning, repenting, lying, admitting, not knowing, swallowing some bitter pills, spitting out both poison and sweet, daring, hiding, trying not to hate, and always, always, reaching for love. Story is this and much more.

Story is what happened to me in Fiesole. The people I met, the ways they spoke with me, how they invited me into their lives, showed me their badges and their scars. Now that was really something. That was as good as paint.

They make me want to honor them by being as honest and as brave as they are. They make me want to do better, be better, in the world I inhabit with them now. It is a world resonant with the past and at the same time as new as every dawn.

"Good morning, good morning," I will say, and step outside into *plein air*, carrying the contessa's easel. I'll remember it was my grandfather's gift to her as it is now her gift to me. It is my inheritance, my responsibility, my—I will dare to say it—joy.

The End

Acknowledgments

With continued and sincere gratitude to Michael James, Christine Horner, Lauren McElroy, Chris Wozney, and Danielle Boschert at Penmore Press.

To Ben Catanzaro, Quinn Atlas Jannetty, and Nancy Bradley, for their patience and technical and design expertise.

Grazie mille to Georgetown University's Fulvio Orsitti, Ph.D., Director of Villa le Balze, Fiesole, for his generous tour and helpful insights. Thanks to the management and staff of the former Hotel Villa Aurora, Fiesole, for allowing me unfettered access to their building and grounds. Gratitude to Stella Soldani, extraordinary guide, Siena, Italy. Thanks to Carol and David Ross of Sophisticated Italy, and Lydia Ganz of Largay Travel.

To writers Rachel Basch, Lou Bayard, Chantel Acevedo, Christopher Castellani, James Benn, Sari Rosenblatt, Midori Snyder, Nan Parson Rossiter, Marly Youmans, Steve Parlato, Carol Snyder, Jackie Bickley, Susan Cossette, Lucia DeFillipis Dressel, Sean Crose, Jocelyn Ulevicus, Lou Aguilar, Helen Hollick, Cosimo Vannini, Jane G. Harlond, Joanna Clapps Herman, Raeleen Mautner, Joan Keyes Lownds, Kerry Sloan, Tracey O'Shaughnessy, Edith Reynolds, Tom Santopietro, Amity Gaige, Tim Watt, Tracie Mauriello, Terence Hawkins, Sandra Lambert, Umberto Mucci, Thomas McDade, Gabe Pietrorazio, Matt Lannon, Liora Wilkins, Kathleen Green,

Christian Lewis, Ryan Aghamohammadi, Faith Christian-Ferrri, KC Chiucarello.

To friends and stalwart supporters Nicola Orichuia of I AM BOOKS, Boston, Anita Graveson of New Orleans, Kyle, Pam, Maura, and Kaden Kahuda, Joe and Leslie Hadam, Lisa Carlson, Molly Emmer, Lindsay Slattum Johnson, Colleen Altenburger, Bob and Liz Cutrofello, Cole Cutrofello, Gus Haracopos, Nedra and Rich Gusenburg, Doreen Kiefer-Kopecky and Tomas Kopecky and family, Ann Gygax, Diana Smith, Judith Kellogg Rowley, Martha Kellogg, Gerard and Mary Chiusano and family, Susan, Brendan, and Sue Hemingway, Yasemin Keles, Maria Pecoraro, Sara McConnell, Estibaliz Garria, Lisa Altarescu, Dan Greene, Jesse Lloyd, Andrea Cordovez, Nyasha Chiundiza, Steve Bergin, Joan Ruggiero, Barbara Ruggiero, David Whitehouse, Phil and Barbara Benevento, Frank and Ruth Steponaitis, Elaine Muldowney and Robert Morgan, Dan and Linda Sloan, Rena and Jim Shove, Anna and John Shove, Peggy Columb, Maria and Don Michaud, Louise Bradley, Marion and Robert Bradley, Denise Ryan, the Vance, Alves, and Perrone families, the Bernetsky family, Ann and Don Lengyel, Jane Mis, Sue and Bill Mis, Jan Schuck, Karen and Chip Longo, Wendy and Mark Hopkinson, Sandy and Rich Solomita, Nancy and John King, Amy Davis, Brian Humpal, Jackson Davis, Sheryl and Tom Feducia, Gail and Bill Fredericks, Carmine and Paula Paolino, Becca Paolino and Chris Holshauser, Dante Paolino and Isabella Gonzalez, Janet P. Parlato and Rich Peronace, Rev. Martin Breski, OFM Conv., Rev. Ricky Manalo, CSP, Rev. Aloysius P. Kelley, SJ, Rev. Charles H. Allen, SJ, Rev. Leonard J. Kvedas, Rev. Mathai Vellappallil, SDB, Rev. Joy Jacob, SDB, Rev. Ronald A. Ferraro, Sister Kathleen Dorney, CND, Deacon Victor and Kathleen Lembo, Janet Canepa, Frank and Jennifer Ficko, Stephen Haessler, Theresa Fratamico, Pam Hull and Mark Eastridge, Patricia and John Philip, Suzanne Noel and Jim Wigren, Sharon and Dan Wilson, Joyce D'Alessio, Rick and Joanne

Waldron, Ivy Bennett, Cathy Buxton Holmquist, Lila Lee Coddington, Peggy Healey, Kathy LaPorta DiCocco, Marilyn LaPorta Baker, Greta Solomon, Ray Solomon, Sam and Linda Lazinger, Ken and Carla Burgess, Pam and the late Howard Burros, Dennis and Michelle Lapadula, Nancy O'Brien, Robin Masciewicz-Morehouse, Nina and Görgen Gostas, Wim Caers and Charlotte Smekens, Antonella Rocchini, Federico Manetti, John Tkacik, Jim and Jeanne Dansereau, Karl Mallick, Bill Boemmels, Laura DeFrancesco, the Ritrivi family, the McCavitt family, Robb and Robyn Moran, Kelly and Sam Hahn, Susan LaJoie, Renée Donnarumma, Sun Mee Steiskel Ryan, Lisa and Joe South and family, Lyn and Ron Ryan and family, Susan Bogart, Michael O'Rourke, the Zavala and Acevedo families, Tom and Bev Pratt, Linda and Mark Narowski and family, Kathy and Tom Niezelski, Don and Alice Baldwin, Diane Betkoski, Barbara Betkoski, Tony and Alice Smith, John and Kate Smith, the Lombardo family, Michael Peloquin, Sam Bacco, Tom, Lori, and Olivia Alosco, Lenny, Kelly, and Samantha Crone, Steve, Karen, and Rosemary Minkler, the Harte, Butler, and Johnson, Feldman, and Brayton families, Taleesha Christian.

To the families, administration, faculty, and staff of the former Sacred Heart High School, Waterbury, Connecticut, for welcoming me into an unmatched community during the challenging 2020-2021 academic year. My utmost gratitude, respect, admiration, and affection.

To my beloved students, past and present.

To the late Ruth Kipp, seventh-grade teacher, who suggested I use my own words to tell stories. To Daniel D'Alessio, eighth-grade teacher, who revealed the power and possibility of 26 letters and to this day encourages and inspires.

To Jeanne Basile and Dave Dostaler, David Dostaler and Giavanna Brunelle, Scott Basile, Kory Basile, Rosie Alexander, Gino Basile.

To the Pelosi, Ciampi, and D'Avino families of Frigento; Italy, the Gubitoso family, the Crupi, Pesino, Mitchell, Chiucarello, Ferraro, and Giordano families.

To the Fabry, Cohen, and Plasko families; the Horny, Petlock, Kane, Ohrin, Janoski, Swatkoski, and Hurn families, the Lychock, Johnson, and Sudy families, the Sarnik family of Prague;

To Fran and Maureen Donnarumma, Ed and Teresa Wasil, Mike and Ellen Donnarumma; Alessandra Donnarumma and Chris Ryan, Egon Donnarumma and Sara Slayton O'Rourke, Matthew and Caroline South, Colin Donnarumma and Andrea Donnarumma Zavala; Emily Wasil, Ethan Wasil, George Donnarumma, Erin Donnarumma.

To Cashen, Connor, and Joseph South, Clara and Henry Donnarumma, Linnea and Huxton Ryan.

To my late, loving, cheerleading parents, Louise and Carmen Donnarumma, and the inspiring aunts and uncles and godparents and cousins who enjoy eternal life with them. I miss you more and more. To my loving mother-in-law, Veronica Sharnick, and my late father-in-law, Robert Sharnick, who never missed a book talk. Intrepid and generous supporters all.

"You may have the universe if I may have Italy," said Giuseppe Verdi.

With unending thanks, palpable joy, and deepest love to my husband, Wayne, who gives me Italy again and again.

Suggested Listening to Accompany
The Contessa's Easel

"Always", Irving Berlin

La Bohème, Puccini

The Four Seasons, Vivaldi

Canon in D Major, Pachelbel

Violin Sonata No. 9 in A Major, Beethoven

Clair de Lune, Debussy

Grand Duo Concertante No. 1 for Two Violins, Beriot

The Lark Ascending, Vaughan Williams

Lucia di Lammermoor, Donizetti

"Can't Help Falling in Love", Hugo Peretti, Luigi
    Creatore, and George David Weiss

ABOUT THE AUTHOR
MARY DONNARUMMA SHARNICK

Mary Donnarumma Sharnick is the author of five novels, the first of which, *Thirst*, is being adapted for the operatic stage. She was a recipient of a Wesleyan Writers' Conference Fellowship in 2008, as well as a fellowship from the Hartford Council for the Arts Beatrice Fox Auerbach Foundation in 2010.

Orla's Canvas and *Painting Mercy*, the first two novels in the ORLA PAINTS QUARTET, were awarded prizes from the Connecticut Press Club and the National Federation of Press Women in 2016 and 2018. *Orla's Canvas* was also a Finalist for a Kindle Award in 2017. Mary lives in Connecticut with her husband, Wayne Sharnick. She may be reached at www.marysharnick.com

If You Enjoyed This Book

Please place a review as this helps the author
and visit the website of

PENMORE PRESS
www.penmorepress.com

All Penmore Press books are available directly through
our website,

Coming Soon: Book Four of the Orla Paints series:
En Plein Air

Painting Mercy

By

Mary Sharnick

In Painting Mercy, the sequel to prize-winning Orla's Canvas, Orla, now twenty-four, has been studying and painting in New York City. It is 1975. Saigon has fallen to the Communists, and Vietnamese refugees have been invited to settle in New Orleans by Archbishop Hannan, a former paratrooper and military chaplain in WW II. Orla's childhood friend and forever confidant, Tad Charbonneau, is practicing immigration law in New Orleans, where he mitigates challenging adoption cases involving children, many of them bi-racial, recently airlifted from Saigon and in need of new families. On her way back home for Katie Cowles' wedding and a summer painting in misspelled St. Suplice, Orla reconnects with Tad and contemplates her future. While she anticipates marriage and family with her undisputed soul mate, she discovers upsetting news about Tad's sexuality and learns that her forty-three-year-old mother is pregnant. Adding to her troubling personal revelations, Orla becomes involved in the devastating costs of war for former GI and Katie's brother Denny Cowles and Mercy Cleveland, a Vietnamese orphan who eventually becomes as essential to Orla as her art. Orla once again calls upon her art to make sense of loss and gain. Through her craft she reimagines how Love and Home might look, finally charting a future for herself she had not previously considered possible.

PENMORE PRESS
www.penmorepress.com

Orla's Canvas

By

Mary Sharnick

Narrated by eleven-year-old Orla Gwen Gleason, Orla's Canvas opens on Easter Sunday, in St. Suplice, Louisiana, a "misspelled town" north of New Orleans, and traces Orla's dawning realization that all is not as it seems in her personal life or in the life of her community. The death of St. Suplice's doyenne, Mrs. Bellefleur Dubois Castleberry, for whom Orla's mother keeps house, reveals Orla's true paternity, shatters her trust in her beloved mother, and exposes her to the harsh realities of class and race in the Civil Rights-era South. When the Klan learns of Mrs. Castleberry's collaboration with the local Negro minister and Archbishop Rummel to integrate the parochial school, violence fractures St. Suplice's vulnerable stability. The brutality Orla witnesses at summer's end awakens her to life's tenuous fragility. Like the South in which she lives, she suffers the turbulence of changing times. Smart, resilient, and fiercely determined to make sense of her pain, Orla paints chaos into beauty, documenting both horror and grace, discovering herself at last through her art.

PENMORE PRESS
www.penmorepress.com

Mistress Suffragette

by

Diana Forbes

A young woman without prospects at a ball in Gilded Age Newport, Rhode Island is a target for a certain kind of "suitor." At the Memorial Day Ball during the Panic of 1893, impoverished but feisty Penelope Stanton draws the unwanted advances of a villainous millionaire banker who preys on distressed women—the incorrigible Edgar Daggers. Over a series of encounters, he promises Penelope the financial security she craves, but at what cost? Skilled in the art of flirtation, Edgar is not without his charms, and Penelope is attracted to him against her better judgment. Initially, as Penelope grows into her own in the burgeoning early Women's Suffrage Movement, Edgar exerts pressure, promising to use his power and access to help her advance. But can he be trusted, or are his words part of an elaborate mind game played between him and his wife? During a glittering age where a woman's reputation is her most valuable possession, Penelope must decide whether to compromise her principles for love, lust, and the allure of an easier life.

PENMORE PRESS
www.penmorepress.com

The Measure of Ella
by
Toni Bird Jones

The islands frightened her with their uncivilized rawness. They looked like a place where anything could happen, a godforsaken outcrop at the end of the world.

Sea-faring chef Ella Morgan is an honest woman — until her life falls apart. When her dream of owning a restaurant is shattered by the death of her father and loss of her inheritance, she is suddenly alone in the world. Desperate for money, she signs on as crew for a Caribbean drug run, only to find herself fighting for her life in an underworld ruled by violent men.

Set in the Caribbean, The Measure of Ella is a dramatic story of love, murder, high-seas action, and the consequences of pursuing a dream at all costs. Like Patrick O'Brien's novels, including Master and Commander, The Measure of Ella captures the breathtaking and perilous world of blue-water sailing. Like Girl on the Train, it unwinds with gripping suspense from a woman's point of view. With its brave, strong, complex female protagonist at the helm of a high seas adventure, the novel is entirely unique.

PENMORE PRESS
www.penmorepress.com

ÆGIR'S CURSE

BY
LEAH DEVLIN

A thousand years ago, the Viking colony of Vinland was ravaged by a swift-moving plague ... a curse inflicted by the sea god Ægir. The last surviving Norseman set the encampment and his longboat ablaze to ensure that the disease would die with him and his brethren.

In present-day Norway, a distinguished professor is found murdered, his priceless map of Vinland missing. The ensuing investigation leads to the reclusive world of Lindsey Nolan, a scientist and recovering alcoholic who has been sober for five years. Lindsey reluctantly agrees to help the detective who's hunting the murderer, but she has a bigger problem on her hands: a mysterious disease that's spreading like wildfire through the population of Woods Hole. As she races against a rising body count to discover the source of the plague, disturbing events threaten her hard-won sobriety—and her life. Will Lindsey be the next victim of Ægir's curse?

Leah Devlin is rapidly establishing herself as a writer of modern day mystery-thrillers. This story is as tight as a piano wire. Life at a seaside town in New England is full of treacherous undercurrents and peril, as residents are threatened by a menace from a thousand years ago. Murder, romance and deceit are a potent mix in this gripping novel, which I didn't want to put down.—James Boschert, author of the Talon Series and *Force 12 in German Bight*

PENMORE PRESS
www.penmorepress.com

Penmore Press

Challenging, Intriguing, Adventurous, Historical and Imaginative

www.penmorepress.com

CPSIA information can be obtained
at www.ICGtesting.com
Printed in the USA
BVHW082235240721
612192BV00002B/3

9 781950 586813